THE BEAR TRUTH

The Dilbian called The Hill Bluffer opened his large mouth again, and put a further aspect of the matter out for John's consideration.

"You know," said the Bluffer, "you can't get Greasy Face back from the Terror without fighting him?"

Greasy Face, John remembered, was the Dilbian's nickname for the human woman the Streamside Terror had kidnapped. "*Fighting* him??" he echoed.

"Yep," said the Bluffer. "Man-to-man. No weapons. No holds barred."

John blinked. He looked past the Dilbian postman's head at the puffs of white clouds. They had not moved. They were still there. So were the mountains. It must be something wrong with his ears.

"Fighting him?" said John again, feeling like a man in a fast elevator which has just begun to descend.

"A man's got his pride," said the Bluffer. "If you take Greasy Face back, his mug's spilt all over again." He leaned a little toward John. "That is, unless you whip him in a fair fight. Then there's no blood feud to it. You're just a better man than he is, that's all. But that's what I haven't been able to figure in this. You aren't bad for a Shorty. You pulled a good trick with that beer on those drunks last night. You got guts."

He looked searchingly at John. "But I mean— Hell, you can't fight the Terror. Anybody'd know that. I mean— *Hell*!" said the Bluffer.

John was wishing he could express to the postman how much he agreed with him.

"So what," inquir⬛⬛⬛⬛⬛⬛⬛⬛⬛⬛⬛⬛ to do when I deliver ⬛⬛⬛⬛

John thought ab⬛

THE RIGHT TO
ARM BEARS

GORDON R. DICKSON

Spacial Delivery copyright © 1961 by Ace Books, Inc., *Spacepaw* copyright © 1969 by Gordon Dickson, "The Law-Twister Shorty" copyright © 1971 by Ben Bova. First unitary edition.

A Baen Book

Baen Publishing Enterprises
P.O. Box 1403
Riverdale, NY 10471
www.baen.com

ISBN: 0-671-31959-0

Cover art by Richard Martin

First Baen printing, December 2000
2nd printing, May 2001

Distributed by Simon & Schuster
1230 Avenue of the Americas
New York, NY 10020

Production by Windhaven Press, Auburn, NH
Printed in the United States of America

CONTENTS

Spacial Delivery

CHAPTER 1

The Right Honorable Joshua Guy, Ambassador Plenipotentiary to Dilbia, was smoking tobacco in a pipe, an old-fashioned, villainous habit for such a conservative and respected gentleman. The fumes from the pipe made John Tardy cough and strangle. Or perhaps it was the fumes combined with what the Rt. Hon. Josh Guy had just said.

"Sir?" wheezed John Tardy.

"Sorry," said the dapper little diplomat. "Thought you heard me the first time." He knocked his devil of a pipe out in a hand-carved bowl of some native Dilbian wood, where the coal continued to smoulder and stink only slightly less objectionably than it had before. "What I said was that, naturally, as soon as we knew you were safely drafted for the job, we let out word to the Dilbians that you were deeply attached to the girl. In love with her, in fact."

3

John gulped air. Both men were talking Dilbian to exercise the command of the language John had had hypnoed into him on his way here from the Belt stars, and the Dilbian nickname for the missing Earthian girl sociologist came from his lips automatically,

"With this Greasy Face?"

"Miss Ty Lamorc," corrected Joshua, smoothly slipping into Basic and then out again. "Greasy Face to Dilbians, of course. But you mustn't pay too much attention to the apparent value of these Dilbian nicknames. The two old Dilbian gentlemen you're about to meet—Daddy Shaking Knees, Mayor of Humrog, here, by the way, and Two Answers—aren't at all the sort they might sound like from name alone. Daddy Shaking Knees got his name from holding up one end of a timber one day in an emergency. After about forty-five minutes someone noticed his knees starting to tremble a bit. And Two Answers is not a liar, as you might expect, but a wily sort who can come up with more than one solution to a problem."

"I see," said John.

"Miss Lamorc is quite a fine young woman. I would not at all be ashamed to have her for a daughter, myself. Lots of character."

"Oh, I'm sure she has," said John, hastily. "I'm not objecting to the situation here. I don't want you to think that. After all, the draft is necessary in emergency situations, particularly in areas where we're in close competition with the Hemnoids. But I don't understand what this has to do with my decathlon record? I thought I'd put all that sports business behind me after the last Olympics. As you know, I'm actually a fully qualified biochemist, and . . ."

"Names," said Joshua, "have their chief value around here as an index to what the Dilbians think of you. I, myself, now, am referred to as Little Bite; and you will undoubtedly be christened yourself with a Dilbian nickname, shortly."

"Me!" said John, startled. He thought of his own red

hair which surmounted an athletically stocky body. He had always hated to be called Red.

"It should not be too humiliating, provided you are careful not to make yourself ridiculous. Heinie, now—"

"I beg your pardon?"

"I beg yours," said Josh, starting to refill his pipe. "I should have used his full name of Heiner Schlaff." He puffed fresh clouds of smoke into the air of the small, neat office with the log walls. "He lost his head first time he stepped out alone on the street. A Dilbian from one of the back-mountain clans who'd never seen a human before, picked him up. Heinie lost his head completely. After all, he was never able to poke his nose outdoors without some Dilbian picking him up to hear him yell for help. The Squeaking Squirt, they named him; very bad public relations for us humans. Particularly when Gulark-*ay*, the Hemnoid in charge of *their* embassy locally here, gets an advantageous handle hung on him like the Beer-Guts Bouncer. There he goes now, by the way."

Joshua pointed out the office window that fronted on the main street of Humrog. Coming down its cobblestones, John saw, a sort of enormous robed, Buddha-like parody of a human being. The Hemnoid was a good eight feet in height, enormously boned, and while not as tall as the Dilbians themselves, fantastically padded with heavy-gravity muscles. The Hemnoids, John remembered, came from an original world with one-fourth again the gravity of Earth. Since Dilbia's gravity was about a sixth less than Earth's, that gave humanity's chief and closest competitors quite an advantage in this particular instance.

"He may stop—no, he's going past," said Joshua. "What was I saying? Oh, yes. Keep your head in all situations. I assume someone who's won the decathlon in the All-Systems Olympics can do that."

"Well, yes," said John. "Of course, in biochemistry, now—"

"You will find the Dilbians primitive, touchy, and insular."

"I will?"

"Oh, yes. Definitely. Primitive. Touchy. And very much indifferent to anything outside their own mountains and forests; although we've been in touch with them for thirty years and the Hemnoids have for nearly twenty."

"I see. Well, I'll watch out for that," said John. "It struck me they wouldn't know much about chemistry, to say nothing of biochemistry—"

"On the other hand," Joshua brushed the neat ends of his small grey mustache with a thoughtful forefinger, "you mustn't fall into the error of thinking that just because they look like a passel of Kodiak bears who've decided to stand on their hind legs at all times and slim down a bit, that they're bearlike completely in nature."

"I'll watch that, too," said John.

"There are intelligent individuals among them. Highly intelligent. There's one," said Joshua, indicating a three-dimensional on his desk, the transparent cube of which showed the scaled-down frozen images of three Dilbians, the middle one of the trio—at whom Joshua was pointing—being a good head taller than either of his companions. Since John's hypno training had informed him that the average male adult Dilbian would scale upwards of nine feet, this made the one Joshua was pointing at a monster indeed. "He's shrewd. Independent and open-minded. Experienced and wise, to say nothing of being influential with his fellow-Dilbians. Is this pipe bothering you, my boy?"

"No. No," said John, coughing discreetly. "Not at all."

"Have to put it out shortly when we meet Daddy Shaking Knees and Two Answers. Dilbians are quite sensitive about human odors, even mild ones like tobacco. To get back to what I was saying: We *must* influence Dilbians like that chap or the Hemnoids are going to get the inside track on this planet. And the Dilbian system, as I'm sure your hypno training didn't omit to inform you, is absolutely necessary as a supply and reequipment stage for further expansion on any large scale beyond the Belt

Stars. If the Hemnoids beat us out here, they've got the thin end of a wedge started that could eventually chop our heads off. Which they would be only too glad to do, you know."

John sighed. It was the sigh of a very human, young, recent graduate in biochemistry who would have liked nothing better than to live and let live.

"You'd think there'd be room enough in the universe for both of us."

"Apparently not, in the Hemnoid lexicon. You must read up on their psychology sometime. Fascinating. They're actually less like us than the Dilbians are, in spite of their greater physical resemblance."

"I understand they can be pretty dangerous."

"They've an instinctive streak of cruelty. Do you know what they used to do to the elderly among their own people until just the last hundred years or so of their history—"

Beep, signaled the annunciator on Joshua's desk.

"Ah, that'll be Shaking Knees and Two Answers, in the outer office now," said the diplomat. "We'll go on in." He knocked out his pipe and laid it, regretfully, in the carved wooden bowl among the ashes.

"But what's it all about?" said John desperately. "I just got off the spaceship four hours ago. You've been feeding me lunch, and talking about background; but you haven't told me what it's all about!"

"Why, what's *what* all about?" asked Joshua, pausing halfway to the door to the outer office.

"Well—everything!" burst out John. "Why was I drafted? I was all set to trans-ship to McBanen's Planet to join my government exploration outfit, and this girl from the local embassy on Vega Seven where I was, came up and pulled my passport and said I was drafted to here. Nobody explained anything."

"Dear me! They didn't? And you just came along to Dilbia here by courier ship, without asking—"

"Well, I'm as good a citizen as anyone else," said John,

defensively. "I mean I may not like the draft, but I realize the necessity for it. They said you needed me. I came. But I'd just like to know what it's all about before I start getting into the job."

"Of course, of course!" said Joshua. "Well, it's really nothing. Miss Lamorc, this young sociologist girl, the one I was talking about, got kidnapped, that's all. By a Dilbian. We want you to go bring her back. Old Shaking Knees in the next room is the father of Boy Is She Built. And it was the fact that the Streamside Terror wanted Boy Is She Built that caused all this ruckus which ended up with the Terror kidnapping Miss Lamorc. You'll see," said Joshua, starting off toward the door again, "it's all very simple. It'll all straighten out for you once you get into it."

"But I don't see—" insisted John, doggedly, following him.

"What?" Joshua hesitated with his hand on the door latch.

"What all this has to do with my work. Why do you want a biochemist to bring back some woman who'd been kidnapped?"

"But we don't particularly want a biochemist," said Joshua. "What we want is a rough, tough laddie with excellent physical reflexes of the kind that would take top honors in a decathlon competition. It isn't your brains we want, Mr. Tardy, it's your brawn." He opened the door. "You'll find it's all very simple once you get the hang of it. Come along, my dear boy. After you."

CHAPTER 2

Politely but firmly herded forward by the little diplomat, John found himself pushed into the large outer office of the Human Embassy on Dilbia, at Humrog, his head still spinning from Joshua's last words and the odd Dilbian names. Who, he wondered confusedly and in particular, was Boy Is She Built? The obvious conclusion, in terms of a seven foot-plus Dilbian female accoutered in little more than her natural furry pelt, was a little mind-shaking to imagine.

The moment, however, was not the proper one for imaginings, no matter how mind-shaking. Reality was being too overpowering to leave room for anything else. The first thing to strike John as the door closed behind him, was the scale of the room he was entering. The inner office had been a reassuringly human cell tucked away

9

in a corner of gargantuan Dilbian architecture. Desk and chairs had been to John's own fit.

This outer office, for reasons of diplomatic politeness, was furnished in the outsize Dilbian scale. The heavy wall logs allowed for headroom up to fifteen feet below the log rafters. The bottom of the crudely glazed windows were on a level with John's chin. Several tables and straight-backed chairs fitted the rest of the furnishings by being of the same uncomfortable (by human standards) largeness. A quart-sized ink pot, and a hand-whittled pen holder about sixteen inches long on one of the tables, completed the picture.

Not this, though, *nor* the hypno training, quite served to prepare John adequately for his first close-up encounter with a pair of the Dilbian natives. These two were standing not a dozen feet inside the door as John came through it; and their appearance assaulted his senses in all ways, immediately, and without warning.

To begin with, they *smelled*. Not overpoweringly, not even unbearably, in fact rather like dogs that have been out in the rain for the first time in several weeks during which they had not had a bath. But, definitely, they smelled.

It did not help, either, for John to notice that the two were faintly wrinkling their large black noses at him, in turn.

And on top of this odor, there was the fact of the bigness of the room; which, after ten seconds, pulled a double switch on the senses; so that, instead of John feeling that he was the same size he had always been and the room was unnaturally big, the first thing he knew he was feeling that *it* was normal in dimensions and *he* had shrunk, all of a sudden, to the stature of a six-year old boy.

But last and not least was the center of all this, the two adult male Dilbians themselves, looking indeed like a pair of Kodiak bears who had stood up on their hind legs and gone on a diet. True, their brows were higher and more intelligent than bears. Their noses were shorter, their lower jaws more human-like than ursinoid. But their thick coats of brownish-black hair, their lumbering stance, massive shoulders and forearms and the fact that they wore nothing to speak of beyond a few leather straps and metal ornaments, shouted *bear* at you, any way you looked at it. If it was up to me, thought John . . .

"Ah, there, Little Bite!" boomed the larger of the two furry monsters in native Dilbian, before he could finish the thought. "This is the new one? Two Answers and I shook a leg right over here to give him the eye. Kind of bright colored up top there, ain't he?"

"Hor, hor, hor!" bellowed the other, thunderously. "Belt me, if I'd want one like him around. Liable to burn the house down! Hor, hor, hor!"

"Some of we humans have hair that color," replied Joshua. "Gentlemen, this is John Tardy. John, this gentleman with the sense of humor is Two Answers. And his quiet friend is Shaking Knees."

"*Quiet!*" roared the other Dilbian, exploding into gargantuan laughter. "Me, *quiet*! That's good!" He shook the heavy logs with his merriment.

John blinked. He glanced incredulously from the imperturbable Joshua to these oversize clowns in fur. What kind of goof-up, he wondered, could have put Guy in an ambassadorial post like this. A sharply tailored, fastidious little dandy of a man—and these lolling, shouting, belching, king-sized, frontier-type aliens. It was past belief.

For the first time there crept into John's mind the awful suspicion that the whole thing—Joshua Guy being ambassador in a post like this, the kidnapping of the female sociologist, and his being drafted to do a job that he was in no way experienced or prepared for—all this just part of one monstrous blunder that had its beginnings in the Alien Relations Office, back in Governmental Headquarters on Earth.

"Haven't laughed like that since old Souse Nose fell into the beer vat in the Mud Hollow Inn!" Two Answers was snorting, as he got himself back under control. "All right, Bright Top, what've you got to say for yourself? Think you can take the Streamside Terror with one paw tied behind your back?"

"I beg your pardon?" said John. "I understood I was here to bring back—er—Greasy Face, but—"

"Streamside won't just hand her over. Will he, Knees?" Two Answers jogged his companion with a massive elbow.

"Not that boy!" Shaking Knees shook his head, slowly. "Little Bite, I ought never have let you talk me out of a son-in-law like that. Tough. Rough. Tricky. My little girl'd do all right with a buck like that."

"I merely," said Joshua, "suggested you make them wait a bit, if you remember. Boy Is She Built is still rather young."

"And, boy is she built!" said her father, fondly. "Yep, I know it made sense the way you put it then." He shook his head a little. "You sure got the knack for coming up on the right side of the argument with a man. Still, now I look back on it, it's hard to see how that little girl of mine could do better." He peered suddenly at Joshua. "You sure you ain't got something hidden between your claws on this?"

Joshua spread his hands expressively.

"Would I risk one of my own people?" he said. "Maybe two, counting John, here? All for nothing but the fun of making the Terror mad at me?"

"Don't make sense, does it?" rumbled Shaking Knees. "But you Shorties are tricky little characters." His words rang with an honest admiration.

"Now, you people are pretty sly yourselves," said Joshua. They both turned and spat over their left shoulders. "Well, now," went on Joshua, "compliments aside, anybody know where the Terror is?"

"He headed west through the Cold Mountains," put in Two Answers. "He was spotted yesterday a half day's hike north, pointed toward Sour Ford and the Hollows. He probably nighted at Brittle Rock Inn, there."

"Good," said Joshua. "We'll have to find a guide to there for my friend here."

"Guide? Ho!" chortled Shaking Knees. "Wait'll you see what we got for your friend." He shouldered past Two Answers, opened the door and bellowed. "Bluffer! In here!"

There was a moment's wait. And then a Dilbian even leaner and taller than Shaking Knees shouldered his way through the outer doorway into the office, which with this new addition, and in spite of its original size, began to take on the air of being decidedly crowded.

"Here you are, Shorties!" said Shaking Knees, waving an expansive furry hand at the newcomer. "What more could you ask for? Walk all day, climb all night, and start out fresh next morning after breakfast. Right, Hill Bluffer?"

"Right as rooftops in raintime!" sonorously proclaimed the newcomer, rattling the windows about the walls. "Hill Bluffer, that's my name and trade! Anything on two feet walk away from me? Not over solid ground or living rock! When I look at a hill, it knows it's beat; and it lays out flat for my trampling feet!"

"Well, how do you like that, Little Bite? Eh? How?" boomed Shaking Knees.

"Mighty impressive, Knees," replied Joshua. "But I don't know about my friend keeping up if the Hill Bluffer here moves like that."

"Keep up? Hah!" guffawed Shaking Knees. "No, no, Little Bite, don't you recognize the Hill Bluffer? He's the government postman from Humrog to Wildwood Peak. We're going to mail your Shorty friend here to the Terror. Guaranteed delivery. Postage: five pounds of nails."

"Nobody stops the mail." The Hill Bluffer swept the room with a glare that had a professional quality about it. "Nobody monkeys with the mail in transit!"

"Well . . ." said Joshua, thoughtfully. "Five pounds, of course, is out of the question."

"Out of the question?" roared Shaking Knees. "A guaranteed, absolutely safe government mailman—!"

"I can hire five strong porters off the street for that."

"Sure you can. Sure!" jeered Shaking Knees. "But can any of them catch up with the Terror?"

"Can the Bluffer catch up?"

The Hill Bluffer bellowed like a struck bull.

"Well," said Joshua, "a pound and a half. That's fair."

The bargaining continued. John began to get a headache. He wondered how Joshua had kept from going deaf all these months in the embassy, or however long he had been billeted here. Then he noticed the older man was wearing a sound dampening coil behind each ear. It had not of course, thought John a trifle bitterly, occurred to him to suggest the same protection for John.

The price was finally settled at three and a quarter pounds of steel nails, size and type to be at Shaking Knees' discretion, at some future date.

"Well, now," said Joshua, "the next thing is—how's the Bluffer going to carry him?"

"Who? Him?" boomed the Bluffer, focusing down on John. "Why, I'll handle him like he was a week-old pup. Wrap him up real careful in some soft straw, tuck him in the bottom of my mail pouch and—"

"Hey!" cried John.

"I'm afraid," said Joshua, "my friend's right. We're going to have to find some way he can ride more comfortably."

The meeting adjourned to the embassy warehouse adjoining, to see what could be rigged up in the way of a saddle.

"I won't wear it!" the Hill Bluffer was trumpeting, two hours later. They were all standing in the Humrog main street by this time, in front of the warehouse; and the cause of the Bluffer's upset, a system of straps and pads arranged into a sort of shoulder harness to carry John, lay on the cobblestones before them. A small number of local Dilbian bystanders had gathered; and their freely offered basso comments were not of a sort to bring the Hill Bluffer to a more reasonable frame of mind.

"Now, that's a real good system for my old lady to tote the youngest pup around," one Dilbian with a grey scar jaggedly across his black nose, was saying.

"Good training for the Bluffer, too," put in another blackfurred monster. "Have pups of his own, one of these days."

"Unless," said the scar-nosed one, judiciously, "this here little feller actually is a pup of the Hill Bluffer's, already."

"You don't mean to actually tell me!" said the other. He squinted at John. "Yep, there's a resemblance all right."

"You want your ear tore off," roared the infuriated Bluffer, pausing in the midst of his hot argument with Shaking Knees and Two Answers. "This here piece of mail's a Shorty!"

John backed off a little from the bellowing group and tried to shut the voices out of his mind, even if shutting them out of his ears was somewhat impractical. He was in that stage of helplessly worn-out exasperation which often results when naturally independent and strong-willed people are pushed around without explanation and without the chance for natural protest.

He turned his back on the shouting group and gazed off through the thin, clear air of the Dilbian mountains that made everything seem three times as close as they actually were, to a snow-laden peak thrusting up above the pinelike trees surrounding Humrog.

"At least try the unmentionable thing on!" Shaking Knees was roaring at the Hill Bluffer a dozen feet away.

Here, thought John, he had been hauled off the ship that was to take him out to his job with a government exploration team; it was work he had always wanted and just finished seven years of college-level study for. Instead he was on a citizen's draft which left him no chance to object. Well, yes, John had to admit to himself, the Draft Law provided he could refuse if he could charge the

Drafting Authority—in this case, Joshua—with incompetence or misinformation. John snorted under his breath. Fine chance he had of doing that when he couldn't even find out what was going on. He had just stepped off his spaceship a few hours ago; and Joshua had yet to give him five minutes opportunity to formulate questions.

At the same time, thought John, there was something awfully screwy about the way things were going on. As soon as this business of the saddle had been settled, he was going to haul Joshua aside, if need be by main force, and insist on some answers before he went any further. A citizen had some rights, too . . .

"Arright, arright, arright!" snarled the Hill Bluffer barely six inches behind John's ear. "Buckle me up in the obscenity thing, then!"

John turned to see Joshua pushing the system of straps up on the back of the Hill Bluffer, who was squatting down. Instinctively, he moved to give the little diplomat a hand.

"That's better!" growled Shaking Knees. "Don't blame you too much. But, you listen to me, pup! I happen to be your mother's uncle's first cousin, one generation up on you. And when I speak for a relative of mine of the second generation, he stays spoken for!"

"I'm doing it, ain't I?" flared the Bluffer. He wiggled his shoulder experimentally. "Don't feel too bad at that."

"You'll find it," grunted Joshua, buckling a final strap, "easier to carry than your regular pouch."

"Not the point!" growled the Bluffer. "A postman's got dignity. He just don't wear—" a snicker from the scar-nosed Dilbian cut through his speech. "*Listen, you—Split Nose!*"

"I'll take care of him." Shaking Knees rolled forward a couple of paces. "What's wrong with you, Split Nose?"

"Just passing by," rumbled Split Nose, hastily backing into the crowd as the Humrog village chief took a hand in the conversation.

"Well, then just pass on, friend. Pass on!" boomed

Shaking Knees; and Split Nose trundled hastily off down the street with every indication that his hairy ears were burning.

While this was going on, John, at Joshua's urging had seated himself in the saddle to see how it would bear his weight. The straps creaked, but held comfortably. The Hill Bluffer looked back over his shoulder.

"You're light enough," he said. "How is it? All right up there?"

"Fine," said John.

"Then, so long everybody!" boomed the Hill Bluffer.

He rose to his feet in one easy movement. And before John had time to do more than grab at the straps of the harness to keep from falling off, and catch his breath, they were barrelling off down the main street at the swift pace of the Bluffer's ground-eating stride, on their way to the forest trail, the mountains beyond which rose that distant peak John had just been watching, and the elusive and inimical Streamside Terror.

CHAPTER 3

If it had not been for the hypno training John had undergone, sitting with a large, bell-shaped helmet completely covering his head in the cramped little government scoutship, while on overdrive from the Belt Stars to Dilbia, he might instinctively have protested the Hill Bluffer's sudden departure. As it was, his pseudomemories of Dilbian life stood him in unexpectedly good stead. As it was, he had barely opened his mouth to yell, "Hey, wait a minute" when he suddenly 'remembered' what consequences this might have and shut his lips firmly on the first syllable. As it was, the startled sound in his throat was enough to make the Hill Bluffer check his stride momentarily.

"Whazzat?" growled the Dilbian postman.

"Nothing," said John, hastily. "Clearing my throat."

18

"Thought you were going to say something," grunted the Bluffer, and swung back into his regular stride.

What John had suddenly 'remembered' was one of the little tricks possible under Dilbian custom. He, himself, had not expected to start out after the Lamorc girl until the next morning at the earliest; and then not without a full session with Joshua Guy in which he would pin that elusive little man down about the whys and wherefores of the situation. As a citizen of the great human race it was his right to be fully briefed before being sent out on such a job.

That is, as a human citizen it was his right. As a piece of Dilbian mail, his rights were somewhat different—generally consisting of the postman's responsibility to deliver him without undue damage in transit to his destination.

Therefore, the little trickiness of the Hill Bluffer. As John had noticed, the postman had lost a great deal of his enthusiasm for the job on discovering the nature of the harness in which he would be carrying John. The Bluffer could not, of course, refuse to carry John without loss of honor, the hypno training informed John. But if a piece of mail should try to dictate the manner in which it was being delivered, then possibly Dilbian honor would stand excused, and the Bluffer could turn back, washing his hands of the whole matter.

So John said nothing.

All the same, he added another black mark to the score he was building up in the back of his mind against Joshua Guy. The Dilbian ambassador should have forseen this. John thought of the wrist phone he was wearing and began to compose a few of the statements he intended to make to that particular gentleman, as soon as he had a moment of privacy in which to make the call.

Meanwhile, the Bluffer went away down the slope of the main street of Humrog, turned right and began to climb the trail to the first ridge above the town. He had not been altogether exaggerating in his claims for himself as someone able to swing his feet. Almost immediately, it seemed to John, they were away from the great log buildings of the approximately five thousand population town of Humrog, and between the green thicknesses of the pinelike trees that covered the mountainous part of the rocky planet.

The Bluffer's long legs pistoned and swung in a steady rhythm, carrying himself and John up a good eight to ten degree slope at not much less than eight to ten miles an hour. John, swaying like a rider on the back of an elephant, concentrated on falling into the pattern of the Bluffer's movements and saving his own breath. The Bluffer, himself, said nothing.

They reached the top of the ridge and dipped down the slope into the first valley crossed by the trail. Long branches whipped past John as he clung to the Bluffer's shoulder straps and they plunged down the switchback trail as if any moment the Dilbian might miss his footing and go tumbling headlong off the trail and down the slope alongside.

Yet in spite of all this, John felt himself beginning to get used to the shifts of the big body under him. He was, in fact, responding with all the skill of an unusually talented athlete already experienced in a number of physical skills. He was meeting in stride the problems posed by being a Dilbian-rider. In fact, he was becoming good at it, as he had always become good at such things—from jai alai to wrestling—ever since he was old enough to toddle beyond the confines of his crib.

Realizing this did not make him happy. It is a sort of inverse but universal law of nature that makes poets want to be soldiers of fortune, and soldiers of fortune secretly yearn to write poetry. John, a naturally born physical success, had always dreamed of the day his life could be exclusively devoted to peering through microscopes and writing scholarly reports. Fate, he reflected not without bitterness, was operating against him as usual.

"What?" demanded the Hill Bluffer.

"Did I say something?" asked John, starting guiltily back to the realities of his situation.

"You said *something*," replied the Hill Bluffer darkly. "I don't know what, exactly. Sounded like something in that Shorty talk of yours."

"Oh," said John.

"That's what I figured it was," said the Bluffer. "I mean, if it had been something in real words, I would have understood it. I figure any talking you'd be doing to me would be in regular speech. A man wouldn't want anyone making cracks behind his back in some kind of talk he couldn't understand."

"Oh, no. No," said John, hastily. "I was just sort of daydreaming—about things back on the Shorty world where I come from."

The Hill Bluffer absorbed this information in silence for a moment or two, during which he reached the bottom of one small valley and started up its far side.

"You mean," he said, after a moment, "you been *asleep* back there?"

"Uh—well—sort of dozing . . ."

The Bluffer snorted like a small laboratory explosion and put on speed. He did not utter a word for the next two hours. Not, in fact, until someone beside John appeared on the verbal horizon to offer an excuse for conversation.

This new individual turned out to be another Dilbian, very much on the shaggy side, who appeared suddenly out of the woods on to the path ahead of them as they were crossing the low-slung curve of one of the interminable valleys. The stranger was carrying over one shoulder one of the local wild herbivores, a type of musk ox, large by human rather than Dilbian standards. In his other hand swung an ax with a seven foot handle.

The head of the ax was a thick, grey triangle of native iron, one leading side forming the edge of the blade, and the point at the far end being drawn back into a hook.

A wicked-looking tool and weapon which John's hypno training now reminded him was carried and used on all occasions of civil and police matters.

But never used in brawls or combats. The Dilbians considered reliance on any weapon to be rather unmanly.

The Dilbian who had just appeared, waited agreeably in the path for them to catch up. John's nose, which was getting rather used to the Hill Bluffer by this time, discovered the newcomer's odor to be several notches more powerful than that of the Dilbians he had met so far. This Dilbian also had a couple of teeth missing and was plentifully matted about the shoulder and chest with blood from the dead animal he was carrying. He grinned in gaptoothed interest at John; but spoke to the Bluffer, as the Bluffer stopped before him.

"Bluffer," he said.

"Hello, woodsman," said the Bluffer.

"Hello, postman." The tap-toothed grin widened. "Anything for me in the mail?"

"You!" The Bluffer's snort rang through the woods.

"Not so funny!" growled the other. "My second cousin got a piece of mail, once. His clan was gathering at Two Falls; he was a Two Faller through his mother's blood aunt . . ." the woodsman went on heatedly in an apparent attempt to prove his cousin's genealogical claim to have received the piece of mail in question.

Meanwhile, John's attention had been attracted by something else back in the trees from which the woodsman had just emerged. He was trying to get a clearer view of it without betraying himself by turning to look directly at it. It was hard to make out there in the deep shadow behind the branches of the trees, but there seemed to be two other individuals standing back out of sight and listening.

Neither one was a human being. One seemed to be a Dilbian, a small, rather fat-looking Dilbian. And the other, John was just about prepared to swear, was a Buddha-like Hemnoid. It was infuriating that just as he was about to get a clear glimpse of this second individual, a breeze or movement of the air would sway a branch in the way of his vision. If it were a Hemnoid . . .

John's hypno training, possibly by reason of the general snafu that seemed to effect anything having to do with John and Dilbia in general, had omitted to inform him about the Hemnoids. Accordingly, all he knew about this race, which were neck-and-necking it with the humans in a general race to the stars, was what he had picked up in the ordinary way through newspapers and chance encounters.

The Hemnoids looked exactly like jolly fat men half again the size of a human. Only what looked like fat was mostly muscle resulting from a heavier-than-earth gravity on their home world. And they were not—repeat, not—jolly, in the human sense of the word. They had a sense of humor, all right; but it was of the variety that goes with pulling wings off flies. John's only personal encounter with a Hemnoid before this had been at the Interplanetary Olympiad in Brisbane, Australia, the year John had won the decathlon competition.

The Hemnoid ambassador, who had been in the stands that day to witness the competition, came down afterwards to be introduced to some of the athletes; he amused himself by putting the shot two hundred and twenty feet, making a standing broad jump of twenty-eight feet, and otherwise showing up the winners of the recent events. He had then laughed uproariously and suggested a heavy-fat diet such as he followed himself, and also hard physical labor.

If he had time, he said, he would be glad to train a school of athletes who would undoubtedly sweep the next Olympics. Alas, he had to get back to his embassy in Geneva. But let them follow his advice, which would undoubtedly do wonders for them. He had then departed, still chuckling.

While over by the sawdust pit of the pole vault, half the Italian track team were engaged in restraining one of their number, the miler Rudi Maltetti, who had gotten his hands on a javelin and was threatening to cause an interstellar incident.

"So that's the Half-Pint Posted."

John came back to the present with a start, suddenly realizing that the words the woodsman had just spoken were in reference to himself. He turned and stared over the Bluffer's shoulder at the other Dilbian, who was grinning at him in almost Hemnoid fashion. John had, it seemed, already been nicknamed as Joshua had predicted.

"What do you know about him?" the Bluffer was demanding.

"The Cobbly Queen told me," said the other, curling up the right side of his upper lip in the native equivalent of a wink. John recalled that the Cobblies were the Dilbian equivalent of elves, brownies, or what-have-you. He wondered if the woodsman could be serious. John decided the Dilbian wasn't, which still left the problem of how he had recognized John.

"Who're you?" demanded John, taking advantage of the best Dilbian manners, which allowed anybody to horn in on any conversation.

"So it talks does it?" said the woodsman. The Hill Bluffer snorted and threw a displeased glance over his own shoulder. "They calls me Tree Weeper, Half-Pint. Because I chops them down, you see."

"Who told you about me?"

"Ah, that's telling too much," grinned the Tree Weeper. "Call it the Cobbly Queen and you've half of it, anyway. You knows why they call him the Streamside Terror, don't you, Half-Pint? It's because he likes to do his fighting alongside a stream, and pull the other man in the water and get him drowned."

"Oh?" said John. "I mean—sure, I know that."

"Does you now?" said the other. "Well, it ought to be something to watch. Good luck, Half-Pint, then; and you, too, road walker. Me for home and something to eat."

He turned away; and as he did so, John got a sudden

glimpse past him in between the trees at the two who
waited back in the shadow. The Dilbian he did not identify; but the Hemnoid was a shorter, broader individual
than Gulark-*ay*, one who evidently had his nose broken
at one time or another. Then, the Hill Bluffer started up
again with a jerk. John lost sight of the watchers.

The Tree Weeper had stepped in among the brush and
trees on the far side of the road and was immediately out
of sight. A few final sounds marked his going—it was
surprising how quietly a Dilbian could move if he wanted
to—and then they were out of hearing. The Hill Bluffer
swung anew along his route without a word.

John was left sorting over what he had just discovered.
He searched his Dilbian 'memories' for the proper remark
to jolt the Hill Bluffer into conversation.

"Friend of yours?" he inquired.

The Hill Bluffer snorted so hard it jolted John in his
saddle.

"Friend!" he exploded. "A backwoods tree-chopper? I'm
a public official, Half-Pint. You remember that."

"I just thought—" said John, peaceably. "He seemed
to know a lot about me, and what was going on. I mean,
about the Streamside Terror and the fact we're after him.
But nobody's passed us up—"

"Nobody passes me up," said the Bluffer, bristling
apparently automatically.

"Then, how—"

"Somebody leaving just ahead of us must've told him!"
growled the Bluffer.

But he fell unaccountably silent after that, so that John
could get nothing further out of him. And the silence
lasted until, finally, they pulled up in the late afternoon
sunlight before the roadside inn at Brittle Rock, where
they would stay the night.

CHAPTER 4

The first thing John did on being free once more of his saddle was to take a stroll about the area of the inn to stretch the cramps out of his legs. He was more than a little bit unsteady on his feet. Five hours on top of a hitherto unknown mount is not to be recommended even for a natural athlete. John's thighs ached, and his knees had a tendency to give unexpectedly, as if he had spent the afternoon climbing ladders. However, as he walked, more and more of his natural resilience seemed to flow back into him.

Brittle Rock Inn and grounds constituted, literally, a wide spot in the mountain road which John and the Hill Bluffer had been traveling. On one side of the road was a rocky cliff face going back and up at something like an eighty degree angle. On the other side was a sort of flat, gravelly bulge of the kind that would make a scenic

highway parking spot in the mountain highways back on
Earth. On this bulge was situated the long, low shape of
the inn, built of untrimmed logs. Behind the inn was a
sort of trash and outhouse area stretching about twenty
yards or so to the edge of a rather breathtaking dropoff
into a canyon where a mountain river stampeded along,
pell-mell, some five hundred feet below. A picturesque
spot, for those in the mood for such.

John was not in the mood. As soon as his legs began
to feel less like sections of rubber tire casings and more
like honest flesh and bone, he walked up along the bulge
toward the spot where it narrowed into a road, again.
Here, in relative isolation, he called Joshua on his wrist
phone.

The ambassador responded at once. He must, thought
John, have been wearing a wrist phone himself.

"Hello? Hello!" said Joshua's voice tinnily from the tiny
speaker on John's wrist phone. "John?"

"Yes, sir," said John.

"Well, well! How are you?"

"Fine, thanks," said John. "How are you?"

"Excellent. Excellent. But I suppose you had some
reason for calling?"

"I'm at Brittle Rock," said John. "We just got here.
We're going to stay the night. Can you talk freely?"

"Talk freely? Of course I can talk freely, why shouldn't
I?" The wrist phone broke off suddenly on a short barking
laugh. "Oh, I see what you mean. No, I was just having
a drink before dinner, here. Quite alone. What did you
want to say?"

"Why, I thought you might have some instructions for
me," said John. "The Hill Bluffer ran off with me back
at Humrog before you really had a chance to brief me.
I thought you could tell me now."

"Tell you?" said the phone. "But my dear boy! There's
nothing to tell. You're to run down the Streamside Terror and bring back Miss Ty Lamorc. What else do you
need to know?"

"But—" began John, and stopped. He did not know what he needed to know; he merely felt the need of a large area of necessary knowledge like a general ache or pain. At a loss to put this effectively into words, he was reduced to staring at his wrist phone.

"No sight of the Terror, yet?" inquired the phone, politely filling in the gap in the conversation.

"No."

"Well, it'll probably take several days to catch up with him. Just feel your way as you go. Things will undoubtedly work out. Follow your nose. Play it by ear. Otherwise, just relax and enjoy yourself. Beautiful scenery up there around Brittle Rock, isn't it?"

"Yes," said John numbly.

"Yes, I always thought so, myself. Well I'll ring off, then. Call me any time you think you might need my help. Good-bye."

The voice in the phone broke the connection with a click. John shut off the power source at his end. A little sourly, he headed back toward the inn. It was against all known rules of biology, but he wondered if Joshua might not be part Hemnoid, from one of the sides of his family.

The mountain twilight had been dwindling as he talked; but his eyes had automatically adjusted to the failing light so that it was not until he stepped in through the hide curtain that protected the front entrance to the inn, that he realized how dark outside it had become. The thick, flaring candles around the room, the smells and the noise struck him as he entered, leaving him for a moment half-stunned and blinded.

The ordinary Dilbian inn, his hypno "memories" told him, was divided into a common room, a dormitory, and a kitchen. He had just stepped into the common room of this one; and he found it a square crowded space, jammed with wooden benches and tables like picnic tables at which three or four Dilbians could sit at once. There were about twenty or so Dilbians seated around it, all of them drinking and most of them arguing. The Hill Bluffer, he discovered, was off to one side arguing with a female Dilbian wearing an apron.

"But can't you tell me what to feed it?" the innkeeperess or whatever she was, was demanding, wringing her oversized, pawlike hands.

"Food!" roared the Hill Bluffer.

"But what kind of food? You haven't had the children dragging in one pet after another, like I have. I know. You feed it the wrong thing, and it dies. You're going to have to tell me exactly what—"

"How the unmentionable should I know exactly what?" bellowed the Bluffer, waving his arms furiously in the air and vastly entertaining those other guests of the inn who were nearby. "Give him something. Anything. See if he eats it. Some meat, some beer. Anything!"

"Talking about me?" inquired John.

They all looked down, discovering his presence for the first time. "Where'd he come from?" several of them could be heard inquiring audibly; although John had practically stepped on their toes on the way in.

"It talks!" gasped the inkeeperess.

"Didn't I say he did?" demanded the Bluffer. "Half-Pint, tell her what you want to eat."

John fingered the four-inch tubes of food concentrate clipped to his belt. Joshua had handed them to him in a rather off-hand fashion that very morning; but with no suggestion that he might be shortly using them. Apparently there had been something more than coincidence at work, however. John's hypno training reminded him now that while Dilbian food would nourish him, it might also very well trigger off some galloping allergy. He was not, at the present moment, in the mood for hives, or a case of eczema. The tubes would have to do. With something for bulk.

"Just a little beer," he said.

He could sense the roomful of Dilbians around him warming to him, immediately. Beer-drinking was a man's occupation. This small, alien critter could not be, they seemed to feel, *too* alien if he enjoyed a good drink.

The innkeeperess went off to fill John's order and John climbed up on one of the benches, put his elbows on the table and found himself more or less in the position of a five-year-old on Earth whose chin barely clears the parental tabletop. The beer arrived in a wooden, foot and a half high mug that smelled as sour as the most decayed of back-lot breweries. There was no handle. John looked about him.

The others were all sitting, Dilbian polite fashion, with one furry leg tucked underneath them, watching him, and waiting. John pulled his right leg up under his left, seized the mug in both hands, tilted its top-heavy weight, and gulped. A bitter, sour, flat-tasting liquid flowed down his throat. He swallowed, hastily, suppressing an urge to sputter, and set the mug back down, wiping his lips appreciatively with the back of his hand.

The room buzzed approval. And returned to its regular business.

John, left alone, swallowed a couple of times, finding the aftertaste not so bad as he had feared. Beer, in the sense of a mildly alcoholic beverage brewed from a fermented cereal, is after all, beer. No matter where you find it; and now that the first shock was over, John's taste buds were discovering similarities between this and other liquids of a like nature that they had encountered aforetime.

John surreptitiously uncrooked his leg, which was beginning to cramp, and turned to the Hill Bluffer to ask whether there had been any word of the Streamside Terror having passed, or news of his captive. But the Dilbian postman had disappeared.

Thoughtfully, John took another, and smaller, drink from his mug absentmindedly noting that this one was not so bad. It occurred to him that the Hill Bluffer might just have stepped out somewhere for a moment. In any case, John himself would be safer to stick where he was than go incautiously running around among the guests, most of whom had already finished eating and settled down to a serious evening of drinking.

But the Hill Bluffer did not return. John found his mug was empty. A few minutes later the inkeeperess replaced it with a full one, whether on the Bluffer's orders or her own initiative, John did not know. John was rather surprised to find he had drunk so much. He was not ordinarily a heavy drinker. But it was hard not to take large gulps from the clumsy and heavy mug; and it was hard to take human-sized swallows when all around him Dilbians were taking a half-pint at a sip, so to speak.

The common room, John decided, was after all, a rough, but friendly place. The Dilbians were good sorts. What had ever given him the idea that wandering around among them might not be safe? It occurred to him abruptly that it might be a clever move to go find the Bluffer. Bring the postman back to the table here. Buy him a beer and under the guise of casual conversation find out how the Dilbians really felt on the human-versus-Hemnoid question. John slipped down from the bench and headed off toward the inner door through which the inkeeperess had just disappeared.

The door, like the one outside, had a hide curtain. Pushing the heavy mass of this aside, John found himself in a long room, halfway down the side of which ran an open stone trough in which charcoal was burning. A rude hood above this ran to a chimney that sucked out most of the smoke and fumes to the quick overhead whip of the constant mountain winds.

Various Dilbians of all ages, mostly female or young, he noted, were moving around the fires in the trough and a long table that paralleled it, running down the room's center. Produce and carcasses hung from the wooden ceiling rafters and kegs were racked up near the back entrance of the kitchen. He recognized the innkeeperess through the steam and smoke, busy filling a double handful of mugs from one of the kegs; but the Bluffer was nowhere in the room. Those who were, ignored him as completely as had the spectators in the common room earlier, before he had spoken up. He waited until the inkeeperess was done and headed toward her. Then he stepped directly into her path.

"Eeeek!" she said, or the Dilbian equivalent, as she recognized him. She stopped dead, spilling some of the beer. "What are you doing in here? Get out!" She looked at him, uncertainly. "That's a good little Shorty," she said, changing the tone of her voice. "Go back to your nice table, now."

"I was looking for the Hill Bluffer—" began John.

"Bluffer's not here. Now, you go back to your table. Is your mug all empty? I'll bring you some more in just a minute."

"Just a second. As long as I've got you," said John, "can you tell me if the Streamside Terror came through here yesterday? He'd have had a Shorty like myself along. Did they stay here for the night?"

"He just stopped in for some meat and beer. I didn't see any Shorty," said the inkeeperess, a hint of impatience creeping into her tone. "In fact, I didn't see him. Wouldn't have cared if I did. I've no time for hill-and-alley brawlers. Fight, fight, that's all they think of! When's the work to get done? Now, shoo! Shoo!"

John shooed, back toward his table. The Hill Bluffer was still among the missing in the common room; but as John was climbing with a certain amount of effort back up onto his bench, he felt himself seized from behind and lifted into the air. Craning his head back to look over his shoulder, he saw he was being carried by a large male Dilbian with a pronounced body odor reminiscent of the woodchopper's, and a large pouch slung from one shoulder. This Dilbian seemed rather more than a little drunk.

Whooping cheerfully, the Dilbian staggered across the room, carrying John and came bang up against another table where two more villainous-looking characters like himself were waiting.

CHAPTER 5

John found himself dropped on top of the table between
them, as the Dilbian who had brought him over thumped
down heavily on a bench behind John. Instinctively, John
scrambled to his feet. He found himself surrounded by
three large, furry faces in a circle about three feet in
diameter. One of the faces had halitosis.

"There he be," said the one who had brought John
over. "A genuine Shorty."

"Full-growed, do you think?" inquired one of the others, a Dilbian with a broken nose and a scar creasing the
fur of his face. It was the third one at the table, evidently,
who needed to brush his teeth.

"Sure, he is," said the drunken one, indignantly. "You
don't think they'd let him run around here unless he was
all the way grown up?"

33

"Give him some beer," interjected the halitosis one, hoarsely.

A mug was thrust at John, who in prudence took it and tilted it to his mouth.

"Don't drink much," said Halitosis, after John had set the mug down, his already somewhat alcoholized head swimming after what had actually been a healthy human-sized draft of the liquid. "Like a bird. Like a little bird."

"Built man-shape, though," commented the one with the broken nose. "I wonder if he . . ." The question was of purely physiological significance.

"Not likely, at that size," said the drunken one. "Here he's chasing this here Shorty female the Terror's got, though. You reckon . . . ?"

One of the others—it was Halitosis again—hoarsely regretted the fact that they did not have the Shorty female there as well. It would, in his opinion, provide an opportunity for interesting and educative experimentation.

"Go to hell!" said John, instinctively in Basic Human.

"What?" asked the one with the pouch, drunkenly, behind him.

John made the most forceful translation into Dilbian that he could manage. The three Dilbians exploded into laughter.

"Have another drink," said Broken Nose; and a further pint or so of the beer was forced down John's throat. Broken Nose turned to his friends. "He better not get too tough with me, though!" He made a few humorous swipes with one huge hand in the air over John's head. John felt his hair fanned by the blows, which would have had little trouble splitting his skull wide open if they had connected.

Everybody laughed.

"I wonder, can he do tricks?" asked Halitosis.

"How about it, Shorty?" demanded the drunken Dilbian with the pouch, who seemed to have adopted an air of ownership toward John.

"Sure," said John.

"Show 'em one!"

"Give me a full mug of beer, then," said John. The three contributed from other mugs until one was brimming full—amongst guesses, polite and impolite—as to what the trick might require the beer for. When the mug was full, John reached down and hefted the gallon and a half container in his arms, taking a good grip on it.

"Now, watch closely," he said. "I take a firm hold here, rock back on my heels like this, and—"

He spun suddenly on one heel, swinging the mug around and sloshing a wave of beer into all three faces. As they ducked and pawed at their eyes, he leaped off the table, dodged under the nearest bench, and continued in a sort of broken-field run for the door. At any minute, he expected a large hand to reach down and capture him; but although he found himself forced to give opportunities for this, no one else seemed inclined to halt him. The rest of the common room of the inn was roaring with laughter at the three belonging to the table he had just left. And these were cursing, rooting around and overturning nearby benches under the evident impression that John was still in their immediate area. The door to the outside loomed before John. He ducked gratefully under its hide curtain and into the safety of the outer darkness.

He did not immediately halt on gaining the security of the night, but continued around the side of the inn toward the bare patch of trashyard behind it that stood between the inn and the dropoff into the gorge, down in which he could hear the unseen mountain river even now, brawling on its nighttime way.

He wanted room. Once behind the inn, he dropped into a sitting position in the shelter of some empty kegs that, with other junk, filled the area. Off to his right, a rectangle of light framed the hide curtain covering a door to the inn. From that door came the odors of cooking and the sound of quarreling voices. A back kitchen entrance, apparently.

John sat, breathing heavily and trying to pull himself

together. To his annoyance, he was more than a little drunk. The quart or so that the three at the table had forced him to drink on top of what he had already had, was now piling up inside him to give him a noticeable fuzziness. It would not last too long since it was the result of fast, rather than heavy, drinking. But for the moment it put him at a definite disadvantage in any contest where his only defense against overwhelming size and strength would be his natural speed and alertness. He decided to sit still where he was until his head was clear again, even if that took a couple of hours or so. Then carefully reconnoiter the place for the Hill Bluffer, in whose shadow he could enjoy some security.

He had just made up his mind to this, and was beginning to get his breath back, when there was a sudden flash of light from the hide curtain. Looking up, he caught sight for a moment of a female Dilbian figure, a small one, framed in silhouette for a second against the glare within. Then, swiftly, the curtain fell back into place, leaving only its pencil outline of yellow illumination.

But John had a sudden, uncomfortable feeling that the female he had seen had remained outside, rather than within. Quickly and quietly, he got to his feet in the darkness.

No sound from the direction of the door reached his ears; but he remembered how quietly the Tree Weeper had gone off through the woods as he left John and the Bluffer. And there had been no reason for the woodsman to hide the noise of his passage. If that was any index, and the Dilbian he had seen in the doorway was actually out there hunting him for any reason, John would have to rely on more than his ears for warning of any approach.

He lifted his nose and sniffed, cautiously. The kitchen odors had pretty much taken charge of the night air, but . . . yes, he was sure he caught a whiff of the peculiar Dilbian body odor.

And just at that moment, not ten feet from him, he heard clearly the sound of a double sniff.

Mentally kicking himself for his stupidity in forgetting that where human and Dilbian were concerned, two could play at this nose game, John moved speedily and silently away from the spot where he had been resting. The thing to do now, he thought, was to get upwind of his hunter, or huntress—if indeed it was the small female he had seen silhouetted, and then try to dodge past and get around once more to the front of the inn. Even Halitosis and his friends would be safer company than he was enjoying out here.

John began to move cautiously around to his right, toward the unseen and sounding river below the edge of the dropoff. No noise followed him; and this silence by itself was disturbing. John breathed shallowly and quietly, straining his eyes against the obsidian dark. He thought he saw something moving—black against black—but he was not sure. With the utmost possible silence, he began to back away, crouching. If he could find the edge of the cliff without falling over it, and work back along to a point level with the end of the inn, perhaps a quick dash from that spot for the inn's front door—

The odds were against him. Just at that moment, he tripped and fell over a broken hoop from a keg.

The thud and clatter of his fall cried out in the tense silence. There was a sudden, tearing rush at him by something large and invisible; he rolled frantically free, stood up and ran.

There was no moon showing over this part of Dilbia in this season of the year, and the starlight gave little illumination. Still, what there was was enough to show him the ragged edge of the dropoff. He skidded to a halt, just short of tumbling headlong into the canyon. He stopped and turned, half-crouched, holding his breath and listening.

His heart hammered. There was no other sound.

End of round one, his brain suggested idiotically. And beginning of round two. Seconds out of the corners.

He held his breath and went on listening. For a long minute or two he heard nothing. Then, at some short distance behind him, he heard again the faint but unmistakable sound of sniffing. He froze. He was between the wind blowing up over the edge of the dropoff, and whoever hunted him. That sniffing nose would lead the pursuer straight to him.

Step by step, like a cat cautiously crossing a basket of eggs, he began to back up along the lip of the cliff. He had been blocked off from escape around the near end of the inn. Possibly he could retreat and make another try, this time around the far end. That is, if the hunter didn't catch up with him before he got that far, as was more than likely.

John took a moment now to wish that he had picked up a piece of barrel hoop, or some sort of a weapon from the trash lying about the yard. The female he had seen framed in the doorway was not so much bigger than he that something in the way of a club might not give him a fighting chance. He stretched out his hands as he went, sweeping the ground, in hopes of encountering something that could be put to use defensively.

His fingers trailed over the stones of the ground; then touched something hard, but a moment's feeling about showed it to be the end of a complete keg, and useless for his purposes. A little farther, he encountered a barrel hoop, but it was complete and roundly harmless. It was not until the third try, that he found something useful.

It was a chunk of what was probably kindling wood to one Dilbian size, a length of split, dried log about four inches thick and about two and a half feet long. It was better than nothing and John's hand closed gratefully about it, taking it with him.

He was three-quarters of the way to the far end of the inn, now. A little farther, and perhaps he would not need the chunk of kindling after all. A little farther . . .

He had backed clear to a point level with the end of the inn, and its front side was less than thirty yards away. One quick dash and he would be safe. John froze and sniffed silently. He listened.

Silence held the night.

John turned his head slowly from right to left, scanning the darkness behind him and the darkness between him and the inn. Over the rushing of the waters far below he could hear, through the bones of his inner ear, the creak of his tense neck muscles moving in the ringing silence of the waiting hush.

Nothing could be seen. Nothing moved. End of round three, whispered his brain. Beginning of round four. Seconds out of their corners. Still holding the club, he got up on his toes and knuckles like a sprinter about to start.

There was a sudden movement. A rearing up in the darkness before him. He tried to dodge, felt his feet slipping in the loose gravel and rock, struck out with the club and felt it connect . . .

And something indescribably hard smashed down onto his head, sending him swirling down and away, into starshot blackness.

CHAPTER 6

John opened his eyes to bright sunlight.

Dilbia's sun, just above the snow-gilt peaks of the mountain horizon, was shining its first clear rays of the day directly into his eyes. He blinked sleepily, and started to roll over onto his side, turning his back to the penetrating dazzle of the light—

—and grabbed with every ounce of strength he could summon at the rough trunk of a stubby tree growing sideways out of the granite rock beside him.

For a long second, he hung there sweating. Then he wriggled back a ways, but without releasing his grip on the little tree, until he felt himself firmly wedged in among the rocks around him. Then—but still not letting go of the tree—he risked another look.

He lay on a narrow ridge several hundred feet above a mountain river and eternity. The water was far below.

How far, he did not take the time or trouble to estimate. It was far enough.

He turned over and looked up. Just above him, a slight overhang came to an end, than there was about fifteen feet of jagged rock cliffside, then a steep slope, and some small sweaty distance beyond that, the haven that was the edge of the inn's backyard. A bit of rusty hoop overhanging the edge identified it as such.

Swallowing a little convulsively, John relaxed his grip on the tree.

He was wide awake now, and in condition to notice a number of scrapes and gouges. There was one plowed groove that started up from his wrist and almost made it to his elbow. For a second John almost regretted not being back comfortably asleep again. Then he remembered the gorge below and was glad he was not. He looked up at the cliff face above him once more, and began to pick out a route by which he could ascend it.

He found it easily enough. The climb was not one which called for mountaineering experience, though John had that, along with other sports qualifications. But, thought John as he climbed, it was not exactly what everybody would pick for exercise before breakfast.

He made it up over the lip of the yard and lay there for a second, panting. In the daylight, the yard looked very small and ordinary. It was hard to believe that it had been the lengthy and dangerous arena where he skulked and fought for his life the night before. John got to his feet, brushed himself off, and limped around to the front of the inn, where some commotion seemed to be in process, and stumbled upon a scene that made him blink.

The entire populace of the inn, guests and help alike, were drawn up in the road before it. They stood in fairly orderly ranks before an open space in which a grizzled and lean old Dilbian sat on a bench placed on top of a table. Between this individual and the crowd—among which John recognized the inkeeperess in a clean apron— were John's three tormentors of the night before, looking hangdog between two large Dilbians carrying axes over their shoulders. What, from its stained and gouged appearance looked ominously like a chopping block, was in position a little in front of the prisoners.

Across from the prisoners, the Hill Bluffer was windmilling his arms and orating in tones of outrage.

"The mail!" he was roaring, as John tottered around the corner of the inn into the full sight of everybody. "The mail is sacred. Anyone laying hands upon the mail in transit—"

At that moment, he caught sight of John; and broke off. The total assemblage, including the judge, turned and stared at John as he limped forward into their midst.

"There!" burst out the inkeeperess. "Didn't I say it? The poor little fellow—probably frightened out of his wits. Been up a tree all this time, no doubt. No reason at all for chopping three poor men who're just having a friendly drink. But, that's it for you, a man can't get beyond his middle years but he has to be playing judge at every opportunity. And every man who ever wore a mail pouch ranting and raving as if there wasn't anything in the world but letters—much good letters do anyone, anyway. And those who can't wait to waste their good time standing around at a trial and an execution not much better. Poor little Shorty." She swooped down on John, fluttering her apron at him. "Now you just get right inside there and have your morning beer. *Men!*"

John let himself be herded inside. In addition to all his other aches and pains, he had just discovered himself to be the possessor of a walking hangover. And the Dilbian beer was at present the quickest—and only—cure for that.

Later, after John had drunk his breakfast and washed off a certain amount of dried blood, he and the Hill Bluffer got under way again. The long-legged Dilbian had fizzed and popped with the effervescence of throttled outrage for the first fifteen minutes or so following John's return. But on being shut up by the inkeeperess, he had lapsed into a thoughtful silence, and he continued to be silent during the first few hours of their trip.

Meanwhile, thanks to a generally good physical condition and possibly in some measure to the beer and the food concentrates, John was recovering rapidly. Their way from Brittle Rock led through the highlands toward Knobby Gorge, the Bluffer had informed John, earlier. After that they would begin the gradual descent down the far, forested side of the Cold Mountains to Sour Ford and the Hollows. The Hollows was clan-country for the Streamside Terror, and their hope was to catch up with him before he reached it.

The first part of the day's trailing after they left Brittle Rock led by narrow mountainside paths and across swinging suspension bridges over deep cuts in the rock that ended, far below, in rushing currents of white water. The Hill Bluffer trod this way for the first couple of hours, not merely with the casualness of someone well-used to it, but with the actual absent-mindedness of a person in deep thought.

"Hey!" said John, finally, when for the fifth time that morning the Hill Bluffer had shown signs of intending to walk off the path on to several hundred feet of thin air.

"Huh? What?" grunted the Hill Bluffer, saving them both with a practiced twist of an ankle. "What's that? Something on your mind, Half-Pint?"

As a matter of fact, thought John, there was. The notion born out of the fumes of the beer the previous evening when he had sat in what he thought was momentary safety in the inn's backyard—before whoever it was had come out the kitchen door to hunt him—had returned to mind this morning as not a bad idea after all. Why not, he thought again, find out an honest Dilbian point of view about the human-Hemnoid struggle to make friends with the natives of this world? It was something that might not only rate him a commendation after all this was over; but might furnish him some valuable pointers on his present situation. These first two hours of no conversation had given him a chance to turn the matter over in his mind and try to think of how to frame the question.

He had finally come to the conclusion that, considering the Dilbian character, a direct approach was probably the best.

"Yes," he said to the Hill Bluffer now. "I've been trying to figure out why you Dilbians like the Hemnoids better than us Shorties."

The Bluffer did not rise to the bait, as John had half-hoped by immediately denying that the Dilbians played favorites.

"Oh, that," said the Hill Bluffer, as calmly as if they were talking about a law of nature. "Why, it stands to reason, Half-Pint. Take the Beer-Guts Bouncer, now; or that new little one—"

"What new little one?" asked John, sharply, remembering the Hemnoid back in the woods when they had stopped to talk to Tree Weeper.

"What's his name—Tark-*ay*, I guess they call him. The one who's supposed to have been quite a scrapper back on his own home territory. You take someone like him, for example."

"What about him?" asked John.

"Well, now," said the Bluffer, judiciously, "he's nowhere near the proper size of a man, of course. But he's not ridiculous, like you Shorties. Why, two of you wouldn't make a half-grown pup. And if people don't lie, he's strong enough to stand up to a man and holler for his rights—yes and back them up, too, if he had to, win or lose."

"That's important?" said John. "To you Dilbians?"

"Why, of course it's important to any man!" said the Bluffer. "A man might lose. Bound to lose sometime, to someone, of course. But if he stands up for his rights, then there can't be anything worse happen to him but get killed. I mean, he's got standing in the community."

"We Shorties stand up for our rights, too," said John.

"Sure. But—hell!" said the Bluffer. "Besides, what do

you mean, you all stand up for your rights? What about
the Squeaking Squirt?"

"Well . . ." said John, uncomfortably.

He had, for the moment, forgotten Heiner Schlaff, that
blot on the human escutcheon where Dilbia was concerned. Now, here Schlaff was being thrown in his face,
as he must have been to Joshua on a number of occasions. For the first time, John felt a twinge of sympathy
with the dapper little ambassador. How do you go about
explaining that one man's reactions are not typical of a
race's?

Attack, thought John.

"Oh, you never knew a man from Dilbia, here, who
lost his head or got scared?" he said.

"I never knew one who yelled just because he was
picked up!" snorted the Bluffer.

"Who'd pick one up? Who's big enough to?" said John.

That apparently stopped the Bluffer for a moment. He
did not immediately answer.

"You just imagine something big enough to pick you
up and tell me if there aren't some men just as big as
you who'd lose their head if something like that picked
them up?"

"They'd be pretty poor if they did," growled the Bluffer.
He muttered to himself for a minute. "Anyway," he said,
"that's not the point. The point is, it doesn't matter. It's
just plain ridiculous, even if a Shorty like you'd *try* to
stand up for his rights. Any idiot could see you wouldn't
have a chance against a real man."

"Oh, you think so," said John; wondering what in the
galaxy was making him pretend that the Bluffer was not
a hundred per cent correct. After a second's thought, he
concluded it was probably much the same human-type
reaction that had sent Rudi Maltetti diving for the javelin in Brisbane, on the occasion with the Hemnoid
ambassador.

The Bluffer snorted with laughter.

"Now," he said, when he had got his humor off his

chest, "one of those Fatties, there's be some point to an argument. But someone like you, why I couldn't take a shove at someone like you. It'd be like swatting a bird."

He brooded for a second.

"Besides," he said. "Some of you Shorties may not be too bad; but a real man doesn't take kindly to critters that got to go around using all kinds of tools for things. Fighting with tools, taking advantage with tools, getting ahead of somebody else by using tools. But particularly fighting with them—that's just plain, downright yellow; the way we see it!"

"Is that so?" said John. "Well, listen to me for a minute—"

"Hold on. Hold on." The Bluffer held up a pacific lump of a hand. "I can't go fighting with my own mail; besides, didn't I say some of you Shorties weren't too bad? Why, you know how Little Bite got his name, and—"

"Who?" said John. And then his hypno training informed him that Little Bite was the Dilbian nickname for Joshua Guy. But the hypno training was silent on how the name had been selected. "Oh, no, I don't."

"You don't?" ejaculated the Bluffer.

"No," said John, suddenly cautious and wondering what he had blundered into.

"Everybody knows that," said the Bluffer.

There was no help for it.

"I don't," said John.

Slowly, the Bluffer turned his head to look back over his shoulder. The eye that met John's was alight with sudden puzzlement and suspicion.

"You're pretty strange, even for a Shorty," said the postman slowly. "What're you trying to pull? Everybody knows how Little Bite got his name. And you're a Shorty yourself and you *don't?*"

He stopped dead in the trail and stood, still staring back at John.

"What're you trying to pull?" he said again.

CHAPTER 7

"Let me down," said John.

"What?" said the Bluffer. "What's that you say?"

"I said," repeated John evenly through his teeth, even though his heart was rising into his throat, "let me down. I've had it."

"Had what?" said the Bluffer; and this time there was more puzzlement than suspicion in his voice.

"I've sat up here," said John, letting his voice climb on a note of anger—not much, but noticeably. "I've sat up here, hung up in this harness and had you insult us Shorties by saying we're all like the Squeaking Squirt. I've had you call me yellow. But I'll be roasted over a slow fire if I have to sit up here and have you imply I'm pulling something just because Little Bite didn't have time to tell me how he got his name. Just let me down on solid ground and by my paternal grandfather—"

"Hey-hey-hey—*hey!*" cried the Bluffer. "I told you I couldn't go fighting with my mail. What're you getting so hot about?"

"I don't have to take this!" shouted John.

"Well, don't!" shouted the Bluffer. "I didn't mean anything against you, personally. You asked me, didn't you? The smaller they are, the touchier they are! I was surprised you didn't know how Little Bite got his name, was all. I was just going to tell you."

"Well, then, why didn't you tell me?" said John in a calmer tone.

"I will—I will!" said the Bluffer, grumpily, taking up the trail again. John relaxed in his saddle and surreptitiously wiped his brow. His hypno training and the Bluffer together had let him know that the Dilbian mail was sacrosanct, but whether that meant from assault by the postman himself, he had not been completely sure, even then. But evidently, even that was true.

"Actually," the Bluffer was saying in a calmer tone, "nearly everybody down at Humrog and through the mountains thinks all right of Little Bite. He's a guest at Humrog, now; and nobody'd dare touch him. But this was back in the first days after he came here—"

A chuckle erupted momentarily into the Bluffer's story.

"—Old Hammertoes, down at Humrog. That old coot's always getting hot about something. Well, he was talking about the good old days, one day. He was drinking some, too . . ."

John, after the night before at the inn, found himself with a rather graphic mental image of what "drinking a little" might amount to in the case mentioned.

"He was about half loaded, and got himself all riled up over the thought that we had foreigners like Shorties and Fatties all over the place, nowadays. The old world was going to pot, he said; there ought to be a law. He was about half-drunk and he headed uptown."

John's graphic mental image staggered out into the cobblestone street of Humrog as he remembered it.

"He was all set to put Little Bite—only everybody called him just the Shorty, in those days—back in his shell and kick him clear back into the sky where he came from. Well, he went up and knocked on Little Bite's door. Little Bite opens it; and Hammertoes leans down and shouts in his face:

" 'All right, Shorty! I'm packing you off to your own hole, now!'

"And he made a grab at Little Bite through the door. But Little Bite had this sort of chain on the door so it wouldn't open up all the way; and Hammertoes couldn't get much more than one arm inside. So there he is, half-drunk, hollering 'Come here, you Shorty! You can't get away. I'll get you; and when I get hold of you—' "

John winced. His mental image was becoming so graphic as to be almost painful.

"Then Little Bite, who's picked up something sharp, takes good aim at that big hand of Hammertoes, and cuts Hammertoes a couple times across the knuckles, practically to the bone. Old Hammertoes yells bloody murder and yanks his hand back." The Bluffer began to laugh. "Little Bite slams the door."

The Bluffer was laughing so hard he could not go on. He slowed down and stopped, leaning against the cliff side with one hand while he whooped at the memory. His whole body shook. John held on to his saddle with both hands. It was very disconcerting to be bucked around by the equivalent of a horse that was telling him a funny story at the same time.

"Any—anyway," gasped the Bluffer, getting himself partially back under control, "Old Hammertoes comes back up to the bar, there, dripping blood and sucking on his knuckles.

" 'Why, what happened?' says everybody else at the bar.

" 'Nothing,' says Hammertoes.

" 'Something must've happened. Look at your hand,' says everybody.

" 'I tell you, nothing happened!' yells Hammertoes. 'He

wouldn't let me in there where I could grab a hold on him. So I come away. And as for my hand—that's got nothing to do with it. He didn't hurt my hand, hardly at all. All he done was to give it a little bite!' "

The Bluffer went off into another fit of laughter that necessitated stopping and leaning against the cliff. But this time, John found himself laughing too. The story *was* funny—or it seemed funny to John, at least. They laughed together; and when they had both run down, rested a moment in a silence that was almost companionable.

"You know," said the Bluffer, after a moment's silence. "You aren't too bad, for a Shorty."

"You're all right, yourself—for a man," said John.

The Bluffer fell silent again. But he did not move on. After a moment, he sat down on a nearby boulder.

"Climb down," he said, over his shoulder. "I got something to talk to you about; and I can do it better if I'm looking at you while I'm at it."

John frowned, hesitated; but climbed down. He walked around in front of the Dilbian and found that, with the Bluffer seated, and himself standing, they were as close to eye to eye as they would normally ever expect to be.

"What is it?" asked John.

"You know," said the Bluffer with an effort, "you're not bad for a Shorty as I say and—"

However, having got this far, he was stuck. It was rather hard for a human like John to read embarrassment on a Dilbian face; but if such a thing was possible, John thought he spotted that emotion on the Hill Bluffer now. He avoided the postman's eyes and simply waited. Looking off past the big head, he saw, far beyond the sharp mountain peaks, a few white puffs of clouds, looking peaceful and innocent.

"What I mean is," said the Bluffer finally, after an apparent inner struggle. "The Streamside Terror's had his drinking mug spilt."

For a moment, John did not understand. And then he did, his hypno training coming once more to the rescue. To have one's drinking mug silt, in Dilbian terms, was to endure a deadly affront to personal honor. In short, someone had given the Streamside Terror reason for starting a blood feud. John had a sinking feeling as to whom it might be.

"By me?" said John. "But he's never seen me."

"No. By Little Bite," said the Bluffer. "But you're sort of hauled into it. It's real peculiar."

"I'll bet," said John, thinking about the small ambassador back at Humrog.

"You see," said the Bluffer, "Little Bite's a guest at Humrog nowadays."

"I know. You told me," said John.

"Let me finish. Now, since he's a guest, his fights are Humrog's fights. But Little Bite shamed the Terror, when he told old Shaking Knees the Terror shouldn't have Boy Is She Built. Because that meant the Terror was being called not worthy. Well, now what's the Terror going to do? He can't get mad at Shaking Knees for not letting him have Boy Is She Built. A man's got a right to look out for his daughter. He could get mad at Little Bite; but nobody in his right mind—even somebody like Streamside—is going to start a blood feud with a town of five thousand.

"I mean, Clan Hollows could back him up, and that's more of a match; but Clan Hollows would be crazy if they did—when most of the stuff they sell gets sold in and to Humrog. No, what'd happen is that the grandfathers of Clan Hollows'd declare it a personal matter and Streamside'd have a choice of hiding out in Clan Hollows territory for the rest of his life, or being up by the heels before the year was out."

"I see," said John. And he did. He was thinking deeply. Up until this point he had simply refused to accept the notion that Joshua could be deliberately at fault in sending him out on this mission. Mistakenly so, that was imaginable. But to plan to draft a man and send him out to cover up what had evidently been a diplomatic error on the little man's part—it was staggering. Men of sufficient stature to be appointed ambassadors, particularly to posts like this, did just not descend to such unethical tactics to hide their dirty linen. The job Joshua had given John to do was absolutely illegal; and John was under absolutely no compulsion to go through with it.

He opened his mouth to say so, to tell the Bluffer that they should return immediately to Humrog—and closed it again, slowly, without having uttered a word. He had suddenly remembered how cleverly Joshua had him trapped. The Bluffer would certainly not just turn around on John's say-so and head back for the town. He had contracted to deliver a piece of mail to the Streamside Terror; and his Dilbian honor was at stake.

The Hill Bluffer had been waiting the several seconds it took John to think this out. Now, he opened his large mouth again, and put a further aspect of the matter out for John's consideration.

"You know," said the Bluffer. "You can't get Greasy Face back from the Terror without fighting him?"

The words went in John's ears and knocked the problem of Joshua clear back out of sight.

"*Fighting* him??" he echoed.

"Yes," said the Bluffer. "Man-to-man. No weapons. No holds barred."

John blinked. He looked past the postman's head at the puffs of white clouds. They had not moved. They were still there. So were the mountains. It must be something wrong with his ears.

"Fighting him?" said John again, feeling like a man in a fast elevator which has just begun to descend.

"A man's got his pride," said the Bluffer. "If you take Greasy Face back, his mug's spilt all over again." He leaned a little toward John. "That is, unless you whip him in a fair fight. Then there's no blood feud to it. You're just a better man than he is, that's all. But that's why I haven't been able to figure this. You aren't bad for a Shorty. You pulled a good trick with that beer on those drunks last night. You got guts."

He looked searchingly at John.

"But I mean—Hell, you can't fight the Terror. Anybody'd know that. I mean—*Hell*!" said the Bluffer, explosively finding his vocabulary insufficient to describe his overcharged feelings.

John was wishing he could express to the postman how much he agreed with him.

"So what," inquired the Bluffer, "are you going to do when I deliver you to Streamside?"

John thought about it. He took a deep breath and blew it out again.

"I don't know," he said, at last.

"Well, not my problem," said the Bluffer, getting to his feet. "Go on around and climb on by the rock, there. Oh, by the way," he added as John followed this instruction. "Know who it was pitched you over the cliff last night?"

"Who?" asked John. He had explained the evening adventures and his waking up to the Hill Bluffer over the morning beer; but the Bluffer had made no comment, then.

"The Cobbly Queen. You on, back there?"

"Yes. Who?" said John, remembering how the woodsman had winked at them while mentioning the same mythical character yesterday.

"Boy," said the Bluffer, a little grimly, "Is She Built. The same little wagtail that sends postmen messages to make a five mile sidetrip to pick up special mail, while she's back at the inn monkeying with the mail he was carrying to start off with. I'd sure like," said the Bluffer, "to figure out how she could leave with enough head start to be there ahead of us, and still know that was where we were going."

So, thought John, pricking up his ears at this information, did he.

"Well, let's go."

And the Hill Bluffer swung off again once more down the trail. Swinging and bouncing in the saddle on the Dilbian's broad back, John mulled over this new information that had just been supplied him. It occurred to him that it might be a wise idea, on all accounts to phone Joshua Guy back at Humrog, and let the ambassador know John had just uncovered the whole of his seamy little scheme.

There was no doubt now that Joshua Guy, inadvertently or not, had got himself into a bad diplomatic situation with the Streamside Terror with his advice to the father of Boy Is She Built. It had been none of the human's business to begin with whom Boy Is She Built got paired off with. In fact, it was just this sort of monkeying in private alien affairs that had gotten humanity into hot water before. A human representative who goofed like that stood in a fair way of being chopped, himself, back home once the news got out, and provided it could be proved against him. Blunders like that had cost human lives before and might well again.

It came home to John, suddenly, with a repetition of the elevator feeling he had experienced a little before, that one of the lives it might cost in this instance might well be his own.

For if John met the Terror and got mashed, it might solve several things at once for Joshua Guy.

In the first place, it would probably save Greasy Face, since the Terror would have no further reason for holding on to her after his shame had been washed out in John's blood; and Shaking Knees had given the successful warrior Boy Is She Built, after all, as he would be practically obligated to do so under Dilbian mores. That would get Joshua off the hot spot where the life of the female human sociologist was concerned. Also, it would dispose of the only one, John again, who knew what Joshua had been up to and could bring human charges against him. Moreover, it would allow him to sidetrack any blame in the affair by pinning it on John's misman-agement of matters after John had left Humrog.

And the Hill Bluffer was carrying John inexorably to the destination Joshua had planned for him. There was no hope of turning the Dilbian postman.

There was, however, one thing John could do. He could call Joshua on the wrist phone and make it clear that unless Joshua somehow pulled him and Greasy Face out of this, John would spread word among the Dilbians about what was going on. After that, it would be merely a matter of time before the news leaked past Joshua and back to authorities on Earth. A good bluff might get Joshua out here to mend things on the double. After all, if he could stop things now, there would be no capital crime such as would be involved if the Terror killed John or Greasy Face. Joshua would be a fool not to stop things.

Cooled by a sudden rush of relief, John lifted his wrist to his lips. It was then that he noticed something.

The long gouge in his left forearm ran right down under where the strap to his wrist phone had gone around his wrist. And, wherever the wrist phone was now, John, at least, no longer had it.

CHAPTER 8

There are times when the imagination simply gives up. It happened that way with John about this time. It was, he knew, a temporary thing—or he hoped it was—which possibly a good night's sleep or a bit of unexpected luck, or some such thing, could snap him out of. But for the moment, the intellectual, hard-working part of his brain had hung up a notice "Out—Back later" and gone off for a nap.

He simply could not think constructively. Whenever he tried to figure out a way out of his present situation, he came back around to the fact that the Hill Bluffer, whether John liked it or not, was taking him—and nothing could stop the process—directly to the Streamside Terror, who—and nothing could stop that, either—would pick John up and effectively kill him. It was written. Kismet. Give up.

John did. In the end, he slumped in the saddle and dozed.

A sudden stopping on the part of the Hill Bluffer woke John with a start. He sat up and looked around him.

At first he saw nothing but a gorge with vertical sides of light, salmon-colored granite and a thread of a river away down at its base. Then he realized that he was looking over the edge of a ledge that the Bluffer was standing on and he readjusted the angle of his view.

Having done this, he saw that the ledge was actually almost as large as the widening of the road had been at Brittle Rock Inn, only they were standing at the very edge of it. At this edge was one end of a suspension bridge that swooped breathtakingly across the open space of the gorge to a landing on a smaller ledge on the far side. Its further end was anchored high on the face of the rock wall behind the further ledge, where the trail took up again.

At this end there was a small log hut, outside which the Hill Bluffer was now in conversation with a hefty-looking, middle-aged Dilbian.

"Saw him turn off at the fork myself!" this Dilbian was bellowing. "You questioning the word of a public official? Want me to swear on my winch-cable? Eh?" He laid a heavy, pawlike hand on the great drum on which the cables of the bridge were wound, crank-driven through a series of carved wooden gears by a polished wooden handle.

"I was just asking!" roared the Bluffer. "A man can ask, can't he?"

"If he asks politely, all right," said the evident bridgekeeper, stubbornly. "I said I seen him turn off at the fork on this side and go over the bridge there." He pointed along this side of the gorge and John saw where, on this side the trail did split, one way following along the near cliff face, and the other crossing the bridge disappearing through a cleft in the rock. "He headed toward the high country and Ice Dog Glacier."

"All right. All right, I believe you!" said the Bluffer. He turned toward the bridge.

"Hey," said the bridgekeeper. "Your toll."

"Toll!"

The Bluffer spun about in outrage.

"Me? A government postman? Toll?"

"Well," grumbled the other, "after doubting my word like that, I'd think you'd want—"

"Toll!" snorted the Bluffer, in contempt, and turning about, marched off over the bridge without waiting for the bridgekeeper to finish.

"Are we going someplace different?" asked John, as they left the far end of the bridge, and headed into the cleft in the rock.

"Streamside's headed for glacier country," muttered the Bluffer. "Or maybe he plans to double over the mountains the other way at Halfway House, and end up in the Free Forest. Anyway we got to shake a leg to catch him, if that's it. *Toll!*"

He snorted again and put on speed.

Their new road took them steeply up and away from the territory of rivers and deep gorges. After half an hour's climb they began to emerge into an area of wide, stony slopes across which a high-altitude wind blew with the sort of coolness that did not permit sleeping in the saddle.

It was past noon when they came around a bend in the slope three hours later and approached another inn. This one, situated to take advantage of what little natural shelter there was in this exposed area, was built almost exclusively of stone and earth. They stopped for a midday break, and John got down to stretch his legs gratefully. His brain was still refusing to make itself useful by coming up with any plan to frustrate the ambassador; but the cool, keen winds had blown John into physical wakefulness, so much so that he realized he was tired of the saddle. If it had not been clearly an impractical notion, John would have liked to forego riding and walk for a while.

But there was no hope of that. If John should try to make it on foot, the Bluffer would be over the horizon and out of sight inside of half an hour. That is, unless he held his pace down to that of his human companion. And, numb-minded as he was at the moment, John had to smile at the thought of the explosive and impatient Bluffer's reaction, if he was asked to do that.

So, John made the best of it by taking a stroll around the stone inn of Halfway House to take the kinks out of his leg muscles. When he approached the front door of it again, he found the Bluffer on the point of explosion. The cause of this was not John, or anything he had done, but the other visitors at the Halfway House.

They were laughing at the Bluffer.

There were half a dozen of them just outside the door of the House, headed by a relatively short and chunky Dilbian carrying a sort of alpenstock.

"Hor! Hor!" the short Dilbian was bellowing.

"You want to make something out of it?" the Bluffer was roaring.

"What is it?" asked John. Nobody even heard him, of course.

"Fixed you right!" chortled the short Dilbian.

"Fixed me . . . ! I'll show who fixed me!" The Bluffer shook both fists high over his head. It was an awesome sight. "Swore to me as a public official, he did. Said he'd seen the Terror take the fork this way with his own two eyes!"

"He did! Sure he did!" put in somebody else. "Tell him, Snowshoe!"

"Why," said the chunky Dilbian, "he saw the Terror take the right fork, all right. But after that he closed his eyes for a bit there, just like she'd arranged."

"She?" bellowed the Bluffer. "Boy Is She Built?"

"Why, who else, postman? The Terror was waiting for her to catch up with him there.

" 'That long-legged postman's right behind me,' she says.

" 'Don't, now,' she says. 'You can't fight the government mail,' she says. 'I got a better idea.' And she fixed it up with old Winchrope to close his eyes while they come back out of one fork and took the other to the Hollows with the female Shorty they had along." The chunky Dilbian named Snowshoes stopped to laugh again. "Passing by myself at the time. Saw the whole thing. Laugh! Thought I'd split a gut!"

The Bluffer bellowed to the mountain sky. His eyes fell on John and he snatched John up like the package John was officially supposed to be.

The next thing they knew, they were fifteen yards back along the trail they had just come, and gaining speed.

"Hey!" said John. "At least let me get in the saddle."

"What? Oh!" snarled the Bluffer. He checked and waited a few impatient seconds, while John crawled over his shoulder into the saddle. Then he took off again.

Two hours later they were back at the wrong end of the bridge. The word *wrong* was, thought John, used advisedly. For the bridge was now out of their reach.

What had been done was simple enough. Their end of the bridge had its cables fastened to the sheer cliff face some twenty feet back and another twenty feet above their heads. What had been done was to tighten these cables by means of the winch to which they were attached at their other end. The sag of the span had straightened out, lifting the bridge up and out of their reach.

The Hill Bluffer bellowed across the gap. His first forty words were a description of Winchrope's person and morals, his last four an order to put the bridge back down where he and John could reach it, and cross.

There was no answer at the far end. The windlass to which the cables were attached showed no inclination to comply with the order by itself and no one emerged from the bridgekeeper's hut.

"What's happened?" asked John.

"He's in there!" raged the Bluffer. "That bridge isn't

supposed to be cranked up until night—and then only to keep people from sneaking across and not paying their toll. He's in there, all right. He just won't come out and let it down, because he knows what I'll do to him the minute I get over there." He thundered across the gorge again. "Get out here and let down this unmentionable, indescribable bridge, so I can get over it at you and tear your head off!"

The bridgekeeper still showed no eagerness to take the Bluffer up on this invitation. Small wonder, thought John privately, standing prudently back out of arms reach of the wrought-up postman.

The Bluffer stopped shouting and looked up at the bridge overhead. He made a half-hearted motion as if to try reaching for it; but it was obviously many feet beyond even the stretch of his long arms. He dropped them, defeatedly.

"All right!" he roared once more, shaking his fist across the gorge. "I'll climb up the gorge. I'll go along the cliff. I don't need a trail. I'll get to the Hollows before Streamside does! And then I'm coming back for you!"

John stirred suddenly, pricked for the first time out of his mental lethargy.

"Go up the gorge?" he said.

"You heard me!" growled the Bluffer. "Who needs a trail? It's the shortest route. We'll get there in half the time."

John glanced over the Bluffer's shoulder at the sheer walls of the gorge on the edge of which they were standing. There were footholds along it, all right, but even for someone of the Bluffer's skill. And then there was that business of catching up with Streamside faster than expected. John came fully awake.

"Lift me up," he said to the postman. "If I can reach, and climb across and let the winch out—"

The Bluffer's eyes lit up.

"Sure," he said, enthusiastically. He picked up John and they tried it. John, upheld by the ankles and holding his body stiff, stretched upward toward the bare cable near the end of the bridge's flooring slats, but was rewarded only by a throat-squeezing view of the Knobby River, nine hundred feet below.

"Put me down," he said at last. The Hill Bluffer put him down.

John, not in the most cheerful mood in the universe after his scenic view of the gorge, went over and examined the cliff face leading up to the anchor points of the bridge cables. He possessed a fair amount of rock climbing experience and the granite face before him was not too bad, although no one of the bulk and necessary clumsiness of a Dilbian could have made it. It was not that, so much, that was giving him cold shivers, as the fact that once he had reached an anchor point, he would have to work out along the bare cable some twenty-odd feet before he came to the bridge proper.

Oh, well, he thought.

"Hey! Where're you going?" shouted the Bluffer.

John did not answer. He needed his breath and anyway his destination was obvious. After a little time, he reached the near anchor point, and got his arms over the rough, three-inch cable. He rested for a moment and surveyed the situation. The Bluffer was just below him, staring up and looking foreshortened by the angle of John's vision. So was the ledge. John did not look down into the gorge.

After a while, he got his breath back and he climbed up with both arms and legs wrapped around the cable, himself on top, and began to inch his way toward the bridge end, floating in an absurdly large amount of space at a remarkable distance from him. It occurred to him, after he had covered about six or eight feet in this fashion, that a real hero in this situation would undoubtedly have got to his feet and tightrope-walked the really rather broad cable to the end of the bridge proper. This, in addition to impressing the watching Hill Bluffer, would have shortened the time of personal suspense considerably.

John concluded that evidently he was just not the stuff out of which real heroes are made, and continued to inch along.

Eventually, he reached the bridge, crawled out on it and lay panting for a while, then got up and crossed to the far side of the gorge. The far ledge of the gorge was still the home of somebody dodging a process server. John walked over to the winch, and utilizing a handy rock, managed to knock loose the lock-ratchet.

The winch roared loose, the cables boomed like gigantic bowstrings; and the far end of the bridge slammed down, raising a temporary cloud of dust through which the Hill Bluffer was shortly to be seen advancing with a look of grim purpose. He stalked past John and entered the bridgekeeper's abode. Without knocking.

There was a moment of silence; and then sound erupted like a bomb exploding inside the hut.

John looked hastily around for something to climb up on or inside of, where he would be out of harm's way. He had never seen a pair of Dilbians fight; but it was remarkable how accurately his ears interpreted what was going on inside the hut right now.

After a little while, abruptly, there was peace. The Hill Bluffer emerged, dabbing with one big hand at a torn ear, but otherwise looking not unsatisfied.

"What happened?" asked John.

The Bluffer went over and washed off his ear in a large stone trough that ran along side the shack.

"Said it was *his* bridge. Hah!" replied the Bluffer. "Nobody stops the mail. I fixed him." He paused, water dripping from one side of his big head and looked at John. "You did all right, too, Half-Pint."

"Me?" said John.

"Climbing up and out across that cable to the bridge. Never thought I'd see a Shorty, even a good one, doing something like that. Actually took a little guts, I'd say. All right. Climb up and let's get going."

John complied.

"You didn't kill him?" he asked as they headed off up their original fork of the trail toward the Hollows.

"Who? Old Winchrope? Just knocked a little sense into him. Hell, there's got to be somebody around here keep the bridge up and in repair. Hang on. It's all downhill from here, and we're late. But it'll be twilight in two hours and I think we can just make Sour Ford by then."

And the Hill Bluffer, swinging once again into his six-foot, ground-devouring stride, was once more hot on the trail of the Terror.

CHAPTER 9

They made good time.

As the Bluffer had said, from there on it was all downhill. They descended almost immediately into the treed sections of the mountains, the forest part. The trees among which they now traveled were lofty and thick-topped. All underbrush between them had been killed off by the lack of sunlight and they traveled, through what seemed to be an endlessly, sloping, pillared land, dimly lit by no particular source of illumination.

Sound was less where they were, too. There were no insects to feed on the nonexistent small vegetation; and no birds to live off the insects. Occasionally, from high overhead, eighty to a hundred and twenty feet up in the loftily remote crowns of the trees, there would float down a distant chitter or chirp of some unseen animal or winged creature. Otherwise, there was only the trail, an occasional boulder, looking lost here in the wooded dimness, and the unending carpet of dead leaf forms from the trees.

The Bluffer said nothing; and the steady rocking of his body as he swung along over the trail, now soft with earth, swayed John into a dreaminess in which nothing about him seemed real. Not the present scene, and not the whole business in which he had become engaged, seemed to have anything to do with reality. What was he doing here, strapped up on the back of an alien individual as large as a horse and headed for a duel to the death with another horse-sized individual of the same race? Such things did not happen to ordinary people.

But, come to think of it, were there any ordinary people? When you got right down to it, thought John sleepily, nobody was ordinary.

John dozed. An indeterminate, grey time went past; and then he was awakened by the jerk of the Hill Bluffer stopping. He straightened up, blinking, and looked about him.

He saw that it was already dusk. In the fading light, they stood in a large grassy clearing semi-encircled by the forest trees. Directly before him was a long, low log building at least double the size of anything he had seen yet, outside of Humrog. At some short distance behind it, a broad, smooth-surfaced river gurgled, swiftly flowing around a chin of stones that led across it to be lost in the twilight and the tree shadow on the far side of the stream.

"Light down, Half-Pint," said the Bluffer.

Stiffly, John climbed down from the harness. His scrapes and bruises of the night before, had found time to set during his long hours in the saddle. The soft turf felt odd under his bootsoles and his calves were wooden with a mild cramp. He stamped about, restoring his circulation; and then followed the Hill Bluffer's great back as, for an instant, it blocked out the yellow light of an open doorway, in passing into the building's interior.

Inside he found himself in a common room both much

larger and much cleaner than he had been in before. The customers here at Sour Ford Inn also seemed to be quieter and less drunk than those he had encountered in other Dilbian inns, Brittle Rock for example. Gazing around for some explanation of the reason behind this difference, John caught sight of a raised dais at the far end of the room, where in a huge chair was seated a truly enormous Dilbian, grizzled with age and heavy with fat.

Staring at this Dilbian as he walked behind the Bluffer, John ran into a table, recovered himself, and was admonished by the Hill Bluffer.

"Don't go starting any trouble now, Half-Pint."

"Me?" said John, so overwhelmed at the suggestion that someone his size could start trouble with lumbering Dilbians—even if he was crazy enough to want to—that he found himself at a loss for words to protest properly that he had no such intention.

"That's right," said the Bluffer, some moments later, after they had been seated and ordered beer and food (beer only, still, for John). "This here's treaty ground, belonging to a clanless man. Nobody starts trouble here."

"Treaty ground?"

"Yep," said the Hill Bluffer. "One Man, he—" the food, arriving just then, put a cork in the postman's flow of words. He devoted himself to bread, cheese and beer, merely grunting when John tried to continue the conversation.

John sat back, and sipped on his beer. He was cautious with it, this evening. He tried to catch a glimpse of the big Dilbian at the room's end, through the shifting bodies passing in and about the tables in the room, but the way was never clear long enough for him to get a good look.

Suddenly, however, John dropped his mug with a bang on the table and sat bolt upright.

"Hey!" he said, punching the Bluffer.

The Bluffer took another large bite of meat.

"*Hey!*" said John, punching harder.

The Bluffer growled something unintelligible with his mouth full.

"Look up!" said John. "Look over there! Quick!"

The Hill Bluffer looked up, in the direction John was pointing. He did not seem disturbed to see a Hemnoid accompanied by a relatively short, plump Dilbian female, threading their way between the tables toward the enormous patriarch in the chair on the dais.

The Bluffer swallowed.

"Sure," he said casually. "That's that Fatty, Tark-*ay*. The one I was telling you about claims to be quite a scrapper back on his home world?" The Bluffer discovered he needed to dispose of one more swallow, and did so. He pointed with a large finger, while picking up a large chunk of bread with his other hand. "That's Boy Is She Built with him."

"Boy Is She Built?" John stared.

"That's what they all say," muttered the Bluffer through a mouthful of bread. "Like 'em a little skinnier, myself."

"I mean—" said John. "What's she doing here? Let's go get her and make her tell us about Greasy Face, and if Greasy Face is all right—"

"Now, there you go," said the Bluffer.

"Go?" John turned to blink at him.

"Starting trouble."

"Starting trouble?"

"Didn't," said the Bluffer, "I just finish telling you this here's treaty ground? Man's got to be polite on treaty ground. Everybody, even Shorties got to respect the rules."

John fell silent. The Bluffer went back to his eating. John watched the Hemnoid, Tark-*ay*, and Boy Is She Built who proceeded up to the dais, sat down; and evidently fell into a friendly conversation with the oversize patriarch seated there.

John wished he could hear what they were saying.

He looked over at the Bluffer, eating away; and began to try to evolve some kind of scheme which would inveigle the Bluffer into taking him over to meet the giant Dilbian, in turn. And as soon as the Bluffer was finished, John took a cautious sip of beer and went to work.

"Who did you say is that man down in the chair at the end?" he asked.

"Why, don't you know? No, I guess you don't," said the Bluffer. "Why, that's One Man, Half-Pint. This here's all his, at Sour Ford."

"Quite a man," said John.

"You can say that," replied the Bluffer judiciously, draining the last drops from his beer mug.

"I'd like to meet a man like that," said John. "Now, back home—"

"That's good," said the Bluffer, standing up. "Because the waitress passed word I was to bring you over, soon as we were through eating. Come on, Half-Pint."

He headed off between the tables. John shook his head ruefully and followed. The next time, he though, I'll ask first and scheme afterwards.

When they got close to the individual in the chair, John discovered that sometime during their passage across the room, the Hemnoid and Boy Is She Built had disappeared. He did not have much opportunity to wonder about this, however; because his attention was immediately completely taken up by the Dilbian he was about to meet. One Man was that sort of a being.

It was definitely disconcerting, after John had spent a couple of days adjusting to the idea of Dilbian size, to have that adjustment knocked for a fresh row of pins. He was rather like a man who having gotten used to measuring with a yardstick instead of a foot-rule, suddenly finds the yardstick replaced by a fathom line. And he, himself as a fraction of that measurement getting smaller and smaller.

John had accustomed himself to standing about armpit high on the ordinary male Dilbian. Now, here along came a specimen on which John could hardly hope to stand more than midrib height. John's reaction was rather like Gulliver's with the Brobdingnagians. He felt like standing on tiptoe and shouting to make himself heard.

One Man overflowed the massive chair in which he sat; and the greying hair on the top of his head almost brushed against a polished, six-foot staff of hardwood laid crosswise on pegs driven into the wall six feet above the floor, behind him. His massive forearms and great pawlike hands were laid out on the small table in front of him, like swollen clubs of bone and muscle. Attendant Dilbians stood respectfully about him. He looked like some overstuffed, barbaric potentate. Yet his large, grey eyes, meeting John's suddenly and sharply as John and the Bluffer came to stand before him, were alight with an unusual quality of penetrating intelligence.

It was the look John had noticed back home on earth, in the eyes of human politicians of statesman level.

"This here's the Half-Pint Posted, One Man," said the Hill Bluffer, as the Dilbians around passed forth a bench for him and John to sit on. The Bluffer sat down. John climbed up to sit beside him.

"Welcome, Half-Pint," rumbled One Man. His voice was so deep with its chest tones that it sounded like a great drum sounding somewhere off in the forest. "This is the moment we've all been waiting for."

CHAPTER 10

"You've been waiting for me?" John stared at the big Dilbian.

"To be sure," said One Man. "No Shorty has ever been a guest under this roof before." He bent his head with solemn dignity in John's direction. It was all very pompous and empty-sounding; but John got the sudden clear conviction that One Man's first words had been plainly intended to give a double meaning. What was it? A warning? John flicked his eyes about as much as he could without actually turning his head away to look; but he saw nothing but unusually well-mannered Dilbian faces. Tark-*ay* and Boy Is She Built were still not in evidence.

"It's a pleasure to be here," John was saying, meanwhile, automatically.

"You're my guest under this roof," said One Man. "For now and at any time in the future, if you come back."

Again, there was that impression of a double meaning. John was completely baffled as to what there was in what One Man said, or possibly in the way he said it, that was giving him the hint of some undercover message. Also, why would the giant Dilbian be doing such a thing? He undoubtedly did not know John from Adam, or any other Shorty.

"Has the Bluffer told you about me?" One Man was asking.

"Well, not much—"

It's probably just as well." The enormous head nodded mildly. "The past is the past; and I'm an old man dreaming in my chair, here . . ."

John just bet he was. From what he had seen of Dilbians, they did not accord the sort of respect he was witnessing to any ancient hulk, no matter how venerable.

"They call him One Man, Half-Pint," put in the Bluffer, "because he once held blood feud all alone—being an orphan—with a whole clan. And won!"

"Ah, yes. The old days," rumbled One Man, with a faraway look in his eyes.

"One time," said the Bluffer, "five of them caught him on a trail where there wasn't any chance to get away. He killed them all."

"Luck was with me, of course," said One Man modestly. "Well, well, I don't want to bring up past exploits. It'll be more polite to talk about my guest. Tell me, Half-Pint," the grey eyes suddenly became penetrating, zeroing in on John, "what are you Shorties doing here, anyway?"

John blinked.

"Well," he said, "I'm here looking for—er—Greasy Face, myself."

"Of course." One Man nodded benignly. "But what brought her, and the others?" His eyes went dreamily away from John out over the room. "There must be some plan, you'd think." He looked quizzically back at John. "Nobody asked you all to come here, you know."

"Well, no," said John. He felt definitely at a loss. The Diplomatic Service had people like Joshua Guy trained to explain the reasons for human expansion into space. He summoned up what he could remember of his high school civics; and tried to present this to One Man in Dilbian terms. One Man nodded agreeably; but John had a hunch he was not making many points. What, for example, could population pressure mean to a Dilbian to whom a community of five thousand was a big city? And what could "the automatic spread of civilization" convey, other than the sound of some large and complicated words?

"That's very interesting now, Half-Pint," said One Man, when John had finally run down. "But you know what kind of puzzles me about you Shorties," he leaned forward confidentially, "is why you figure people ought to like you."

"Why, we don't—" began John, and then suddenly realized that humans did. It was one of the outstanding— if not the most outstanding—human characteristics. "I guess we do. All right, what's wrong with that? We're prepared to like other people."

One Man nodded sagely.

"I hadn't thought of that, Half-Pint," he said solemnly. "Of course, that explains it." He looked around at the other Dilbians. "Naturally, they expect people to like them, if they like people. Maybe we should have realized that."

The other Dilbians looked back at him in apparent puzzlement. But evidently they were used to being puzzled by this oversize patriarch because nobody objected. John, on his part, frowned; not sure whether he was being made fun of or not.

"I just can't make up my mind about you Shorties," said One Man, with a sigh. It was like a mountain sighing. "Well, well, I'm not being much of a host, making my guest here dig around for the reasons behind things; when I ought to be thinking only of entertaining him. Let's see now, what would be instructive and pleasant . . ." He lifted a big finger suddenly. "I've got it. Its been a long time since I broke my stick for anyone. Will one of you, there, hand it down to me?"

A young Dilbian at one side got up, lifted down the staff from the pegs above One Man's head; and gave it to One Man, who took the six-foot, three-inch-thick young post in both hands. He held it crosswise before him with his hands about three feet apart and his wrists flat on the table before him.

"A little trick of mine," he said confidentially to John. "You might get a kick out of it." He closed his fists firmly about the pole. Then, without moving his arms in any way or lifting his wrists from the table, he twisted both fists to the outside.

The thick hardwood curved up in the center like a strung bow—and snapped.

One Man leaned forward and handed the pieces to John. They were heavy and awkward enough so that John preferred to tuck them under one arm.

"Souvenir for you," said One Man, quietly.

John nodded his thanks, a little numbly. What he had just witnessed was impossible. Even for a Dilbian. Even for a Dilbian like One Man. The lack of leverage forced by the requirement of keeping wrists flat with the table, made it impossible.

"No man except me ever was able to do that," said One Man, closing his eyes dreamily. "Good luck with the Terror, Half-Pint."

John still sat where he was, staring at the broken ends of the wood pieces under his arm, until the Bluffer tapped him on the shoulder and led him off through the room, through another hide curtain and into a long room furnished with two rows of springy branches from the conifer-type trees of the forest outside the inn. The mounds made effective natural springs and mattresses for sleepers. A number of male Dilbians were already slumbering along the room. The Bluffer led John to a mound of branches in the far corner.

"You can turn in here, Half-Pint," he said. "Nobody'll

bother you here." He pointed toward the entrance. "I'll be out there, if you want to find me."

The mound of branches suddenly looked very good to John. He was bone-weary. He laid the pieces of broken staff that One Man had given him, down beside the mound and sat down on it to take off his shoes.

Five minutes later, he was asleep.

At some indeterminate time after that, he awoke suddenly and with all senses alert. For a long moment he merely lay tense and waiting, ears straining, as if for the warning of an instant attack.

But no attack came. After a moment, he sat up cautiously and looked around him.

In the light of the single thick candle burning by the entrance he saw that the dormitory was now full of sleepers. The Dilbians all slumbered with a silence that was amazing, considering their size and their boisterousness during waking hours. Beside John the Hill Bluffer was now asleep on a neighboring mound, lying on his side with one great hairy arm outflung, palm up. But it was hardly possible to tell that the postman was breathing.

John sat looking around the dormitory, trying to imagine what had wakened him. But there was nothing to see. He was isolated and undisturbed. Even his shoes, and One Man's broken staff lay just where John had laid them, beside the mound of branches.

Yet, John's tenseness continued.

The more he thought of it now, the more convinced he was that One Man had been trying to convey some message or other to him under the mask of casual conversation. The giant Dilbian was without a doubt vastly more intelligent than those around him. Also he seemed to occupy a unique position.

John swore softly to himself.

He had just remembered something that had been niggling at the back of his mind ever since he had walked into the Sour Ford Inn and seen the seated shape of its proprietor. One of the reasons One Man had attracted John's attention was that he had looked familiar. And he had looked familiar because John had seen him before—or at least his image.

One Man had been the oversize Dilbian in the cube of the three-dimensional on Joshua Guy's desk in Humrog.

That did it.

Now what was he supposed to think, wondered John bleakly. One Man—friend or foe? If the giant Dilbian was a close friend of Joshua's—and if he was not a close friend of Joshua's, what was the three-dimensional of him doing on Joshua's desk?

John shoved a hand distractedly through his ruffled mass of red hair. As a boy he had eagerly read not only *The Three Musketeers*, and *Twenty Years After*, but everything dealing with Dumas' famous musketeers. Then he had envied D'Artagnan and his three sworded friends for dashing about risking their lives by engaging in high intrigue. Now, fifteen years later and spang in the middle of a similar adventure, he realized they all must have been nuts, to say the least. Like the hired hand in the joke who could plow four hundred acres with ease but had a hard time sorting potatoes, it wasn't the risks in adventure that got you down. It was the decisions.

And this business about the broken staff. Why give the pieces to John? A souvenir, One Man had said; and possibly this was true from the Dilbian point of view, but it was hardly the kind of present for a Shorty headed for a battle *a l'outrance* with a Terror.

John reached down and hefted up the two pieces for another look. It was still impossible, he thought once more, as he examined the broken ends. Physical strength along just wasn't enough.

He checked suddenly and bent to examine the break more closely. There seemed to be a faint stain covering most of the interior area of each broken end. It radiated out around a faint line that went from the edge into the center. In the dim light he bent close over the line, but could make nothing out. He rubbed the tip of his finger over it; it was a faint groove. He put the two ends back together and the grooves matched.

It occurred to John that it would not be too impossible to drill a tiny hole in the center of even a fairly large staff. Then if some corrosive liquid was poured down this hole at intervals over a period of time, it could well result in a definite weakness in the wood at that point. In fact, with experimentation, it might be possible to control the degree of weakness, so that only someone with unusual strength to begin with . . .

Hmm, thought John. He began to consider One Man in a new light.

Now, if I had brains as well as brawn, thought John, in a physically oriented society—and if I was alone in the world, so that these two things were all that I had to go on, what would I do?

Play down the brains and play up the brawn, of course, he answered himself. I might even build myself into a living legend with supernormal attributes, if I was clever; and so give myself protection in my old age when my strength would begin to dwindle.

Query: If I was this sort of individual, would I enter into any associations or alliances with any other individuals or groups?

Answer: No, I wouldn't dare. Too close an association with anyone else would destroy the illusion of supernormality which was my best protection.

Ergo, thought John, One Man could not be on Joshua's side. Or on the Terror's. In which case, it was just barely possible to persuade him to be on John's.

John put on his shoes and got quietly to his feet. It would not be a bad idea, he thought, to hunt up One Man right now and see if they could not have a further, and more private, chat about things.

He went softly down the long length of the dormitory and out through the hide curtain into the common room. There were few Dilbians left at the tables; and One

Man's chair was empty. He had not taken one of the branch-mounds in the dormitory; so either he had separate quarters elsewhere, or perhaps he did not sleep here at the inn. John stood a moment, irresolutely. The few Dilbians in the room were ignoring him, by reason of that particular blindness to someone his size that he had encountered before. They simply were not expecting to see anyone built that close to the ground. In a literal sense, they were all looking over his head.

It occurred to John that One Man might still be around, but have stepped outside, or retired to one of the smaller houses or whatever they were behind the inn. Quietly—after his experience at Brittle Rock Inn he had no wish to call attention to himself—he crossed the room, pushed the heavy hide curtain aside and slipped out.

Outside, he paused to accustom his eyes to the night, moving a little way off from the inn to get away from the door and window light. Slowly, the starlit scene took shape around him, solidifying out of obscurity. The wide face of the river ran silver-dark in the faint light, and the distant woods loomed like the tidal wave of some black sea. The clearing where the Inn and the outbuildings behind it stood, lay pooled in silence.

He turned and found his way cautiously around the main building to its back. Unlike the Brittle Rock establishment, the backyard area here, sloping gradually to the river, was clear of rubbish; and the outbuildings themselves were neatly in good repair. Between them, when the way was close, the shadows were deeper and John had almost to feel his way.

It occurred to him then—and he wondered why he had not thought of it before—that a good share of these were probably private living quarters, not only for One Man, but for the rest of his staff, as well as any female visitors. Females seemed to have little to do with Dilbian inns, except in a service capacity. Now, as he groped among the close dark shapes of these buildings he found himself wondering how he could check on whoever might be in them, without raising some kind of alarm.

Just then he caught sight of a thin blade of yellow light between two hide curtains of a building around the corner from one he had just passed. He turned and went toward the light; but as he passed by a little patch of deeper shadow a hand reached out and took him by the arms.

"Do you *want* to get killed?" hissed a voice.

And of course, it spoke Basic. For both the hand and voice were human.

CHAPTER 11

The grip on John's arm drew him away, deeper into the shadow and around behind a building that blocked him off from the window light. They came on a door of this building and John felt himself led through its hide curtain. In the utter blackness of the interior, the hand left his arm. John stopped, instinctively; completely lost in the leather-smelling obscurity. Then there was a scratch, a sputter, and a candle burst into light only a few feet from him, blinding him.

John blinked helplessly for several seconds against the sudden illumination. Gradually he became able to see again, and when he did, he found himself looking down—for the first time in two days—into the face of one of the prettiest young women he had seen in a long time.

She was perhaps a foot shorter than he was, but at first glance looked taller by reason of her slimness and the

tailored coveralls she wore. To John's Dilbian-accustomed
eyes, she looked tiny, not to say fragile. Her chestnut hair
swept in two wide wings back on each side of her head.
Her eyes were green-blue above marked cheekbones that
gave her a sculptured look. Her nose was thin, her lips
firm rather than full, and her small chin had a determined
shape.

John blinked again.

"Who—?" he managed, after a minute.

"I'm Ty Lamorc," she said. "Keep your voice down!"

"Ty Lamorc?"

"Yes."

"Are you sure?" stammered John. "I mean, you—"

"Who were you expecting to run into away out here
in the center of—oh, I know!" she glared at him. "It's
that Greasy Face name the Dilbians gave me. You were
expecting some sort of witch."

"Certainly not," said John.

"Well, for your information, they just happened to see
me putting on makeup one day."

"Oh."

"That's where the name came from."

"Oh, of course. I never thought—"

"I'll bet you didn't."

"Really," said John.

"Anyway, never mind that now. The point is, what on
Earth are you doing out here? Do you want to get
knocked on the head?"

"I was trying to find One Man—" John suddenly stiffened and lowered his voice. "Is the Terror back here?"

"No, but Boy Is She Built is. She's been guarding me.
And she'll kill you if she gets her hands on you. She hasn't
even told the Terror you're after him."

John stared.

"I don't understand," he said.

"The Terror wouldn't run from a fight. He'd run toward
it. He thinks it's just the Hill Bluffer after him with a
demand from the Humrog mayor that he bring me back.

Boy Is She Built doesn't want the Terror to get into trouble by killing you."

"But she's willing to do it, herself."

"She's in love with the Terror. That's the way she thinks. And she doesn't know—well, how essentially harmless your mission is. Now, what we've got to do is smuggle you back into the dormitory before she catches you. She won't go in there after you. It's treaty ground inside, anyway."

"Hold on a minute," said John, as Ty took hold of his arm again. He did not move. "Aren't we getting this a little mixed up? I mean—who's rescuing who? I came along here to find you and bring you back to Humrog. Well, I've found you. Come along back to the main inn building with me and I'll wake up the Hill Bluffer and explain things—"

"You don't," interrupted Ty with feeling, "understand a blasted thing about these Dilbians, Half-Pint—I mean, Mr. Tardy."

"Call me John," said John.

"John, you don't understand the situation. The Terror left me here because he knew Boy Is She Built would stay on watch. And she will. She'll be back looking for me in ten more minutes; and if I'm not where she left me, she'll be right after us. So even if we did try to get away, she'd catch us. Also, the Bluffer's honor bound to deliver you to the Terror. The Terror's honor bound to fight you when that happens, or any time he finds out you're after him to take me away. So he'd be after us, too. And if she couldn't catch us, *he* certainly could."

"But—"

"*Will* you listen to me?" hissed Ty. "I'm a sociologist. I've put in six months studying these people. What we've got to do is keep you out of danger until the Terror takes me into the Hollows, his own clan territory. Once he does that, it'll be up to the grandfathers of his clan to decide what happens to me, and you and the Terror, and all. I can demand a hearing and explain that I've got no connection by blood or anything like that with Joshua, and then they'll rule that the Terror wasn't within his rights to steal me in retaliation for Joshua's insult; I'm sure they will. Then, there'll be no reason for the Terror to fight you and we can both go back, safely."

"If you're so sure of that," said John, "how come I was sent out here in the first place?"

"Oh, Joshua doesn't understand these people much better than you do."

"I can believe that," said John.

"So, you go back to the main inn building now. And be careful!"

"Well . . ." John hesitated. "I still think I ought to play safe and try to take you away, tonight. With a good start and by wrecking the Knobby Gorge bridge—" He paused and considered her. She was *remarkably* small and fragile-looking. The thought of the Terror grabbing her up and running off with her made him growl a little bit inside, at that. "I just don't think we should take any chances with your safety," he wound up.

Ty Lamorc stood perfectly still for a long second, looking at him. The expression on her face was one he could not fathom.

"Well, John!" she said, finally, and suddenly her eyes were quite soft. She reached out and touched his arm. "That was very nice of you," she said, in a low voice. "Thank you, John."

Then, suddenly, before he could move, she blew out the candle. In the sudden darkness he heard the hide curtain flap and sway.

"Ty?" he said.

But there was no answer. She had gone.

He felt his way out of the hut, and emerged into the dimness of the starlit night outside. He squinted around himself, located the main building and headed through the darkness toward it.

Something large and leathery descended out of nowhere, wrapping around him. A couple of powerful arms lifted him off the ground. He fought, but it was useless. He felt himself being carried off.

Inside the tight folds of the leather enfolding him he began to suffocate. Very shortly, he lost consciousness. Things became soft and pillowy about him. He seemed to swim off into blackness.

Then, there was nothing.

CHAPTER 12

John awoke with the vague impression that he had over-
slept on a work day and was due on the job. Opening
his eyes, he was puzzled and surprised to see the intri-
cate branches of treetops black against the paling grey
of a predawn sky.

How did he get here? he wondered.

His next vague impression was that he had been someplace and drunk too much the night before. He had the
ugly taste in his mouth and dull skullcap of a headache
that goes with a hangover. Then everything to do with
Dilbia came back to his mind with a rush, up to and
including the memory of being carried off after leaving
his talk with Ty Lamorc.

He sat up to look around him, achieving this with a
difficulty that led him to discover that his forearms and
ankles were bound and tied with thick rope.

He found he was seated on damp leaves over damp forest earth, in a little clearing. A small fire was burning about fifteen feet from him. At the fire sat Boy Is She Built and the short, broad Hemnoid, Tark-*ay*.

Boy Is She Built jerked up her head to look as John raised himself into a sitting position, and Tark-*ay's* glance followed in a more leisurely manner. In the wild woods, sitting over the pale fire just as dawn was breaking in the sky, they looked like a scene out of some oriental books of legends, the wise man and the beast. Just then Boy Is She Built opened her mouth and blew the illusion to smithereens.

"He's conscious!" she said. The tone of her voice was accusing.

"To be sure, little lady," responded Tark-*ay*. His voice, like the voice of all Hemnoids, had a heavy, liquid quality. It was somewhat higher in tone than that of a male Dilbian would have been. In fact, he and Boy Is She Built operated in about the same vocal range. "He's been merely asleep for several hours now. I was very careful."

"In the old days," said Boy Is She Built, hopefully, "they used to break the legs of prisoners to keep them from getting away."

"We aren't barbarians, after all though, little lady," protested Tark-*ay* mildly.

"Oh, you're all so stubborn!" said Boy Is She Built, huffily. "It isn't good enough just to hit him over the head. Oh, no! We have to carry him here, and carry him there. My Terror's not like that."

"That," pointed out Tark-*ay*, "is exactly why we don't want your Terror to know this little fellow is after him. If I might remind you—"

"Well, I'm getting tired of waiting, that's all!" said Boy Is She Built. "If the Beer-Guts Bouncer isn't here by an hour after sunrise, I'm going to hit him on the head, and that's that."

"I would have to stop you from doing anything like that, little lady."

"You wouldn't dare!" She glared at him. "I'd tell the Terror!"

"That would be too bad, little lady. But," said Tark-*ay* almost apologetically, "you ought to understand that I would still have to stop you. It would be my duty. And you should also understand that in the regrettable instance of the Terror and I coming to blows, I would have no doubt of emerging the winner."

"You! I can just see you beating up the Terror!" said Boy Is She Built and laughed nastily. "He's twice as big as you are."

"Not twice. Somewhat taller, it's true. But our weights aren't so far apart as most of your people might think. And besides, it would make no real difference—even if Streamside was, in truth, twice my size."

"Why not, smarty?" said Boy Is She Built.

"Because of the high skills and arts of unarmed combat, developed on my world, in which I am an expert. Now, suppose Streamside should rush at me with intent to do me harm."

"He'd swarm all over you."

"Not at all." Tark-*ay* got to his feet in one quick motion. "He comes rushing at me. I meet him, so—!" Suddenly the short Hemnoid twisted, half bent over, and lashed out with a foot. "Then, before he can recover, I am all over *him*!" Tark-*ay* straightened up and bounded forward. His open hands made slashing cutting motions in the air.

"You aren't going to stop the Terror by *slapping* him," said Boy Is She Built. "Oh yes, I can just see you slapping my Terror!"

"Slapping?" said Tark-*ay*. There was a fair-sized length of log near the fire. Tark-*ay* picked it up and leaned it against a close tree. His open hand cut at it, and the log broke loudly into two sections. "You will be happier, little lady," said Tark-*ay* sitting down once more by the fire, "if your Terror never has anything to do with me in an unfriendly way."

He bent to put one of the broken log-pieces on the fire. And John, watching, saw a peculiar glitter in the eyes of Boy Is She Built, as she gazed at the Hemnoid. One furry hand of the young Dilbian female reached for a large rock nearby, hesitated, and then returned to her lap. It occurred to John that Tark-*ay* might be an expert in the high skills and arts of unarmed combat developed on his world; but he was pretty much of a numbskull when it came to female psychology. Boy Is She Built had been going to a good deal of trouble to dispose of John because she thought of him as a threat to Streamside. And now Tark-*ay* had just incautiously revealed that he was also a threat, not only to the Terror's honor, but to his very life and limb.

Of course, a loyal female should perhaps have laughed the matter off, scorning to doubt her husband-to-be. But Boy Is She Built, while loyal enough to suit almost anybody, appeared to have a strong practical streak in her nature as well.

John licked his lips, which were very dry.

"I could use a drink of water," he said out loud.

Boy Is She Built looked up the slope at him.

"Hmph!" said Boy Is She Built. She did not stir.

"Are we barbarians?" cried Tark-*ay*, bouncing to his feet. He went to a canteen hanging from a nearby tree, brought it to John, unscrewed the top, peeled off a sterile cup, filled it and held it to John's lips while he drank.

"How about loosening these ropes?" asked John, after he had gulped a couple of cups of the water.

"I'm sorry. Very sorry," said Tark-*ay* and returned to the fireside.

They all sat in silence, for some little while during which the sky turned pink and the local sun shoved his upper rim into sight behind the surrounding trees. Tark-*ay* got to his feet and began to bounce up and down, clapping his hands over his head. John stared. So did Boy Is She Built.

"What's wrong?" cried Boy Is She Built.

"Nothing, little lady," replied Tark-*ay*, "merely my exercises which I do periodically during the morning hours."

"Well, I thought you'd eaten something!" said Boy Is She Built. She relaxed again. "Or sat on a splinter. Or something."

Tark-*ay* abandoned his initial exercise. He began one in which he leaped up from the ground, clicked his heels, clasped his hands, and winked. As soon as he hit the ground, he bounced up and went through the whole process all over again.

"That's the most ridiculous thing I ever saw," said Boy Is She Built. "What do you do something like that for?"

"It is part of my training, little lady," gasped Tark-*ay*. "A true master of the skills and arts does it once each time before he says anything. It builds character."

"Well, I think it's utterly ridiculous," said Boy Is She Built. She lay down and curled up on her side. "Call me when the Beer-Guts Bouncer gets here. I'm going to take a little nap."

She closed her eyes. Tark-*ay* continued bouncing. He ran through several more exercises before he ran down. Then, wiping his forehead, he waddled over and sat down by John.

"She is a trial, that little lady," he said, nodding at Boy Is She Built.

"Oh?" said John, wondering if this was leading up to something.

"Yes. Irrepressible youth. The eternal juvenile young female whose world is completely oriented to her own parochial ego. Anything that does not fit her own image of the universe is dismissed as unworthy of consideration."

"Is that so?" said John.

"Only too truly so. You come from a civilized race the way I do. You understand me. She is driving me crazy."

"How?"

"She's just so—impossible. She knows nothing. And she thinks she knows everything. I was trying to explain a chance remark I made the other day about psychological pressure. Now, *you* know as well as I do she knows nothing about psychology."

"I wouldn't think so," said John.

"How could she? On this barbaric world? I started to explain what psychology was, to explain my remark. Well, first she got angry and said she knew as much about it as I did."

John was getting interested in spite of the ropes and the situation.

"What did you say to that?" he asked.

"I pointed out that this couldn't be true, since there were no colleges upon her world where she could have learned it."

"That stopped her?"

"No," said Tark-*ay* sadly. "She said, there was, too. She had studied all about psychology at the college at Blunder Bush."

"Blunder Bush?"

"There's no such place," said Tark-*ay*, "of course. I told her this, and she claimed that I just didn't know about it. That it was highly secret. It must have been plain to her that I was seeing through all this, so she went on, piling her fictions higher. Her whole family were college graduates, she told me. She had been offered a teaching position herself. She wound up telling me that the Streamside Terror was actually an instructor at his college; and all his running around and fighting was just so people wouldn't suspect his true abilities. Well, well—"

Tark-*ay* sighed heavily, got up, and went back to the fire.

John frowned. He had been expecting the Hemnoid to get even more confidential, and had even hoped he could find some lever in the conversation which he might turn to his own advantage in getting out of this fix. But Tark-*ay* had broken things off too abruptly.

John could have sworn Tark-*ay* had settled down beside

him with intentions for an extended conversation. What had made the short Hemnoid change his mind?

Then John heard the distant crackling of footfalls among the dry leaves under the trees a little distance off. They were approaching behind John, and he found he was too tightly trussed to turn around. At the fire, Tark-*ay* busied himself breaking up small pieces of wood and adding them to the blaze. He did not look up.

The footfalls approached. They came right up behind John and stopped. John heard the slow, even sound of deep breathing, above and behind his head.

Then the feet moved whoever it was around in front of John and he saw a great yellow moon-face beaming down at him from eight feet above the ground.

"Well, well," said a heavy, liquid voice, "so, here's our quarry, trussed and ready for roasting. How should we season him, Tark-*ay*?"

It was the Hemnoid ambassador to Dilbia, Gulark-*ay*.

CHAPTER 13

"You'll think of something, Mr. Ambassador, I'm sure," replied Tark-*ay* and the two Hemnoids chuckled together like a couple of gallon jugs of machine oil poured out on the ground.

The sound woke up Boy Is She Built. She sat up.

"Here you are!" she said to Gulark-*ay*.

"Absolutely right, Boy Is She Built," replied the Hemnoid ambassador. "Here, indeed, I am. You don't look pleased?"

"I don't know why we had to wait for you," she said.

"Because," said Gulark-*ay*, "there's more to this than simply throwing someone you don't like over a cliff. Remember? You were only supposed to take his wrist radio there at Brittle Rock, not drop him into a five hundred foot canyon."

"It would have saved a lot of trouble," said Boy Is She Built. She looked rebellious.

"So you think. But, as you would have found out, if you'd been successful, what it actually would have done would have been to cause a lot of trouble. Do you think the Shorty authorities are going to let one of their people get killed here on your world and not want to know what happened?"

"They wouldn't dare make a fuss," said Boy Is She Built. "They need to make friends with us real people. Just like you Fatties do. If they attacked us, you'd just like the excuse to back us up." She snorted. A curiously feminine version of the Hill Bluffer's favorite emotional outlet. "They wouldn't dare make trouble over one little Shorty."

"Never mind," said Gulark-*ay*. "Life's a little more complicated than you think, Boy Is She Built. You don't get things without paying for them. And, believe me, you can't just kill a Shorty on a whim without paying for that, either."

"Oh, you sound just like my father!" said Boy Is She Built, furiously.

"Thank you," said Gulark-*ay*, dryly. He turned away from her and sat down by John on the ground, spreading his robes over his enormous knees.

"And how is our cat's-paw doing?" he asked.

"You're talking to me?" said John.

"Of course," said Gulark-*ay*. "Didn't you realize that's what you've been all along?"

"To tell you the truth," said John, "and now that you ask me, no, I didn't."

"Such trust," said Gulark-*ay*.

"And faith," said John. "To say nothing of experience." He pointed out something. "I'm a little bit older and more widely traveled than Boy Is She Built, for example."

"What's he saying about me?" said Boy Is She Built, lifting her head up. "What's travel got to do with it?"

"But I'm only telling you what's true," said Gulark-*ay*,

bassly and liquidly. "How do you think Tark-*ay* here, and Boy Is She Built happened to be waiting for you on the trail your first day out? How do you think Boy Is She Built happened to know enough to deprive you of your wrist phone?"

"Now, that's an interesting point," said John. "You say she took my wrist phone off. Why? When she was going to throw me over the cliff, anyway?"

"She wasn't supposed to do anything but get the wrist phone," said Gulark-*ay*. "As to why she still bothered to do that after deciding to kill you, is something you'd have to ask her."

"They told me to," said Boy Is She Built sulkily.

"But you miss the point," said Gulark-*ay* to John, "which is how we knew where you were going to be and when. Aren't you going to ask me who tipped off Boy Is She Built?"

"You did."

"Not at all. Your ambassador, Joshua."

John looked at him sourly.

"You expect me to believe that, don't you?"

"Why not?" Gulark-*ay* spread his enormous hands.

"For one reason, because you wouldn't have any reason for telling it to me unless to convince me of something that wasn't true."

"Not at all," said Gulark-*ay*. "Don't you know about us Hemnoids? We're a cruel people. We enjoy seeing others suffer. I enjoy dashing your faith in Joshua Guy— particularly because I've no doubt in the back of your mind, you've been planning on using action by him, in the event of your death, as a threat to make me let you go."

John had. But he kept his face bland.

"Seems to me," he said, "you protest your cruelty too much."

Gulark-*ay* shook his head. He seemed to be quite earnest and enjoying the conversation.

"That's because," he said, "according to your mores it

is immoral to make someone else suffer. But according
to my mores it is not only moral, but eminently respectable. It is a skill, a high art."

"Do you jump up in the air and click your heels before
beginning?" asked John, sourly.

For the first time, Gulark-*ay* looked slightly baffled.
Tark-*ay*, busily poking the fire with his head down, did
not offer to interpret the remark for his ambassador.

"We seem to be drifting off the subject," said Gulark-
ay. "The point I am laboring to get across to you is that
your Joshua Guy is to be no help to you. He had you
written off from the beginning."

"Are you sure you aren't judging according to Hemnoid
mores?" said John. "Human ambassadors usually operate
a little differently."

"No doubt, no doubt," said Gulark-*ay* chuckling richly.
"But there are special reasons in the case of Mr. Guy.
You're a draftee, aren't you, my friend?"

"That's right," said John. "A willing draftee, I might
point out."

"No doubt, no doubt," said Gulark-*ay* chuckling richly,
and chuckled again. "Well, so is your ambassador to
Dilbia."

"Guy? Drafted?"

John blinked in spite of himself. There was, of course,
no technical reason why you couldn't draft a man with
the proper talents into a diplomatic post. It was just kind
of farfetched, that was all.

"Quite right," said Gulark-*ay*. "Joshua Guy, three years
ago, had retired after a full lifetime in the diplomatic
service. He was planning to spend the rest of his life
cultivating certain species of your native flora—I don't
remember just what. Roses, or some such name. However, his government thought they needed him on Dilbia,
and so they sent him here."

John accepted this in silence, without arguing or
accepting. But he was busy thinking.

"Of course," went on Gulark-*ay*,—and he did, indeed,

seem to be enjoying himself—"Joshua has been very eager all this time to get relieved of his duties and be allowed to return to his roses, or his turnips, or whatever. And of course you realize, the only way for anyone like him to get relieved would be to—how do you put it?—goof up so badly that he would have to be replaced. He fomented this whole fuss with Boy Is She Built just to create the proper kind of trouble."

"In that case he didn't need me," said John. "Ty Lamorc being kidnapped by the Terror was trouble enough."

"Ah, yes, but you see, he found he had misplaced his hand in the case of Ty. That young female was sent out here by a different branch of your government. One which would be only too glad to pin something on the Diplomatic Service. If anything happened to Ty, it began to look as if Joshua might face not merely retirement, but trial for manslaughter, or worse. On the other, by throwing you to the Terror, he could more or less ransom Ty. And an obscure young biochemist with no connections could be spared with only the routine amount of reprimand and investigation."

"Very interesting," said John. "And you undertook to mess up Guy's plans just out of your natural, healthy instinct for cruelty? Tell me another fairy tale."

"You misjudge me!" said Gulark-*ay* sharply. "I have my personal pride and pleasures; but first and foremost, I am a servant and representative of my people. It's as important to our plans as to the plans of you humans, to get the inside track on friendship with the Dilbians. A bad and an unwilling human ambassador such as Guy is just what we're pleased to see on Dilbia. It was my duty to back up Guy's superiors in this matter and see that he failed in trying to arrange for his own retirement."

"Well, then," said John. "Since we're all working together in this, why don't you just cut these ropes off; and we can all go back to Sour Ford Inn for breakfast."

Gulark-*ay* quivered and shook with sudden laughter. His

laughing was so infectious that shortly Tark-*ay* and Boy Is She Built had joined in the humor. And John, to his own surprise, had to fight back the beginnings of a smile.

"Well, now!" chortled Gulark-*ay*, running down at last. "If that doesn't—! Let you go! We couldn't do that, Mr. Tardy. You see, you're the price of Boy Is She Built's assistance. She wants you out of the way, permanently. We promised this; and she promised to talk the Terror into giving Miss Lamorc up without argument, when his clan grandfathers order him to do so." He looked at John. "Which," he said, delicately, "they will undoubtedly do when you are found dead within their clan territory of the Hollows, just over the river."

John looked at Gulark-*ay*, gave a short incredulous laugh and looked away.

"Good! Very good, Mr. Tardy!" cried Gulark-*ay* bursting into a fresh gallon-jug's worth of laughter. "Oh, it's going to be a pleasure to work on you, Mr. Tardy, when we get down to actual business. Well—" he heaved himself erect and went over to sit down by Tark-*ay* and Boy Is She Built at the fire.

"Well!" he said again, clapping his big hands together, briskly. "I don't believe in being a hog about these things. All good suggestions are welcome. How'll we do it?"

"If you don't mind, Mr. Ambassador," said Tark-*ay*, with polite eagerness. "There's a new technique my cousin was reading about recently. He wrote me about it in his last letter. A sort of peeling-back of the fingernails."

"Well now, that sounds interesting," said Gulark-*ay*. "I'm no expert, more's the pity on human nerve-endings, particularly in the fingertip areas; but we can assume a basic similarity. We'll put that on the list. Now, I myself, have a small specialty involving the inside of the mouth, if no one objects?" He looked at the other two.

"Why don't we just hit him over the head?" said Boy Is She Built.

Tark-*ay* gave her a look or scorn.

"We aren't barbarians!" he said.

CHAPTER 14

The discussion went on in lively fashion for some time. And an amazing thing happened to John. He dozed off. The subject matter might have been enough to keep him awake; but the two Hemnoids had become unintelligibly technical; and the tone had become the tone of in-group discussions the universe over. Half the wrangling was over authorities and precedents, rather than about the actual performance contemplated. Moreover, John had had two rough nights and days in a row. His body made up his mind for him. It went to sleep.

When he reawakened, the sun was well up over the trees, and he found that he was not the only one who had become tired of the discussion. Boy Is She Built was reading the two Hemnoids the riot act.

"—and I think you're disgusting, both of you!" she was informing them, in anything but well-modulated tones.

"And crazy! And stupid! I keep telling you why don't you just hit him over the head? But, oh no! Not you! It's got to be first we'll do this. And then we'll do that. And then—oh, no, we can't do that, because it'd finish him off too quick—or somebody else tried it and it didn't work out too well."

"Little lady," began Tark-*ay*.

"You give me a pain!" cried Boy Is She Built. "And you aren't even *mad* at him, that's what gets me! If it wasn't for Streamside, I don't think I'd even let you have him! You're just—just—you're disgusting, both of you!"

"You don't understand," said Gulark-*ay*. "The point is—"

"Well, I'm glad I don't. If this is the way you Hemnoids are, I'm not sure I don't like Shorties better, after all. I'll bet if it was *him* helping me and you two tied up over there, he'd tell me to go right ahead and hit you over the head. He wouldn't go on arguing about doing this first, and doing that second." Boy Is She Built made an unsuccessful effort to imitate the deep liquidity of the Hemnoid voices gloating over a particularly attractive idea. " 'and we moost try thees. Oh, wee surleee moost!' You both give me a pain!"

Tark-*ay*, glancing helplessly away from her, found his glance meeting that of John's; and shrugged helplessly at the human.

"Well," said Gulark-*ay*, shaking his head and getting to his feet, "there's no help for it. We'd just be wasting him to go to work now. I have to get on to see the grandfathers of the Hollows clan; and I can't get back until late afternoon, now. Let's put it all off until this evening. I'll bring some supplies from my stuff, when I get back, something good in the way of food and drink, and we can make a bang-up night of it. How does that strike you, Tark-*ay*?"

"Mr. Ambassador," said Tark-*ay*, his voice full of deep emotion, "you are a gentleman!"

"Thank you, thank you indeed," said Gulark-*ay*. "Well,

I'm on my way, then. Traveling in my direction, Boy Is She Built?"

"I should think so!" Boy Is She Built jumped to her feet. "I was supposed to meet Streamside just two hours after the sun was up, and I forgot all about it. He gets awfully impatient. Maybe he went off and left that Shorty female alone."

And without even waiting for Gulark-*ay*, Boy Is She Built hurried off.

"Mr. Ambassador," said Tark-*ay*, looking after her. "You don't know. You just don't know."

"Cheer up," said Gulark-*ay*. "It'll be all remembered to your advantage in my reports." He rearranged his robes. "I'll be back this evening, then."

"May the hours fly until then, Mr. Ambassador."

"Indeed," said Gulark-*ay*; and departed in his turn.

Tark-*ay* left alone with John, sighed heavily. He produced a curved knife from his robe, with which he proceeded to clean his fingernails, meanwhile heaving another occasional heavy sigh. Finished, he stuck the knife into a piece of firewood beside him and tapped its hilt with his finger to make it vibrate back and forth. After a while he gave even this up. His eyes closed. He dozed.

John, lying still, watched the Hemnoid carefully from fifteen feet of distance. It had not occurred to John before, but Tark-*ay* had probably not had a good night's sleep either for some time. He waited.

Tark-*ay* slid down the tree against which he was leaning. He began to breathe heavily with a whistling overtone which John took to be the Hemnoid equivalent of a snore. He lay sprawled out. John's eyes went to the knife, still stuck in the chunk of firewood.

As quietly as he could, John slid down flat on the ground himself. Luckily, it was downhill. He rolled over once. Twigs crackled and pebbles rattled away from him. But Tark-*ay* did not wake up. John rolled over a second time.

Three minutes later he was rubbing his bound wrists against the blade of the upright knife blade. It was not as easy as it looked in the pictures John had seen. He did a pretty good job of slicing up his wrists in the process, and the rope was thick. Also, he discovered, it is not easy to get pressure against the blade of a knife stuck upright in a piece of wood. The angle is all wrong.

Nevertheless, some ten minutes after he had first started his roll downhill, he was cutting his feet loose from their bindings, knife in hand. He got the foot-tyings parted, stuck the knife in his belt and took off, as quietly as he could up the slope into the trees.

Tark-*ay* had not stirred.

John was just about to congratulate himself on having gained his freedom without mishap, when an infuriated roar behind him stopped him in his tracks. Instinctively, he dodged behind a nearby tree, turned and looked back.

A Dilbian with coal-black fur was just charging into the clearing John had just left, forty feet below. Tark-*ay* was scrambling to his feet.

"Where is he?" roared this Dilbian. "Point him out!"

"What are you doing here?" said Tark-*ay*.

"Don't try to pretend you don't know. I found out! When Boy Is She Built didn't come back in time, I went looking for her. When I found her coming out of these woods she had some explaining to do. I know it all now. Where's this Shorty who's been acting as if I was running away from him?"

"You're too late," said Tark-*ay*, not without a certain tone of satisfaction in his voice, it seemed to John. "He's escaped." And he pointed to the cut sections of the rope that had bound John.

"Escaped?" The Dilbian, who could be no other than the Streamside Terror, had gone ominously quiet. John, peering at the two of them from around the tree, was trying to make up his mind whether to make a run for it, or lie quiet and hope they would not come searching this way.

He decided to lie quiet. It would give him a chance to case the Streamside Terror and see, if possible, what gave that Dilbian his reputation as a battler. So far, there had been no indications. The Terror was by no means the biggest Dilbian John had seen; he was considerably shorter, for example, than the Hill Bluffer. Perhaps his unusualness was a matter of reflexes.

"You let him escape?" said the Terror, mildly.

"Alas," said Tark-*ay*, a trifle smugly.

"WHY?" roared the Terror.

Hemnoids were no more without nerves than humans, apparently. Tark-*ay* jumped involuntarily, as the Terror erupted with full lung power two feet from his nose.

"That's not for you to question!" snapped Tark-*ay*. "And furthermore—"

There was no furthermore. For just then, the Terror lit into him.

Note: noted John. Terror gives no warning. Does not telegraph punches.

The fight became active in the clearing below John. Tark-*ay* was valiantly attempting to employ his high skills and arts; but seemed somewhat hampered by the factor that the Terror had closed with him immediately and they were both now rolling around on the ground together.

Note: noted John. When no stream available, Terror attempts to batter opponent against handy rocks and trees.

No matter how you sliced it, the battle proceeding below was an awe-inspiring bit of action. The combined weight of the two opponents must have run close to fifteen hundred pounds; both were skilled fighters, and both in top condition.

Note: noted John. Liberal use of nails and teeth gives Terror considerable advantage over opponent not trained to this sort of fighting and not expecting same.

The Terror was definitely gaining the upper hand. Tark-*ay* seemed to be weakening.

Note: noted John. Terror particularly quick for someone so large. Would smallness of human and consequent greater maneuverability of human give human slight advantage in this department however? Possibly. But what good would it do just to keep dodging?

The fight below seemed drawing to its close with the Terror emerging as a clear winner. John suddenly realized that with all this noise going on, now was the ideal time for him to get away from the vicinity and travel.

He traveled.

At first, he merely headed off through the woods in a plain and simple attempt to put as much distance between himself and the place of his recent captivity, as possible.

As soon as he had covered about a quarter mile or so, his first urgency dwindled a bit. He took time out to get a handkerchief out of his pocket, tear it in half and bind up the cuts on his wrists, which had been bleeding somewhat messily, all down his hands. There was no water nearby in which he could wash his hands, but he rubbed them in dry leaves, and got them looking better than they had before.

Then he sat down on a fallen tree to catch his breath and began to think about getting his bearings.

He had no idea in what direction he had been carried the night before after being wrapped up in the leather blanket, or whatever it was that had been used to bundle him up. However, he remembered Gulark-*ay*'s reference to Clan Hollows territory, "just over the river"; and he recalled that Sour Ford Inn had been right at a river. Consequently, the river in question could not be far from him; and once he found it, he could go up or down it until he found Sour Ford Inn and the Bluffer.

John utilized some elementary woodcraft. He hunted for the tallest tree he could find close at hand and climbed it.

From its top he spotted the river, about half a mile

away and almost due west according to the sun. And on this side of the river, a mile or two upstream was some cluster of buildings which was probably Sour Ford Inn.

John climbed down again and headed west, not forgetting to keep his eyes peeled for the Terror or even for Tark-*ay*, assuming the Hemnoid had been left in condition to travel.

However, he met no one. When he reached the river, he found there was a trail running alongside it; and he had hardly proceeded half a mile up the trail before he ran into a group of five Dilbians.

"Hey! Whoop!" hollered the first of these, the minute he got around a bend in the trail and spotted John. "There he is! Where'd you run off to, Shorty? The Bluffer's got half the people between here and Twin Peaks out looking for you!"

CHAPTER 15

"Never," said the Bluffer, as he swung through the forest with John on his back, "again. Nothing with legs. If it's got legs it can deliver itself. The mail's for things that can't get around on its own. That's what the mail's for."

John felt too comfortable to be disturbed by the postman's grousing. He had put his foot down for the first time, when the group he had run into had brought him back to the inn, and insisted on a couple of hours sleep in ordinary fashion. He had gotten them, in the peace of the inn dormitory. When he had woken up, he had decided as well to quit worrying about possible allergies and have something more than paste and pill concentrates to eat.

He had stuffed himself, accordingly. Dilbian bread, he discovered was coarse and full of uncompletely milled kernels, the cheese was sour and the meat tough, with a sour taste to it. It tasted delicious, and he just wished he had been able to hold a bit more. No allergic reactions had showed up so far; and now, with a full stomach, he drowsed on the back of the Dilbian postman, all but falling asleep in the saddle. As he drowsed, he wondered dreamily about his escape from Tark-*ay*. It all seemed almost too good to be true.

They were descending now into a country of lower altitudes, although they were still far above the central plains of this particular Dilbian continent. The central plains, being warmer in the summer than the Dilbians liked, were only sparsely settled. They regarded them as lush, unhealthy places where a man from the uplands lost his moral fiber quickly and fell into unnamed vices. Black sheep from the respectable communities of the clans often ended up down there, where the living was easy and no questions asked about a man's past.

So, the higher Hollows area was regarded as lowlands, in the ordinary sense by the mountain-living Dilbians. And in fact, John noticed that the countryside here did look a lot different. A new type of tree, something like a birch, was now to be seen among the hitherto unbroken ranks of sprucelike coniferoids of the uplands. And fern and brush began to put in an appearance.

All this could have been quite interesting to John if he had not been half-asleep; and if he had not had other things swimming about in the back of his mind, specifically, that apparently unavoidable meeting with the Streamside Terror, to which events and the Hill Bluffer seemed to be rushing him in spite of himself.

He felt like someone who has been caught in an avalanche, and now was riding it down the mountainside— for the moment on top of the moving mass, but with an inevitable cliff edge looming ahead. What the blazes was he to do, he wondered dully out of his half-awake state, when he found himself suddenly shoved, barehanded against the Terror? Doubtless with an impenetrable ring of Dilbian spectators hemming them both in, as well.

And for what? Why? Everybody from Joshua on through Gulark-*ay* seemed to have a different explanation of the reasons for the combat taking place. Everybody's patsy, that's what I am, thought John gloomily and dozed off again. Time went by.

He awoke suddenly. The Hill Bluffer had stopped unexpectedly, with a startled grunt. John sat up and looked around with the uncertainty of a man still fogged by sleep.

They were out of the woods. They had emerged into a small valley in which a cluster of buildings stood in the brown color of their peeled, and naturally weathered logs, haphazardly about a stream that ran the valley's length. Beyond the village, or whatever it was, there was a sort of natural amphitheater made by a curved indentation in the far rock wall of the valley. Past this, the path curved on through an opening in the valley wall and into the further forest.

However, it was not this pleasant little village scene that caught John's attention as he came fully awake.

It was a group of five brawny Dilbians who stood squarely athwart the path before himself and the Bluffer.

Armed with axes.

The Hill Bluffer had not said a word from the moment of John's awakening. Now he exploded. In his outrage he was almost incoherent.

"You—you—" he stuttered, roaringly. "You got the almighty nerve—you got the *guts*—! You dare stop the mail? Who do you think—just *who* is it thinks he's got the right—"

"Clan Hollows in full meeting, that's who," said the middle axman, a Dilbian almost as tall as the Bluffer, himself. "Come on with us."

The Bluffer took two steps backwards and hunched his shoulders. John felt himself lifted on the swell of the postman's big back muscles.

"Let's just see you take us!" snarled the postman. He sounded slightly berserk. Up on his back, John swallowed automatically looking at the Dilbian axes. John was in rather the same position as someone with a drunken or excitable friend who is in the process of getting them both into a fight. Harnessed to the Bluffer the way he was, there was no way he could quickly get down and loose in the case of trouble; and just at the moment the Bluffer did not seem to be thinking of taking time out to put his mail in a safe place before committing suicide.

"Hey!" said John, tapping the Bluffer on the shoulder. He might as well have tapped one of the Dilbian mountains in a like manner, for all the attention he attracted.

"Spread out, boys," said the head axman, hefting his forty-pound tool-weapon. The line began to extend at either end and curve in to flank the Bluffer. "Postman, officially in the name of Clan Hollows, I'm bidding you to immediate meeting. The grandfathers are waiting for you there, postman. And that Shorty you got with you."

The Hill Bluffer ground his teeth together. Seated just back of the Dilbian's mandible hinges the way John was, it made an awesome sound.

"He's mine." The postman sounded like he was talking through clenched jaws. "Until delivered! Come try to take him, you hollow-scuttling, thieving low-land loopers, you Clan Hollows sons of—"

The axmen were beginning to snarl and look red-eyed in turn. Desperate times, thought John, call for desperate measures.

He leaned forward, got the Bluffer's right ear firmly in his teeth. And bit.

"Yii!" roared the Bluffer—and spun about, almost snapping John's head off at the neck. "Who did that—? Oh! What're you trying to pull, Half-Pint." He tried to twist his neck around and look John in the face.

"That's right," said John. "Get in a fight! Get the government mail damaged! Back on my Shorty world they've got better postmen than that."

"They can't do this to me," rumbled the Bluffer, but his voice had noticeably dropped in volume.

"Sure," said John. "Your honor. But duty comes before

honor. How about me? It's as much against my honor to let these axmen take me in. There's nothing *I'd* like better," said John, smiling falsely, "than to get down from your back here and help you take these Hollows unmentionables to pieces. But do I think of myself? No. I—"

"Listen at him," said one of the axmen. "Help take us to pieces! Hor, hor."

"You think that's funny, do you!" flared the Bluffer afresh, spinning to face the tickled axman. "You just remember this is the Shorty chasing down the Terror. How'd you like to tangle with the Terror, yourself, hairy-legs?"

"Huh!" said the other, losing his good humor suddenly, and hefting his ax. However, he did throw a second look over the Bluffer's shoulder at John and stood where he was.

"All right, men," said the leader of the axmen. "Enough of this chit-chat! When I give the word—"

"Cut it! Cut it!" boomed the Bluffer. "We'll go with you. Half-Pint's right. Lucky for you."

"Huh!" said the axman who had laughed before. But as they all fell into a sort of hollow square with the Bluffer and John in the middle, he stayed well to the rear. Together they marched down into the valley and toward the amphitheater at the far end.

They went through the village, which under the bright early afternoon sun seemed to have a fiesta air about it, and to the amphitheater. The main road up which they traveled was alive with Dilbians of all ages moving in the same direction and many questions were thrown at the guard around John and the Bluffer. The guard, marching stiffly, with axes over their shoulders, looked straight ahead to a Dilbian and refused to answer.

They came at last to a long, meter-high ledge of rock on which five very ancient-looking male Dilbians sat on one low bench. The one on the far right was a skinny oldster who seemed slightly deaf, since as they came up he was cupping one ear with a shaky hand and shouting at the Dilbian next to him to speak up. As the Bluffer and John were brought to a halt before them, John was astonished to notice the number of other familiar faces in the forefront of the gathering. One Man was there, seated on a sort of camp stool. Ty Lamorc and Boy Is She Built stood not far from the giant Dilbian. And Gulark-*ay* and Joshua Guy were flanking old Shaking Knees, who—whether in his capacity as mayor of Humrog, or father to Boy Is She Built—was looking important.

"Hey!" cried John, trying to attract the attention of the little human ambassador.

Joshua Guy looked up, spotted John, and gave him a large smile and a cheery wave of one hand.

"Beautiful day, isn't it?" called the ambassador; he went back to chatting in a friendly manner with Gulark-*ay* and Shaking Knees.

"I can't see him. Where is he? Get him out in the open!" the deaf grandfather on the end of the bench was snapping fretfully.

"Sit here," said an axman. The Bluffer sat down on a bench. John climbed down from the saddle and sat beside him.

"There he is!" said the deaf grandfather. "Why didn't someone point him out to me before. What? Hey? Speak up!"

He was nudged by the grandfather adjoining. The grandfathers conferred, for the most part in low voices. Then they all sat back on their bench, and the central one waggled a finger at the head axman, who stepped out into the open space before the ledge and turned to the crowd.

"Clan Hollows is now meeting in open session!" he shouted. "No fighting! Everybody listen!"

The crowd muttered, grumbled, and took about forty seconds to subside to a passably low level of noise.

"Ahem!" The central grandfather, a heavy Dilbian

whose hair was showing the rusty color of age, cleared his throat. "The grandfathers have called this meeting to discuss a matter of Clan honor. In short: is the honor of Clan Hollows involved in the ruckus that one of the Clan Members, the Streamside Terror, has got himself into?"

"Yes!" spoke up Boy Is She Built.

"Who said that?" said the central grandfather.

"She did," said an axman, pointing at Boy Is She Built.

"Keep her quiet," said the grandfather.

"Shut up!" said the axman to Boy Is She Built.

"I apologize for my daughter to Clan Hollows," said Shaking Knees.

"You ought to," said the center Clan Hollows grandfather.

"What'd she say? Hey?" said the grandfather on the end. And they started all over again.

Three minutes later, approximately, things were fairly well straightened out and the meeting underway.

"It seems," said the center grandfather, "that the Terror, wanting this female that just interrupted your grandfather, here, got himself involved with a couple of different types of characters, who may or may not be real people, ended up coming back here with one of the types of characters, known as a Shorty, hot after him, and killing one of the other types of characters, known as a Fatty. Everybody agree to this?"

There was a stir in the forefront of the crowd and Gulark-*ay* spoke up.

"If the grandfathers will allow a stranger to speak—"

"Go ahead," said the center grandfather. "You're the Fatty top man from Humrog, aren't you?"

"I am."

"You don't agree?" said the center grandfather.

"I just," said Gulark-*ay* in a voice that reminded John of heavy maple syrup being poured from a five-gallon can, "wished to point out to the grandfathers of Clan Hollows that the Fatty in question is not quite killed. The Terror apparently left him for dead; but it seems now he will recover."

"Well, then, there's no blood feud involved there!" said the grandfather, sharply. "Why aren't we informed properly about these things?"

"I don't know," said the chief axman.

"Speak when you're spoken to," said the center grandfather. He looked out over the crowd. "Where's the Terror? I don't see the Terror."

"He's waiting at Glen Hollow," said Boy Is She built.

"Shut up," said the axman who had spoken to her before.

"Let her speak now," said the center grandfather. "Unless somebody else can tell us why the Terror's at Glen Hollow instead of here? I didn't think so. Go on, girl!"

"The Terror says the Clan can't force a man to dishonor himself. If he'd known the Half-Pint Posted, this Shorty here, had been after him, he wouldn't have moved a step after taking Greasy Face to avenge his honor against Little Bite—"

"Hold on!" said the center grandfather. "Hold on. Let's get things straightened out here. Who's Greasy Face?"

Boy Is She Built pointed down at Ty Lamorc, beside her.

"This Shorty female, here."

The crowd muttered among itself and craned its necks, looking over the shoulders of those in front of it to get a look at Ty.

"Female!" the grandfather next to him was shouting in the ear of the deaf grandfather on the end. "Shorty FE-*male!*"

"They come in pairs?" the deaf grandfather said, interestedly.

Boy Is She Built went on to explain. It was approximately the same story Joshua had given John originally, except that in Boy Is She Built's version she and the Terror were reported as invariably speaking in tones of great calm and reasonableness; while Shaking Knees,

Joshua, and all others sneered, whined, bellowed, and generally used the nastiest voices they were capable of using, when they were quoted.

"That still doesn't explain," said the center grandfather when she was through, "why the Terror isn't here to speak for himself."

"He says it already looks as if he had been dodging a fight with Half-Pint. He's not going to have it look as if he was hiding behind the grandfathers. He's there waiting for the Shorty now, in Glen Hollow for all the world to see. And if the Shorty doesn't reach him, it isn't his fault!"

"Hmph!" said the center grandfather, thoughtfully. He conferred with the other grandfathers. "Hey? What say?" the deaf grandfather could be heard demanding at intervals. Finally, they all sat back on their bench and the center grandfather spoke out again.

"As far as the grandfathers of the Clan can see," he said, "there's no reason this shouldn't be a personal matter between The Terror and the Half-Pint, here—except for one thing."

He paused and cleared his throat. It was like banging a gavel for order. The crowd became the quietest it had so far become.

"The facts are these," he said. "The Terror has had his mug spilt by a Shorty who is a guest in Humrog." He glanced at Shaking Knees. "Right?"

"Right," replied Shaking Knees, inclining his head as one gentleman of substance to another.

"To hit back, the Terror has tried to spill the mug of the guest Shorty by stealing away a member of the guest's household. That little Shorty female, there, Greasy Face."

Everybody looked at Ty.

"All right. Now, along comes a male Shorty—Half-Pint Posted here—having a claim on Greasy Face, and chases after the Terror to get his female back. And the grandfathers of your clan aren't such unfeeling old geezers—" he paused to glare at the audience "—even though you all seem to think so most of the time, that they'd require him to give her back. So why not let the Terror and the Half-Pint meet? Well, there's only one hitch."

The center grandfather leaned back, readjusting the creases in his large belly and looked right and left for approval. With nods and grunts, his fellow grandfathers gave it to him. Even the deaf grandfather seemed to be fully briefed and in favor as he nodded with one hand cupped about his ear.

"The hitch is this," said the center grandfather. "Now the rules and customs of real men are not set up at random. There is always a purpose behind them. And the purpose behind affairs of honor is to enable real men to live honorably and safely, one with another."

"*I* think it's absolutely ridiculous!" muttered Boy Is She Built. "What *I* think, is—"

"Shut up!" said the axman.

"Therefore, it is not just the honors of two individuals at stake in such instances, but the whole structure of custom by which we live. In this instance, now, it may well be honorable for man to fight with man; but is it honorable for man to fight a Shorty—considering all that a Shorty is, in the way of size and differentness? In short, if we let this Shorty fight the Terror it's the same thing as admitting he's as much a man as any real man among us. And is he? What kind of proof have we got that he deserves to be treated like one of us, like a real man?" The center grandfather paused and looked out over the crowd. "Anybody who has anything they want to say on this question can now speak up."

"Ahem!" said Shaking Knees.

"Mayor?" said the center grandfather. Shaking Knees rolled forward a couple of ponderous paces.

"Just thought I'd clear the record," he said. "I don't claim to be any expert on the Half-Pint here, or Greasy Face, or any other Shorty. But I just thought I'd mention," he rubbed his nose with one large-knuckled hand, "that Little Bite here is a guest in Humrog. And speaking as the Mayor of Humrog, I don't exactly guess that Humrog would be making a guest out of anyone who wasn't entitled to be treated as a real man." He smiled widely around the crowd. "Just thought I'd mention it to you Clan Hollows folk."

The grandfathers consulted.

"Well, now," said the center grandfather, after the huddle was over. "The way the grandfathers of Clan Hollows think is this. Everybody here knows the folks in Humrog, after all we do most of our trading there. And we know that Humrog folks generally know what they're talking about. So if the folks in Humrog are pretty generally sure that Little Bite, there, is the same thing as a real man, the grandfathers of Clan Hollows and the folks of Clan Hollows are willing to go along with the way they think, as far as Little Bite is concerned."

"Thanks. Humrog thanks you," said Shaking Knees.

"Not at all. However," went on the center grandfather, "deciding Little Bite can be taken for a real man, is one thing. Deciding Half-Pint, just because he's a Shorty, too, is a real man as well is something else again. After all, Little Bite didn't come hunting the Terror for an affair of honor—" he broke off suddenly, and his voice took on the first tinge of politeness it had yet shown. "One Man?"

"If I might—" the great basso of One Man rumbled politely off to John's left; and John, turning his head and peering around the bulk of the Hill Bluffer, saw the giant Dilbian rising. "If I might just say a few words to the eminent grandfathers of this ancient clan."

"The honor's ours, One Man," the center grandfather assured him.

"Very good of you," said One Man. The whole assemblage had gone dead silent and One Man's scarcely-raised voice carried easily to all of them. "An old man like myself, now, who has lived long enough to be a grandfather in my own clan, if I had one, and was worthy, sees things perhaps a little differently from you younger people.

It's enough for me nowadays to sit feebly in my corner, letting the fire warm my old bones, and ponder on the world as it goes by me."

"Now, One Man," said the center grandfather, "we all know you're nowhere near's feeble as all that."

"Well, thank you, thank you," said One Man, lifting an arm like a water main in acknowledgement and then letting it drop, as if its weight was too much for him. "I've got a few years left, perhaps. But it wasn't myself I was going to talk about. I was just going to mention something of how things look to me from my chimney corner. You know, as I watch the passing parade I can't help thinking how much things have changed from the old days. The old customs are falling into disuse."

"Never said a truer word!" muttered the deaf grandfather on the end of the bench. He now had both hands cupped behind both ears.

"Children no longer have the old respect for their parents."

"You can bet on that!" growled Shaking Knees, scowling at his daughter.

"Everywhere, the old way of doing things is being replaced by the new. Where this will lead us nobody knows. It may be that the new ways are better ways."

"So there!" said Boy Is She built, tossing her nose up at her father.

"We cannot, at this moment, say. But certainly we seem stuck with a world now in which we are not alone, in which we must deal with Shorties and Fatties, and maybe other creatures, too. This leads me to a suggestion which in my own limited judgment I consider rather sound; but I hesitate to push it on the venerable grandfathers of this Clan, being only an outsider."

"We'd be glad to hear what One Man has to suggest," growled the center grandfather. "Wouldn't we?" He looked around and found the other grandfathers nodding approval.

"Well," said One Man, mildly, "why not let them fight

and make up your minds afterwards whether Half-Pint deserves to be regarded as a man—depending on how he shows up in the fight? That way you don't risk anything; and whichever way you decide, you've got evidence to back you up. For after all, it isn't size, or hair, or where he was born that makes a man among us. It's how he behaves, isn't that correct?"

He paused. The grandfathers and the crowd as well, including such diverse elements as Shaking Knees and Boy Is She Built, muttered their approval.

"A lot of people have thought that it might make somebody like the Terror look foolish, facing up to someone as small as a Shorty. Something or someone that small, they thought, couldn't possibly have a hope of standing up to a toothless old grandmother with a broken leg. But the Terror seems willing. And if the Half-Pint seems willing, too, who knows? The Half-Pint might even surprise us all and actually take the Terror."

There was a roll of laughter from the crowd and One Man sat down. The center grandfather shouted at the chief axman; and the axman shouted for order. When comparative silence was re-established, it was found that Gulark-*ay* had taken several ponderous steps toward the bench of the grandfathers.

"What's this?" said the center grandfather, as the chief axman whispered in his ear. He consulted with his fellow grandfathers.

"Very well," he said at last; and raised his voice to the crowd. "Quiet out there! The Beer-Guts Bouncer's got something to say and your grandfathers can't hear anything short of a thunderstorm with you yelling around like that!"

The crowd noise dwindled to near silence.

"Speak up!" said the center grandfather to Gulark-*ay*.

"Well, now, I kind of hate to shove in like this," said Gulark-*ay* in robust tones very different from the voice he had used to John, that morning before in the forest. He hunched his fat shoulders and was suddenly and amazingly transformed from a sleek Buddha to an over-weight, but clumsily forthright and honest-looking, lout; somewhat embarrassed by being the center of all attention. "I wouldn't want to mess in the business of Clan Hollows, here. And I sure wouldn't want to say anything against that fine suggestion One Man made just now. But fair's fair, I say. I guess I ought to tell you."

"Tell us what, Beer-Guts?" inquired the center grandfather.

"Well, now," said Gulark-*ay*, scuffing the earth with one sandal toe, and turning red in the face. "Nobody likes Little Bite better than I do, but it's a fact, he's getting old."

"Something wrong with that?" inquired the center grandfather, sharply.

"No—no," said Gulark-*ay*. "Nothing wrong with it at all. But you know, Little Bite doesn't say much; but I happen to know he's been wanting to leave his job here and get back to his home on that other world, for a long time."

"What," said the center grandfather, "has all that got to do with us?"

"Well, Little Bite, he wanted to go home. But his people back there, they wanted him to stay here. Well, some little time ago he figured maybe he better just mess things up here a little; and then his people back home would send someone else out to do the job right and he could quit. Well now," said Gulark-*ay*, "I don't blame him. A Shorty his age, with nothing but real people twice his size around him all the time, it's not the sort of thing that would bother me, myself. But I can see how something like that would be for someone his size—like asking a kid to go out and do a full day's work in the fields, same as a man. And, of course, around here he doesn't have his machines and gadgets to make life easier for him. So, as I say, I don't blame him; all the same I wouldn't have done what he did. Didn't seem right."

Gulark-*ay* stopped to mop his face with a corner of his robe.

"Sure is thirsty, standing out here talking like this," he said. "I could go for a drink."

He got a good laugh from the crowd. But the grand-fathers did not join in.

"What do you mean—'done what he did?' What did Little Bite do?" demanded the center grandfather.

"Well, he just thought he'd kick up a little ruckus by mixing into the Terror's business. Then Terror—any real person would have figured on it, of course—took off with Greasy Face and it got a whole lot more serious than Little Bite had bargained for. So he had to call in the Half-Pint there. Well, now, the truth is, the Half-Pint never saw Greasy Face before in his little life. It's all a story about him wanting her back from the Terror, like a real man might."

The center grandfather turned. His eyes focused on Joshua Guy.

"Little Bite?" he said.

"I'm right here," said Joshua, standing up.

"Is what the Beer-Guts Bouncer's telling us, the truth?"

Joshua brushed some pine needles from a fold in his jacket with a casual flick of his hand.

"With all due respect to the grandfathers of Clan Hollows, and the people of Clan Hollows," he said, "I am a guest in Humrog, and a representative of the Shorty people. Accordingly, to dignify the Beer-Guts Bouncer's accusation by taking any notice of it would be beneath my official dignity."

Joshua smiled winningly at the Clan Hollows grand-fathers.

"Accordingly," he said, "I must refuse to discuss it."

And sat down.

CHAPTER 16

There was a moment's dead silence and then the closest thing to a collective gasp that John had ever heard uttered by Dilbians. Being the type of people they were, it was more grunt than gasp—rather the sort of sound that comes from a punch in the stomach.

Then, a knowing babble arose.

The grandfathers sat back on their bench, looking grim. The center grandfather consulted to his left and to his right. Then he addressed the assemblage.

"Quiet down!"

They quieted, eagerly listening.

"Beer-Guts," said the center grandfather, to Gulark-*ay*. "You said Half-Pint here never even knew about Greasy Face until Little Bite got in touch with him. Then maybe you can tell us just why he'd come chasing after her, wanting to fight the Terror."

"He didn't," said Gulark-*ay*.

"He what?"

"Half-Pint," said Gulark-*ay*, "never even knew he'd have to fight the Terror, maybe, to get Greasy back. Little Bite never let on that might happen. If he had, he'd never have got Half-Pint to go after her. You don't think any Shorty would seriously consider tangling bare-handed with—what was it One Man said?—even a toothless old grandmother. Half-Pint wouldn't have been willing at all." He threw a grin at John. "He's not willing now. Find out for yourself. Ask him."

"Hey—" said the Hill Bluffer, shooting suddenly to his feet.

"Sit down!" said the center grandfather.

"Are you giving the government mail orders?" roared the Bluffer.

"Yes, I'm giving the government mail orders!" snapped the center grandfather. "On Clan Hollows ground, in full Clan Hollows meeting, I'm giving the government mail order. Sit down!"

The Bluffer, growling, sat down.

The grandfathers went into session together. They talked for a minute or two, then sat back. The center grandfather spoke out.

"Here's the decision of the grandfathers," he said. "With all respect to One Man and others, this whole business smells a little too fishy to your grandfathers. Accordingly, it's our ruling that Greasy Face be sent back with Little Bite, and Half-Pint along with them. No affair of honor to be allowed between the Terror and the Half—"

"NOW YOU LISTEN TO ME!" thundered the Hill Bluffer, rising like a stone from a catapult. "Clan Hollows or no Clan Hollows. Grandfather or no grandfathers. And if the Beer-Guts Bouncer doesn't like it, he knows where to find the government mail, any time. You think this Shorty here isn't willing to tangle with the Terror?"

"Sit down!" yelled the center grandfather.

"I won't sit down!" the Bluffer yelled back. "None of

you know the Half-Pint. I do. *Not willing!* Listen, when a bunch of drunks at Brittle Rock tried to make him do tricks like a performing animal, he fooled them all and got away. Then Boy Is She Built tried to drop him over a cliff. Does he look dropped? On our way here the bridge at Knobby Gorge was rucked up out of our reach. He climbed up a straight cliff with nothing to hang on to, to get it down and let us over after the Terror."

The Bluffer swung around and flung out a pointing arm at the chief axman.

"And what happened when you and four of the boys tried to take us in just outside the valley here? Who wanted to help me clean up on the five of you? And who didn't have any doubts about the two of us being able to do it, either?" He glared at the chief axman. "Huh?"

He swung around back to John.

"How about it, Half-Pint?" he roared. "The hell with the Clan Hollows and their grandfathers! The hell with anybody but you and me and the Terror? You want to be delivered or not? Say the word!"

John heard the Bluffer, and the swelling roar of the crowd rising behind him. All this time he had been sitting with one thumb rubbing pensively back and forth along the top edge of his belt buckle, listening to what was being said, and thinking deeply. He had time to figure out what was behind most of what was happening; and when the Bluffer had leaped up just now and gone into his impassioned speech, it had rung a bell clear and strong inside John Tardy.

So when the Bluffer bawled his question, John had his answer ready. The words were still in the air when John was on his feet himself, and shouting.

"Show me this skulking Terror!" he shouted. "Lead me to him! Who hides behind his grandfathers and his clan and won't stand and fight like a man!"

CHAPTER 17

The words barely had time to pass John's lips before things began happening. He felt himself snatched from the ground and the whole scene whirled wildly about him as he found himself being carried like a sack of grain away from the amphitheater and the meeting, and toward the forest beyond the valley.

The Hill Bluffer had grabbed him in two large hands and was running with him toward the forest the way a football player runs with a football. A roar of voices surged up and beat behind them. Looking back over the Bluffer's boulder-like shoulder, John saw that the whole mass of people involved in the meeting of Clan Hollows was now at their heels.

The free air whistled past John's face. He was being jolted about with every jarring footfall of the Bluffer; but the landscape was reeling past them both at a rate that must be close to thirty miles an hour; and the crowd behind was not gaining on them. In fact, John hesitated to believe it, considering that the Bluffer was carrying John's extra one hundred and eighty-five pounds in such an awkward fashion, but as the forest wall drew near he was forced to, they were actually running away from their pursuers. Their lead got bigger with each stride of the Bluffer. John felt the glow of competition as he had felt it on the sports field many times before. For the first time, a spark of kinship glowed to life inside him for the Bluffer.

They might be worlds apart, biologically, thought John, but by heaven they both had what it took to outdo the next man when the chips were stacked and wagered.

Abruptly, the shadow of the forest closed about them. The Bluffer ran on a carpet of tree needles, easing back his pace to a steady lope. He lifted John, pushing him back around to the saddle. John climbed into the saddle and hung on. With John's weight properly distributed, the Bluffer ran more easily.

The surf-sound of pursuit behind them began to be muffled by the forest. Moreover it was dropping further behind yet, and fading. The Bluffer ran down the side of one small hollow, and coming up the other, dropped for the first time back into his usual stalking stride of a walking pace. When he reached the crest of the further side, he ran again down the slope to the next hollow. And so he continued, alternately running and walking as the slope permitted.

"How far to the Terror?" asked John, during one of these spells of walking.

"Glen Hollow," said the Bluffer, economically. "Half a—" he gave the answer in terms of Dilbian units. John worked it out in his head to come to just about three miles more.

A little more than ten minutes later, they broke through a small fringe of the birchlike trees to emerge over the lip of a small, cuplike valley containing a nearly treeless, grassy meadow split by a stream, which in the valley's center spread out into a pool some forty feet across at its widest and showing enough dark blueness to its waters to indicate something more than ordinary depth.

By the side of those waters, waited the Streamside Terror.

John leaned forward and spoke quietly into that same ear of the Bluffer's that he had bitten an hour or so earlier, as the Bluffer started down the slope toward the meadow.

"Put me down," said John, "beside the deepest part of that pond."

The Bluffer grunted agreeably and continued his descent. He came down to a point by the wider part of the pool and stopped while he was still about thirty feet from the waiting Dilbian.

"Hello, postman," said the Terror.

"Hello, Streamside," grunted the Bluffer. "Mail for you here."

The Streamside Terror looked curiously past the Hill Bluffer's shoulders and met John's eye.

"That's the Half-Pint Posted, is it?" he said. "I thought he'd be bigger. So the old ones let you come?"

"Nope," said the Bluffer. "We just came on our own."

While the Terror had been peering at John, John had been closely examining the Terror. John had gotten a fair look at the Dilbian scrapper back while he was escaping from Tark-*ay*, but from some little distance. And for most of that time, the Terror had been in pretty constant motion. Now John had a chance to make sure of the picture he had carried away from the Hemnoid camp before.

Once more, John was struck by the fact that the Terror did not seem particularly large, for a Dilbian. The Bluffer was nearly a good head taller. And the impressive mass of One Man would have made two of the younger battler. Streamside was good sized for a male, but nothing more than that. John noted, however, the unusually thick and bulky forearms, the short neck and—more revealing perhaps than anything else—the particularly poised stance and balance of the Dilbian.

It was as if the whole weight of the Terror's body was so easily and lightly carried that the whole effort of moving it into action could be ignored.

John threw one quick glance at the water alongside. The bank seemed to drop directly off into deep water. He slid down from the saddle and stepped around the Dilbian postman, kicking off his boots and shrugging out of his jacket as he did so. His hands went to his belt buckle; and in the same moment, with no further pause for amenities, the Streamside Terror charged.

John turned and dived deep into the pool.

He had expected the Terror to attack immediately. He had even counted on it, reasoning that the Dilbian was too much the professional fighter to take chances with any opponent—even one as insignificant as a red-headed Shorty. John had planned that the Terror should follow him into the water.

But not that the Terror should follow so quickly.

Even as John shot for the dark depths of the pool, he heard and felt the water-shock of the big body plunging in after him, so close that it felt as if the Terror's great nailed hands were clawing at John's heels.

John stroked desperately for depth and distance. He had a strategy of battle; but it all depended on a certain amount of time and elbow room. He changed direction underwater, shot off at an angle up to the surface; and, flinging water from his eyes with a backward jerk of his head, looked around him.

The Terror, looking in the other direction, broke the surface fifteen feet away.

Rapidly, John dived again. Well underwater, he reached for his belt buckle, unsnapped it and pulled the belt from the loops of his trousers. In the process, he had come to the surface again. He broke water almost under the nose of the Terror; and was forced to dive again imme-

diately with half a lungful of air and his bulky enemy close
behind him.

Once more, in the space and dimness of underwater,
he evaded the Dilbian; and this time he came up cleanly,
a good ten feet from where the back of the Terror's big
head broke the water. Turning, John stroked for distance
and breathing room, the length of his belt still trailing
from one fist like a dark stem of water-weed.

Confidence was beginning to warm in John as he dove
again. He had had time, now, to prove an earlier guess
that, effective as the Terror might be against other
Dilbians in the water, his very size made him more slow
and clumsy than a human in possibly anything but straight-
away swimming. John had gambled on this being true—
just as he had gambled on the fact that, true to his
reputation, the Terror would pick a battleground alongside some stream or other. Now, John told himself, it was
time to switch to the attack, choose the proper opening
and make his move.

Turning about, John saw the Terror had spotted him
and was churning the water in his direction. John filled
his lungs and dived, as if to hide again. But underneath
the surface he changed direction and swam directly toward
his opponent. He saw the heavy legs and arms churning
toward him overhead; and, as they passed in the water,
he reached up, grabbed one flailing foot and pulled.

The Terror reacted with powerful suddenness. He
checked; and dived. John, flung surfacewards by the heel
he had caught, released it and dived also, so that he shot
downwards, behind and above the back of the Dilbian.
He saw the wide shoulders, the churning arms; and then,
as the Terror—finding no quarry—turned upwards again
toward the surface, John closed in.

He passed the thin length of his belt around the
Terror's thick neck, wrapped it also around his own wrists
and twisted the large loop tight.

At this the Terror, choking, should have headed toward
the surface, giving John a chance to breathe. The Dilbian

did. But there and then the combat departed from John's plan, entirely. John got the breath of air he had been expecting at this moment—the one breath he had counted on to give him an advantage over the strangling Terror. But then Streamside plunged down again, turning and twisting to get at the human who was riding his back and choking him. And finally, and after all, John came at last to understand what sort of an opponent he had volunteered to deal with.

It is always easy to be optimistic; and even easier to underrate an enemy. John, in spite of all the evidence, in spite of all his experiences of the last three days, had simply failed to realize how much greater the Terror's strength could be than his own. Physically, the Terror in sheer weight and muscle was a match for any two full-grown male Earthly gorillas. And, in addition to this, he had human intelligence and courage.

John clung like a fresh-water leech, streaming out in the wake of the Terror, as the Terror thrashed and twisted, trying to get a grip with his big fingers on the thin belt, sunk in the fur of his neck. While with the other nineteen-inch hand he beat backwards through the water, trying to knock John from his hold.

John was all but out of reach, stretched at arms-length by his grip on the belt. But now and again, the blind blows of the Terror's flailing hand brushed him. Only brushed him—awkwardly, and slowly, slowed by the water—but each impact tossed John about like a chip in a river current. He felt like a man rolling down a cliff side and being beaten all over by baseball bats at the same time.

His head rang. The water roared in his ear. He gulped for air and got half a mouthful of foam and water. His shoulder numbed to one blow and his ribs gave to another. His senses began to leave him; he thought—through what last bit of semiconsciousness that remained as the fog closed about his mind—that it was no longer a matter of proving his courage in facing the Terror. His very life now lay in the grip of his hands on the twisted belt. It was, in the end, kill or be killed. For it was very clear that if he did not manage to strangle the Terror before he, himself, was drowned or killed, the Terror would most surely do for him.

Choking and gasping, he swam back to blurred consciousness. His mouth and nose were bitter with the taste of water and he was no longer holding the belt. The edge of the bank loomed like a raft to the survivor of a sunken ship, before him. Instinctively, no longer thinking of the Terror, or anything but light and air, he scrabbled like a half-drowned animal at the muddy edge of earth. His arms were leaden and weak, too weak to lift him ashore. He felt hands helping him. He helped to pull himself onto slippery grass. The hands urged him a little farther. His knees felt ground beneath him.

He coughed water. He retched. The hands urged him a little farther; and finally, at last completely out on solid land, he collapsed.

He came around after a minute or two to find his head in someone's lap. He blinked upwards and a watery blur of color slowly resolved itself into the face of Ty Lamorc, taut and white above him. Tears were rolling down her cheeks.

"What—?" he croaked. He tried again. "What're you doing here?"

"Oh, shut up!" she said, crying harder than ever.

She began wiping his face with a piece of cloth nearly as wet as he was.

"No," he said. "I mean—what're *you* doing here?" He tried to sit up.

"Lie down," she said.

"No. I'm all right." He struggled up into a sitting position. He was still in Glen Hollow, he saw, groggily. And the place was aswarm with Dilbians. A short way down the bank a knot of them were clustered around something.

"What—?" he said, looking in that direction.

"Yep, it's the Terror, Half-Pint," said a familiar voice above him. He looked up to see the enormously looming figure of the Hill Bluffer. "He's still out and here you're kicking your heels and sitting up already. That makes it your fight. I'll go tell them." And he strode off toward the other group, where John could hear him announcing the winner in a loud and self-justified voice.

John blinked and looked over at Ty.

"What happened?" he asked her.

"They had to pull him out. You made it to shore on your own." She produced a disposable tissue from somewhere—John had almost forgotten such things existed during the last three days—wiped her eyes and blew her nose vigorously. "You were wonderful."

"Wonderful!" said John, still too groggy for subtlety. "I was out of my head to even think of it. Next time I'll try tangling with a commuter rocket, instead!" He felt his ribs, gently. "I better get back to the embassy in Humrog and have a picture taken of this side."

"Oh! Are your ribs—"

"Maybe just bruised. Wow!" said John, coming on an especially tender spot.

"Oh!" Ty choked up again. "You might have been killed. And it's all my fault!"

"All *your* fault—" began John. The dapper, small figure of Joshua Guy loomed suddenly over him.

"How are you, my boy?" inquired Joshua. "Congratulation, by the way. Oh, you must let me explain—"

"Not now," said John. He clutched at the small man's wrist. "Help me up. Now," he said, turning to face Ty, who had also risen. "What do you mean, it was all your fault?"

"Well, it was!" she wailed, miserably, twisting the tissue to shreds. "It was my off-official recommendation. The Contacts Department sent me out here to survey the situation and recommend means for beating the Hemnoids to the establishment of primary relations with the Dilbians."

"What's that got to do with me?"

"Well, I—I recommended they send out a man who conformed as nearly as possible to the Dilbian psychological profile and we worked out a Dilbian emotional situation so as to convince them we weren't the absolute little toylike creatures they thought we were—but people just like themselves. We needed to prove to them we're as good men as they are, aside from our technology, which they thought was sissy."

"Me?" said John. "Dilbian emotional profile?"

"But you are, you know. Extroverted, l-lusty—. They've got a very unusual culture here, they really have. They're really much more similar to us humans when we were in the pioneering stages of culture than they are to the Hemnoids. We had to prove it to them that we could be the kind of people they could treat with on a level. The truth is, they've got chips on their shoulders because we and the Hemnoids are more advanced. But they can't admit to themselves they're more primitive than we are because their culture— anyway," wound up Ty, seeing John was getting red in the face, "it would have been fine except for Boy Is She Built trying to throw you over that cliff. She was only supposed to take your wrist phone. And that altered the emotional constants of the sociological equations involved. And Gulark-*ay* almost got it all twisted to go his own way, and—"

"I see," interrupted John. "And why," he asked, very slowly and patiently, "wasn't *I* briefed on the fact that this was all a sort of sociological power politics bit?"

"Because," wept Ty, "we wanted you to react like the Dilbians in a natural, extroverted, un—unthinking way!"

"I see," said John, again. They were still standing beside the pool. He picked her up—she was really quite light and slender—and threw her in. There was a shriek and a satisfying splash. The Dilbians nearby looked around interestedly. John turned and walked off.

"Of course, she didn't know you then," said Joshua, thoughtfully.

John snorted, Dilbian fashion. He walked on. But after half a dozen steps more he slowed down, turned, and went back.

"Here," he said, gruffly, extending his hand as she clung to the bank.

"Thag you," Ty said humbly, with her nose full of water. He hauled her out.

CHAPTER 18

"I hope," said Joshua Guy, "you still don't consider that I—"

"Not at all," said John. He, Ty Lamorc, and the little ambassador, once more freshly cleaned and dressed, were waiting at the small spaceport near Humrog for the shuttle ship to descend from the regular courier spacer and take John and Ty back to Earth to be debriefed by the Contacts Department, there. It was early morning of a sunny mountain day and a light cool breeze was slipping across the concrete apron of the spaceport and plucking at the cuffs of John's trousers. A few curious Dilbian faces could be seen looking out the wide observation window of the spaceport terminal building, whose white roof glittered in the early sunlight about forty yards off.

"I got suspicious," said John, "when Gulark-*ay* gave me that long story about you when he, and Tark-*ay* and Boy

Is She Built had me prisoner there in the woods. It was a little too good to be true—too good for Gulark-*ay*, that is."

"Oh, by the way, I ran into him as I was coming out from Humrog, this morning," said Joshua. "He told me he was due shortly for rotation to a post back on Chakaa—the second of the Hemnoid home worlds. If you and Ty dropped by, be sure to look him up and he'd show you around."

"No thanks," said John, grimly.

"My dear boy!" said Joshua, in tones of mild shock. "You mustn't confuse what a person does in his official capacity with his character as a private citizen. Drop in on Chakaa as a tourist or on official business, and I'm sure you'd find Gulark-*ay* a superb host. In fact, take my advice and take him up on the invitation. I assure you, you'll enjoy yourselves immensely." He interrupted himself to glance over at the building. "That Dilbian who's going with you two should be here by now. But pardon me for interrupting you. You say you only suspected—?"

"The story was too good to be true," said John, again. "What cooked it, to my mind however, was Tark-*ay* conveniently setting out his knife and going to sleep so I could escape. He and Gulark-*ay* wanted me to get away. I was no use to him in pieces. He wanted me to stand up in front of the Clan Hollows meeting and admit to everybody I was scared spitless of fighting the Terror."

"Lucky for us you weren't," said Joshua. "Actually, Ty and I never intended matters to go so far."

"We estimated that the emotional value of your simply coming after me would have a good effect on the Dilbian group opinion where humans were concerned," put in Ty. "We wouldn't have blamed you a bit if you had let Joshua take the blame of Gulark-*ay*'s story and let the grandfathers send us back without a fight. We didn't expect that kind of courage."

"What do you mean—courage?" said John. "If I hadn't thought of the belt trick, and at that, it was a crazy fool stunt because I'd gotten so used to the Dilbians I'd forgotten how strong they could be. Don't ask me to try it again." He thought of something, suddenly. "The Terror never said anything about being beaten by a weapon, like my belt?" Joshua shook his head.

"He's got his own reason, perhaps," said Ty. "The Dilbian personality—oh, look!"

John and Joshua looked and saw One Man approaching, enormous in the morning light.

"Is *he* the one going with us?" said John. But One Man joined them before Joshua could answer.

"Greetings to you all," rumbled One Man.

"Greetings to you as well," replied Joshua. They smiled at each other, it was rather like a mouse and an orangutan exchanging the time of day.

"Uh—" said John to Ty, "how'd you get that smudge on your nose?"

"Smudge?" said Ty. "Nose?" She effected some feminine sleight of hand which caused a large compact to appear and open in her fingers. She peered into the mirror inside its lid. "Where? I don't see it."

"On the side of your nose there," said John. "It looks," he added, "sort of greasy . . ."

"Greasy!" Ty Lamorc snapped the compact shut indignantly and headed toward the terminal building. "Just a minute—tell the shuttle to wait," she called over her shoulder. The two human men and the single Dilbian one watched her go.

"Attractive girl," murmured Joshua.

"Is she?" inquired One Man.

"By our Shorty standards, very," replied Joshua. "Our young friend here, the Half-Pint—"

"Oh, well," said John, and cleared his throat meaningfully. He looked at One Man. "If I could have a word with you—"

"Excuse me," said Joshua; and discreetly wandered off toward the far fence of the port.

"I wanted to thank you," said John.

"Thank me?" rumbled One Man, in mild basso astonishment.

"For your help."

"Help? Why, Half-Pint," said One Man. "I can't take any credit for helping you. I'm too old to go engaging in help to anyone, and if I did, of course it would be one of my own people. I can't guess what you could be talking about."

"I think you know," said John.

"Not at all. Of course, now that you've given my people a clearer picture of what Shorties are like— Nothing wins like a winner, you know," said One Man, pontifically. "In fact, I'm surprised it took you Shorties so long to realize that. As I said to you once before, who asked you all to come barging into our world, anyway?"

"Well—" said John, uncomfortably.

"And what made you think we all *had* to like you, and welcome you, and want to be like you? Why, if when you were a pup, some new kid had moved into your village; and he was half your size but had a lot of playthings you didn't have, but came up and tapped you on the shoulder and said from now on I'm going to be your leader, and we'll play *my* games, how would you have felt?"

He eyed John shrewdly out of his huge, hairy face.

"I see," said John, after a moment. "Then why *did* you help me?"

"I tell you I don't know what you're talking about," said One Man. "How could I help a Shorty, even if I wanted to?"

"Well, I'll tell you how," said John. "Back home where I come from, we've got a trick with something called a city directory. It's about this thick," John measured several inches between finger and thumb, "and it's about as much a job for one of us Shorties to tear it in half as it is for one of you Dilbians to break that stick of yours. So—"

"Well, now, I can believe it," broke in One Man in a judicious tone. "Directories, sticks of wood, or first class hill-and-alley scrappers; there's a trick, I imagine, to handle almost any one of them. Of course," said One Man, gazing off at the pure snow of the far mountain peaks, "nobody like you or I would stoop to using such tricks, even in a good cause."

There was a moment's dead silence between them.

"I guess," said John at last, "I'll never make a diplomat."

"No," said One Man, still gazing at the mountain peaks. "I don't believe you ever will, Half-Pint." He returned his gaze to John's face. "If you take my advice, you'll stick to your own line of Shorty work."

"I just thought," said John awkwardly, "since you were coming back to earth with us—"

"I?" said One Man. "What an idea, Half-Pint! An old man like me, exposed to all those new-fangled contrivances and being taught to act like a Shorty so I could come back and tell people about it? Why, I'd be just no good at all at something like this."

"Not you?" John stared. "Then who—?"

"I thought you knew," said One Man; and looked past John toward the terminal building. "Look; here he comes now."

John turned and blinked. Coming toward them from the terminal and holding his pace down to accommodate his stride to that of Ty, who was walking alongside him, was none other than the Streamside Terror.

"But—" said John. "I thought he—"

"Appearances," said One Man, "are often deceiving. If you were somebody with brains, among us real people on this world here, and nothing much else but a good set of reflexes, what would *you* do? Particularly if you were ambitious? Unfortunately, our society is a physically-oriented one, where muscles win more attention than wisdom. Streamside is the very boy to visit your Shorty worlds and begin to set up connections. Temperamentally, I can admit to you now, I suppose, you Shorties are a lot more akin to us than those Fatties. But you know how it is," One Man paused and sighed, "close relatives squabble more often than strangers do."

The Terror and Ty were almost to them. There was only time for a private word or two more.

"I hope he isn't feeling a little touchy," said John. "With me, I mean. After our fight, and so forth."

"You mean they didn't tell you?" said One Man. "Why that was one of the Terror's conditions before he agreed to go. You see, evidently you Shorties have high hopes of setting up Dilbian-Humans teams—" John looked at One Man in surprise. He had never heard a Dilbian refer to either his own people, or any others by the human names for them "—and after initial contact work has been done, the Terror wants to pioneer that field, as well."

John frowned.

"I don't understand," he said.

"Why, the Terror's condition was that he be trained in your field and you be drafted to work with him, of course," said One Man. Staring up at the big face in astonishment, John was overwhelmed to see it contort suddenly in what, he realized after a second, was a pretty fair Dilbian imitation of the human expression known as a wink.

"You see," said One Man. "After the little episode in the water at Glen Hollow, he thinks you're pretty well capable. With you he feels *safe*."

Spacepaw

Chapter 1

Spiraling down toward the large, blue world below, in the shuttle boat from the spaceship which had delivered him here to Dilbia. Bill Waltham reflected dismally upon his situation. Most of the five-day trip he had spent wearing a hypno-helmet. But in spite of the fact that his head was now a-throb with a small encyclopedia of information about the world below and its oversize inhabitants—their language, customs, and psychology—he felt that he knew less than nothing about this job into which he had been drafted.

The shuttle boat would land him near the Lowland village of Muddy Nose. There, presumably, he would be met on disembarking by Lafe Greentree, the human Agricultural Resident here, and by Greentree's other trainee-assistant—an Earth girl named Anita Lyme who had, incredible as it seemed, volunteered for her pre-college field training here, just as Bill had originally volunteered himself for the Deneb-Seventeen terraforming project. These two would introduce Bill to his native associate—an Upland Dilbian named the Hill Bluffer. The Hill Bluffer would in turn introduce him to the local Lowland farmers who had their homes in Muddy Nose, and Bill could get down to the apparently vital job for which he had been drafted here. He could hear himself now . . .

" . . . This is a spade. You hold it by this end. You stick the other end in the earth. Yes, deep in the earth. Then you tilt it, like this. Then you lift it up with the dirt still on it and put the dirt aside. Fine. You are now digging a hole in the ground . : ."

He checked the current of his thoughts sharply. There was no point, he told himself grimly, in being bitter about it. He was here now, and he would have to make the best of it. But in spite of himself, his mind's eye persisted in dwelling on the succession of days stretching ahead through two years of unutterable dullness and boredom. He thought again of the great symphony of engineering and development that was a terraforming project— changing the surface and weather of a whole world to make it humanly habitable; and he compared that with this small, drab job to which he was now headed. There seemed no comparison between the two occupations— no comparison at all.

But once more he took a close rein on his thoughts and emotions. Some day he would be a part of a terraforming project. Meanwhile, it would be well to remember that he would be given an efficiency rating for his work on Dilbia, just as if it was the job he had originally intended to do. That efficiency rating could not be high if he started out hating everything about the huge, bearlike natives and everything connected with them. At least, he thought, the Dilbians had a sense of humor— judging by the names they gave each other.

This last thought was not as cheering as it might have

been, however. It reminded Bill of something the reassignment officer had said at the space terminal on Arcturus Three, where his original travel orders had been lifted and new ones issued. The officer had been a tall, lath-thin, long-nosed man, who had taken Bill's being drafted away from the Deneb-Seventeen Project much more calmly than had Bill.

" . . . Oh, and of course," the reassignment office had said cheerfully, "you'll find you've been given a Dilbian name yourself, by the time you get there. . . ."

Bill scowled, remembering. His only experience previously with a nickname had not been a happy one. On the swimming team at pre-engineering school, he had failed to rejoice in the given name of "Ape"—not so much because of anything apelike about either his open and rather ordinary face under its cap of black hair, or his flat-muscled, square-boned body. The name had arisen because he was the only member of the team with anything resembling hair on his chest. Bill made a mental note to keep his shirt on when Dilbians were about, during the next two years—just in case. Of course he reflected now, they had hair all over their own bodies . . .

The chime of the landing signal rang through the shuttle boat. Bill looked out the window beside his seat behind the pilot and saw they were drifting down into a fair-sized meadow, perhaps half a mile away across plowed fields alternating with stands of trees from a cluster of buildings that would probably be the village of Muddy Nose. He looked down below him, searching for a glimpse of Greenleaf or his assistant—but he saw no human figures waiting there. In fact, he saw no figures there at all. Where was his welcoming committee?

He was still wondering that, five minutes later, as he stood in the clearing alone, with his luggage case at his feet and the shuttle boat falling rapidly skyward above his head. The shuttle-boat pilot had not been helpful. He knew nothing about who was to meet Bill, he had said. Furthermore, he was due back at the ship as soon as possible. He had handed Bill's luggage case out the hatch to him, closed the hatch, and taken off.

Bill looked up at the rich yellow of the local sun, standing in the midafternoon quarter of the sky. It was a beautiful, near-cloudless day. The air was warm, and from the stand of trees surrounding him a little distance, some species of local bird or animal was singing in high liquid chirpings. Well, thought Bill, at least one good thing was the fact that Dilbia's gravity was a little lighter than Earth's. That would make carrying his luggage case up to the Residency a little easier. He might as well get started. He picked up the luggage case and headed off in the general direction of the village as he remembered seeing it from the air.

He trudged out of the clearing, through the trees, and had just emerged into a second clearing when he heard a shouting directly ahead of him through the farther stand of trees. He stopped abruptly.

The shouting came again, in a chorus of incredibly deep bass voices, deeper than any human voice Bill had ever heard, and, it seemed to him in that first moment, more threatening.

He was about to change course so as to detour prudently around the noisy area, when his hypnoed information of the Dilbian language somewhat belatedly rendered the shouts into recognizable words and the words into parts of a song. Only "song" was not exactly the word for it, Dilbian singing being a sort of atonal chanting. Very crudely translated into English, the so-called singing he heard was going something like this:

> Drink it down, old friend Tin Ear,
>   Drink it down!
> Drink it down, old friend Tin Ear,
>   Drink it down!
> Here's to you and your sweet wife,
> May you have her all your life!

Better you than one of us.
Drink it down!

Drink it down . . . etc.
Here's to you and your new plow!
Does it make your back to bow?
Well, better you than one of us.
Drink etc . . .

Bill abruptly changed his mind. If the song was any
indication, a happy gathering of some sort was in progress
on the other side of the trees. All the hypnoed information
he had absorbed on the way to Dilbia had indicated that
the Dilbians were normally good-humored and generally
friendly enough—if somewhat boisterous and inclined to
take pride in observing the letter of the law, while carefully avoiding the spirit of it. Besides, Muddy Nose Village had a treaty agreement with the human members
of the Agricultural Assistance Program, and that officially
put him under the protection of any member of that local
community.

So there should be no reason not to join the gathering and at least get directions to the Residency, if not
some help as well in carrying his luggage to the village.
The situation would also give him a chance to size up the
natives before Greenleaf gathered him in and gave him
Greenleaf's own, possibly biased, point of view about
them. Bill was still not clear why a pre-engineering stu-
dent with a prospective major in mechanical engineering
should be needed to explain simple things like hoes and
rakes to the Dilbians.

Accordingly, he picked up his traveling case from where
he had put it down, and tramped ahead in under the trees
before him. The grove was not more than fifty to seventy-five feet thick, and he reached the other side shortly,
stepping out into what appeared to be the front yard of
a log farmhouse.

In the yard a plank table had been set up on trestles,

and at that table were half a dozen towering, bearlike individuals, nearly nine feet tall, and covered with brown-black hair plus a few straps, from which each had hung a monstrous sword, as well as various pouches or satchels. The crowd at the table was eating and drinking out of large wooden mugs refilled constantly from a nearby barrel with its top broken in. A dozen feet or so from the table was a pile of what appeared to be sacks of root vegetables, half a carcass resembling a side of beef, and an unopened barrel like the one from which they were drinking—together with some odds and ends, including a three-legged wooden stool. A small piglike animal was tied by a cord to one of the heavy vegetable sacks, and it was grunting and chewing on the cord. It was plain the creature would soon be loose.

But no one in the farmyard was paying any attention to the animal as Bill joined them. They had stopped singing and their attention was all directed to a smaller, more rounded—you might actually say fat—native, a good head shorter than the nine-footers at the table, and with a voice a good octave or two higher than the rest. From which, in addition to the fact that this one wore no sword, Bill concluded that she was a female. She was standing back a dozen feet from the table and shouting at the others—at one in particular who Bill now noticed was also not wearing a sword, but who sat rather more drunkenly than the others, at the head of the table facing down at her.

" . . . Look at him!" she was shouting, as Bill stepped into the yard and approached the table without any of them apparently noticing him. "He *likes* it! Isn't it bad enough that we have to live here outside the village because he won't speak up for our right to live at the Inn, when he knows I'm More Jam's dead wife's own blood cousin. No, he's got to sit down and get drunk with rascals and no-goods like the rest of you. Why do you put up with it, Tin Ear? Well, *answer me!*"

"They're making me," muttered the individual at the

top of the table who was evidently called Tin Ear. His tongue was a little thick, but his expression, as far as Bill could read it on his furry face, was far from unhappy.

"Well, why do you let them? Why don't you fight them like a man? If I was a man—"

"Impolite not drink guests," protested Tin Ear thickly.

"Impolite! Guests!" shouted the female. "Ex-Upland runagates, reivers, thieves . . ."

"Hold on, there, Thing-or-Two! No need to get nasty!" rumbled one of the sworded drinkers warningly. "Fair's fair. If there's something in that stack there"—he pointed to the pile to which the animal was tied—"you really can't spare, you're free to trot yourself over and talk to Bone Breaker—"

"Oh yes!" cried Thing-or-Two. "Talk to Bone Breaker, is it? He's no better than the rest of you—letting Sweet Thing stick her nose in the air and treat him the way she does! If there were any real men around here, they'd have settled the hash of men like him and you, long ago! When I was a girl, if a girl didn't want to leave home just yet, much she had to say about it. The man who wanted her just came in one day and swept her off her feet and carried her off—"

"Like Tin Ear, here, did to you? Is that it?" interrupted the male with the sword—and the whole table exploded into gargantuan laughter that made Bill's ears ring. Even Tin Ear choked appreciatively on the contents of the wooden mug from which he was swallowing, in spite of being, as far as Bill could see, in some measure the butt of the joke.

Thing-or-Two shouted back at them, but her words were lost in the laughter, which took a few minutes to die down.

"Why, I heard it was *you*, Thing-or-Two, who broke into Tin Ear's daddy's house one dark night and carried *him* off!" bellowed the speaker at the table, as soon as he could be heard, and the laughter mounted skyward again.

This last sally apparently had the unusual effect of rendering Thing-or-Two momentarily speechless. Taking advantage of this, and the gradual diminishing of the laughter, Bill decided it was time to call the attention of the gathering to himself. He had been standing in plain daylight right beside the table all this time, but for some strange reason no one seemed to have noticed him. Now he stepped up to the side of the Dilbian who had been trading insults with Thing-or-Two and poked him in the ribs.

"Hey!" said Bill.

The head of the Dilbian jerked around. Seated, his hairy face was on a level with Bill's and he stared at Bill now from a distance of less than three feet. His jaw dropped. Behind him, the laughter and other sounds died out, giving way to a stony silence as everyone at the table goggled incredulously at Bill.

"Sorry to bother you," said Bill, stiffly, in his best Dilbian, "but I've just got here, and I'm on my way to the Shorty Residency building, in Muddy Nose Village. Maybe one of you would be kind enough to point me in the right direction for the village, and maybe even one of you wouldn't mind coming along and giving me a hand with my luggage case?"

He waited, but they only continued to stare at him in fascinated silence. So he added, cautiously, knowing that bargaining was as much a part of Dilbian culture as breathing:

"I could probably scrape up a half-pint of nails for anyone who'd like to help me."

Again he waited. But there was no answer. Amazingly, the silence of the Dilbians persisted. They were still staring at Bill as if he were some strange creature, materialized out of thin air. Bill felt a slight uneasiness stir inside him. It seemed to him they were gaping at him as if they had never seen a human before, which was strange. His hypnoed information plainly informed him that Shorties—as humans were called by the Dilbians—

were well known to the Muddy Nosers. Perhaps he had made a mistake in stopping here, after all.

"A Shorty!" gasped the Dilbian he had spoken to, finally breaking the silence. "As I live and breathe! A real, walking, talking, little Shorty! Out here, all by himself!"

He turned about in his seat and slowly reached out a long arm, which Bill avoided by backing away out of reach.

"Come here, Shorty!" said the Dilbian.

"No thanks," said Bill, now fully alerted to the fact that there was something very wrong in the situation. He kept backing away. "Forget I asked." It was high time to remind them of his protected status, he decided. The sworded individual he had been speaking to was already beginning to rise from the table with every obvious intention of laying hands upon him.

"It was just a thought—that I might get one of you to help me," Bill said rapidly. "I'm a member of the Residency, myself, you know."

The Dilbian was now on his feet and others were rising. Alarm rang as clearly in Bill as the clanging of a fire bell.

"What's the matter with you?" he shouted at the oncoming Dilbian. "Don't you know we Shorties have a treaty with the Muddy Nosers? According to that treaty, you all owe me protection and assistance!"

The male Dilbians, still rising from the table, froze and stared once again for a long second before suddenly bursting out into wild whoops of laughter, wilder and louder than Bill had yet heard from them.

Bill stared at them, amazed.

"Why, you crazy little Shorty!" cried the voice of Thing-or-Two furiously behind him. "Can't you tell the differences between people, when you see them? These aren't honest folk like us here around the village! They're those thieves and plunderers and no-goods from the Outlaw Valley! They're *outlaws*—and *they* never signed any kind of treaty with *anybody*!"

Chapter 2

Thing-or-Two's shouted warning explained matters, but it came, if anything, a little late. By the time she had finished speaking, the leading outlaw was almost upon Bill, and Bill was already in motion.

He dropped his luggage case and ducked desperately as the big Dilbian hands made a grab for him. They missed, and he spun about only to find himself running in the wrong direction. With whoops and yells the whole crew of outlaws was after him. Every way he turned, he found a towering, nine-foot figure barring his escape.

Not that an immediate attempt to escape would do him any good at the moment, he realized almost at once. Bill's first reaction had been that of any small animal being chased by larger ones—to duck and dodge and take advantage of his reflexes, which were faster simply because he was smaller. The Dilbian outlaws, being all nearly twice

Bill's size and several times his weight, were by that very fact slower and clumsier than he was. In fact, after the first leap to escape, he found himself evading their clutches with relative ease.

But even as he realized he could do this, he saw the spot he was in. At first he had been dodging about only in order to find a clear space in which he could make a run for the forest. Now he realized that simply running away was no solution. The reflexes of the Dilbians might be slower than his, but their huge strides could cover the same among of ground at double his speed. They could catch him in no time if he simply tried to outrun them in a straight-away chase.

His only hope, he realized now, still dodging desperately about the farmyard, was to keep evading them in this small area until they began to grow winded, and then take his chances on outrunning them. If he could only keep this up, he thought—ducking under a flailing dark-furred arm as thick as a man's thigh—for just a few minutes more . . .

"Hold it!" the outlaw leader was shouting. "Don't let him run you ragged. Circle him! Circle him! Herd him into a corner!"

Bill's hopes took a nose dive. He dodged and spun about, but without finding an opening. Already the outlaws were forming a semicircle, long arms extended sideways, that was herding him back against the front wall of the house. They were closing in, now . . .

Bill made a feint toward the right end of the semicircle, and then made a dash toward the left end, with the wild thought of diving between the legs of the outlaw leader, standing at the corner of the house. But at the last second the outlaw stepped forward and whooped in a powerful voice Bill had come to recognize.

"*Got you, Shorty!*"

Bill braked to a frantic halt. Glancing over his shoulder, he saw the rest of the semicircle closing rapidly on him. He looked back at the outlaw leader, standing crouched now and ready by the interlaced butt ends of the logs at the corner of the house. The leader spread his arms and reached forward—

—And went suddenly flat on his face with a furry figure atop him, as a wild war cry split the air.

"*I'm* a Muddy Noser and proud of it!" roared the still-drunken voice of Tin Ear, in triumph. "*Run*, Shorty!"

But there was no place to which Bill could run. Other outlaws had rushed over to bar the escape route opened up by the fallen leader. Glancing wildly about, Bill looked up and saw that where the roof of the house joined the wall there was an opening leading to some dark interior, probably a loft or attic. The alternating ends of the logs in the front and side walls of the house were notched and interlocked together so that they stuck out like the tips of the fingers of two hands, interlaced at right angles to each other. They were as good as a ladder to someone Bill's size. He had not won a climbing medal in Survival School, back on Earth, for nothing. He went up the log ends like a squirrel.

A second later he had dived into the dark, loftlike area to which the opening he had seen gave entrance. For a moment he simply lay there, panting, on what seemed to be a rough bed of poles, which was probably a roof to the room or rooms below. Then, as he began to breathe easily once more, he squirmed about, crawled back to the entrance, and looked down and out.

Tin Ear was slumbering or unconscious on the ground at the spot where he had jumped the outlaw leader. The leader himself was on his feet with the other outlaws clustered around the corner of the house, and one of their number was trying to climb the sixteen or eighteen feet up the same ladder of log ends Bill had used.

However, the log ends were too small for the big feet and hands of the Dilbians. The climber was finding fairly good support for his toes, but he was able to hang on to the log ends higher up only by his fingertips. His attention was all on those fingertips, and Bill had a sudden inspiration. Leaning out and reaching down the short couple of feet that separated the climber's head from the entrance, he put his hand on the top of the hard, furry skull and shoved outward with all his strength.

The head went back, and the climber's fingertips lost their precarious grip. There was a yell and a thud, and the climber landed on his back in the farmyard dirt. Roaring with rage, he scrambled to his feet as if he would climb again, but checked himself at the foot of the log corner, and dropped his upreaching arms.

"It's no use!" he growled, turning away toward the outlaw leader. "There's nothing you can really get a grip on. You see what he did to me?"

"Go get some fire from the stove inside," said the outlaw leader, struck by a happy thought. "We'll burn him out of there!"

"No, you don't!" trumpeted the voice of Thing-or-Two in the background. "Paying outlaw-tax is one thing, but you're not burning down our house! You try it and you'll see how fast I get to Outlaw Valley and tell Bone Breaker on you! You just try!"

Her words stopped a concerted move toward the front door of the house. The outlaws muttered among themselves, occasionally glancing up to the opening from which Bill was looking down. Finally, the leader looked up at Bill's observing face.

"All right, Shorty!" he said, sternly. "You come down out of there!"

Bill laughed grimly.

"What's so funny?" glowered the outlaw leader.

Bill had a sudden, desperate inspiration. His hypnoed information had just reminded him of a double fact. One, that preserving face—in the human, Oriental sense— meant a great deal to the Dilbians, since an individual Dilbian had no more status in the community than his wit or his muscles could earn for him. Two, that in Dilbian conversation the more outrageous statement you could get away with, the more face-destroying points you were able to score on an opponent. Maybe he could bluff his way out of this situation by making it so humiliating for the outlaws that they would go off and leave him alone.

"You are!" he retorted. "Why'd you think I stuck around here instead of running off? Laugh? Why, I could hardly keep from splitting my sides, watching all of you falling all over yourselves trying to catch me. Why should I come down and stop the fun?"

The outlaws stared at him. The leader scowled.

"Fun?" growled the leader. "Are you trying to tell us you did all that running around for fun?"

"Why, sure," said Bill, laughing again, just to drive the fact home, "you didn't think I was scared of you, did you?"

They blinked at him.

"What do you mean?" growled the leader. "You weren't scared?"

"Scared? Who? Me?" said Bill heartily, leaning a little farther out of his hole to talk. "We Shorties aren't scared of anything on two legs or four. Or anything else!"

"Oh? Then how come you don't come down from that hole now?" demanded one of the other outlaws.

"Why, naturally," said Bill, "there's six or seven of you and only one of me. If it wasn't for that—"

"Hey, what's up?" boomed a new voice, interrupting him. Bill raised his eyes to look beyond the outlaw group and the outlaws themselves turned to stare. Strolling out of the woods was the tallest, leanest Dilbian Bill had seen so far. He was unarmed, but he was as much taller than the general height of the sword-bearing outlaws as they were taller than Thing-or-Two, and his fur was a light, rusty-brown in color.

"Some of your business, Uplander?" growled the outlaw leader.

"Why, not if you say it's not," responded the new-comer genially, strolling up to the group. "But you look like you got something cornered up in Tin Ear's roof, there, and—"

"It's a Shorty," growled the outlaw leader, turning to

look once more at Bill, and apparently accepting the newcomer without further protest. "He's got up in there and if you try climbing up, holding on with your finger and toenails, he shoves you off. And he just sits up there laughing at us."

"That a fact?" said the tall Dilbian. "Well, I know how I'd get him out of there."

"You?" snorted the leader. "Who says you could get him down if we can't?"

"Why, because I wouldn't have to climb," said the tall Dilbian, easily. "You see, I'm just a hair or two bigger than the rest of you. Want me to try?"

"You can try for all I care," grumbled the leader, and the rest of the outlaws muttered agreement. On the ground, Tin Ear was beginning to sit up and look about himself, somewhat dazedly. "But it won't do any good."

"Think so?" said the tall Dilbian, unruffled. "Let me just take a little look, first." He moved to directly below Bill's bolthole. "Look out up there, Shorty—here I come!"

With these last words he crouched suddenly, then sprang, flinging up his unbelievably long arms at the same instant. Bill ducked back from the entrance, instinctively, as with a thud, ten powerful, furry fingers appeared, hooked over the bottom log of his entrance. A second later and the face of the newcomer rose to stare in interestedly at him.

Still holding himself by his grip on the entrance, the tall Dilbian performed the further muscular feat of sticking his head partway into the hole. Bill braced himself to resist capture. But, astonishingly, what came from the intruder was nothing more than a hoarse whisper.

"Listen! You're the Pick-and-Shovel Shorty?"

"Well—uh," Bill whispered back, confused. "My Shorty name's actually Bill Waltham, but they warned me I'd be given—"

"Sure!" whispered the Dilbian immediately. "That's what I said. You're Pick-and-Shovel. Now, listen. I'm going to

get them to back off. When they do, you take a leap out
of there, and I'll get you away from them. Understand?"

"Yes, but—"

Bill found himself talking to empty air. A thud from
the ground outside signaled that his interviewer had
dropped to earth. Bill crept forward and looked out. Below
him, the tall Dilbian was muttering to a close huddle of
the outlaws, all of them with their heads down. Apparently the muttering was supposed to be confidential, but
the words of it came clearly to Bill's ears.

" . . . You got to be tricky with these Shorties," the tall
Dilbian was saying. "Now, I told him I'd talk you all into
going away and leaving him alone. So the rest of you go
hide around the corners of the building, and when he
climbs down, I'll get between him and the corner of the
house here, and the rest of you can run out and catch
him. Got it?"

The outlaws muttered gleeful agreement. Heads were
lifted.

"Well," yawned the outlaw leader, in a loud voice,
pointedly not looking up in Bill's direction, "guess we
better be moseying along back to the valley. Let's go,
men."

All pretending elaborate unconcern, the outlaws wandered off around the other front corner of the house
leaving their pile of loot behind them; and a moment later
Bill could plainly hear the heavy thud of a number of
Dilbian feet, running around the back of the building to
just out of his sight behind the corner below him, and
stopping there.

"Well, Shorty," said the tall Dilbian in loud tones looking up at Bill. "Like I told you, they've all gone back to
the valley"—his voice suddenly dropped to an undertone,
and the held out his two enormous paws—"all right, Pick-
and-Shovel, come on! Jump!"

Bill, who had been crouching poised in the entrance of
his hiding place, hesitated, torn over the decision of whether
to believe what the tall Dilbian had said to him or believe

what the same individual had just told the outlaws below. He remembered however, the hypnoed fact that Dilbians would go to almost any lengths to avoid the lie direct, although perfectly willing to twist the truth through any contortions necessary to produce the same effect.

The tall Dilbian had said he would get Bill away from the outlaws. Having said it, he was almost duty-bound to perform at least the letter of his promise. Besides, Bill remembered in the nick of time, the outlaws had first addressed the newcomer as "Uplander"—and Bill's information had it that there was little love lost between Uplanders, or mountain-dwelling Dilbians, and the Lowlanders.

Bill jumped.

The big hands of the Uplander fielded him with the skill of an offensive end in professional football. And a second later they were running.

Or rather, the Dilbian was running, and Bill was joggling up and down in his grasp.

Behind them, Bill could hear the sudden, furious shouts of the outlaws. Craning his head around a pumping hairy elbow, Bill saw the outlaws swarming out from behind the farmhouse in pursuit. At the same time he felt himself lifted up over the shoulder of the tall Dilbian.

"Climb—on to my back—" grunted that individual, between strides. "Sit on the dingus, there! It's the same one I used for the Half-Pint-Posted. Then I can get down to some serious moving!"

Staring down over the furry shoulder, Bill saw something like a crude saddle anchored between the straps crossing the Dilbian's back. Hanging on tight to the thick neck beside him, he climbed on over the shoulder and, turning around, got himself seated down on the saddle. He grabbed the shoulder straps for added support and anchored his legs in the back straps below.

"All set," he said, finally, the words jolted out of his mouth into the other's ear.

"All right," grunted the other. "Now we leave them eating dust. Watch a real man travel, Pick-and-Shovel!"

The rhythm of the tall native's stride changed—it was a difference like that between the trot and the gallop of a horse. Bill, clinging to the straps, looked back and saw they were drawing away almost magically from their pursuers. In fact, even as he watched, some of the outlaws began to slow down to a walk and drop out of the chase.

"They're giving up!" he said in the ear of his mount.

"Sure, they would," answered that individual. "I knew they'd see it right off—they couldn't catch me. No one can catch me, Pick-and-Shovel. Never could, never will—Lowlander, Uplander, nobody!"

He slowed to a steady, swinging walk. Bill looked shrewdly at the back of the furry head eight inches in front of his own nose.

"You're the Hill Bluffer, aren't you?" he inquired.

"Who else?" snorted the other. Bill got the idea that the Hill Bluffer would have been impressed only if Bill had failed to recognize him. The Dilbian went into a half-chant. "Hill Bluffer, that's my name and fame! Anything on two feet walk away from me? Not over solid ground or living rock! When I look at a hill, it knows it's beat, and it lays out flat for my trampling feet!"

"Er—yes," said Bill.

"You're lucky to get me," stated the Hill Bluffer in a more conversational tone, but with no show of false modesty. "Just luck you did. When the other Shorties decided to bring you in here, they looked me up right away. Could I take a leave of absence from carrying the mail between Humrog Village and Wildwood Peak, and come down to the Lowlands here to take care of another Shorty? Well, it wasn't an easy thing to do, but I just happened to have an experienced substitute handy to take over the mail route. So I came on down. The ten pounds of nails was all right, but it didn't have much to do with it."

"It didn't?" asked Bill.

The Hill Bluffer snorted. It sounded like a small factory explosion and shook Bill upon his saddle perch like a small earthquake.

"Of course not!" said the Hill Bluffer. "That's good pay, but a man wants more than that. This was a matter of reputation. After having taken care of a Shorty once before, could I let another one get himself into all kinds of trouble down here without me? Of course not!"

"Well . . . thanks," said Bill. "I appreciate it."

"You'll appreciate it more by the time you're done," said the Hill Bluffer cheerfully. "Not that you'd have needed me just for protection against these fat-muscled, weak-livered Lowland folk with their sticks and their knives and their swords and their shields and such-like. Can you beat it? No, it wasn't protection you needed down here, Pick-and-Shovel. It was experience, and a good clean-thinking tough cat of a mountain man like myself to back it up. Well, here we are at Muddy Nose Village."

Here, in fact, they were.

Now he looked up and saw, indeed, that they were beginning to travel down the miry main street of some kind of native settlement village. Bill could see how the village had gotten its name.

At first, as they moved between the two rows of log buildings that lined the street, they attracted little attention. But soon they were spotted by the various other Dilbians Bill saw lounging around the fronts of the buildings, and deep bass shouts began to summon other local inhabitants from the interior of the structures. Bill found himself and the Hill Bluffer being bombarded by questions, most of them humorous, and few of them polite, as to his identity and his immediate intentions now that he had arrived at his destination.

He had, however, no chance to answer, for the Hill Bluffer strode swiftly on, grandly ignoring the tumult around them, like an aristocrat taking a stroll among peasants whom it would be beneath his dignity to notice. Bill tried to imitate the postman's indifference. The Bluffer came at last to the far end of the village street, and to a rather wider, more modern-looking log structure there, which sat back a little ways from the other buildings of the village. Bill, finding his wits sharpened by events since he had landed on this world, noticed that the door to this final building was cut in the generous proportions necessary to admit a Dilbian, even a Dilbian as tall as the Hill Bluffer. But, by contrast, the windows in the building were cut down low enough so that a human being would be able to look out of them.

"All right. Here we are," he said, halting. "Light down, Pick-and-Shovel, and get whatever Shorty-type gear you'll need. Then you can get the story straight from Sweet Thing herself, and we'll be off to Outlaw Valley to see about getting Bone Breaker to turn loose Dirty Teeth."

Bill slid down the broad, furry back, relieved to have his feet on a solid surface once more. He found himself standing in a pleasantly sunlit sort of reception room with some Dilbian-sized benches around the walls and a good deal of empty space between them. He looked toward a half-open door, which evidently led deeper into the building.

"What?" he answered, as the Hill Bluffer's last words registered on him. "Wait a minute. I don't think I better go anyplace right away. I'll be expected to stay here until I talk to the Resident and his—I mean—the other Shorty who's staying here."

"Are you deaf, Pick-and-Shovel?" boomed the Hill Bluffer, exasperated.

Surprised, Bill turned to face him.

"Didn't you hear what I was just saying to you?" demanded the Bluffer. "You can't just sit down here and wait for either Dirty Teeth or the Tricky Teacher. Don't you Shorties ever know anything about each other? You can sit here all you want, but neither one of *them's* going to show up."

Bill stared at the tall Dilbian. His scrambling mind finally evoked the hypnoed information that Tricky Teacher was the Dilbian name of the Resident, Lafe Greentree, and that Dirty Teeth was the name the natives had pinned on Greentree's female trainee-assistant—apparently because she had been observed brushing her teeth one day and the Dilbians had jumped to the obvious conclusion that anyone who cleaned their teeth like that as a regular practice must have strong need to do so. But even with this additional knowledge, the Bluffer's last words made no sense.

"Why not?" Bill was reduced to asking, finally.

"Why, because the Tricky Teacher broke his leg a couple of days ago, and a box like the one that always drops out of the sky to bring you Shorties and haul you away took him off to get it fixed!" said the Bluffer, exasperatedly. "That left Dirty Teeth in charge, and of course she had to go out to Outlaw Valley and get mixed up in this hassle between Sweet Thing and Bone Breaker—just like a female. And of course, once he got her in the valley, Bone Breaker just kept her there to make Sweet Thing come to her senses. Well, you Shorties can't let an outlaw like Bone Breaker hang on to one of your females like that and think the farmers around here are going to pay any attention to you when you try to teach them tricks with those picks and shovels and plows and things you brought them!"

He broke off and stared down at Bill from his lean ten feet of height.

"—So, what you've got to do is get going right now out to Outlaw Valley and get Dirty Teeth back. With the Tricky Teacher gone, there's no one else to do it," the Bluffer said. "And we better get moving soon as you've talked to Sweet Thing if we want to get in today. Those outlaws bar the gates to their valley at sundown, and anyone trying to get in or out gets himself chopped. Well, what's holding you?" roared the Bluffer as Bill still stood there. "You're not going to let a Lowlander outlaw hang on to one of your females like that and do nothing about it? You're going after her, aren't you?"

Chapter 3

"No," said Bill automatically.

It was an instinctive reply. Out of the welter of odd names and odder statements that the Hill Bluffer had just been throwing at him, the only thing that stood out clearly was that Bill was being asked to do something besides instruct Dilbians in how to use agricultural implements. Apparently Lafe Greentree had broken his leg and had been taken off-planet for medical treatment, leaving Anita Lyme in charge. And evidently she had interfered, where she should not, in native affairs, and been made a prisoner.

The Hill Bluffer roared, jerking Bill's attention back to the tall Dilbian.

"*No!*" exploded the Hill Bluffer incredulously. Bill with some relief—he had been ready to start running again—realized that the other was not expressing fury so much

163

as he was expressing outrage. "*No*, he says! Here, a female Shorty's got herself captured, and you say you won't go after her! Why, if I'd known you weren't anything like the Half-Pint-Posted, I'd never had let myself in for this job! I'd never even have considered it!"

"Half-Pint-Posted?" echoed Bill, as the Dilbian paused for breath.

"Of course!" snorted the Bluffer. "He was just a Shorty too, but did he hesitate to take on the Streamside Terror? I ask you?"

"I don't know," answered Bill, half-deafened by the other's voice in this enclosed space. "Who's the Streamside Terror?"

"Why, just the toughest Upland hill-and-alley brawler between Humrog Village and Wildwood Peak!" said the Bluffer. "Just the roughest—why, the Terror'd chew this Bone Breaker outlaw up for breakfast—" The Bluffer's voice abruptly lowered, and became judicious, "not that Bone Breaker's an easy match, of course. It's just that he's used to fighting with that blade and shield of his in the sissy Lowland fashion. Barehanded, I'll bet the Terror could take him any day. And the Half-Pint-Posted took the Terror."

Bill's mind staggered under the impact of this additional, improbable information.

"You mean this Shorty—a human like me," said Bill, "fought this Streamside Terror you talk about, without weapons?"

"Didn't I say so?" demanded the Bluffer. "Bare-handed and man-to-man. Not only that, but beside a mountain creek—the Terror's favorite spot. And Half-Pint licked him."

"How do you know—" Bill was beginning, when the Bluffer interrupted him.

"How do I know?" shouted the Bluffer in fresh outrage. "Didn't I carry Half-Pint on my back until we caught up with the Terror? Didn't I stand by him and watch while they tangled? Are you questioning my word,

Pick-and-Shovel—the word of the official postman between Humrog Village and Wildwood Peak?"

"No—no, of course not," said Bill, still bewildered. "It's just that I hadn't heard—about it before now." As he spoke, his mind was racing. There must be more to it than the Bluffer was telling. Probably there was some kind of gimmick that had kept the match from being the simple massacre of a human being that by rights it would have had to have been.

Also—a new thought struck him—if Greenleaf was actually gone and his assistant was honestly in trouble, then he did indeed have a responsibility to do whatever was necessary to get her out of it. At least, to begin with, he could go and talk to this Dilbian who had taken her, and who evidently was an individual of importance among the outlaws—if not their chief. If nothing else, he could stall until the Resident returned. An ordinary broken leg should not keep the man away from his job much more than the three or four days of the round trip required to take him to a hospital ship and bring him back here.

Bill scrambled about in his mind for words to explain his first refusal to go to Outlaw Valley to help Dirty Teeth. He was neither a quick nor easy liar and excuses did not come readily to him. Luckily, at that moment he remembered that underneath the wild improbabilities of the situation here on Dilbia, there still existed the prosaic organization of any off-world project. Project Spacepaw might be the most fouled-up human endeavor ever to take place beyond Earth's orbit around the Sun, but behind it there had to exist the ordinary official machinery of equipment and regulation.

"Now, listen to me!" he said to the Hill Bluffer. "I'm as good a Shorty as this Half-Pint-Posted or any other one of us you've met; and I'm not going to let one of my own people be held against her will if I can help it. But you've got to remember I'm not the head Shorty here. Before I go dashing off to Outlaw Valley, I've got to see if the Tricky Teacher left me any message telling me what to do. If he did, I've got to do what he said. If he didn't, then I can do things my own way. You're just going to have to wait until I see if he left that message."

"Well, why didn't you say so?" demanded the Hill Bluffer, obviously relieved. "You don't have to explain things twice to an official postman, where something like a message is concerned. If the Tricky Teacher left you a piece of mail to read before you started out, that comes before anything. Though what he should've done was give it to me to deliver to you. It wouldn't have cost him anything extra, and that way he'd be sure you got it right off. Of course," said the Hill Bluffer, suddenly interrupting himself, "come to think of it, he couldn't. Because I just got here yesterday and he was already gone; and probably he didn't want to trust it to any of these Lowlanders. Why, one of them's just as liable to lose it down a well, or go off and leave it lying someplace—"

He checked himself again.

"Anyway, you go read your message, Pick-and-Shovel," he said, "and I'll go dig up Sweet Thing and bring her back here."

He headed toward the door.

"Just a minute," Bill called after him. "Who's Sweet Thing, anyway?"

"Thought you knew," replied the Bluffer, surprised, opening the door. "More Jam's daughter, of course— More Jam's the innkeeper here in town. Passable enough female, I suppose, but like any Lowland woman, talk your head off, even if she hadn't been listening to those crazy notions of Dirty Teeth. Well, see you in a few minutes—"

Out he went. Bill spun around and headed back through the halfway open door into the living quarters of the Residency.

He knew what he was looking for first, whether Greenleaf or Anita Lyme had actually left him a message or not. Somewhere in this building there would be the official daily log of the project—and the odds were strongest he would find it in the room holding the off-plant communications equipment and project records.

It took him four or five minutes of opening doors before he discovered the room for which he searched. It was a square, white-walled room with office equipment and the two banks of consoles which severally operated the Residency computing equipment and the off-planet communications equipment. On one of the room's two desks, he saw the heavy, black-bound book which would be the project log. He sat down hastily at the desk and flipped it open, searching for the latest entries.

He found them within seconds, but they proved to be unusually uninformative, merely listing equipment loaned to the farmers and the times and subjects of conferences between either Greenleaf or Anita Lyme and the local natives. There was none of the diary-like chattiness that isolated project members usually added to the log entries in situations like this on Dilbia, and which might have told Bill a great deal more than he now knew about Greenleaf and the girl. Three days ago, there was a brief entry in Greenleaf's upright, hard-stroked hand:

. . . fell from ladder climbing to replace blown-away roofing shakes on Residency roof above north wall. Broke leg. Have called for medical assistance.

The next entry, the following day, was in a sloping, more feminine hand.

0800 hours, local time. Resident Greenleaf evacuated by shuttle from nearby courier ship, for transportation to closest available hospital ship, for treatment of broken leg.

1030 hours. Leaving for conference with Bone Breaker at Outlaw Valley.

Anita Lyme, Trainee Assistant

That was the last entry in the log, two days ago. There was no message for Bill from either Greenleaf or Anita, though it was highly irregular of the girl to go off without leaving one. Unless, that is, she had honestly expected to be back the same day.

Bill closed the log, got to his feet, and stepped over to the communications equipment. It was a standard console, arranged to put whoever used the equipment in touch with a relay station orbiting the planet, which would in turn re-broadcast the message at multilight velocity to its interstellar destination. Bill had been checked out on its use, as he had been checked out on most general equipment in use on off-world projects. He flipped the power switch and pressed the microphone button.

Nothing happened. The power light on the console did not go on. The microphone did not give out the signal hum that announced it as being in operating condition.

The set was dead.

For a second, Bill stared at it. Then, quickly, he ran over the console, flipping check switches and trying to locate the malfunction. But nothing responded. His hands flew to the toggle-nuts holding the face of the panel in place. Somewhere in the building there would be test equipment and with it, given time, even he ought to be able to trace down what was keeping the set from operating.

"PICK-AND-SHOVEL!"

It was the voice of the Hill Bluffer, roaring for him from the reception room. A second later, it was reinforced by a lighter toned, female Dilbian voice, also calling him. Grimly, Bill dropped his hands and turned away from the console. Fixing the communications equipment would have to wait.

He went rapidly out of the room and down the hall toward the front of the building. A moment later, he stepped into the reception room and found the Bluffer there with his female companion, who was the first to break off shouting for Bill as he came through the door.

"Well, there you are, Pick-and-Shovel!" said Sweet Thing—for this short, compact newcomer could only be that Dilbian female whom the Bluffer had gone to get, thought Bill. "It's high time you got here to Muddy Nose!"

"You knew I was coming?" asked Bill, in the sudden silence as the Bluffer stopped his shouting in turn and nodded genially at Bill.

"Why, of course we knew you were coming!" said Sweet Thing sharply. "Didn't *She* say *She* was sending for you? Of course *She* did. She knew how to handle the situation even if no one else did. As *She* said, the time had come to strike a blow for our rights. What *She* said was—"

"Let him get a word in edgewise, will you?" roared the Bluffer, for Bill had valiantly been trying to speak in the face of this torrent of talk.

"Who's *She*?" asked Bill hurriedly into the moment of silence that followed Sweet Thing's snort.

"*She*?" answered Sweet Thing, on a rising note. "Why Dirty Teeth, of course! *She* who has roused us at last to strike for our rights against men who have been telling us what to do all the time!"

The Hill Bluffer snorted.

Sweet Thing snorted.

"Wait—" said Bill hastily, before the situation could degenerate into a private argument between the two Dilbians. "What I want to know is, why is Dirty Teeth being held by Bone Breaker, in the first place?"

"Why, because *She's* the champion of us women!" said Sweet Thing swiftly. "It comes from listening to Fatties, that's what it does! Bone Breaker wants to force me to go live in that robber's roost of his. Well I won't do it! You can tell him so. Not if he should chop Dirty Teeth up for fish bait. I've got my principles!"

Once more, Sweet Thing's nose elevated itself toward the ceiling.

Bill had felt his heart lurch a little bit at the mention of Dirty Teeth being chopped up for fish bait. The matter seemed to be more serious than he had thought at first. What listening to "Fatties"—the Dilbian name for Hemnoids—had to do with it, was another mystery.

Ignoring that for the moment, however, Bill decided to stick to his main line of questioning.

"You mean the only thing that will save Dirty Teeth is if you go live in Outlaw Valley?" Bill demanded.

"Of course not!" retorted Sweet Thing. "All you have to do is go and take Dirty Teeth back from him. Why do you think *She* sent for you?"

"Well, as a matter of fact . . ." Bill's voice trailed off. He had been about to protest that it had not been Dirty Teeth at all who was responsible for his being here. Just in time, it had occurred to him that the situation was complicated enough already. There was no telling what harm he might do if he revealed that he was not specially appointed by this girl, who appeared to have become something of a local heroine to Sweet Thing, if not to the other females of Muddy Nose. "You say I just go in and get her?"

"Well, I'd certainly teach him a lesson while you're about it—Bone Breaker, I mean," said Sweet Thing. "Imagine the idea of holding prisoner someone like Dirty Teeth! It's just what you'd expect of some scruffy outlaw. Tell him you'll hit him one for me, too!"

"Hit him one—I don't understand—" Bill was beginning, when Sweet Thing exploded.

"Well, I don't see what there is not to understand!" she cried angrily. "I've been explaining and explaining until even a Shorty like you ought to be able to follow it. I won't marry that Bone Breaker unless he gives up his outlaw ways and settles down to being a farmer here in Muddy Nose, like you Shorties say everybody in the Lowlands should do. It's all nonsense about a girl having to go where her husband says. It's only women like Thing-or-Two that pretend to believe the world's coming to an end if any of the old customs get changed. Hah! Why she's really all for the old customs is that if she can get me out of the Inn, she'd have a right as female relative next-of-kin to move into it as inn-keepress in my place. She'd drive my poor old daddy crazy in a week!

No, no—Dirty Teeth explained it all to us! We've just as much right to say where we're going to settle down as the men have! Bone Breaker's as bad as the rest, but he really made a mistake when he decided to make Dirty Teeth a prisoner out in the valley. I wish I could see his face when you do it!"

"Do what?" demanded Bill, baffled.

"Challenge him, of course!" snapped Sweet Thing, turning on her heel and opening the street door. "Naturally, he's not going to give Dirty Teeth back to you unless you fight him for her and win, like the Half-Pint-Posted did with that mountain man who ran off with a Shorty female. So you better get out there to the valley and do it. I've waited long enough for Bone Breaker as it is, and it's a cinch there's no one else around Muddy Nose with nerve enough to take him on!"

She went out, slamming the door behind her.

A second later, it opened again, and she stuck her nose back in.

"Don't worry about having to get him all riled up before you challenge him," Sweet Thing added. "He knows what you're coming out there for. I sent word to him to expect you a couple of days ago."

Chapter 4

Sweet Thing's nose disappeared. The door slammed shut again. Bill stared at it, with his head swimming. If there was one thing he had absolutely no intention of doing, it was challenging the head man, or whatever, of outlaws like those from whom he had run and hidden in Tin Ear's farmyard earlier in the day.

"Well, so you see," said the Hill Bluffer behind him heavily. Bill turned to look at the postman and the Bluffer nodded at the closed door. "Crazy as a spring storm. And with a father who thinks more of his belly than he does of his daughter, or she wouldn't be able to get away with these wild, Shorty ideas—"

He broke off, glancing at Bill apologetically.

"—No offense to you, of course, Pick-and-Shovel," he rumbled. "As for Sweet Thing's ideas—"

"Wait a minute," interrupted Bill hastily. "Can't the village get together and help someone like Tin Ear—"

"Well, now, that's an idea for you!" said the Hill Bluffer indignantly. "Sure, if a neighbor yells for help, you might run over and give him a hand—when you hear him yell. But put yourself and all of your family into blood-feud for someone who's no kin at all? Well, a man'd be crazy to do that. After all, these are pretty honorable outlaws. Bone Breaker sees to that. They take their outlaw-tax out of what the Muddy Nosers can spare—they don't go taking what the local people have to have to stay alive. If they did that, then I suppose the Muddy Nosers would get together in blood-feud, if they had to declare themselves a clan, temporarily to do that. We've got to get going to make that valley before the gates are closed." He turned his massive, furry shoulders to Bill and squatted down. "Climb on, Pick-and-Shovel."

Bill hesitated only a second, and then climbed into the saddle on the postman's back. Listening to Sweet Thing, he had come to the conclusion that whatever he did, he could not avoid at least going to the valley and talking to the outlaw chief. But he certainly had no intention of challenging Bone Breaker, no matter what Sweet Thing thought. What he could and would do, would be to spin out negotiations until Greenleaf got back, which would certainly be within four or five days at most.

"—Of course," said the Bluffer, unexpectedly breaking the silence as the trees closed about them, "naturally, that's why the Tricky Teacher hasn't been having much success getting these Lowlanders to use all these tools and things you Shorties have brought in."

Bill, by this time, was beginning to get used to the unexpectedness of Dilbian conversation. It required only a little thought on his part to realize that the Bluffer was continuing the conversation begun inside the Residency after Sweet Thing's departure.

"What's why?" Bill asked, therefore, interested.

"Why, the fact there's no point in these farmers learning

all sorts of new tricks so they can grow more food," answered the Bluffer. "The outlaws just take anything extra, anyway. The more extra food they raised, the more extra outlaws they'd just be supporting."

"How far is it to the valley?" Bill asked.

"Just a step or two," answered the Bluffer economically.

However, a step or two by the Bluffer's standards seemed to be somewhat more of a distance than the term implied to human ears. For better than half an hour, the Bluffer strode rapidly into rougher and rougher country. The Dilbian sun was close to the tops of the hills and peaks ahead of them, when the Bluffer at last made an abrupt turn and plunged downward into what looked like an ordinary ravine, but which suddenly opened up around a corner to reveal, ahead and below them down a narrow ravine, a parklike, green valley, walled in all other directions by near-vertical cliffs of bare stone from fifty to a hundred feet in height. Softly green-carpeted with the local grass, the valley glowed in the late afternoon sun, the black log walls of a cluster of buildings at its far end soaking up the late light.

That light fell also on a literal wall made of logs about thirty feet high, some fifty yards ahead down the path. This wall was pierced by a heavy wooden door, now ajar but flanked by two Dilbians wearing not only the straplike harness and swords Bill had seen on those at Tin Ear's farm, but with heavy, square, wooden shields hanging from their left shoulders, as well. Sweet Thing's words about challenging Bone Breaker came uncomfortably back into Bill's mind.

The Hill Bluffer, however, had evidently come here with no sense of caution. As he approached the two at the gate, he bellowed at the two outlaws on watch.

"All right, out of the way! We've got business with Bone Breaker!"

The guards, however, made no move to step aside. Their nine-foot heights and a combined weight of probably over three-quarters of a ton, continued to bar the entrance. The Bluffer necessarily came to a halt before them.

"Step aside, I say!" he shouted.

"Says who?" demanded the taller of the guards.

"Says me!" roared the Bluffer. "Don't pretend you don't know who I am. The official postman's got right of entry to any town, village or camp! So clear out of my way and let us through!"

"You aren't being a postman now," retorted the Dilbian who had spoken before. "Right now you're nothing but a plain, ordinary mountain man, wanting into private property. Did anybody send for you?"

"*Send for us*?" the Bluffer's voice rose to a roar of rage, and Bill could feel the big back and shoulder muscle of the Dilbian bunching ominously under him. "This is the Pick-and-Shovel Shorty who's here to tangle with Bone Breaker if necessary!"

"Him? Tangle with Bone Breaker?" the guard who had been talking burst into guffaws. "Hor, hor, hor!" His companion joined in.

"So you think that's funny!" snarled the Bluffer. "There were a few of you valley reivers at Tin Ear's farm earlier today who got made to look pretty silly. And lucky for them, that was all that happened—" The Bluffer's voice took on an ominous tone. "Remember it was a Shorty just like him that took the Streamside Terror!"

Startlingly enough to Bill, this reminder seemed to take the wind out of the sails of the two guards' merriment. Apparently, if Bill found it impossible to believe that a Shorty could outfight a Dilbian, these two did not think so. Their laughter died and they cast uneasy glances over the Bluffer's shoulder at Bill.

"Huh!" said the talkative one, with a feeble effort at a sneer. "The Streamside Terror. An Uplander!"

Bill felt the saddle heave beneath him as the Bluffer took a deep breath. But before that breath could emerge in words, the talkative guard abruptly stood aside.

"Well, who cares?" he growled. "Let's let 'em go in, Three Fingers. Bone Breaker will take care of them, all right!"

"High time!" snarled the Bluffer. But without staying to argue anymore, he set himself in motion through the gate, and a second later was striding forward over the lush slope of grass toward the log buildings in the distance, all these things now reddened by the setting sun.

As they drew closer, Bill saw that there was considerable difference in the size of some of the buildings. In fact, the whole conglomeration looked rather like a skiing chalet, with a number of guest cottages scattered around behind it. The main building, a long one-story structure, stood squarely athwart their path, the big double doors of its principal entrance thrown wide open to reveal a perfectly black, unlighted interior. As the Bluffer approached the building Bill could smell the odor of roasting meat, as well as several other unidentifiable vegetable odors. Evidently it was the hour of the evening meal, which Bill's hypnoed information told him was served about this time of day among the Dilbians. Once inside, the Bluffer stepped out of line with the open doorway, and stopped abruptly; evidently to let his eyes adjust to the inner dark.

Bill's eyes were also adjusting. Gradually, out of the gloom, there took shape a long narrow chamber with bare rafters overhead, and a large stone fireplace filled with crackling logs in spite of the warmth of the closing day, set in the end wall to their right. There was a small, square table with four stools set before the fireplace, just as there were other long tables flanked by benches stretching away from it down the length of the hall. But what drew Bill's eyes like a magnet to the table with four stools in front of the fireplace was not the tall Dilbian with coal-black fur sitting on one of the stools, talking, but his partner in conversation, sitting across from him.

This other was not a Dilbian. Swathed in dark, shimmering cloth, his rotund body was scarcely half a head shorter than that of the Dilbian. Standing, Bill guessed that he could be scarcely less than eight feet tall, a foot or so below the average height of a male Dilbian. His face, like his body, bulged in creases of what appeared to be fat. But Bill knew that they were nothing of the kind. Seated, talking to the black-furred Dilbian was a member of that alien race which was most strongly in competition with the humans for influence with the natives on worlds like Dilbia, and for living space in general between the stars.

The being to whom the black-furred Dilbian was speaking was a Hemnoid, and his apparent fat was the result of the powerful muscles required by a race which had evolved on a world with half again the gravity of Earth.

Abruptly and belatedly, the meaning of Sweet Thing's obscure reference to taking the advice of Fatties became clear to Bill. A cold feeling like a cramp made itself felt at the pit of his stomach.

It was Bone Breaker, apparently, who had been taking the advice of Fatties—or of this one Fatty in particular. Unexpectedly, Bill found himself facing a Hemnoid in exactly the sort of ticklish interracial situation that the Human-Hemnoid treaty of noninterference in native Dilbian affairs had been signed to prevent. Too late now, he realized that he had intruded on the type of incident that should be dealt with by no human below the rank of a Resident in the Diplomat Service. Let alone a trainee-assistant in mechanical engineering who was like a fish out of water in being assigned to an agricultural project. And let alone a trainee-assistant who had been unable to contact his superiors by off-planet communications, and who was operating totally without authority and on his own initiative.

"Turn around!" Bill hissed frantically in the Hill Bluffer's ear. "I've got to get out of here!"

"Out? What for?" said the Bluffer, surprised. "Anyway, it's too late now."

"Too late—?"

Bill never finished echoing the Bluffer's words.

From just outside the door behind him there came a sound like that of a large, untuned, metal gong being struck. A voice shouted:

"Sun's down! Close the gates."

There was only a second or two of pause, and then floating back from the far distance of the valley entrance with a clarity that only the lung-power of a Dilbian could provide with such pressure, came the answering cry:

"The gates are closed!"

Chapter 5

The long drawn-out cry from the valley gate had barely
died away, before the Hill Bluffer was in motion, heading toward the short table in front of the fireplace. Bill
opened his mouth to protest, then quickly shut it again.
Now he saw that the room was crowded with Dilbians
of all sizes, and probably of both sexes, both standing
about and seated at the various benches. At first this
crowd had not noticed the Bluffer and Bill, standing just
inside the doorway. But as they began to move toward
the small, square table at the head of the room, before
the fireplace, they drew all eyes upon them, and silence
spread out through the room like ripples from a stone
flung into a pond. By the time the Bluffer reached the
table where the Hemnoid and the black-furred Dilbian
sat, that silence was absolute.

The Bluffer stopped. He looked down at the seated Hemnoid and the seated Dilbian.

"Evening, Bone Breaker," he said to the Dilbian, and transferred his gaze to the Hemnoid. "Evening, Barrel Belly."

"Evening to you, Postman," replied Bone Breaker. His unbelievably deep, bass voice had an echoing, resonant quality that made it seem to ring all around them. The outlaw chief was, Bill saw, almost as outsize for a Dilbian as was the Hill Bluffer. Probably not quite as tall as the Bluffer, judged Bill, as he tried to estimate from the seated figure of the outlaw, but heavier in the body, and certainly wider in the shoulders. A shiver trickled coldly down Bill's back. There was an air of competence and authority about this one Dilbian that was strangely at odds with the appearance of other members of that same race that Bill had met so far. The eyes looking at him now out of the midnight black of the furry face had a brilliant, penetrating quality. Could someone like this be holding prisoner a human being for such emotional and obvious reasons as Sweet Thing had attributed to him?

But he had no chance to ponder the question. Because the Hemnoid was, he found, already talking to him, gazing up at him over the Bluffer's furry shoulder, and speaking in a voice which, while not so deep as those of the Dilbians, had the ponderous, liquid quality of some heavy oil, pouring out of an enormous jug.

"Mula-*ay*, at your service," gurgled the Hemnoid with a darkly sinister sort of cheerfulness. He was speaking Dilbian, and the fact he did so, alerted Bill to answer in the same language—and not fall into the social mistake of speaking out in either human or Hemnoid, of which latter alien tongue he also owned a hypnoed knowledge.

"Or, 'Barrel Belly,' as our friends here call me," went on Mula-*ay*. "I'm a journalist, here to do a series of articles on these delightful people. What brings you among them, my young, human friend?"

"Bill Waltham," answered Bill cautiously. "I'm here

as part of our agricultural project at Muddy Nose."
Mula-*ay* might indeed be a journalist, but it was almost
certain he was also a Hemnoid secret agent—that was
the Hemnoid way.

"Just part of it?" Mula-*ay* gave a syrupy chuckle as he
answered, like a hogshead of molasses being emptied into
a deep tank. There was a note of derision in his chuckling. A note that seemed to invite everyone else to join
him in laughing over some joke at Bill's expense. This in
itself might mean something—or it might not. A love of
cruelty was part of the Hemnoid character, as Bill knew.
It was a racial characteristic which the Hemnoid culture
praised, rather than condemned. Nonetheless, it was not
pleasant to be the butt of Mula-*ay*'s joke, whatever it was.
Feeling suddenly ridiculous, Bill took his feet out of the
back straps of the Bluffer's harness and slid down to stand
on the floor.

Now on his feet and facing both the seated Mula-*ay*
and Bone Breaker, Bill found he could look slightly down
into the face of the Hemnoid, although his eyes glanced
level with the eyes of Bone Breaker.

"Have a place at my table, Pick-and-Shovel," rumbled
the outlaw chief. His tone was formal, so that the words
came out very like a command. "You too, Postman."

Without hesitation, the Bluffer dropped down on one
of the unoccupied stools. Bill walked around and hoisted
himself up on the other empty seat. He found himself
with Bone Breaker close at his right elbow; while at his
left elbow, with only a few feet between them, sat the
gross form of Mula-*ay*, his Buddha-like face still creased
in a derisive smile. Opposite, Bill's single ally, the Hill
Bluffer, seemed far away and removed from the action.

With the fire lashing its red flames into the air at one
side of them, throwing ruddy gleams among the sooty
shadows of the bare rafters above them and the outsize
figures surrounding him, there came on Bill suddenly a
feeling of having somehow stumbled into a nether world,
peopled by dark giants and strange monsters. A

momentary feeling of helplessness washed through him. All around him, the situation seemed too big for him— physically, emotionally, and even professionally. He broke out rashly and directly to Bone Breaker, speaking across a corner of the table.

"I understand you've got a Shorty here—a Shorty named Dirty Teeth!"

For a long second, the outlaw merely looked at him. "Why, yes," answered Bone Breaker. Then, with strange mildness, "She did wander in here the other day and I believe she's still around. Seems I remember she told me yesterday she didn't plan to leave for a while—whether I liked it or not."

He continued to gaze at Bill, as Bill sat, momentarily shaken both by his own lack of caution and by Bone Breaker's astonishing answer. Now, while Bill was still trying to collect his scattered wits, Bone Breaker spoke again.

"But let's not get into that now, Pick-and-Shovel," said the outlaw chief, still in that tone of surprising mildness. "It's just time for the food and drink. Sit back and make yourself comfortable. We'll have dinner first. Then we can talk."

Mula-*ay*, Bill saw, was still grinning at him, evidently hugely enjoying Bill's confusion and discomfiture.

"Well . . . thanks," said Bill to Bone Breaker.

A couple of Dilbian females were just at this moment coming to the table with huge platters of what appeared to be either boiled or roasted meat, enormous irregular chunks of brown material that seemed to be some kind of bread, and large wooden drinking containers.

"What's the matter, Pick-and-Shovel?" Bone Breaker inquired mildly, as the wooden vessels were being poured full of a dark brown liquid, which Bill's nose told him was probably some form of native beer. "Nothing wrong with the food and drink, is there? Dig in."

"Quite right," Mula-*ay* echoed the Dilbian with an oily chuckle, cramming his own large mouth full of bread and meat and lifting the wooden tankard to wash the mouthful down. "Best food for miles around."

"Not quite, Barrel Belly," replied Bone Breaker, turning his deceptive mildness this time upon the Hemnoid. "I thought I told you. Sweet Thing is the best cook in these parts."

"Oh yes—yes," agreed the Hemnoid hastily, swallowing with a gulp, and beaming hugely at the outlaw, "of course. How could it have slipped my mind? Good as this is, it isn't a patch on what Sweet Thing could cook. Why, sure!"

Bone Breaker, Bill thought, must possess an iron fist within the velvet glove of this apparent mildness of his, judging by the reaction of the Hemnoid. Now the black-furred outlaw's eyes were coming back to Bill. Bill hastily picked up a chunk of meat and began gnawing on it. Oh well, he thought, nothing ventured, nothing gained.

Conversation in general had ceased, not merely at their own head table, but about the hall, as the Dilbians present settled down to the serious business of eating. Their industry in performing that task was awesome enough from a human's point of view. Bill had never thought of himself as a particularly light eater—in fact, at Survival School, he had been accused of just the opposite. But compared to these Dilbians, and to the Hemnoid at his left elbow, his performance as a trencherman was so insignificant as to seem ridiculous.

To begin with, somewhere between six and eight pounds of boiled meat had been dumped upon his wooden plate, along with what looked like about the equivalent of two loaves of bread. The wooden flagon alongside his plate looked as if it could hold at least a quart or two of liquid, and it had been generously filled.

After a first attempt at trying to keep up with the oversized appetites and capacities of those around him, Bill gave up. He scattered the food around on his plate as much as possible to make it look as if he had eaten, and resigned himself to pretending to be busy with the drinking flagon, which, as it became more and more empty, got easier to handle.

He had just, somewhat to his own surprise, managed at last to drain the final mouthful of liquid from this oversized utensil and set it back down on the table, when to his dismay he saw Bone Breaker turn and lift a pawlike hand. One of the serving Dilbians came over and refilled the flagon.

Bill gulped.

"Very good. Very good," gurgled Mula-*ay*, tossing off at a gulp his own refilled flagon, which if anything was a little bit bigger than Bill's. "Our Shorty is quite an eater and drinker"—he added in a deprecating tone—"for a Shorty."

"Man don't lick the world by filling his belly," growled the Hill Bluffer.

An instinct warned Bill against glancing appreciatively in the Bluffer's direction. Nonetheless, he warmed inside, at this evidence of support by the lanky Dilbian.

"But a man's got to lick the world sometime," said the Hemnoid, chuckling richly as if this was some rare kind of joke. "Isn't that so, Pick-and-Shovel?"

Bill checked himself on the verge of answering, and picked up his heavy drinking utensil in order to gain time.

"Well . . ." he said, and put the vessel to his lips.

As he pretended to swallow, over the circular wooden rim of the container, he unexpectedly caught sight of a small slim, non-Dilbian figure moving along next to a far wall, until it reached the big double doors which still stood open to the twilight without. It passed through those doors and was gone. But not before Bill, staring after it over the rim of his drinking vessel, had identified the figure as human—and female, at that.

Hastily, he replaced the drinking container on the table, turning to Bone Breaker.

"Wasn't that—" he had to think a moment to remember the Dilbian name for her, "Dirty Teeth, I just saw going out the door?"

The huge Dilbian outlaw chief stared back down at Bill with dark, unreadable eyes.

"Why, I don't know, Pick-and-Shovel," answered Bone Breaker. "Did you say you saw her?"

"That's right," replied Bill, a little grimly, "she just went out the doors there. You didn't see her? You're facing that way."

"Why," said Bone Breaker mildly, "I don't remember seeing her. But as I said, she's around here some place. It could have been her. Why don't you take a look for yourself, if you want?"

"I think I'll do just that," replied Bill. He swung around on the stool and dropped to the floor. To his discomfort and dismay, he discovered that the dangling of his legs in midair over the sharp edge of the stool had put the right leg to sleep. A sensation of pins and needles was shooting through it now, and it felt numb and unreliable. Trying not to hobble, he turned and headed toward the big, open, double door.

Finally he reached the wide-open doors and stepped thankfully into the twilight outside. Looking first right and then left he saw that even the guards who had been lounging there were gone now. For a moment, as his gaze swept the gloaming that was settling down over the barricaded valley, a feeling of annoyance began to kindle in him. He could not discover anywhere that slim, girlish figure he had seen passing within the hall. Then abruptly his eyes located her—hardly more than a dark shadow against the darkening loom of the wall of an outbuilding some fifty feet away.

He went down the steps at a bound and headed toward her at a run, just as she turned the corner of the outbuilding and disappeared.

The soft turf all but absorbed the sound of his thudding boots as he ran. He reached the corner of the building and came swiftly around it. Suddenly, he was almost on top of her, for she had been merely idling on her way, it appeared, her head down as if she was deep in thought.

What do you say in a situation like this, wondered Bill, as he hastily put on the brakes; and she, still deep in thought, continued to wander on, evidently without having heard him. He searched his mind for her real name, but all that would come up from his memory in this winded moment was the nickname of Dirty Teeth that the Dilbians had given her. Finally, in desperation, he compromised.

"Hey!" he said, moving up behind her.

She jumped, and turned. From a distance of only a few feet away, in the growing dimness of the twilight, he was able to make out that her face was oval and fine-boned, her hair was brown and smooth, fitting her head almost like a helmet, and her eyes were startling green and wide. They widened still further at the sight of him.

"Oh, here you are!" she cried in English. "For heaven's sake, what do you mean by coming here, of all places? Didn't you know any better than to charge into a delicate situation like this, the moment you landed, like a bull into a china shop?"

Chapter 6

Bill stared at Anita Lyme, wordlessly.

He was not wordless because she had left him with nothing to say. He was wordless because he had too many things to say at once, and they were all fighting each other in his mind for first use of his tongue. If he had been the stuttering kind, he would have stuttered—with incredulity and plain, downright fury.

"Now, wait!" he managed to say at last, "you got yourself into this place, here—"

"—And I knew what I was doing! You don't!" she snapped back, neatly stealing the conversational ball from his grip. "You're just lucky I was here to get you out of it. If I hadn't heard from the outlaw females about Sweet Thing's message to Bone Breaker that you were coming, you'd have been committed to a duel with Bone Breaker right now! Do you know why you aren't? Because the

187

moment I heard, I went to Bone Breaker and told him that I was enjoying my visit here with the females and I wasn't going to leave for anybody! You couldn't very well fight over my being here after that!"

"No," said Bill grimly. "But as it happens, I wasn't planning to. Meanwhile, you're still stuck here, Greenleaf is off-planet, and I'm left with a Residency and a project I've been drafted to and don't know anything about. I'm not one of your agricultural or sociological trainee-assistants. My field's mechanical engineering. What do I do—"

"Well, you find that out for yourself," she said. "Just call Lafe and ask him—"

"The communications equipment's dead. It won't work." She stared at him.

"It can't be," she said at last. "You just didn't get it turned on right."

"Of course I got it turned on right!" said Bill stiffly. "It's not working, I tell you!"

"Of course it's working. It has to work! Go back and try it again. And that's the point—" she said, checking herself suddenly. "The point is, you shouldn't ever have come here in the first place. Common sense should have told you—"

"Sweet Thing said you needed rescuing from Bone Breaker."

"Did you have to believe her, just like that? Honestly!" said Anita, on an exasperated note. "You should have immediately called Lafe—"

"I tried to. I tell you—" said Bill, almost between his teeth, "the communications equipment doesn't work!"

"I tell you it does! It worked when I left the valley here, two days ago—and what could have happened to it since? Wait—" Anita held out her hand in the gathering dusk to stop him as he was about to explode into speech. She lowered her own voice to a more reasonable tone. "Look, let's not fight about it. The situation here is too important. The point is, I've saved you from fighting

Bone Breaker. Now, the thing for you to do is get back to the village as fast as you can, and stay there. Get busy at your real job."

"What real job?" ejaculated Bill, staring at her.

"Organizing the villagers to stand up all together to the outlaws, of course!"

"What!"

"That's right." She lowered her voice still further, until it barely carried to his ear. "Listen to me—ah—Mr. Waltham—"

"Call me Pick-and-Shov—I mean, Bill," answered Bill, lowering his own voice in turn. "What are we whispering for?"

She glanced around them at the gathering dusk.

"That Hemnoid understands English as well as you or I understand Hemnoid," she murmured. "Let me explain a few thing to you about Project Spacepaw—Bill."

"I wish you would," said Bill, with deep emotion.

"Oh, stop it! There's no need to keep getting a chip on your shoulder!" said Anita. "Listen to me now. This started out here as a perfectly ordinary agricultural project, taking advantage of the fact that when the original Human-Hemnoid Non-Interference Treaty on Dilbia was signed, neither the Hemnoids nor we knew that there were any sizable Dilbian communities that weren't organized and disciplined by the clan structure you find among the Dilbians in the mountains—where ninety percent of the native population lives."

"I know that," interrupted Bill. "I spent five days on the way here wearing a hypno-helmet. I can even quote the part about the project aims. *The project name 'Spacepaw,' refers to the hope of giving technology a foothold among the Dilbians—literally translated into Dilbian, it comes out meaning 'helping hand from the stars'—except that since the Dilbians consider themselves to be the ones who have hands—Shorties and Fatties are referred to as having 'paws.'* I already know all about that. But I was sent here to teach the natives how to use farm tools, not to organize a—" he fumbled for a word.

"Civil defense force!" supplied Anita.

"Civil defense . . ." he goggled at her through the increasing darkness.

"Why not? That's as good a name for it as any!" she whispered, briskly. "Now, will you listen and learn a few things you *don't* know? I said this *started out* like an ordinary project. The Lowland Dilbians here at Muddy Nose come from fifty or sixty different Upland clans. They don't have the clan organization, therefore, and they don't have any Grandfathers of the Clan, to exert a conservative control over the way they think and act. Also, they don't have the Upland Dilbian's idea that it's sissy to use tools or weapons. So it looked like they were just the community to let us demonstrate to the mountain Dilbians that tools and technology in general could raise more crops, build better buildings, and everything else—start them on the road to modern civilization."

"And, incidentally, make them closer friends of ours than they are of the Hemnoids," put in Bill skeptically.

"That, too, of course," said Anita. "At least, if the Dilbians have some knowledge of modern technology, they'll be better able to understand the psychological difference between us and the Hemnoids. We're betting that if we can raise their mean technological level, they'll want to be partners with us. The Hemnoids don't want them to become technologically sophisticated. They'd rather take the Dilbians into the Hemnoid sphere of influence, now while they're still safely primitive and they'd have to be technologically dependent."

"You were going," pointed out Bill, "to tell me something I didn't know."

"I am, if you'll listen!" whispered Anita fiercely. "When we started to make a success of this project, the Hemnoids moved to counter it. They sent in Mula-*ay*, one of their best agents—"

"Agents?" echoed Bill. He had suspected it, of course,

but finding himself undeniably up against a highly trained alien agent sent an abruptly cold shiver snaking its way between his shoulder blades.

"That's what I said. Agent. And Mula-*ay* didn't lose any time in taking advantage of the one local condition which could frustrate the project. He moved in with the outlaws, here, and pointed out to them that the more the villagers could produce from their farms, the more surplus the outlaws would be able to take from them. The outlaws only take what the farmers can spare, you know. Dilbian custom is very strict on that, even without Grandfathers—"

"I know," muttered Bill impatiently. "Why wasn't I told about the Hemnoid being here and being an agent, though? None of the hypnoed information mentioned it."

"Lafe was supposed to brief you after you got here—that's what he told me, anyway," she said, in so low a voice that he could hardly hear her. "The Hemnoids are too good at intercepting and decoding interstellar transmissions for the information I'm giving you now to be sent out for inclusion in ordinary hypno tapes. The point is that word of what Mula-*ay* told the outlaws got back from the outlaws to the villagers, and the villagers began to ask themselves what was the point of using tools, if making a better living simply meant making a better living for the outlaws. You see, the outlaws go around collecting their so-called tax and the Muddy Nosers can't stop them."

"Why not?" asked Bill. "There must be more of them than there are of outlaws—"

"That's what I've been trying to tell you," whispered Anita. "There *are* more of them than there are of outlaws. But without a clan structure they won't combine, and the outlaws raid one farm at a time and take whatever the farmer has to spare. The farmer doesn't even fight for his property—for one thing he's always outnumbered. For another, most of them rather admire the outlaws."

"Admire them!"

"That's right," said Anita. "They complain about how the outlaws take things from them, but when they're telling you about it, you can see they're halfway proud of having been robbed. It's been a sort of romantic interlude, a holiday in their lives—"

"Yes," said Bill, suddenly thoughtful. He remembered Tin Ear's drunken but happy grin as he had sat at the table, being forced to swallow his own beer.

"The point is," wound up Anita, "agriculture isn't going to be improved around Muddy Nose as long as this nest of outlaws continues to exist. We've got a stalemate here—outlaws balanced off against the villagers, the Hemnoid influence balanced off against ours. Well, I've had some success with bringing the local females around to a human point of view. Lafe told me our superiors think maybe someone—er, mechanically oriented—like you, could have some success with the village males. So—as I say, you go back and try to organize them into a civil defense force—"

"I see," said Bill. "Just like that, I suppose?"

"You don't have to sneer at the very notion," she retorted. In fact, a note of enthusiasm was beginning to kindle in her own voice as she talked—almost as if, Bill thought, she was falling in love with her own idea. "All the village males really need is a leader. You can be that—only, of course, you'll need to operate from behind the scenes. But why don't you talk to the village blacksmith to begin with? His name's Flat Fingers. He's big enough and strong enough to be a match for Bone Breaker himself, if they went at it without weapons. You get him on your side—"

"All right. Hold on a minute!" interrupted Bill. "I don't know what this business of raising a civil defense force has to do with the situation, but it's not the reason I came here. For your information, I was drafted while I was en route to a terraforming project on Deneb Seventeen, and what I was drafted for was to instruct the Muddy Nose villagers in the use of farming tools. In short, those were my orders and no one in authority has changed them. Until someone does—"

"*So!*"

It was the first time Bill had ever actually heard the word hissed. He stopped his own flow of words out of sheer surprise.

"So—you're one of those, are you!" Anita's voice was bitterly accusing. "You don't really care a thing about your work out between the stars! All you want to do is put in your two years and get your credit so that you can enter a university back home and get a general instead of a restricted professional license when you graduate! You don't care what happens to the project you work on, or the job it's trying to do—"

"Now hold on—" began Bill.

"—You don't care about anything but putting in your time the easiest way possible—"

"If you want to know," began Bill, "the way I feel about the terraforming of a whole world, with—"

"—and to blazes with anyone else concerned, human or native! Well, it happens I *do* care about the Dilbians— I care too much to let the Hemnoids stand in the way of their developing into an expanding, technological society and joining us and the Hemnoids not just as poor country cousins, but as an independent, self-sufficient, space-going race—"

"If you'll listen a minute, I didn't mean to say—"

"So nobody's given you any orders, have they" furiously whispered a spot in the by-now pitch-darkness, twelve inches in front of and eight inches below Bill's nose. "Well, we'll just fix that! You're a trainee-assistant, aren't you?"

"Of course," he said, when he was able to get the words out.

"And I'm a trainee-assistant. Right? But which one of us was here first?"

"You, of course," said Bill. "But—"

"Then who's senior at this post? *Me*. You go back to the village tonight—"

"You know I can't get back tonight!" said Bill desperately. "The gates were closed at sundown!"

"Well, they'll be opened up again, if Bone Breaker says so—ask him!" snapped Anita. "Then go back to the village tonight and stay there and start organizing the villagers to defend themselves against the outlaws! That's not a suggestion I'm giving you, it's an *order*—from *me* as your superior! Now go do it and good night, Mr. Pickham—I mean, Mr. Billham—I mean—oh, *good night!*"

There was a feminine snort or rage almost Dilbian in its intensity, and Bill heard the sound of shod human feet stamping off across the turf away from him in the blackness.

Bill stood where he was, stunned. It was part and parcel of the ridiculously unorthodox way in which things had been going ever since he had landed on Dilbia that he should find himself at the orders of a female trainee-assistant who apparently was stark, raving unreasonable on the subject of the local natives. Now what? Should he follow Anita's orders, organize the Dilbians of Muddy Nose—even if he was able to accomplish that—into a fighting force, and end up being tried under out-space law for unwarranted interference with natives' affairs on Dilbia? Or should he go back to the village, instruct the locals in the uses of picks and shovels, and end up being tried under out-space law for refusing to obey an order of his immediate superior?

Chapter 7

It was too much to figure out now. Bill gave up. Tomorrow, he would think the whole matter through. Meanwhile, there was the business of getting back to the village tonight—and into a human-style bed at the Residency, which he was far from unwilling to do. Maybe Anita was right about his only having to ask Bone Breaker to let himself and the Bluffer out after hours.

He turned about uncertainly, peering through the night, and to his relief, discovered the lights shining out of the windows of the outlaw buildings like beacons, a little way off. He went toward them, and as he got close, he discovered that he was coming up on the rear of the main building. He swung out around the closer end of it and headed toward the front entrance.

As Bill approached, he saw a number of Dilbian figures standing in front of the entrance steps—among them, standing a little apart, was the obese-looking figure of one who could only be the Hemnoid, Mula-*ay*, and with him two unusually tall Dilbians, one taller and thinner than the other, who should be Bone Breaker and the Hill Bluffer. Bill went up to them. As he got close, the large moon poked itself farther and farther above the mountain peak, and the silvery illumination in the fortified valley increased—so that by the time he stopped before all three of them, he was able to see their expressions clearly.

"Well, well, here he is," chuckled Mula-*ay* richly. "Did you find your little female, Pick-and-Shovel?"

"I spoke to her," replied Bill shortly. He turned toward the outlaw chief. "She suggested I could ask you whether you wouldn't let the Hill Bluffer and myself out of the gate, even if it has been closed for the night. I'd like to get back to the village before morning."

"She did?" answered Bone Breaker, with that same deceptive mildness of tone. It was impossible for Bill to tell whether the Dilbian was intending to agree or refuse to let Bill and the Bluffer leave. The Hill Bluffer chuckled—for no reason apparent to Bill. Mula-*ay* chuckled again, also.

"You mean," Mula-*ay* said, "you're going to go off and leave the little creature here, after all?"

Bill felt his ears beginning to grow hot.

"For the moment," he said, "yes. But I'll be back, if necessary."

"There you are!" said the Hill Bluffer happily. "Didn't I say it? He'll be back. And I'll bring him!"

"Anytime, Pick-and-Shovel," rumbled Bone Breaker mildly. "Just so it's in the daytime."

"Of course I'll come in the daytime," he said. "I wouldn't be leaving now, but after talking to—ah—Dirty Teeth, we decided—that is, I decided—to get back to the village tonight."

"And why not?" trumpeted the Bluffer, in something very like a challenging tone of voice.

"No reason at all," said Bone Breaker mildly. "Take all

the time you want. Come on, the two of you, and I'll see the gate opened and both of you let out."

The outlaw chief headed off toward the end of the valley where the wall and the gates were. The Hill Bluffer absently started after him, and Bill was forced to run in an undignified fashion after the Dilbian postman and jerked at the belt of his harness in order to alert the Bluffer to the fact that Bill could not keep up with his strides.

"Oh?—sorry, Pick-and-Shovel," chuckled the Bluffer, as if his attention had wandered. He paused to scoop up Bill in his two big paws and plump him down in the saddle on his back. "You kind of slipped my mind for the moment . . . are you all set, up there?"

Bill replied in the affirmative and the Hill Bluffer once more started off after the Bone Breaker.

For the first time, Bill began to realize what kind of favor the Bone Breaker was doing by letting him out after hours. Opening the gate was far from a simple procedure. First the guards had to find torches of resinous wood and light them. Then with the help of Bone Breaker and the Hill Bluffer they removed two heavy cross-beams from the inner side of the gates. Finally, with a great deal of heaving, puffing, and shoving, the gates were forced to rumble open, squeaking and roaring as they each traversed on a sort of millstone arrangement, with one round wooden wheel rotating upon the flat surface of another. At last, however, the gates stood open.

"Well, good night and good traveling, Bluffer. You too, Pick-and-Shovel," said Bone Breaker.

Bill and the Bluffer returned the good night, and the Bluffer headed out into the patch of outer darkness beyond the gates and the reach of the flickering torches. As that darkness swallowed them up, Bill could hear the gates once more rumbling shut on the millwheel-like arrangement behind them, and over this rode a powerful shout, which could only have come from the lungs of Bone Breaker.

"Remember, Pick-and-Shovel!" he heard. *"In the daylight!"*

"What's the matter, Pick-and-Shovel," growled the Bluffer underneath Bill. "Aren't you going to promise him?"

"Oh—" said Bill, startled. He raised up in his stirrups, turned his head, and shouted back as loudly as he could. "I promise—by daylight, Bone Breaker!"

The Bluffer chuckled. Behind them, Bill could see the outlaw chief nodding in satisfaction. Bill turned his head back toward the front, and sank down into his saddle, adjusting himself to the sway and plunge of the big body of the Hill Bluffer, striding beneath him. The lanky Dilbian postman said nothing except to chuckle once or twice to himself. Since Bill was too tired to inquire what the joke was, neither one of them said anything further, until they were once more treading the main street of Muddy Nose Village and the Residency loomed before them in the moonlight.

"All right, light down here," said the Bluffer, stopping abruptly before the Residency's front door. Bill complied.

"Are you staying here—" Bill began, but the Bluffer was ahead of him.

"I'm off down to the Village Inn, myself," the Dilbian replied. "If you want me, that's where you'll find me—from now until dawn, that is," grumbled the Hill Bluffer.

"Well—ah—I'll probably have lots of things to keep me busy early in the morning here—"

"You can say that, all right!" interrupted the Bluffer. "They say this blacksmith called Flat Fingers, here in the village, is a pretty good workman, but it's my guess you're going to have to stand over him all the time he's at it. Well, I'll stand there right beside you. We'll mosey up to his forge tomorrow morning and see what kind of promises we can get out of him."

"Flat Fingers?" echoed Bill, puzzled. "Blacksmith? What would I be wanting a blacksmith for?"

The Bluffer chuckled slyly.

"Why, to make you one of those sissy Lowlander fighting tools they call a sword—and a shield, of course! You didn't think they had things like that just lying around so you could go pick one up when you needed it? You Shorties take too much for granted."

"Sword?" echoed Bill, by this time thoroughly confused. "Shield?"

"I don't blame you," said the Hill Bluffer, but chuckling again. "It'd gall me to the very bone, too, to have to fight with gadgets like that. But there's no choice." He paused, peering down at Bill in a way that was almost sly. "After all, you were the one who challenged Bone Breaker, so he's got choice of place and style—and you can bet he isn't going to tangle without his blade and buckler. Trust a Lowlander for that."

Bill stood, frozen, staring upward at the big furry shape of the Dilbian, looming over him.

"*I* challenged the Bone Breaker to a fight with swords?" he managed to get out, finally.

The Hill Bluffer released his inner glee in a sudden roar of laughter that shattered the sleeping silence of the darkened village.

"Thought you'd missed out on the chance, didn't you?" he sputtered, finally calming down. "I could have told you different as soon as we left the valley, but I thought I'd let you chew on your hard luck for a while first. Didn't I tell you you were lucky to have me? The minute I heard Bone Breaker say Dirty Teeth was staying there because she wanted to, I saw what was up. She'd got some female notion about not wanting you to tangle with Bone Breaker. That was it, right? So later on after you'd gone out to talk to her, I got Bone Breaker alone in a corner and put in a few good words."

"Good words . . . ?" echoed Bill, an uneasy suspicion beginning to form in his mind.

"You can bet I did," said the Bluffer. "I said it was a real shame you and he weren't going to be able to tangle after all—especially as you'd said you'd find it interesting, and I was sure he felt the same way. I pointed out that after all we didn't have to have a real spelled-out challenge, just as long as folks thought there'd been one. I said he could tell his folks you'd said to me that it was a lucky thing Dirty Teeth didn't need rescuing, because you could have taken him with one paw tied behind your back."

Bill gulped.

"And he could say," went on the Bluffer gleefully, "that the minute he'd heard this from me he told me that he'd never believed the story about the Half-Pint-Posted and the Streamside Terror—that he didn't believe any Shorty could last two seconds with a man like him—and he didn't mind if I passed the word along to you. And I did, and you challenged him, naturally, right away, swords or anything he wanted."

"Swords . . ." said Bill dazedly.

"I know how you feel," said the Bluffer with sudden sympathy. "Kind of sickening, isn't it, when a man's still got the teeth and nails he was born with? Anyway, we can get you one made, and the duel's on. Everybody knows about it by now. That's why Bone Breaker and I arranged for him to holler after you through the gate to come back in the daylight, and I nudged you to holler back you would, meaning you'd be around to tangle as soon as it was convenient, in daylight and in front of witnesses. But I agree with you about those swords. It's sure a measly way to fight."

The Hill Bluffer sighed heavily.

"Of course, maybe I shouldn't worry about it," he said brightening. "Maybe you Shorties *like* fighting with tools. You seem to use them for just about everything else. Well, grab yourself a good night's sleep—and I'll see you at dawn!"

Chapter 8

Bill awoke from a confused dream of rolling thunder, as in a heavy thunderstorm, in which Kodiak bears had risen up on their hind legs, put on armor, and begun a sort of medieval tournament which he was being compelled to join. Then he became more fully awake and realized that the thunder was the roaring of a Dilbian voice, shouting Bill's own Dilbian name of Pick-and-Shovel, and that the nightmare was no dream but merely the dream-twisted facts of his previous day on Dilbia.

He opened his eyes to the sight of one of the Residency's spare bedrooms. Scrambling out of bed, he pulled on his pants and stumbled down the hall in his bare feet to open a door and step into the reception room at the front of the Residency. Standing in the middle of the room and still shouting for him was a Dilbian. But it was not the Hill Bluffer, as Bill had automatically assumed it would be. Instead, it was the strangest-looking member of Dilbia's native race that Bill had so far encountered.

He was the widest being on two legs that Bill had ever seen, in the flesh or in any reproduction of any alien race humans had discovered. Bill had so far adjusted to the size of the Dilbians in his one day among them that he had felt prepared for anything the race might present him with. But the individual he looked at now was beyond belief.

He was a Dilbian who made Mula-*ay* look skinny. This, in spite of the fact that he must have been a good head taller than the Hemnoid. What he must weigh was beyond the power of Bill's imagination to guess. Certainly, at least double the poundage of the ordinary Dilbian male. So furry and round was he, that he had a jovial, if monstrous teddy-bear look to him; but this impression was immediately diluted by the fact that, hearing Bill come through the door, the fat Dilbian whirled to face him, literally on tiptoe, like a ballet dancer, as if his enormous weight was nothing at all.

"Well, well, there you are, Pick-and-Shovel!" he beamed, chortling in a voice like the booming of some enormous kettledrum. "I had a hunch if I just stood still and yelled about for you, a bit, you'd come running sooner or later."

"Grnpf!" growled Bill, deep in his throat. He was only half awake, and he had never been one to wake up in an immediate good humor. On top of this, having been summoned from sleep, and down the long cold floor of a hallway in his bare feet, by someone who seemed to be using the same technique a human might use to call a dog or cat to him, did not improve his morning temper. "I thought you were the Bluffer!"

"The postman?" the laughter of the roly-poly Dilbian shook the rafters. "Do I look like that skinny mountain cat? No, no—" His laughter subsided, his humor fled, and his voice took on a wistful note. "No bluffing of hills for me, Pick-and-Shovel. Not these many years. It's all I can do to waddle from place to place, nowadays. You see why?"

He gazed down at his vast stomach and patted it tenderly, heaving a heavy sigh.

"I suppose you'd guess from the looks of me that I enjoyed my food, wouldn't you, Pick-and-Shovel?" he said sadly.

Bill scowled at him. Then, remembering the duty he owed as a trainee-assistant assigned to this area, he managed to check the instinctive agreement that was about to burst from his lips.

"Well, I—ah—" he began uncomfortably.

"No, no," sighed the Dilbian. "I know what you think. And I don't blame you. People herebouts have probably told you about poor old More Jam."

"More Jam?" echoed Bill frowning. He had heard that name somewhere before.

"That's right. I'm the innkeeper here," said More Jam. "You've already talked to my little girl. Yes, that's exactly who I am, Sweet Thing's poor old father; a widower these last ten years—would you believe it?"

"Sorry to hear it," muttered Bill, caught between confusion and embarrassment.

"An old, worn-out widower," mourned More Jam, sitting down disconsolately on one of the room's benches that were designed for Dilbians—which, however, in spite of its design, creaked alarmingly underneath him as his weight settled upon it. He sighed heavily. "You wouldn't think it to look at me now, would you, Pick-and-Shovel? But I wasn't always the decrepit shell of a man you see before you. Once—years ago—I was the champion Lowland wrestler."

"Long ago?" echoed Bill, somewhat suspiciously. He was waking up, automatically, remembering Dilbian verbal ploys. The unkind suspicion began to kindle in his mind that More Jam was protesting his weakness and age a bit too much to be truthful. He remembered the lightness and quickness with which the rotund Dilbian had spun about on his toes as Bill entered the room. If More Jam could still move that mass of flesh he called a body with that much speed and agility, he could hardly be quite as decrepit and ancient as he claimed.

Not only that, thought Bill, watching the native now through narrowed eyes, but Bill's experience on Dilbia so far had begun to breed in him a healthy tendency to take a large grain of salt with anything one of them claimed about himself.

"Tell me," Bill said now, becoming once more uncomfortably conscious of the iciness of the boards under his bare feet, "what did you want to see me about?"

More Jam sighed again—if possible, even more sadly than he had managed to sigh before.

"It's about that daughter of mine, Sweet Thing," he answered heavily. "The apple of my eye, and the burden of my declining years. But why don't you pull up a bench, Pick-and-Shovel, and we can go into this matter in detail?"

"Well—all right," said Bill. "But if you'll wait a moment or two, I'd like to get some clothes on."

"Clothes?" said More Jam, looking genuinely surprised. "Oh, those contraptions you Shorties cover yourselves up with. You and the Fatties. Never could understand that— but go ahead, don't mind me. I'll just wait here until you're ready."

"Thanks. Won't be a minute," said Bill gratefully.

He ducked back through the door and down the hall back into his bedroom, where he proceeded to get the rest of his clothing on. Now at least dressed and shod— he returned to the reception room where More Jam was waiting.

Before he had fully traversed the hall, and long before he had opened the door to the reception room, a booming of Dilbian voices informed him that More Jam was no longer alone. Even with this warning, however, he was not prepared for the sight that greeted his eyes as he stepped back into that room. Two more Dilbians had

appeared. One of them was the Hill Bluffer. Another was
a Dilbian with grayish-black, rather singed-looking hair
on his forearms, who was fully as large as Bone Breaker.
It was not, thought Bill as he stepped into the room
without being noticed at all by the three natives, that any
of them were larger than he might have expected. It was
just that all three of them together seemed to fill the
reception room well past the overcrowding point. Not only
this, but the sound of their three voices, all talking at
once, was deafening.

"There he is!" said the Hill Bluffer proudly, being the
first to notice him. "Pick-and-Shovel, meet Flat Fingers—
the blacksmith in the village here. The one I was telling you about."

"That him, hey?" boomed the blacksmith in a decidedly hoarse voice. He squinted down at Bill. "Why if I
was to make him a regular blade, it'd be bigger than he
was! And a shield—why if I was to make him a shield
and it fell over on top of him, he'd plumb disappear!"

"You too, huh?" roared the Bluffer, making Bill's ears
ring. "Didn't you ever hear about the Shorty that took
the Streamside Terror? Didn't I tell you about him?"

"I heard. And you told me several times." Flat Fingers rubbed his bearlike nose thoughtfully. "Still and all,
it stands to reason. I say a regulation sword and shield's
too big for him. Who's the expert here, you or me? I've
been shoeing horses and arming men and mending kettles
for fifteen years, and what I say is, a regular blade and
buckler's too big for him. And that's that!"

"All right!" shouted Bill quickly, before the Hill Bluffer
could renew the argument. "I don't care what size my
sword and shield are. It doesn't make any difference!"

"There!" boomed the Bluffer turning on the blacksmith.
"I guess that shows you what these sissy fighting weapons of you Lowlanders are worth! Even a Shorty doesn't
care what they're like, when he has to use them! I'd like
to see some of you iron-carriers wander up into the
mountains bare-handed some of these days and try your

luck man-to-man in my district. Why, if I wasn't on official duty, more or less, with Pick-and-Shovel here—"

"Ahem!" More Jam interrupted at this point by clearing his throat delicately—delicately, that is, for a Dilbian. However, the sound effectively stopped the Bluffer and brought his eyes around toward the wide-bodied individual.

"Far be it from me to go sticking my oar into another fellow's argument," said More Jam sadly. "Particularly seeing as how I'm old and decrepit and fat, and have a weak stomach and I've long forgotten what it was like back in my wrestling days—"

"Come on now, More Jam," protested Flat Fingers. "We all know you aren't all that old and sickly."

"Nice of you to say so, Flat Fingers," quavered More Jam, "but the truth is with this weak stomach of mine, that can't hardly eat anything but a little jam and bread or something like that—though I do try to force down some regular meat and other things just to keep myself alive—I'm lucky if I can leave the house. But it's true—" He looked sidelong at the Hill Bluffer, "that once I'd have taken on any mountain man, bare-handed."

"No one's putting *you* down, More Jam," rumbled the Hill Bluffer. "*You* never used to tangle with a lot of sharpened iron about you!"

"True, true," sighed More Jam. "And true it is, that our younger generation has kind of gotten away from the old way of doing things. Just like it's true that I never had anything in the way of a weapon about me—that time I happened to be up in the mountains and ran into One Man."

He pronounced this name with a peculiar emphasis, and Bill saw both the blacksmith and the Hill Bluffer stiffen to attention. The Hill Bluffer stared at him.

"*You* tangled with One Man?" the Bluffer said, almost in a tone of awe. "Why, nobody ever went up against One Man alone. Nobody!" He glanced aside at Bill. "There never has been anybody like One Man, Pick-and-Shovel," he explained. "He's a mountain man like myself, and he's called One Man because in spite of being an orphan, with no kin to help, he once held feud with a whole clan, just by himself—and won!"

The Hill Bluffer turned back to More Jam almost accusingly.

"You *never* tangled with One Man!" he repeated.

More Jam sighed regretfully.

"No, as a matter of fact, I never did, the way things worked out," he rumbled thoughtfully. "I'd heard of him, up there in the mountains, of course. Just as he'd heard of me, down here in the Lowlands. Then one time we just happened to run into each other in the foothills back a ways from here, and we got a look at each other for the first time."

More Jam paused, to sigh again. Flat Fingers and the Hill Bluffer were staring at him.

"Well, go on, More Jam!" boomed Flat Fingers, after a moment of stillness. "You met him you say—and you didn't tangle?"

"Well, no, as it happened. We didn't," said More Jam; and his eyes swung about to catch and hold the eyes of Bill with a particular intensity. "It's quite a little story— and as a matter of fact, that's what brought me up here this morning to talk to Pick-and-Shovel. I got to remembering that story, and it began preying on my mind—the strange things that could happen to keep a couple of bucks from tangling, in spite of all their being primed and hardly able to wait to do it!"

Chapter 9

"You mean—?" the Bluffer stared down at More Jam. "In spite of both of you being in the same place and eager to go, something happened to keep the fight from coming off?"

"Well, yes. In fact a couple of things happened . . ." said More Jam, rubbing his nose thoughtfully. "The place One Man and I happened to run into each other was a place called Shale River Ford—"

"I know it. Good day's walk from here," said the Bluffer promptly.

"Yes, I guess you would know it, Postman," said More Jam. "Well, there was a sort of celebration of some kind going on when we both landed there at the same time— I forget what it was. But the minute the folk there saw One Man and I had run into each other, at last, they asked us to put off our little bout until the next day. So they could get word out to all their friends and kin to come watch. Well, now, we couldn't be so impolite as to say no—but what am I thinking about?"

More Jam broke off suddenly in mid-sentence, his gaze returning to Flat Fingers and the Bluffer.

"Here I am yarning away like the old dodder-head I am," said More Jam, "never thinking you two men must have come over here to talk some kind of important business with Pick-and-Shovel. Well, I won't hold you up a moment longer. You go right ahead with your business and I'll hold my story for another day."

"No business. That is, nothing that can't wait," broke in the blacksmith hastily. "Go on with the story. I never heard it before."

"Well, maybe I've got a duty to let everyone know about what happened, at that," said More Jam thoughtfully. "Though, as I say, I just wandered down here to tell it to Pick-and-Shovel, and actually it's more for him than for telling back up in the mountains anyway. I was just saying . . . where was I?"

"The Shale River Forders had asked you and One Man to hold off the fight until the next day," prompted the Hill Bluffer.

"Oh, yes . . . well, as I said earlier, it was really a couple of things that happened to keep us from tangling." More Jam's eyes drifted around to hold Bill's strangely once more. "One to each of us, you might say. You see, as long as we had to wait until the next day, there was no reason we shouldn't have a party the night before. So the Shale River Ford people got a rousing time going. Well, after a bit, One Man and I went for a walk outside, so we could have a chance to hear each other talk. You know how it is when you meet somebody in the same line of business, so to speak . . ."

More Jam glanced at Flat Fingers and the Hill Bluffer. The blacksmith and postman nodded with the seriousness of dedicated professionals, each in their own lines of business.

"Happened, we had quite a talk," continued More Jam. "I might say we even got to know each other pretty well. We finally split up and headed for a good night's rest, each of us looking forward to the fight the next morning, of course."

"Of course," rumbled Flat Fingers.

"But then it happened," said More Jam. He gazed sadly at the Bluffer and at Flat Fingers, and then, unaccountably, his eyes wandered slowly back again to meet the eyes of Bill.

"It?" demanded the Bluffer.

"Would you believe it," demanded More Jam, staring at Bill, "after I'd left One Man—it was a pitch-black night out, of course—on the way back to the Inn, I bumped into someone who told me that my maternal grandmother had just died back down here at Muddy Nose?"

"You grandmother?" began Flat Fingers, wrinkling his nose in puzzlement. "But I thought—"

"Well, of course," went on More Jam smoothly, ignoring the blacksmith and keeping his gaze on Bill, "no ordinary person would ever have thought of trying to get from where I was all the way back to Muddy Nose to pay my last respects to my grandmother, and still make the trip back again in time for the fight the next day. No ordinary person, as I say. But in those days I was in pretty good shape, what with one thing and another. And I didn't hesitate for a minute. I just took off."

"But your grandmother—" Flat Fingers was attempting again, when More Jam smoothly interrupted him once more.

"—Wasn't dead at all as it turned out, of course," said More Jam, his eyes still fixed on Bill's. "As folks around here know, she lived to be a hundred and ten. It was just some kind of a rumor that this stranger had picked up and passed on. And of course, it was so dark out when he told me that I didn't know what he looked like. So I was never able to find him again."

"Good thing for him I bet!" muttered Flat Fingers. "So

you went all the way home and didn't get back in time for the fight? Was that it, More Jam?"

"Not exactly," said More Jam. "As I say, I was in pretty good shape in those days. I turned right around when I found out the truth, and headed back toward the foot-hills. And I made it back, too. I got back to Shale River Ford just as dawn was breaking. But you know, when I hit the door of the Inn, I sort of collapsed. I just fell down and passed out. It was plain for one and all to see that after a round trip like that, I was in no condition to fight."

"True enough," said the Hill Bluffer, with an expert traveler's judiciousness.

"So that's why you didn't fight One Man?" interposed Flat Fingers.

"Well . . . yes, and no," said More Jam mildly. "You see a funny thing had happened to him, too—I found out after I woke up. Just as One Man was heading back to the Inn, himself, the night before, after talking to me—I told you how dark it was out—"

"You told us," put in Flat Fingers.

"Well, dark out as it was," said More Jam, "One Man didn't see this hole in the ground. And he stepped right into it and twisted his ankle. Broke it, I think, although it was kind of hard to tell; his legs were so muscley. Of course," added More Jam, deprecatingly, with a glance at Flat Fingers and the Bluffer, "nobody was about to call One Man a liar if he said he thought his ankle was broken."

"Ha!" snorted the Bluffer. "That's right enough!"

"And, of course," added More Jam mildly, "nobody would think of doubting *my* word that I'd actually had somebody come up to me in the dark who I couldn't see, and tell me a false rumor about my grandmother being dead."

"I'd like to see them try it!" growled Flat Fingers. "That'd be something to see!"

"So, one way and another," wound up More Jam, his gaze returning to Bill, "neither One Man nor I was fit to have that fight after all. And the way it worked out, we never did meet again. Though I hear he's still alive, up there in the mountains."

"He sure is," said the Hill Bluffer. "Says he's all worn out now and decrepit! Him—decrepit!" The Bluffer snorted again, disbelievingly.

"You shouldn't jump to conclusions though, Postman," put in More Jam, almost primly. "You young men in the prime of life, you don't know what it's like when your bones start creaking and groaning. Why, some people might even look at me and think I might have as much as a shadow of my own old strength left. But I tell you, if it wasn't for my daughter's cooking—and my stomach's so delicate nowadays I can't handle anything else—I'd have been dead long ago. You may not believe One Man's being cut down by age, but an old hulk like me knows better."

The Bluffer muttered something, but not loudly enough, or in a tone disbelieving enough, to emerge as obvious challenge to the innkeeper's statement.

"But there you have it, Pick-and-Shovel," said More Jam sadly, turning back to Bill. "That story of mine, of how I had my chance at One Man and then missed out on it—through no fault of my own—has been preying on my mind for a couple of days, now. I just figured I had to step up here and tell you about it, so it could be a caution to you. I know you can't hardly wait to get at Bone Breaker, just like I couldn't hard wait to get at One Man, and vice-versa. But things you wouldn't believe can crop up to interfere with the most promising tangle in the world."

He sighed heavily, apparently remembering Shale River Ford.

"So I just wanted to put you on your guard," he went on. "Something just might come up that'd threaten to keep you from meeting Bone Breaker for that duel. But if it does, let me tell you, you only have to turn and call for More Jam for anything his old carcass can manage by way of help. Because it means a lot to me, your taking Bone Breaker, it really does."

"It does?" said Bill puzzled. "Why to you, in particular?"

"Why, because of this delicate stomach of mine," said More Jam, patting the stomach in question tenderly. "Oh, I know some folks in Muddy Nose think I'm going against tradition, when I back up my little daughter in refusing to let herself be taken off to Outlaw Valley to live. But if Bone Breaker takes her away, who's going to cook for poor old More Jam? I can't move out there with her and turn outlaw at my time of life—even if my old bones would stand the hardships. On the other hand, if he'd do like she wants and settle down here in Muddy Nose, I know I'd always have a bench at their table. Or maybe he'd even want to go into the inn business with me. So, as I say, if you ever find yourself in a position where you have to think about not tangling with Bone Breaker—for his sake, of course—just stop and think instead about More Jam, and see if it doesn't help!"

He closed his eyes, patted his mountainous stomach again, very tenderly, and fell silent. Bill stared at him, baffled.

"All right, Pick-and-Shovel!" said the blacksmith's voice.

Bill turned to find Flat Fingers stooping over him with a leather cord in his two, huge furry hands.

"Hold your arm out, there," rumbled the big Dilbian, "and I'll get you measured for your little blade and buckler—though much good they're likely to be to you—"

Bill's mind had been whirling ever since More Jam had finished talking. What it was spinning about, mostly, was the strange glances the rotund Dilbian had kept shooting at him while telling the story about his own near-fight with the mountain champion, One Man. Clearly, More Jam had been trying to convey some sort of message. But what was it? Bill tried to make some kind of connection between the story of the near-duel and what Anita Lyme had said to him the evening before. Maybe there was more to this business of organizing the villagers to defy the outlaws than he had thought. On the other hand, clearly More Jam was offering to be an ally of some sort. But just how was he supposed to do that? Flat Fingers obviously had a pretty low opinion of Shorties, physically at least. The blacksmith was not likely to accept as a leader someone with whom he was not impressed, and how could Bill impress him—particularly, physically? Offhand, he could think of nothing in which he could even begin to put up a showing against one of the huge, male Dilbians. He certainly could not outrun them, nor outjump them, nor—

Bill's mind broke off in mid-thought. A bit of information about the level of Dilbian science and technology from the hypnoed information had just sat up and clamored for attention in the back of his head. Dilbians, he remembered suddenly, had never heard of a block-and-tackle. He turned to the blacksmith, and taking advantage of a split-second pause in the argument between that individual and the Bluffer, he threw in a few words of his own.

"So you don't think much of me?" he said.

The attention of both Dilbians returned to him. The blacksmith burst into sudden, thunderous laughter.

"No offense to you either, Pick-and-Shovel," he said, still laughing. "But you really don't expect me to take you for being the equal of a real full-grown man. Now, do you?"

"Well, no," retorted Bill, drawling the words out. "I kind of hoped you'd take me for something better than a real man—one like you, for instance!"

The blacksmith stared at him. For a moment, Bill thought that he had overdone the brashness and insult, which, the hypnoed information in his head had informed him, passed for everyday manners of conversation among the Dilbians. Then the Hill Bluffer broke the silence in his turn with a booming and triumphant laugh.

"Hor, hor, hor!" bellowed the Hill Bluffer, giving the blacksmith a mighty slap between the shoulder blades. "How do you like that? I told you! I told you!—and here you were thinking he was just as meek and mild as some little kid's pet!"

The swat on the back, which would probably have broken Bill in two, plus the Hill Bluffer's words, apparently woke the blacksmith out of the stunned condition into which Bill's words had thrown him.

"You?" he said incredulously. "Better than *me*?"

"Well, we don't have to fight about it to find out," said Bill, with the best show of indifference he could manage. "I suppose you think you can lift something pretty heavy?"

"Me? Lift?" Flat Fingers' hoarse voice almost stuck in his throat under the combination of his astonishment and outrage. "Why I could lift twenty times what you could lift, Shorty!"

"I don't think so," said Bill calmly.

"Why, you—" stuttered the blacksmith, balling a huge furry fist ominously. The Hill Bluffer shouldered between him and Bill. "You actually want to try—" words failed Flat Fingers. He tried again. "You want to try to outlift me?"

Bill had a sudden inspiration—born of the fact of the Dilbians being strict about the letter of the law, while playing free and loose with the spirit of it.

"Well, of course," said Bill in a deprecating voice, and borrowing a page from More Jam's technique, "I'm just a Shorty, and I'd never have the nerve to suggest that I might be able to *outlift* you ordinarily. But I just might be able to *outdo* you at it if I had to, and I'm ready to prove it by moving something you can't move!"

Flat Fingers stared at him again.

"Why, he's sick!" said the blacksmith in a hushed voice, at last turning to the Hill Bluffer. "The poor little feller's gone completely out of his head!"

"Think so, do you?" said the Hill Bluffer smugly.

"Suppose we all just go up to that forge of yours, get something heavy, and find out!"

"Uh—not right away," said Bill hastily. "I've got a few things to do around here, first. How about just after lunch?"

"Suits me . . ." said the blacksmith, shaking his head and still looking at Bill peculiarly, as if Bill had come down with some strange disease. "After lunch will do fine, Pick-and-Shovel. Just wander up to the forge, and you'll find me there. Now, hold out your arm."

Shaking his head, he proceeded to measure Bill, making knots in the cord to mark the various lengths he took. Then, without a further word, he turned toward the door and went out.

"Don't worry about a thing, Pick-and-Shovel!" said the Hill Bluffer reassuringly, as he turned to follow the blacksmith. "I'm out to spread the word, myself. I'll see that the whole village is there to watch; as well as everybody else who's close enough to get here by midday."

He, in his turn, went out. The door crashed shut behind him and Bill found himself left alone with More Jam, who seemed to have fallen asleep on his bench. He turned swiftly and went back through the inner door to the rear rooms of the Residency.

He wasted no time—for the moment, even on the matter of his upcoming weight-lifting contest with the blacksmith. Instead, he went directly to the communications room and bent to work removing the console panel. Once it was off, he started the process of checking the components of the equipment, one by one.

Dismantling and checking took time. Bill began to perspire gently as that time crawled by, and unit after unit that he examined had its small quartz window intact. The perspiration did not cease when he finally reached the end of his checking without finding any unit out of order.

It was impossible—but there was only one other place to look.

As rapidly as possible, he reassembled the equipment

units and replaced the console panel. Then he started to trace the power cable leading from the wall beside the console.

His search led him out and down the corridor until at last he stepped into a large room in the rear of the Residency, packed with storage cases. The cables there led to a so-called lifetime battery set. It was simply not possible that one such battery set could fail, or have its stored power exhausted in the ordinary lifetime of a project like this one at Muddy Nose—and Bill's hypnoed information told him that this project was less than three years old. But when he came close to the battery set, he saw why the communications equipment was not working.

The power cable leading to the communications equipment had been disengaged from its battery set terminals.

It had not been wrenched or broken off. Someone had used a power wrench to unscrew the heavy connection clamps.

—And no Dilbian would know how to operate a power wrench, even if he or she recognized the purpose for which the tool had been designed.

Hastily, Bill found a power wrench among a rack of tools in one corner of the storage room which seemed to have been fitted up as a workshop area. There were not only hand tools there, but a hand-laser welding torch and a programmed, all-purpose lathe. With the wrench, he reconnected the power cable and ran back to the Communications Room. This time, when he sat down before the control console and keyed it into action, the ready light glowed amber on the panel in front of him. A second later, a computer's mechanical voice, somewhat blurred by static, spoke to him from the overhead grill of the speaker.

"Station MRK-3, Station MRK-3 . . ." said the voice. "This is Overseer Unit Station 49. Repeat, this is Overseer Unit Station 49. I am receiving your signal, Station MRK-3. I am receiving your signal. Is this the Resident at Muddy Nose Village, Dilbia?"

"Overseer Unit Station 49, this is Station MRK-3," replied Bill, speaking into the microphone grill of the console before him. "This is the Residency at Muddy Nose Village, Dilbia. But I am not the Resident. Repeat, not the Resident. I am trainee-assistant William Waltham, just arrived at this Residency yesterday. The only other Trainee-Assistant here is unavailable, and I understand the Resident has been taken off-planet for medical attention for a broken leg. Can you locate him, please? I would like to talk to him over this relay. If he cannot be located will you connect me with my next available superior? Will you connect me with the Resident or my next available superior officer? Over to you, Overseer Unit Station 49."

"This is Overseer Unit Station 49. This is Overseer Unit Station 49. Your message received, Station MRK-3, Trainee-Assistant William Waltham. We can relay your communication only to Hospital Spaceship Paar. Repeat, communication from your transmitting point can be relayed only to Spaceship Paar. Please hold. Repeat, please hold. We are relaying your call to Hospital Spaceship Paar."

Overhead, the voice ceased. Bill settled back to wait.

"Station MRK-3, Muddy Nose Village, Dilbia, Trainee-Assistant William Waltham, this is Hospital Spaceship Paar, Information Center, accepting your call on behalf of Patient Lafe Greentree. This is Hospital Spaceship Paar—" It repeated the statement several more times. Then it continued. "Are you there, William Waltham at Station MRK-3?"

"This is Trainee-Assistant William Waltham at Station MRK-3," replied Bill. "Receiving you clearly, Hospital Spaceship Paar, Information Center. Please go on."

"This is Hospital Spaceship Paar Information Center Computer Unit, answering for Patient Lafe Greentree."

"May I speak to Mr. Greentree, please?" asked Bill.

There was a slightly longer than usual time lag, before the Computer Unit answered again. "Patient Greentree," it announced, "is not able to communicate at the moment. Repeat, the patient is not able to communicate. You may speak with the Computer Unit which now addresses you."

"But I have to speak with him," protested Bill. "If I can't speak with him, will you relay my call to my next nearest superior?"

"Patient Greentree is unable to speak," replied the voice after the usual pause. "I have no authority to relay your call to anyone else. You may speak with the Computer Unit now addressing you."

"Computer Unit! Listen!" said Bill desperately. "Listen to me. This is an emergency. *Emergency! Mayday! Emergency!* Please bypass normal programming, and connect me at once with my nearest superior. If you cannot connect me with my nearest superior, please connect me with any other human aboard the Hospital Spaceship! I repeat, this is an emergency. Bypass your usual programming!"

Again, there was a longer than usual pause. Then the Computer Unit's voice replied once more.

"Negative. I regret, but the response must be negative. This is a military ship. I cannot bypass programming without instructions from proper authority. You show no such authority. I cannot, therefore, bypass programming. I cannot let you speak to Patient Greentree. If you wish, I can give you the latest bulletin on Patient Greentree's condition. That is all."

Bill stared, tight-jawed, at the communications equipment. Like any other trainee-assistant he had been taught to operate such sub-time communicators. But of course he had not yet been informed on local code calls and bypass authorization procedures. That information would have to come to him in the normal course from the Resident himself. He was exactly in the position of a man who picks up a phone and finds himself connected with an automatic answering service, stubbornly repeating its recorded message over and over again.

"All right," he said, finally, defeated. "Tell me how

Resident Greentree is, and how soon he'll be coming back to his duty post, here."

He waited.

"Patient Greentree's condition is stated as good," said the machine. "The period of his hospitalization remains indefinite. I have no information on when he will be returning to his post. This is the extent of the information I can give you about this patient."

"Acknowledged," said Bill grimly. "Ceasing communication."

"Ceasing communication with you, Station MRK-3," said the speaker.

It fell silent.

Numbly and automatically, Bill reached out to shut off the power to the equipment. After it was shut off, he sat where he was, staring at the unlighted console. The suspicion which had first stirred in him yesterday when he had arrived to find a deserted Residency was now confirmed and grown into a practical certainty.

Something was crooked in the state of affairs on Dilbia, particularly within the general vicinity of Muddy Nose Village; and no more evidence was needed to make it clear that he was the man on the spot, in more ways than one. If he had only had time to check the communications equipment out thoroughly on his arrival, he would never have left the Residency without discovering that crookedness before he got himself irretrievably involved in local affairs.

The power cable, detached by either Hemnoid or human hands, had kept him in ignorance of his actual isolation here just long enough for him to get himself into trouble. As it stood now, he was cut off from outside human aid, cut off even from his immediate superior, Greentree, and faced not only with a captive co-worker, plus a highly trained and experienced enemy agent, but the prospect of a duel which meant death as certainly as stepping off the top of one of the vertical cliffs walling in Outlaw Valley.

One thing was certain. Whatever other aims there might be in the mind or minds of those who had planned this situation for him, one thing was certain. His own death or destruction was part of the general plan. It would ruin any scheme if he was left alive to testify to what had happened to him. Possibly Anita's death was scheduled, too, for the same reason.

He was faced with essentially certain death, in a situation involving aliens with which he was unfamiliar, on a world for which he had not been trained; and he was left to his own devices. From here on out, he must save himself as best he could, and with no help from off-planet.

—Which just about threw out all the rules.

Chapter 10

Bill did not sit for long, thinking in front of the console. A glance at his watch woke him to the fact that he had less than four hours until the noon meal, and it was right after that meal that he had promised to outdo the village blacksmith. It was high time he was getting busy. He got up from his chair before the power console panel of the communications equipment, and went out of the room. He headed toward the storeroom containing the battery set at the back of the Residency, where he hoped he would find what he needed.

Bill had very little trouble finding what he looked for first. He discovered a coil of quarter-inch rope among the farming tools, and measured out and cut off forty feet of it. Then he started to look for a second item—an item he was pretty sure he would not find.

Indeed, he did not. What he was looking for was

nothing less than a ready-made block-and-tackle. But after some forty minutes had gone by without his finding one, he realized he could spend no more time looking for it. He would have to make his own block-and-tackle.

This was not as difficult as it might have seemed to someone with both a theoretical and practical knowledge of such a simple machine. Earlier, as he had stepped into the dim storeroom with its warehouselike smells of plastic wrappings and paper boxes, he had identified a self-programming lathe over against the wall in the one corner that seemed to be a general work area, fitted out with several machines and a multitude of tools racked and hung about the walls.

Now he hunted for some metal stock, but was not able to find what he wanted. He would have to use something else. The outer walls of the Residency, like the walls of most Dilbian buildings, were made of heavy logs. Detaching a power saw from the tool rack on the work-area wall, Bill took it over to a doorway in the back wall of the building. Opening the door, he used the power saw to cut off a four-foot section of one of the logs that ended against the frame of the doorway.

Bill took the log back to the lathe and cut it up into four sections, approximately one foot in length and a foot in diameter. Then he put the sections aside, and turned on the programming screen of the lathe. Picking up the stylus he began to sketch on the screen the pulley-wheel sections that he wanted to construct.

The parts took shape with approximate accuracy in three dimensions, and the programming section of the lathe took it from there. Eventually a red light lit up below the screen, revealing the black letters of the word "*ready*." Bill pressed the replay button, and before him on the screen there appeared completed and corrected, three-dimensional blueprints of the components for a block-and-tackle.

The lathe was now prepared to go to work. Bill fed his log sections to it, one by one, and ended up fifteen minutes later with twelve lathe-turned, wooden parts which he proceeded to join into two separate units by wood-weld processing. The first unit consisted of two double pulleys welded together, or four movable pulleys. This was the fixed block and had a brake and lock as well as a heavy wooden hook welded to the top of it. The other unit was the movable block which contained three pulleys. The two units, combined with the rope, together should give Bill a block-and-tackle with a lifting power seven times whatever pull he could put upon the fall rope. Flat Fingers, being a little bigger than most Dilbians, outweighed Bill by—Bill calculated—about five to one. In other words, the village blacksmith could probably lift about his own body weight of nine hundred pounds. However, the block-and-tackle Bill had constructed gave him a seven-times advantage. Therefore, if he could put upon the rope he would be holding a pull equal to *his* own human body weight of a hundred and sixty-five pounds, he should be able to lift well over a half-ton. Bill looked at what he had constructed, feeling satisfied.

He looked at his wristwatch. The hands, recalibrated to Dilbian time, stood at about half an hour short of noon. He was reminded, suddenly, that he had had no breakfast, and no evening meal the day before except for the Dilbian fare he had choked down in Outlaw Valley. He remembered seeing a well-stocked kitchen in his earlier exploration of the Residency. He turned away from the block-and-tackle, leaving it where it was on the workbench, and opened the doorway to the hallway leading back to the living quarters of the building. The hallway was dim, but as he stepped into it he thought he saw a flicker of movement from behind the door as it opened before him.

But that was all he saw. For a second later a smashing blow on the back of his head sent him tumbling down and away into spark-shot darkness.

When he opened his eyes again, it was at first with the confused impression that he was still asleep in his bed at the Residency. Then he became conscious of a head-ache that gradually increased in intensity until it seemed to fit his head like a skullcap, and, following this, he was made aware of a sickly taste in his nose and mouth, as if he had been inhaling some sort of anesthetic gas.

Cautiously he opened his eyes. He found himself seated in a small woodland clearing, by the banks of a stream about fifteen or twenty feet wide. The dell was completely walled about by underbrush, beyond which could be seen the trunks and the trees of the forest.

He blinked. For before him, seated crosslegged like an enormous Buddha on the ground with his robe spread about him, was Mula-*ay*. Seeing himself recognized, the Hemnoid produced one of his rich, gurgling chuckles.

"Welcome back to the land of the living, ah—Pick-and-Shovel," said Mula-*ay* cheerfully. "I was beginning to wonder if you were ever going to come to."

"What do you mean, knocking me on the head and bringing me here—" Bill was beginning, when the thunder of his own voice and the working of his own jaw muscles so jarred his skullcap of headache pain that he was forced to stop.

"I?" replied Mula-*ay*, in a tone of mild, if unctuous surprise, folding his hands comfortably upon his cloth-swathed belly. "How can you suspect me of such a thing? I give you my word I was simply out for a stroll through these woods, and noticed you tied up here."

"Tied up—?" began Bill, too jolted by the words to pay attention to the stab of pain that the effort of speaking sent through his skull, from back to front. He became aware that his hands were pulled around behind him, and a moment's experimentation revealed that his wrists were tied together on the opposite side of the narrow tree trunk that was serving him for a backrest.

"You can't get away with this sort of thing!" he stormed at Mula-*ay*. "You know no Dilbian would do something like this. You're breaking the Human-Hemnoid treaty on Dilbia. Your own superiors will have your hide for this!"

"Come now, my young friend," chuckled Mula-*ay*. "As I say—my superiors are reasonable individuals. And where are the witnesses who can call me a liar? I was merely wandering through the woods and happened to see you here, and sat down to wait for you to wake up."

"If that's true," said Bill, his headache by this time completely disregarded, "how about untying my hands and turning me loose?"

"Well, now, I don't know if I could do anything like that!" said Mula-*ay* thoughtfully. "That might be interference in native affairs—expressly forbidden, as you yourself point out, by the Hemnoid-Human agreements. For all I know you've been caught in the act of committing some crime, and the local inhabitants have tied you up here, until you can be taken back to face their native justice." He shook his head. "No, no, my dear Pick-and-Shovel. I couldn't take it on myself to untie you—much, of course, as I'd like to."

"You can't get away with claiming something like that!" exploded Bill. "You—" He became aware abruptly of a sheer look of enjoyment on the round face opposite him, and checked himself with sudden understanding. He was rewarded by seeing a slight shade of disappointment overshadow the smile with which Mula-*ay* had been regarding him up until now.

"All right," said Bill, as coolly as he could. "You've had your fun. Now suppose you tell me what this is all about. I suppose you want to make some kind of deal with me, and your idea in kidnapping me and tying me up here is to start me out at a disadvantage. Is that right?"

Mula-*ay* chuckled again and rubbed his large hands together.

"Very good," he said. "Oh, very, *very* good, young Pick-and-Shovel! If you'd only had a little more training and experience, you might have made quite a decent under-cover agent—for a human, that is. Of course, that was the last thing your superiors wanted, in this case— someone with training and experience. Oh, the last thing!"

He chuckled once more.

"Cut it out!" said Bill in a level voice. "I told you, you've had all the enjoyment out of me you are going to have. Quit hinting and come right out with whatever it is you've got to say. I'm not going to squirm just to please you."

Mula-*ay* shook his head, and his smile evaporated.

"You really *are* uninformed, aren't you, Pick-and-Shovel?" he said seriously. "Your knowledge of my race is only that kind of half-rumor that circulates among humans who have never done anything but listen to tall tales about Hemnoids. Do you seriously think that my business here on Dilbia would allow me to engage in that special and demanding art form among my people which you humans consider to be merely the exercise of a taste for deliberate cruelty? To be sure, I'm mildly pleased by your responses when they verge on *sana*, as our great art is known among us. But any serious consideration of such is impossible in this time and place."

"Oh, is that a fact?" said Bill ironically.

"Indeed," said Mula-*ay* steadily, "it *is* so. Let me try to draw you a parallel out of your own human experience. You humans have a response called *empathy*—the emotional ability to put yourself in another's skin and echo in your own feelings what that other is feeling. As you know empathy, we Hemnoids do not have it. But our *sana* is a comparable response, among us, even though you humans would consider it quite the opposite. *Sana*, like empathy, is a response that puts two individuals into a special relationship with one another. Like your empathy, it requires a powerful involvement on the part of the individual engaging in it."

"Only you don't happen to feel like engaging in it right now, I suppose?"

"Your skepticism," said Mula-*ay* steadily, "shows a closed mind. You humans do not empathize lightly, and neither do we engage in *sana* easily or casually. I would no more consider you a subject of *sana* on the basis of our casual acquaintance here, than you would be likely to empathize with—say—Bone Breaker, or any of the Dilbians, on the slight basis of the acquaintanceship you have with them so far."

Bill stared at the Hemnoid. Mula-*ay* was apparently being as frank and honest as it was possible for him to be, in his own terms. And the Hemnoid's argument was convincing. Only, just at that moment, something inside Bill suddenly clamored like an alarm bell in denial of something Mula-*ay* had just said.

"So—you understand," Mula-*ay* was going on, "and you can put your own interior human fears to rest on that subject. Just as," Mula-*ay* chuckled again briefly, "you can abandon the idea that I brought you here to make some kind of deal with you. My dear young human, you are not one of those with whom deals are made. You are only a pawn in the game here on Dilbia—an unconscious pawn, at that."

He stopped speaking and sat beaming at Bill.

"I see," said Bill, while the back of his mind was still busily digging, trying to identify the note of misstatement he had sensed in Mula-*ay*'s earlier explanation. Suddenly he wanted very much to hear more from the Hemnoid. "I'm supposed to ask you why I'm here, then? Well, consider I've asked it."

"Oh, but you haven't, you know," chuckled Mula-*ay*, gazing upward at the fleecy clouds spotting the blue sky above the treetops surrounding their clearing.

"All right!" said Bill. "Why did my superiors send me here—according to you?"

"Why," Mula-*ay* brought his gaze back from the clouds to Bill's face, "to get you killed by Bone Breaker in a duel, of course!"

Bill stared at him. But Mula-*ay* did not seem ready to offer any more conversation without prompting.

"Oh, sure!" said Bill at last. "Do you think I'll believe that?"

"Eventually. Eventually, you will . . ." murmured Mula-*ay*, still watching Bill's face. "Once you let the idea sink in and consider the fact that you are alone here, with no communication off-planet to your superiors. Yes, I know about that. And committed to the duel I mentioned. Don't you think it strangely coincidental that the Resident should be off-planet with a broken leg just when you get here, and that your young female associate should be an involuntary house-guest, so to speak, in Outlaw Valley? Don't you think it strange that you should be placed in the almost identical position of that earlier young human whom the Dilbians call the Half-Pint-Posted, who had a hand-to-hand battle with a native champion in another locality? Come, come now, Pick-and-Shovel; surely your intelligence is too adequate to blink those facts away!"

In fact . . . in spite of himself a distinctly cold feeling was forming somewhere under Bill's breastbone. The facts were overwhelming—and they were the very facts he had been facing as he had sat in front of the communications console earlier this day. It was unbelievable that there could exist an official human conspiracy to get Bill himself killed. But nonetheless the facts were there and . . .

"Why?" said Bill, as if to himself. "What reason could they have? It doesn't make sense!"

"Oh, but it does, Pick-and-Shovel," said Mula-*ay*. "The situation here between Resident Greentree and myself has become—how shall I put it—stalemated." Mula-*ay* chuckled again, softly, as he used the very word Anita had used to Bill the night before. "There's no further gain to be gotten from this Muddy Nose Project for you humans. The local farmers won't accept your help, and the outlaws under Bone Breaker are only enjoying the situation—with my modest help."

He beamed at Bill.

"The best thing for your superiors, in fact," he went on, "is to close this ill-planned project before it turns even more sour. But how to do that without losing face, both with the Dilbians and on an interstellar level? It would be like acknowledging we Hemnoids have won a round here at Muddy Nose. The answer, of course is to close the project—but first to find a suitable excuse for doing so. And what would make the most suitable excuse?"

He stopped and beamed once more at Bill.

"All right," said Bill grimly. "I'll ask. What would?"

"Why, for some untrained, unfortunate youngster to join the project, and—through no fault of his own, but through a series of unlucky accidents—make an irretrievable mess of the situation with the local Dilbians. To the extent, in fact, of getting himself involved in a duel and killed by the local champion, Bone Breaker."

Mula-*ay* stopped and chuckled so heartily that his whole heavy shape shook.

"What a perfect situation that would be!" he said. "For one thing, it would require the humans to close down the project and withdraw its personnel, temporarily—of course, it would never be started up again, nor would they return. For another, there would be no loss of face with the Dilbians; for, even though their foolish young man got himself killed, still he *did* show the combativeness necessary to tangle with Bone Breaker, and therefore the Shorties' record for personal courage on this world would not be impaired."

Bill stared at him.

"You seem pretty sure I'm bound to lose," he said although the cold feeling was back under his breastbone again. "The Half-Pint-Posted didn't."

Mula-*ay* chuckled, undisturbed.

"To be perfectly frank, Pick-and-Shovel," he said, "that is one small caper pulled off by you humans that we haven't been able to figure out, yet. But we have no doubt—and you need have no doubt either—that there was something more at work in that victory than simply one of you small creatures outgrappling a Dilbian. In fact, you hardly need the assurance of our belief. I ask you— can you picture a human who could win such a victory, without some unseen, unethical advantage?"

It was true, Bill could not. The cold feeling under his breastbone increased.

"No, no . . ." Mula-*ay* shook his head. "The very thought of a human winning any physical fair fight between himself and a Dilbian is unthinkable to the point of ridiculousness. But don't worry, little Pick-and-Shovel. I'm going to save you from your cruel and heartless superiors, as well as from Bone Breaker."

Bill stared at him.

"You . . . ?" he began, and then remembered to hide his emotions just in time.

"To be sure," said Mula-*ay*, rising softly to his feet and cocking his ear toward the noises of the forest behind him. "And here, unless I am mistaken, comes the means of that rescue, now. Reassure yourself, Bone Breaker won't kill you."

"Oh, he won't?" said Bill, speaking as coldly and unconcernedly as he could. For at that moment, he had heard what Mula-*ay* had just heard. It was the noise of heavy Dilbian feet approaching.

"No, indeed," said Mula-*ay*, "you will lose your duel and your life, instead, to the most feeble and decrepit Dilbian that the local area provides. Let your superiors try to save face, after that—following your foolish challenge of the best fighter for miles around!"

He half-turned from Bill. At that moment there burst into the clearing two female Dilbians and a scrawny, tottering male so old that his body fur was gone in patches. Of the two females with him, one was short and plump—and disturbingly familiar-looking, and the other was younger, somewhat statuesque of build, and almost tall enough to be a male.

They came to a halt, their eyes roaming the little dell, and fastened all together on Bill.

"There he is!" said the old male with a (for a Dilbian) high-pitched cackle of satisfaction. "Right where we want him!" And he rubbed his hands with glee.

"I leave you in good hands, Pick-and-Shovel,"

murmured Mula-*ay*. With a wink and a nod, but no words spoken, in the direction of the three Dilbians who had just arrived, he glided softly off into the surrounding brush and disappeared.

Chapter 11

"All right, Pick-and-Shovel," said the aged Dilbian male, as the three of them reached him and stopped, standing over him, "are you ready to stand trial, hey? Are you ready to submit yourself to the judgment of a Grandfather—"

A snort from the tall, young-looking female interrupted him. He turned angrily on her.

"Don't you go getting smart with me, Perfectly Delightful!" he shouted. "Got grandchildren, haven't I? I got just as good right to be a Grandfather as anyone!"

"Thank goodness," replied Perfectly Delightful, with the Dilbian equivalent of a ladylike sniff, "at least I'm not one of them!"

"Perfectly Delightful," said the older, plumper female sternly, in a voice which Bill suddenly recognized from the episode in Tin Ear's farmyard, "you leave Grandpa

Squeaky alone! He's here to do a job, that's all. If you keep bothering him, he'll never be able to do it!"

Grandpa Squeaky burst into sneering laughter.

"That's right, Thing-or-Two!" he cackled. "Tell the young biddy a thing or two! Go ahead! Thinks she's so good-looking she can get away with murder! Well, it may work with the young squirts, but it doesn't work with old Grandpa Squeaky. And judging by the way things have been going, it hasn't worked too well with Bone Breaker either! The last I heard," he added in a jeering tone, "he was still hankering after Sweet Thing!"

"Is that so!" cried Perfectly Delightful, on a rising note, furiously turning upon the aged male, who slipped behind the stout body of Thing-or-Two with prudent alacrity. "Some people," spat out Perfectly Delightful, "will say anything! And some other people will repeat it! But that doesn't change things. It's *me* Bone Breaker's always liked best."

She lifted her head and craned her neck, looking down rather complacently at herself. "After all," she went on in a calmer tone, "I *am* Perfectly Delightful. Everyone's always said so. Is it sensible that a tall, powerful man like Bone Breaker would want some little chunky creature like Sweet Thing? Oh, she can *cook* all right. I don't deny that. I believe in giving everyone their due. But there's more to life than eating, you know."

"Never mind that now, Perfectly Delightful!" snapped the older female. "We aren't here to talk about Bone Breaker. We're here to settle this Shorty's hash. Bear in mind, both of you, if you please, that it's the ancient and honorable customs of our village that's at stake here. We're not going to keep this Shorty from helping Sweet Thing get Bone Breaker, just to please *you*, Perfectly Delightful!"

"Hey, never mind that!" broke in Grandpa Squeaky, jittering with what appeared to be eagerness. "Let me at him, hey? I'll judge him! I'll rule on what's to be done with him!"

Grandpa Squeaky approached Bill and bent down until his breath fanned the hair on Bill's forehead. Bill held his breath—for Grandpa Squeaky, it seemed, had a rather bad case of halitosis.

"Hey, you Shorty! Pick-and-Shovel!" demanded Grandpa Squeaky.

"What is it?" demanded Bill, turning his face away. To his relief, the aged Dilbian stood upright, removing both his face and his breath to a bearable distance.

"Answers to his name, all right," commented Grandpa Squeaky to the two females. "That takes care of the part about who he is."

"Why don't we find a rock and hit him on the head?" queried Perfectly Delightful, in a pleasant tone of voice.

"Go on, I say!" insisted Thing-or-Two to Grandpa Squeaky. Grandpa Squeaky swallowed, and obeyed.

"Here, you, Pick-and-Shovel," he said, "you come in here, helping Dirty Teeth and the Tricky Teacher upset all our honorable old ways of living. We let you get away with that, and you think you can get away with even worse. Now, didn't you take Sweet Thing's side against a fine young buck like Bone Breaker, encouraging a young female to dispute where her husband-to-be wants her to live? Didn't you interfere, hey, in something that wasn't your concern? And besides, didn't you go and challenge our village blacksmith to a weightlifting contest at noon today?"

"Certainly I did!" retorted Bill. "And I was just about to head for his forge—"

"Never mind about that!" interrupted Thing-or-Two. "Go on, Grandpa Squeaky."

"I'll find a rock in a minute, and then we can shut him up," put in Perfectly Delightful brightly. She was searching around among the grassy open area of the dell.

"Sure you did!" said Grandpa Squeaky. "And then you sneaked off to the woods here and hid out, so you wouldn't have to face him—I mean Flat Fingers—thereby injuring the honor of our village."

"Hey!" shouted Bill. "What do you mean, sneaked off? Can't you see my hands are tied behind me here?"

"Nonsense! Go on," said Thing-or-Two. "You can't see his hands from where you're standing, can you? So you've only got his word for it, haven't you? And you aren't going to take the word of a moral wrecker, who thinks our young women can start telling their future husbands how to come and go and where they're supposed to live after they're married? Well, are you?"

"Of course not," said Grandpa Squeaky. He straightened up, squared his shoulders, and addressed Bill once more in a rather more grand manner. "This acting Grandfather—me, that is—finds you guilty as all get out on all counts. Accordingly, he sentences you—this acting Grandfather, who's me—to have your head chopped and your body left at that Residency building for the next Shorty that comes along to take care of."

He dropped his grand manner for a more colloquial one.

"I left the axes back in the woods a-ways. I'll go get them now."

Grandpa Squeaky turned away toward the brush, just as Perfectly Delightful came up with a rock the size of a small cantaloupe.

"Knock him on the head with this," she suggested helpfully, "that way he can't dodge around—"

"No, we don't!" snapped Thing-or-Two. "Grandpa Squeaky's got to chop him, and nobody'll believe it was a fair fight if we've got a dead Shorty with a large bump on his head—"

"Wait!" shouted Bill, desperation adding volume to his voice. "Are you crazy? You can't go killing me, just like that—"

"Why, sure we can, Pick-and-Shovel," interrupted Grandpa Squeaky, staggering back under the double load of a pair of heavy Dilbian axes, massive, with triangular heads made of gray, native iron. "It's not as if you don't have a chance. Seeing I'm just an acting Grandfather, I'm giving you a chance to fight for your life, instead of just chopping you like that. I'll take one ax and you can have the other. Here!"

He dropped one ax in front of Bill, and its handle thudded to the earth six inches from Bill's crossed legs.

"What do you mean?" cried Bill. "I told you, I'm tied up! Can't you see my hands are tied—"

"What do you mean, tied?" demanded Thing-or-Two. Looking at the older Dilbian female, Bill discovered that she had her eyes tightly shut. "*I* don't see any ropes on his hands. Do you, Perfectly Delightful?"

"Neither do I!" exclaimed Perfectly Delightful, shutting her own eyes. "You know what I think? I think the Shorty's scared. He's just scared—that's why he won't pick up the ax."

"All right, Pick-and-Shovel!" piped Grandpa Squeaky, doing a kind of feeble war dance, tottering around with his own ax. "What's the matter, hey? Scared of me, hey? Come on and face up to me like a man! The witnesses don't see any ropes on your hands—" Hastily, he shut his own eyes. "Neither do I! Grab your ax, if you've got the guts to face me, or I'll start to chop you anyway. This is your last chance, Pick-and-Shovel—"

At that moment, however, he was interrupted by a voice. It burst upon them all like a shout of thunder.

"WHAT ARE YOU DOING WITH MY SHORTY?"

For a second the three Dilbians facing Bill stiffened in mid-movement. Then they spun about to face in the direction from which the voice had come, and, in turning, moved enough apart so that Bill could see between them.

Breaking into the clearing through the brush at its edge was another Dilbian, a female, shorter than either Perfectly Delightful or Thing-or-Two. For a moment, he had no idea who this was, though the voice that had just shouted at them rang on his ear with accents of familiarity. He was suddenly aware, however, that he seemed to have found a friend, if not a rescuer, and that was all that was important at the moment.

Then Thing-or-Two unconsciously, if conveniently, came to his aid.

"Sweet Thing!" the other Dilbian female exploded, on an indrawn, snarling note.

"You just bet it's me!" snarled Sweet Thing in return, advancing into the clearing. She stopped some fifteen feet from the other three. She did not put her hands on her hips, but Bill got the strong impression that if this had been a Dilbian gesture, she certainly would have done so. "And here you are with my Shorty!" Her eyes scorched them all, but ended upon Grandpa Squeaky. "*You!*"

"Hey, now," protested Grandpa Squeaky, with a perceptible quaver in his voice. A quaver of tremulous old age which contrasted markedly with his energy of a moment before.

"What were you doing to Pick-and-Shovel?"

"None of your business!" snapped Thing-or-Two.

"Pick-and-Shovel!" called Sweet Thing. "What were they doing to you here?"

"They seemed to be putting me on trial—or something," shouted Bill back. He found himself wondering how he could have originally have wondered, on first seeing Sweet Thing, what made her attractive to the outlaw. Right now she was looking decidedly beautiful to him. In fact, the only individual who could have looked much more beautiful would have been Lafe Greentree, himself, with a cast on his broken leg if necessary, but with a handgun in his fist. "This Grandfather here—"

He tried to point at Grandpa Squeaky with his head, but both the pointing and the finishing of the sentence were unnecessary.

"Grandfather!" cried Sweet Thing, scorching Grandpa Squeaky with her eyes again. "*You*, a Grandfather!" She laughed scornfully. "A fine, squeaking Grandfather you'd make, with your nose in a beer cup all day long! You, a Grandfather! Wait'll I tell my father! I'll just tell More Jam that you've been pretending to be a Grandfather—"

"No!" cried Squeaky Grandpa, agonized. "Sweet Thing, you wouldn't do that to an old man? You wouldn't tell your father about a little harmless joke like this? You wouldn't—"

"You better get out of here fast, then," said Sweet Thing ominously.

"I'm going—I'm going—" Squeaky Grandpa lost no time in putting his words into action. He was across the clearing and into the brush, in a sort of tottering rush before he had finished repeating himself the second time. Sweet Thing's eye swung to the other two females. These, however, did not show the satisfactory sort of response that Grandpa Squeaky had exhibited.

"For your information, Sweet Thing," said Thing-or-Two grimly, "you can tell your father about this every day and twice on Sunday, and much it'll mean to me!"

"How much will it mean to you, though," said Sweet Thing, in a surprisingly gentle voice, "when my father tells the whole village how you've been making fun of them by putting up poor old Grandpa Squeaky to act like he's the sort they might pick for a Grandfather? Don't you think that might bother you just the least little bit?"

"Why—" Thing-or-Two broke off sharply. She hesitated. "Why, they'd never believe such a thing. Never in a lifetime!"

Nonetheless, Bill noted, a good deal of the fire had gone out of her tone of voice.

"They won't believe it?" echoed Sweet Thing in a voice filled with innocent wonder. "Not even when More Jam tells them he saw it with his own two eyes?"

"Saw it?" Thing-or-Two darted a sudden, nervous glance around her at the silent brush enclosing the dell. Her voice stiffened. "More Jam wouldn't lie to the whole village. He wouldn't do such a thing!"

"Not if I just refused to cook for him until he did?" queried Sweet Thing, in the same innocent and wondering tone. "Of course, Thing-or-Two, you're a lot older than I am and you know best. But I should think that if I really told my father I wouldn't do any more cooking for him, that he wouldn't hesitate about telling everybody what he really saw with his own two eyes here in this clearing."

Thing-or-Two stared angrily back at the younger female. But after a second, the stiffness seemed to leak out of her. She snorted angrily—but also she began to move. With her head in the air, she marched across the clearing and into the brush, and Bill heard her moving away from them. He looked back at Sweet Thing, who was now facing Perfectly Delightful, the only one of the original three conspirators left in the dell.

"You can go, too," said Sweet Thing, in a voice that suddenly had become very ugly.

"Oh, I don't know," replied Perfectly Delightful lightly. "Everybody knows what an obedient young girl I am. Naturally I had to do what my elders said—like when Thing-or-Two and Grandpa Squeaky told me to come along here."

"They aren't telling you what to do now," said Sweet Thing.

"Oh, I don't know," repeated Perfectly Delightful, gazing absently at the same white clouds drifting overhead that had earlier interested Mula-*ay*—but without failing to watch Sweet Thing at the same time out of the corners of her eyes. "They told me earlier to see that Pick-and-Shovel, here, didn't get loose and run away. They haven't told me anything to change that. They've just gone off. Maybe they're going to be back a little later. Or maybe they figure I'd stay here and guard the Shorty for them. I really don't know what else I can do," said Perfectly Delightful, helplessly withdrawing her eyes from the clouds at last and fixing them firmly on Sweet Thing, "but stay right here and see that nobody tampers with this Shorty."

As Perfectly Delightful had been talking, Sweet Thing had begun to move forward slowly. However, as she came to just beyond arm's reach of the other young Dilbian female, she began to circle to her right. So it was that

Perfectly Delightful, while still speaking, began to turn so as to face Sweet Thing. Gradually, they were beginning to circle each other like a couple of wrestlers, and after Perfectly Delightful had stopped talking, they continued to circle in silence for a number of seconds.

Bill, watching in fascination with his hands tied behind the tree trunk, was made suddenly aware of the fact that he was unable to get out of the way in case trouble should erupt. It was true that Perfectly Delightful, though tall for a female, would hardly have been able to raise the crown of her head above the point of the Hill Bluffer's shoulder, and that Sweet Thing was a head and a half shorter than her opponent. Nonetheless, either one would have considerably outweighed and outmuscled any two good-sized professional human wrestlers, and they seemed to possess the same willingness as Dilbian males to get down to physical brass tacks when a question was in dispute. Added to this was the fact that the nails on their hands and feet were rather more like bear claws, and their teeth rather more like the teeth of grizzlies than those of humans. So that in sum, the situation was one that made Bill devoutly wish he was on the other side of the tree to which he was tied.

The two had been circling for some little time, shoulders hunched, heads outthrust, arms half flexed at the elbow, when Perfectly Delightful broke the tense silence with a musical laugh.

"So you think this is funny?" inquired Sweet Thing lightly, but without at all pausing in her movement, or relaxing her attitude.

"Oh this? Not necessarily," replied Perfectly Delightful merrily—but equally without pausing or relaxing. "It just crossed my mind what a stubby little thing you are, and I imagined how you must look through the Bone Breaker's eyes."

"Oh, I don't think he finds me so stubby," replied Sweet Thing conversationally. "Maybe you won't find me so stubby either." And she laughed merrily in her turn.

They continued to circle, now almost within arm's reach of each other.

"But, really," protested Perfectly Delightful. "To be stubby is bad enough, but can you imagine what you'll look like with an ear torn off, too?"

For the first time, Bill became uncomfortably aware of how much taller and heavier Perfectly Delightful was than Sweet Thing. Up until now, he had been concerned with himself mainly as an anchored spectator of what might happen. Now, suddenly, his imagination galloped ahead a little further and began to consider what should happen if Perfectly Delightful should end up the victor in any combat that should occur.

"But I plan to keep my ears, both of them," Sweet Thing was saying sweetly. "I expect to have both my ears for many years after today—pardon me, I meant to say, after you have lost your teeth. You know, I've often heard my father and other men talking about how funny a woman looks with her teeth knocked out."

"Oh, you have, have you!" retorted Perfectly Delightful shortly. Evidently, in the contest between the two to see who should lost her temper first, Perfectly Delightful was beginning to crack. "If you get close enough to my teeth to try knocking them out, you'll wish you hadn't!"

Meanwhile, in a cold sweat, Bill was struggling for the first time and seriously to see if he could not wriggle his hands loose from the rather thick rope that seemed to be tying them together. He had been tied rather tightly, but he now discovered the thickness of the rope was such in comparison with the size of his wrists that it might be possible for him to slide his right hand free. Evidently, the smallness of the human wrist compared to the Hemnoid one was something that Mula-*ay* had not taken into account. He managed to get his right hand halfway out through its bonds—but there it stuck.

Agonizedly, he looked back at the center of the dell, where the two were still circling each other and trading insults. The tempers of both were sparkling now and sarcasm had given way to direct, untranslatable Dilbian epithets.

"*Snig!*" Perfectly Delightful was hissing at Sweet Thing.

"*Pilf!*" Sweet Thing was snarling back at Perfectly Delightful.

Suddenly, far off in the woods, came the sound of possible rescue, falling sweetly upon Bill's ears. It was the stentorian shout of a male Dilbian. It was more than that. It was the voice of the Hill Bluffer, shouting.

"*Pick-and-Shovel! Pick-and-Shovel—where are you?*"

"Here!" roared back Bill, with all the volume his chest and throat could muster. "Here! This way! I'm over here!"

"I hear you!" floated back the shout of the Bluffer. "Keep yelling, Pick-and-Shovel, and I'll get there in a moment! Just keep shouting!"

Bill opened his mouth to do so. But before he had the chance to make a sound, his shouting to the Bluffer had become as impossible as it was unnecessary as a source of sound to guide the postman to him.

The period of insults between Sweet Thing and Perfectly Delightful had come to an end. With a sound like that of an old-fashioned Western movie brawl between at least half-a-dozen homesteaders and as many cattlemen, Sweet Thing and Perfectly Delightful had closed in battle in the center of the clearing.

Chapter 12

Bill shrank back against his tree. There was little else he could do but make himself as small as possible and watch the action. The action, however, turned out to be wonderful to behold.

Not at first. At first, all Bill saw was a rolling tangle of furry bodies, arms and legs, glinting claws and flashing teeth, rolling this way and that on the ground—and occasionally threatening to roll in his direction. But then the whole tangle rolled over the bank of a little stream running through the clearing and splashed into the water; at which point it immediately separated into two individuals. But the battle was not ended. Sweet Thing and Perfectly Delightful wasted no time climbing out onto the bank and joining in combat again.

Only this time there was a difference. Apparently, the first time around, Sweet Thing had been too worked up to use whatever knowledge she had about fighting. Now, cooled off by her dip in the stream, she proceeded to demonstrate something very like a judo chop to the lower ribs, a forearm smash to Perfectly Delightful's jaw, a knee in the stomach, and finally a shoulder throw that flipped Perfectly Delightful completely over in the air and brought her down flat with an earth-shaking thud on her back in the grass.

It was at this point that the Hill Bluffer burst out of the surrounding bushes and accidentally ran directly into Sweet Thing.

Sweet Thing, either blinded by rage, or perhaps confusing the Bluffer with some ally of Perfectly Delightful's, threw her arms around the postman and attempted to execute the same shoulder throw with him. This time though, the results were not so satisfactory. Sweet Thing was trained and willing enough, but in the Hill Bluffer she had taken hold of an opponent even longer-limbed than Bone Breaker himself. She was in somewhat the same position, it occurred to Bill, as a five-foot woman attempting to throw down a man six and a half feet tall. The theory was excellent, but the practice ran into problems involving the weight and length of the intended victim.

Sweet Thing did manage to get one of the Bluffer's long legs off the ground and toppled him off balance. However, one of the Bluffer's equally long arms propped him off the ground, keeping him from falling even while she still had him in only a half-thrown position and a second later the postman had—more or less gently—pried her arms loose from their grip upon him, and was holding her by the biceps, out at the length of his own arms and facing away from him.

This should have settled matters, since Sweet Thing was no longer in a position to do any damage with teeth, nails, arms, or legs. But so intense was her fighting fury by this time that she literally ran off the ground into the air in her efforts to get loose, and the Bluffer was forced to trip her, get her down on the ground, and sit on her, pinning her arms so that she could not reach back and grab him.

Bill continued to look on, awed. Sweet Thing, no longer able to make effective use of any of her other natural weapons, had fallen back upon her tongue. She was busy telling the Bluffer what she would do to him the moment he turned her loose. It was a question that also interested Bill. It was all very well for the Bluffer to have Sweet Thing immobilized as she was at the moment. But sooner or later he would have to let her up—and what would happen then?

" . . . My father . . . Bone Breaker . . . limb from limb . . ." Sweet Thing was informing the lanky postman. Bill did not see how the Upland Dilbian could possibly get out of his present awkward situation with life and limb intact. But he was about to learn that Dilbian emotional responses were somewhat adaptable in these circumstances. The Bluffer waited patiently until Sweet Thing paused for breath, and then said, apparently, exactly the right thing.

"I've really got to ask you to forgive me for interrupting that beautiful fight of yours," he observed genially. "Where'd a girl like you learn to tangle like that?"

There was a long moment of silence from Sweet Thing. Then she spoke.

"More Jam," she said in a much calmer and obviously pleased voice. "Don't you remember? My father was champion Lowland wrestler."

"Why, of course," said the Bluffer, letting her up, "that explains it."

Sweet Thing bounced hastily to her feet.

"Where is she?" Her face fell. "Oh, she got away."

Bill also looked around the clearing. It was a fact. Perfectly Delightful had disappeared.

"Oh well," said Sweet Thing philosophically. "She'll be around. I can catch her anytime I want to."

She and the Hill Bluffer both turned to look at Bill.

"How about untying me?" demanded Bill.

"Why, sure," said the Bluffer. He walked around behind the tree to which Bill was anchored, and began untying the ropes binding his wrists together.

Bill endured, without really feeling, the rather bruising and painful business that the Hill Bluffer's big fingers made of clumsily jerking loose the knots that tied Bill's hands. His mind was busy, and once he was on his feet, he had a question for both of the two Dilbians facing him.

"How did you happen to find me?" he asked.

"Well, I don't know how *he* did," said Sweet Thing, sniffing slightly, "but Thing-or-Two and Perfectly Delightful had been looking too pleased for words all day long, so I knew something was going on. When they and Grandpa Squeaky ducked off into the woods instead of joining everybody else up at the forge, I just followed them. I lost them in the woods for a few minutes, but I just poked around—and here they were, with you."

"So that's what it was," said the Hill Bluffer, looking down at her admiringly. "Your old dad, More Jam, came rolling up to me when I was waiting at the forge.

" 'Word in your ear, Postman,' he said to me, and led me off behind a shed. 'Haven't seen that daughter of mine around any place, have you?' he asked me.

" 'No,' I said, 'Why should I?'

" 'Because it's all a little peculiar, that's all,' said More Jam, sort of thoughtful. 'I just saw Perfectly Delightful and Thing-or-Two, with Grandpa Squeaky, sliding off into the brush a few minutes ago, and that daughter of mine right behind them. Naturally, I didn't pay much attention, except that it was just about time for me to have a little, hot something to settle this delicate stomach of mine, and Sweet Thing might not be around to fix it for me—' and he patted his stomach, the way he does. 'It sure is peculiar, particularly when you figure that Pick-and-Shovel ought to have shown up at the blacksmith's by this time.'

"Well," said the Bluffer, looking meaningfully at Bill,

"it'd been on my mind, too, that it was high time you were showing up at the forge. So I asked him where he'd seen all this going on—and in what direction Sweet Thing and the others had taken off. Then I went down to the Residency and looked for you. But you weren't there. So I just took off in the woods the way I'd been told everybody else'd gone, and after a while I figured it wouldn't do any harm to sort of yell your name a bit and see if you answered. Well," wound up the Bluffer, "you did. And here I am."

"I see," said Bill. "I wonder how it was More Jam just happened to be watching, to see what he did?"

Sweet Thing and the Hill Bluffer stared back down at Bill with noses wrinkled in every evidence of puzzlement.

"Guess he just happened to, Pick-and-Shovel," said the Bluffer.

"I see," said Bill again. There were a number of questions that were coming to his mind right now that he would like to have answered by Sweet Thing and the Bluffer—particularly by the Bluffer. But he remembered that he had unfinished business back at the village.

"Better let me get back up in that saddle," he said to the Bluffer now. "I'm a good three hours overdue at the forge."

The Bluffer stared at him in consternation, as did Sweet Thing. There was a moment of silence.

"Why, Pick-and-Shovel," said the Bluffer, finally, "you can't go back there now!"

Bill stared up at him.

"Why not?"

"Why? Well, because you—just can't!" said the Bluffer in a shocked tone of voice. "Why, they'd laugh you out of town if you showed up now, Pick-and-Shovel. Here you went and set up a weight-lifting contest, and then you didn't show up for it when the time came."

"But it wasn't my fault I wasn't there," said Bill. Tersely, he told them about being hit on the head and brought into the woods and tied up by the Hemnoid. However, to his surprise, when he finished, the long looks on the faces of Sweet Thing and the Bluffer did not lift. The Bluffer shook his head slowly.

"I might've figured it was something like that," said the Bluffer heavily. "But it doesn't make any difference, Pick-and-Shovel. No doubt you had a good reason for not being there on time—but the point is you *didn't* show up. How're folks to be sure you didn't just duck out of it and make this whole story up as an excuse? I believe you, because I know something about the kind of guts you Shorties've got. But these Muddy Nosers aren't going to believe you. They'll figure you probably knew you couldn't outlift Flat Fingers, so you just didn't show up."

"Well, I'll outlift him now," said Bill.

But the Bluffer still shook his head.

"You don't understand, Pick-and-Shovel," he said. "Flat Fingers isn't going to stick his neck out by agreeing to lift weights with you again. He did once and you ducked out—all right, I know it wasn't your fault. But he's going to be thinking—suppose he agrees to lift again, and you duck out a second time, or fall down and play sick, or something? If it happens twice in a row that you get out of it, people are going to start laughing at him for letting himself be fooled that way."

The Bluffer shook his head.

"No, I wouldn't go back to the village right now if I were you, Pick-and-Shovel," he said. "What you and I better figure on doing is camping out here in the woods for a few days. I'll go in and get your sword and shield made by the blacksmith—that's business, he won't mind making those. Then, when you've got these weapon things of yours, you can go and have the duel with Bone Breaker, and after you win that maybe they'll let you back in Muddy Nose Village without falling over and rolling way down the street, laughing, every time they see you."

"So," observed Bill grimly. "Barrel Belly managed to get me in bad with the villagers, after all, did he? Your rescuing me didn't help at all, then, did it?"

Both the postman and Sweet Thing looked uncomfortable. Sweet Thing, however, was quick to recover.

"Well, why don't you think of something, then?" she demanded. "You Shorties are all supposed to be so tricky and sneaky! Tricky Teacher was supposed to be so smart at thinking up things and getting around people; but where is he when *She* needs him? Not here, that's where he is! Instead, you're here, Pick-and-Shovel. So why don't you think up something? I know why! It's because you're a male Shorty. *She'd* think of something, if *She* were here. I know *She* would. *She*—"

The continued emphatic repetition of the word "She" was doing little to improve Bill's temper which had already been worn rather threadbare by events. The single thought that was in his mind at the moment was that palm trees would be flourishing on the Weddell pack ice of Antarctica, back on Earth, before he would let any combination of events keep him out of Muddy Nose Village. He interrupted Sweet Thing roughly.

"All right," he retorted. "I've thought of something. Let's head for the village."

Chapter 13

The Hill Bluffer still hesitated.

"Are you sure you know what you're doing, Pick-and-Shovel?" he asked. "Like I say, Flat Fingers won't lift weights with you now—"

"That's what he thinks!" said Bill.

The Hill Bluffer lit up suddenly.

"You mean you figured a way to make him?" said the Bluffer, happily. "Why didn't you say so?" He turned on Sweet Thing. "There, how do you like that? You and your female Shorties!"

Sweet Thing sniffed disdainfully.

"Oh, well," she said. "*She* would have thought of it right away."

"Climb up in the saddle, Pick-and-Shovel," said the Hill Bluffer, ignoring this, and turning his back on Bill. "And we'll get going."

Bill scaled the Bluffer's back by means of the straps of the Dilbian's harness, and seated himself. The three of them started back through the woods toward the village.

As they went along, the heads of Dilbians out on the street turned to look at them, and the sounds of comments, ribald and otherwise, began to float to Bill's ears. He held on to the straps of the Bluffer's harness, before him, looking neither to right nor left. He noticed that Sweet Thing and the Hill Bluffer were not particularly pleased, either—even though they themselves were not the target of the jeers and catcalls that pursued them as a group. The Bluffer snorted once and swung half-around, as if ready to turn back and give battle to those who were criticizing. More Jam was not to be seen, Bill noted.

However, in due time they ran the long gauntlet of the street and arrived at the blacksmith's property. Flat Fingers paid no attention to them as they came up. He studiously avoided looking at Bill, and only grunted in response to the greeting of the Hill Bluffer.

"Well," said Bill, as cheerfully as he could manage, in the Bluffer's ear, "I'll get down here."

Flat Fingers was busy at the forge, beating rather savagely upon a piece of red-hot iron. The Bluffer was seated on the bench and Sweet Thing was standing near the Bluffer. Just outside the shed where they all stood, a crowd of villagers was beginning to gather. These stood and watched; silently, but grinning widely, and obviously expecting the worst. Bill felt a return of the coldness inside him he had felt with Mula-*ay*. However, he smiled and turned his back on them with as much an appearance of unconcern as he could muster.

"Well," he said loudly to the Bluffer, ignoring the blacksmith, who had now ceased hammering and thrust the beaten piece of red-hot iron, hissing, into a dark and dirty-looking barrel of water alongside the forge, "so this is Flat Fingers' place, is it?"

"That's right, Pick-and-Shovel," replied the Bluffer curiously.

Bill did not say anything more immediately. Instead he began to wander among the piles of wood and iron that were stacked up under the shed roof, stopping here to finger a broken candlestick—there to run his finger along the edge of a broken sword. Flat Fingers, having laid aside the piece of iron he had been working on before, now had picked up what apparently was a broken barrel hoop and was scowling at it.

"Mighty interesting around here," commented Bill loudly, examining the rafters of the shed overhead. They were very stout rafters indeed, made of logs and a good twelve feet in the air, well out of his reach unless he climbed up on a stack of five- and six-foot lengths of foot-diameter logs—firewood, probably—that were piled up a little distance from him. He drifted over to the logs and began to examine them. Then he turned back to Sweet Thing and pulling her head down to approximately the level of his own mouth, spoke quietly into her ear for a second. Sweet Thing went off through the crowd, followed by the curious stares of those nearby, who watched her disappear in through the front door of the Residency. They might have gone on watching, if Bill had not started talking again and drawn their attention back to him.

"Yes," he said thoughtfully, staring at the logs. "It's a shame I couldn't get here in time to have that weight-lifting contest with the blacksmith."

"Sure was!" spoke up a voice from the crowd, producing a chorus of bass-voiced laughter.

"Yes, a real shame," went on Bill, ignoring the reaction and nodding at the Hill Bluffer. "It would've been something to see."

He looked over at Flat Fingers, who had moodily shoved both the broken ends of the hoop into the bed of coals at his forge and was grimly pumping the bellows attached to it.

"Yes . . ." went on Bill, fingering one of the logs and trying to estimate its weight. It was about five feet long and looked as if it might weigh pretty close to a hundred pounds. The logs underneath it were similar in size, and their weight should be about the same, "An appointment like that's an *appointment*. If you miss it, that's that. I wouldn't insult Flat Fingers by suggesting he lift weights with me now, since I already missed one chance at it."

"That's playing it safe, Shorty!" boomed another voice from the observing crowd, and a new burst of laughter followed.

"No," said Bill thoughtfully. "That'd look like I might be trying to pull the same trick all over again. So I guess there isn't much for me to do—" He broke off as Sweet Thing shouldered her way importantly back through the crowd, the block-and-tackle Bill had made slung over one shoulder. There was a hum of interest at the sight of her, and it; but she ignored the reaction. She came up to Bill and dumped the block-and-tackle into his arms.

"There!" said Sweet Thing. She went over and sat down on the bench beside the Hill Bluffer, as if she had just done something remarkable to put everyone in their place. The crowd stared with interest at Bill and the block-and-tackle. Even Flat Fingers, over by the forge, shot a surreptitious glance in Bill's direction.

"On the other hand," went on Bill, as if to himself, but loud enough to be heard by everyone standing around, "I suppose I could just lift something around here, anyway, and sort of leave it lying where I've lifted it, and maybe Flat Fingers would notice it later—and maybe he wouldn't."

With these last words, thrown away in the best style of More Jam, Bill climbed up on the small pile of logs and tossed one end of the rope attached to the block-and-tackle over one of the rafters, and then tested it to see if it would slip easily. The rafter, being itself a smooth round section of log with all the bark peeled off, allowed the rope to slide around it almost as well as if it, too, was a pulley.

Bill climbed down, took the rope at the bottom end

of the block-and-tackle, and ran a loop around five of the logs. He slid the loop to their center, and tied it down tight there, with the lower block of the tackle perhaps six inches above the tie. He then secured the upper part of the block-and-tackle by a separate rope to the beam itself, and once more flung over the rafter the long, operating end of the rope running into the sheaves of the block-and-tackle.

The crowd had quieted down and had been watching in interested silence while he went through these maneuvers. Out of the corner of his eye, Bill could see Flat Fingers, also watching.

"Well," he said, when he was done, "let's see if I can lift those five pieces of wood, now."

He took a good grip and started to draw down upon the rope to the block-and-tackle running over the rafter overhead. The rope creaked and moved. The wooden pulleys of the block-and-tackle also creaked and whined under the strain. The rope from the pulley moved jerkily through his hands, but at first the five logs did not seem to move.

"You got to try harder than that, Shorty!" whooped a voice from the crowd, followed by another burst of laughter—but then the laughter broke off suddenly. For, as all those who were watching could see, the tied-together bundle of logs had stirred and jerked. Abruptly, they were no longer resting on the logs below, but visibly swaying in the air, a fraction of an inch above them. A few more heaves on the rope by Bill, who was beginning to perspire, and the five logs swung obviously into the air above the pile beneath.

There was a deep-voiced babble of amazement and approval from the group around. Leaving the logs swinging there, held by the brake in the block-and-tackle itself that prevented the line from running out again in reverse order, Bill dusted his hands and walked over to the Bluffer. The onlookers quieted to hear what he might say.

"What do you think, Hill Bluffer," Bill asked conversationally. "You think a man the size of Flat Fingers could lift that?"

The Bluffer squinted thoughtfully at the bundle of five logs.

"Yes," he said at last, "I'd have to say I'd think he could, Pick-and-Shovel."

"Well, I'll guess I'll have to add another log or two," said Bill. He went back to the pile and let the bundle back down. Then he loosened the ropes about the five logs, wrestled another into position on top of them, tightened the loop, and using the block-and-tackle, proceeded to lift the heavier load. Once more he went back to the Bluffer.

"What do you think now, Hill Bluffer?" he asked. "You think Flat Fingers could lift that much?" He spoke airily, but the back of his neck was creeping slightly with the knowledge that Flat Fingers was standing only half a dozen feet behind him, taking it all in. The closeness of the blacksmith, however, did not seem to bother the Bluffer. He took his time about once more examining the bundle of logs.

"If you want my opinion, Pick-and-Shovel," he said at last, judiciously, "I think the blacksmith could lift that much and—say, two more logs, as well."

"Would you say he could lift that much and *three* more logs?" asked Bill.

The Bluffer considered.

"Well," he drawled finally. "I'd have to say no, I don't think he could."

"Suppose I added four logs to that stack," said Bill. "You'd be pretty sure than he wouldn't be able to lift them?"

"Sure I'd be sure," said the Bluffer promptly.

"Well, I'll just add those other four logs on, then," said Bill.

He went back to the stack of logs and did so. As he took hold of the rope running over the rafter to the block-and-tackle, and began to put his weight on it, a trace of uneasiness crept into him for the first time. There was over half a ton of dead weight at the other end. The block-and-tackle might be able to lift it—but the question was, could he? For one thing, the added weight was making the friction between the rope and the rafter over which it ran a not inconsiderable item to be dealt with. At his first tug, it seemed as if the load would not move. Then—Bill remembering the fury that had been born in him back in the woods into which Mula-*ay* had kidnapped him. He set his teeth, wound his hands in the rope—and *pulled*.

For a long second, nothing happened. Then the rope gave, first a little, then a little more. Soon he was able to change his grip and the rope began coming steadily down toward him. Still, he did not count the battle won until a sudden gasp from the crowd behind him told him that the stack of ten logs had finally swung free and clear of the pile below it, visibly into the air.

Gratefully, he let go of the rope, and turned to look. Sure enough, the load he had just lifted showed daylight between it and the top of the log pile.

"Well, there it is," said Bill mildly. "I guess I did manage to lift a little bit, after all."

He dusted his hands together, turned back, and released the brake on the block-and-tackle. The load it was supporting fell with a crash back on to the top of the stack beneath. Bill surreptitiously locked the brake in place with a thrust of his thumb against the ratchet he had provided for that purpose. Then he turned back and walked over to the bench where the Hill Bluffer was still sitting.

"Well," Bill said, "I guess you and I might as well be wandering back on down to the Residency. I just wanted to show what I could do if I had a mind to do it. But I can't really expect Flat Fingers to go and try and lift that same weight, too. So I'll just leave it there; and we'll be going—"

The Bluffer had gotten to his feet, and Bill had already

turned toward the Residency when an angry snarl behind him turned him back.

"Just a minute there, Pick-and-Shovel!" snapped the blacksmith. He strode over to the rope still hanging from the opposite side of the beam from which the block-and-tackle itself depended, and grasped it firmly in his two huge, furry hands.

Then, without warning, he threw all his weight upon it. The rope twanged, suddenly taut—and alarm leaped inside Bill. The rope he had chosen was perfectly adequate to the task of lifting the load he had just lifted—otherwise it would have broken. But he knew how a rope that will not break under a steady pull will part under a sudden jerk that snaps it. For a moment, hearing the bass-viol note of the rope as it straightened out, Bill was sure that this was what had happened in Flat Fingers' huge hands.

But then he saw that the rope had held. Not only that, but although the great shoulder muscles under the black fur of Flat Fingers were bunching heroically, and the block-and-tackle was creaking painfully, the load was not lifting.

The line was now as taut and straight as a bar of iron. The whole body of the blacksmith vibrated with the effort he was making. But, as the long seconds slipped away, it became obvious he was not going to be able to do it.

A single, jeering laugh rang out from the surrounding crowd. With a speed of reflex that seemed unbelievable in one so big, Flat Fingers suddenly let go of the rope, spun around and took three long strides into the crowd, to reappear a second later dragging forward by the neck and arm a somewhat smaller, male Dilbian. Having got the other out where there was room to swing him, the blacksmith shook him like a terrier shaking a rat.

"You want to try it, Fat Lip? You and one of your friends, together, want to try to lift it?" roared Flat Fingers.

He let the other go, and Fat Lip staggered for a

moment before gaining his feet. Then, however, licking his lips, he took a look at the rope, and turned to shout a name into the crowd.

In response to that name another Dilbian of about the same size came forward. Together, grinning, they hauled on the rope.

However, for them as for the blacksmith, the lock held the brake on the block-and-tackle in place. Instead of the rope running through the pulleys as it had for Bill, they—like Flat Fingers—were reduced to trying to lift by main strength the dead weight not only of the logs but of the block-and-tackle itself. They did not succeed. In fact, a third Dilbian was needed to help them before the bundle of logs could be swayed, creakingly, up into the air.

A mutter, a rumble, a general sound of awe ran through the crowd. They stared at Bill with strange eyes.

"Well, Blacksmith!" said the Bluffer, with something very like a crow of triumph in his voice. "I guess that settles it?"

"Not quite, Postman!" replied the blacksmith. He had stepped back to the forge and picked up a rather long sharp knife from a small table near it. Now, approaching the tied-up bundle of logs, and shoving the three who had lifted it out of his way, he cut the rope above the block-and-tackle and below it, tossed it aside and retied the cut end of the lifting rope directly to the rope binding the load together. Then he stepped back, and turned to Bill.

"All right, Pick-and-Shovel," he said ominously. "Let's see you lift it now."

Bill did not move. But his heart felt as if it had just stopped beating.

"Why should I?" he asked.

"I'll tell you why!" said Flat Fingers. He reached down and picked up the block-and-tackle in one large hand and shoved it before Bill's eyes. "Did you think a professional man like me could have something like this pulled right under his nose and not know what's going on? The only reason you could lift those logs was because you used *this*! This gadget, right here!" He shook it, fiercely, almost in Bill's face. "I don't know how you made it work for you, and not work for me—but this is how come you managed to lift those logs!"

"That's right," said Bill calmly. The sweat was prickling under his collar.

"Hey!" cried the Hill Bluffer in alarm. "Pick-and-Shovel, you aren't saying—"

"Let him answer me, first," rumbled the blacksmith dangerously. In the mask of his furry face, his eyes were suddenly red and bloodshot.

"I said," repeated Bill distinctly, "of course I did. As you all know"—he turned toward the crowd of Dilbians just outside the shed—"my main job here is to teach you all how to use the tools that us Shorties brought you in order to make your farming less work, and made it produce more crops. Well, I just thought I'd give you a little example of what one our gadgets can do."

He pointed at the block-and-tackle, which the blacksmith still held.

"That's one of them," he said, "and you just saw how easy it made lifting those logs. Now wouldn't you all like to have a gadget like that—"

"Hold on!" snarled Flat Fingers ominously. "Never mind changing the subject, Pick-and-Shovel! You set up a weightlifting contest. You claimed you could outlift me. But when it came down to it, you used this. You *cheated*!"

The word rang out loudly on the warm afternoon air. From the crowd around there was dead silence. The accusation, Bill knew, was the ultimate one among Dilbians.

It was the old story of the spirit versus the letter of the law, again. What held true for laws held true also for verbal contracts and personal promises. Bill had conceived the block-and-tackle as a clever way of discharging an apparently impossible promise. But what Flat Fingers was saying was that Bill had promised one thing but delivered another.

There was all the Dilbian world of difference between the two things. What Bill had intended to pull off was something clever—and therefore praiseworthy. What Flat Fingers was claiming was anathema to all Dilbians.

The absolute inviolability of the letter of the law was the cement holding the Dilbian culture together. It was the one thing on which farmers, outlaws, Lowland and Upland Dilbians agreed instinctively. Not even the Hill Bluffer would stand by Bill if it was agreed that he had done what the blacksmith said. The penalty for *cheating* was death.

The crowd about the forge was silent, waiting for Bill's reply.

Chapter 14

Silently, Bill blessed the inspiration that had come to him earlier when he had originally begun to challenge the blacksmith. That inspiration should get him out of his present fix now, he told himself firmly. But in spite of that inner firmness, he felt his stomach sink inside him as he looked around at the grim, furry faces ringing him in. He forced himself to maintain his casual voice, and the careless smile on his face.

"Oh, I wouldn't say that," he said lightly. He turned and looked into the crowd. "Where's More Jam?"

"What's More Jam got to do with it?" growled Flat Fingers, behind him.

"Why, just that he was there when you and I had our little talk," answered Bill, without turning. "He's my witness. Where *is* More Jam?"

"Coming!" huffed a voice from the back of the crowd.

And a moment later, More Jam himself shoved his way through the front ranks and joined Bill and the others under the shed roof.

"Well, now, Pick-and-Shovel," he said. "You were passing the shout for me?"

"Yes, I was," said Bill. "You were over at the Residency this morning and maybe you were listening when I had my little talk with Flat Fingers. I wonder if you could think back and see if you remember just what I said I'd meet him here at noon to do? Did I say I'd *outlift* him?"

"Let's see, now," rumbled More Jam. "As I remember it, what Pick-and-Shovel here said was—'*I'm just a Shorty and I'd never have the nerve to suggest that I might be able to outlift you ordinarily. But I just might be able to outdo you at it if I had to, and I'm ready to prove it by moving something you can't move.*'"

More Jam cocked his head at the blacksmith.

"Sorry not to be able to back a fellow townsman up, Flat Fingers," said Sweet Thing's father sadly, "but that's what Pick-and-Shovel said, all right. And he suggested that you get together after lunch and you said 'Suits me . . .'" More Jam continued, repeating the conversation with as much accuracy as if he had been a recording machine.

Bill let a slow, silent sigh of relief escape him. The Dilbians, he knew, had the rather elementary written language that made the Bluffer's job as postman possible and necessary. But Bill had gambled on the fact that, like most primitive cultures, it was the Dilbian custom and habit to depend on the memories of living witnesses to any agreement or transaction.

However, the verdict, Bill noted, was not in yet. The crowd was still silent.

Bill's breath checked in his chest once more—but just then a swelling wave of thunderous, bass-voiced Dilbian laughter began to rise and ring about Bill's ears from every direction. Everybody was laughing—even, finally, Flat Fingers himself. In fact, the blacksmith showed an alarming intention of slapping Bill on the back in congratulation—

an intention Bill only frustrated by hastily backing up against the stout belly of More Jam.

"Well, well, well!" chortled the towering blacksmith finally, as the laughter began to die down. "You sure are a sneaky little Shorty, at that—and I'm the first man to admit it! No offense about my flying off the handle and saying you cheated, I hope? If you feel we ought to tangle about it, right now—"

"No, no—no offense!" said Bill quickly. "None at all!"

General sounds of approval from the surrounding crowd greeted this magnanimous attitude on Bill's part. By this time the shed was completely hemmed in by the villagers. It occurred to Bill that this might be a good time to try to get them on his side against the outlaws, striking while the iron was hot, so to speak. He stepped up on a pile of logs.

"Er—people of Muddy Nose," said Bill. For a second, his voice threatened to stick in his throat. For all the crowd's present good humor, Bill could not forget the ominous quiet that had hung over them a moment earlier when the blacksmith had accused him of cheating. It was a little like public speaking to a convocation of grizzlies. Nevertheless, Bill fell back upon his innate stubbornness and determination, and went doggedly ahead with what he had intended to say.

"—As you all know," he said, "my main job here is to help all of you to make your farms turn out bigger and better crops. But as you all know, too, I haven't been able to do anything about this yet because I've been tied up with a problem about Dirty Teeth and a bunch of outlaws headed by Bone Breaker—whom you all know well.

"But I'm sure you can all understand how this could keep me busy," went on Bill, "because these same outlaws have been keeping you people here around Muddy Nose busy for some time.

"So, I just wanted to mention that perhaps the time has come for you and me to join forces and see about settling the hash of these outlaws once and for all," said

Bill. "When I first landed in this community, I was given to understand that you might not be too interested in following a Shorty that wanted to do away with the community menace up in Outlaw Valley. I can understand that—you didn't know anything about me. But now, though I do say it myself who shouldn't—you've seen me have this little competition here with your village blacksmith, who's as good a man as they come—"

Bill paused to wave in Flat Fingers' direction, and Flat Fingers scowled from right to left—that being the male Dilbian way of taking a bow when referred to on public occasion.

"At any rate, I thought that maybe now we might get together and start to make some plans about cleaning out the outlaws . . ." For the first time, Bill began to be conscious of a good-natured, but rather obvious, lack of response from the crowd before him. In fact, from his elevated position on top of the logs, he now saw some of the outer members of his audience beginning to turn away and amble off.

"Believe me," he said, raising his voice and speaking as earnestly and forcefully as he could, "Muddy Nose Village can't get better and richer and stronger until those outlaws are settled. So what I thought was that we might get together a town meeting . . ."

The crowd, however, was visibly breaking up. Individually and in small groups they began to scatter, turning their backs on Bill and drifting off into the body of the village. Bill continued to talk on, almost desperately. But it was plainly a losing cause. Very shortly, his audience was down to its hard core. That is to say—Sweet Thing, More Jam, the Hill Bluffer, and Flat Fingers. Feeling foolish, Bill stopped talking and climbed down from the pile.

"I guess I don't convince people very well," he said in honest bewilderment to those who remained.

"Don't say that!" said Flat Fingers strongly. "You convinced *me*, Pick-and-Shovel! And I'm as good as any three other men in the village, any day—" He checked himself, looking apologetically at Sweet Thing's male parent. "—men my own age, that is."

"Why thanks, Blacksmith," said More Jam with a heavy sigh. "Nice of you not to include me—though of course I'm only a shadow of my former self." He turned his head to Bill, however, and his voice became serious. "In fact, you've got a friend in me too, Pick-and-Shovel—just as I told you yesterday. But that doesn't change things. If you figured this village to fall in line behind you in a feud with the outlaws, you should've known better."

"You sure should have!" interrupted the Bluffer emphatically. "Why I could've told you, Pick-and-Shovel, you'd never get anywhere impressing these people by being tricky. They *know* Shorties can be sneaky as all get out. The Tricky Teacher proved that. What they want to see if what you can do in the muscle-and-guts department. What you've got to do is just what you're set up to do— and that's tangle with Bone Breaker. Lay him out! *Then* these people will back you against the outlaws."

"I'll get started right away on that blade and buckler, Pick-and-Shovel," put in Flat Fingers. "Let's see if I can find something around here that's particularly good blade material."

"Guts-and-muscle department . . ." muttered Bill thoughtfully, echoing the Bluffer's words. That was certainly the department in which everyone seemed to be eager to have him operate—including whoever or whatever was responsible for his being in this place and situation in the first place.

It was hardly to be considered that Mula-*ay* had been telling the truth, this morning in the woods, when he had claimed Bill had been deliberately put on the spot by human authorities simply to save face in the case of the Muddy Nose Project. On the other hand, some of the things the Hemnoid had said had chimed uncomfortably well with some of the things Anita had said when he spoke to her in Outlaw Valley.

Either Anita had been as badly misled about the true situation here as Bill had, or . . . It occurred to Bill that the cards might be stacked more heavily against him than he had thought, even when he had sat thinking in front of the communications console after his unsuccessful attempt to contact Greentree or anyone else off-planet. There seemed to be no way out of his duel with Bone Breaker unless he could figure out who or what had put him in this situation, and what the true aims and motives of everyone concerned were.

In any case, Anita was going to have to provide him with some answers. That meant he must talk to her again, which meant another penetration of Outlaw Valley, which could hardly be done in the broad light of day . . .

"Muscle-and-guts department?" he repeated again, looking up at the Bluffer. "I suppose it would take a little muscle—and guts too—to get in and out of that Outlaw Valley after it's been shut up for the night?"

The Bluffer stared back at him in astonishment. Sweet Thing and More Jam also stared. Some little distance away the blacksmith raised his head in astonishment.

"Are you crazy, Pick-and-Shovel?" demanded Flat Fingers. "The gate to that valley is locked and barred the minute the sun goes down and there are two armed men on guard until it's opened up at dawn. *Nobody* goes in and out of that valley after the sun's gone down!"

"I do," said Bill grimly. "I think I'll just drop in there tonight; and I'll bring back that piece of metal outside the outlaw's dining hall they use as a gong, to prove I've been there!"

Chapter 15

"Will we get there before dark?" Bill asked.

"Before dark?" The Bluffer, striding beneath Bill, squinted through the trees at the descending sun now, gleaming redly through black-looking trunks and branches, close to setting. "Well, it'll be dark down in the valley. But up on top of the cliffs there'll be some daylight, still. And it's the north clifftop you want, isn't it?"

"That's right," said Bill. "If it's still light there, that's all I'll need."

"All you need, is it?" muttered the Bluffer. "Mind telling a man how you're going to get into that valley, anyway?"

"I'll show you when we get there," said Bill.

In fact, while he was fairly confident that he would make it, one way or another, Bill himself would not know for sure until he actually got to the top of the cliff and

made some measurements. There was a hundred feet of
soft, quarter-inch climbing rope wound around his waist
under his shirt, and with the help of the programmed
lathe he had produced some homemade pitons, snap rings,
and a light metal hammer with an opposed pick end.
These latter items were in a knapsack on his back.

As the postman had predicted, when they reached the
north wall overlooking Outlaw Valley, the sunset was only
falling on the buildings of the valley floor below them.
The Bluffer stopped and let Bill down, but with a strong
air of skepticism.

"What're you going to do, Pick-and-Shovel," the Postman asked. "*Fly* down into that valley?"

"Not exactly," said Bill. He had produced a jackknife
from his pocket and opened it. Now, while the Bluffer
watched with unconcealed curiosity, Bill found and cut
off a couple of small tree branches with y-shaped ends.
The branching ends he trimmed down to vee's; and stuck
the long end of the branches in the ground, one in front
of the other, with the vee's in line, pointing out across
the valley.

Bill then found and cut another straight stick, long
enough to lie in the two vee's, so that it lay like an arrow
pointing across at the top of the opposite valley wall.
Digging into his knapsack, he came up with one of his
homemade pitons, looking like a heavy nail with one end
sharpened and the opposite end bent into a loop. He tied
one end of a length of string to the loop and the other
end to the center of the stick resting in the forks of the
two stakes he had driven into the earth. Then he adjusted
the stakes until the piton hung straight up and down and
in line with the two stakes, over a point midway between
them.

"What is it?" demanded the Bluffer, unable to conceal
his interest.

"Another of our Shorty gadgets," said Bill. There was,
in fact, no Dilbian word for what he had just built—which
was a sort of crude surveyor's transit. The dangling piton

acted like a plumb bob which allowed him to check whether his line of sight—which was along the straight stick in the two forks of the stakes—was level. Now assured that it was, Bill knelt at the back end of the stake, so that he could sight along its length at the top of the valley wall opposite. It seemed to be almost directly in line. That should mean that the two valley walls were roughly of the same height.

From his pocket he took out a protractor he had located back at the Residency, and with this held against the end of the straight stick in the stake forks he rotated it through its angles of declination, making an attempt to get a rough approximation of the angle subtended by the height of the opposite cliff from its valley bottom to its tree-clad top.

He got the angle, and abandoned the transit for a pencil and a notebook. In the notebook, he jotted down the angle he had just observed. Then, using his eye, he made an attempt to judge the distance of the opposite cliff from where he stood.

Since both cliffs were more or less vertical, the gap between the point where he stood and the top of the cliff directly opposite should be roughly the same as the width of the valley floor at that point. His memory of the outlaws' eating hall down below enabled him to estimate its overall length to be about eighty feet. Just about twelve such eating halls placed end-to-end would be required to stretch from this cliff to the other one. Twelve times eighty was nine hundred and sixty—call it a thousand feet roughly between the cliffs.

He sat back, with his notebook and his pencil, and—closely observed by the Hill Bluffer who had hunkered down nearby—performed the simple geometric calculation that gave him an approximate measurement of the opposite cliff as being some sixty feet in vertical height. If the other cliff was sixty feet high, it could hardly be much more than that from where he sat right now to the valley below. He had brought with him a hundred feet of rope, so he had more than enough to let himself down into the valley once darkness fell.

"Well, I suppose I might as well tell you," Bill said. "What I plan to do is climb down this cliff here into the valley, and climb back up after I've gotten hold of the gong I said I'd bring back."

The Bluffer stared at him. For a moment, it seemed that even the Dilbian postman was finally at a loss for words. Then he found his voice.

"*Down* the cliff!" he echoed.

He got to his feet; and, screened by the bushes that grew thickly along the lip of the cliff, and by the trees surrounding, he moved to where he could peer over the edge of the cliff as Bill had earlier done. He peered for a long moment and then came back shaking his head sadly.

"Pick-and-Shovel," he said, "you're either plumb crazy, or better than any man or Shorty I've ever seen."

Bill had expected just this reaction. The cliff was a vertical face but not a smooth one. The dark granitic rock of which it was composed was roughened and broken by outcroppings and fissures large enough to supply adequate hand-holds for someone like Bill who had had rock-climbing experience. With a couple of other experienced climbers to help him and proper equipment, Bill would have felt quite confident about tackling it without any further aid. However, what were adequate hand- and foot-holds for someone with mountaineering experience were not necessarily sufficient to make climbable such a route for another human, without mountaineering experience—let alone a Dilbian, with his much greater weight and clumsiness. Consequently, it was not surprising that the Bluffer found the notion ridiculous—as undoubtedly would the outlaws themselves, or any of the other Dilbians resident in the neighborhood.

To tell the truth, Bill found it a little ridiculous himself. Not the idea of scaling it in full daylight with a team and proper equipment—but the idea of doing it by himself, with his few homemade devices, alone and in the dark. However, he had the rope up his sleeve—or rather, around his waist—which he now decided to keep secret even from the Bluffer.

"It's dark down in the valley now," he said as casually as possible. "Let's walk along the cliff until we find a good place for me to start down."

They started out together, the Dilbian postman shaking his head, with a renewed air of skepticism. A little further along the edge of the cliff, in the rapidly gathering gloom, they came to a place where part of the rock had fallen away, leaving a notch about eight feet wide going down, narrowing as it went into the dimness below.

"Here's a good spot," said Bill with a cheerfulness that he did not completely feel. "Suppose you come back for me here about sunrise. I'll be waiting for you."

"It's your neck," said the Bluffer, with philosophy. "I'll be here. I hope you are."

"Don't worry about me," said Bill. As the Bluffer watched curiously, he began to climb cautiously backward down into the cleft—the notch in the edge of the cliff.

Setting himself securely, with his feet braced and his left hand firmly locked around a projection of the rock, with his right hand he unbuttoned his shirt and began to unwrap the rope from around his waist. It took a matter of some few minutes for him to get it all unwound. He was left at last with the rope lying in coils upon and between his feet and with one end in his grasp. He searched around him for some strong point of anchor.

He found it in a projecting, somewhat upward-thrusting boss of rock about half a foot to his right, just outside the cleft itself. He wrapped his end of rope several times securely around the boss and tied it there. Then, cautiously, bit by bit, he put his weight on the anchored rope until all of his weight was upon it.

The rope held firm around the boss. Gingerly, with his breath quickening in spite of all of his determination and experience, Bill abandoned the security of the cliff for the open rock-face with the rope as his only support.

For a moment, he swung pendulumlike, giddily upon the rope. Then his feet, catching the cliff face, stopped his movement. Slowly, carefully, he began to let himself down the vertical wall of rock, his hands holding firmly to the rope, and his feet walking backward down the vertical surface.

Both the valley floor and all its walls were in deep darkness now. The sun had been set for some minutes, and, so far, no moon had risen. In the obscurity, Bill lowered himself cautiously down the rope, stopping only now and then, when he encountered secure footholds, to rest his arms—which alone took the weight of his body upon the rope. By this procedure, slowly and with a number of pauses, Bill went down into darkness.

He had made knots in the rope at ten-foot intervals. He had counted off more than seven of these—which would make the distance from himself to the bottom of the cliff alone higher than he had figured the cliff face to be. He was wondering with the first, fine, small teeth of panic nibbling at his nerves whether his calculations might not have been badly in error and there was more cliff than he had rope, when, stepping down, his foot jarred suddenly upon a flat and solid surface.

Peering about, he saw that he had reached the valley floor.

Bill stepped down with his other foot and let go of the rope. With a sigh of relief, he turned about and stood supported by his own two legs alone. Now that he was on level ground, he could barely make out the black-against-black of bushes and trees nearby. Cautiously, he began to feel his way among them—not without a scratched face and scratched hands from the spidery limbs and branches he encountered.

Pausing, he turned and looked back up the cliff down which he had come. By the moonlight, he was able to make out the notch at the top of the cliff where he had started his climb down into the valley. It stood out clearly, now that the moon was risen, and he marked it in his

mind—for he would have to find his rope again in order
to get back out of the valley.

Having located himself, Bill turned about and peered
through the open dimness of the valley floor, still in
shadow from the rising moon. Some five hundred yards
away, and barely discernible, chunks of heavier darkness,
with here and there a little crack of yellow light showing about their walls where light from within escaped
through the gaps of a high curtain, he made out the
buildings of the outlaw settlement.

He went toward them.

As he got closer, it was easy for him to distinguish the
large eating hall from the others. It was still occupied,
for not only was light showing here and there through
its curtains, but the sounds of cheerful, if argumentative,
Dilbian male voices came clearly to his ear. Giving the
building a wide berth, Bill circled to his left and began,
one by one, to examine the smaller buildings as he
encountered them.

Peering through a crack in one set of curtains where
yellow light showed, Bill discovered what appeared to be
nothing less than a regiment of young Dilbians evidently
engaged in something between a pillow fight and a general
game of Red Rover, for which purpose they had divided
into two teams, one at each end of the building—from
which they raced at intervals to the other end, roaring
at the top of their lungs and batting out furiously at any
other runner who came within reach.

Fascinated—for Bill had not seen any of the younger
generation of Dilbia's natives until this moment—he stood
staring through a gap in the curtain until the sound of
a door opening at the far end of the room and the appearance of an adult Dilbian not only brought the game to
a close but reminded him that he was an intruder here.
He turned back to his searching.

He had investigated all of the buildings but two, when
distantly—but unmistakably—the sounds of a human voice
fell on his ear. Turning about, he followed it to one of

the buildings not yet investigated, found a window, and peered in through an opening—actually a tear—in the hide curtain.

He had found Anita. But, unfortunately, she was not alone. She was seated in a circle with at least a dozen powerful and competent-looking Dilbian females, working on what looked like a large net.

Dominating the group was a heavy-bodied, older female who looked like a small, distaff edition of More Jam. The group had all the cozy appearance of a ladies' sewing circle back on Earth. Bill could hardly stick his head in the door and ask Anita to step outside and talk to him. On the other hand, every minute he stood about out in the open in Outlaw Valley increased the chance of some local inhabitant stumbling over him.

And the rapidly rising moon would be shining full on the valley floor very shortly.

Chapter 16

As he continued to watch through the tear in the curtain, undecided as to what he should do, Bill's hypnoed information came to mind with the advice that this was a net of the sort used by Dilbians to capture the wild, musk-oxlike herbivores that roamed the Dilbian forest. Anita apparently had been entertaining the others with some kind of a story. For, as Bill put his eye to the rent in the curtain, all the rest burst into laughter hardly less rough and boisterous than Bill had heard from their male counterparts at the eating hall.

"—Of course," said Anita when the laughter died down, apparently referring back to the story she had just been telling, "I wouldn't want Bone Breaker to lose his temper, and string *me* up by the heels."

"He'd better not try," said the fat matriarch meaningfully, looking around the circle. "Not while we're around. Eh, girls?"

There was a chorus of assent, grim-voiced enough to send a shiver down the back of Bill, watching at the window.

"*My* father—Bone Breaker's great-grandfather—" went on the speaker, looking triumphantly around the circle, "was a Grandfather of the Hunters Clan near Wildwood Peak," went on Bone Breaker's great-aunt. "And *his* father, before him was a Grandfather."

"What about Bone Breaker's own grandfather?" queried the smallest of the female Dilbians, sitting almost directly opposite Anita, who was at the left of Bone Breaker's great-aunt in the circle. "Was he a Grandfather too?"

"He was not, Noggle Head," replied Bone Breaker's great-aunt majestically. "He was a tanner. But a very excellent tanner, one of the toughest men who ever walked on two legs and a good deal sneakier than most, if I say so myself who was his blood sister."

"Indeed, No Rest," spoke up another comfortably upholstered female a quarter of the way around the circle from Anita, "we all know how you lean over backward, if anything, where your relatives are concerned."

Mutters of agreement, which Bill could not be sure were either real or feigned, arose from the rest of the group.

"But to get back to little Dirty Teeth here," said No Rest, turning to Anita. "The last thing we'd want to do is be without you and these interesting little tales you tell us about you Shorty females." The circle muttered agreement. "Some of the funniest things I've ever heard, and so—*educational*."

The last word was uttered with a particular emphasis that brought a hum of approval from the other females.

"Oh, well," said Anita modestly, her hands, like the hands of the females about her, busy at tying knots in the net as she spoke, "of course, as you know, under our

Shorty agreement with the Fatties, I'm not supposed to mention anything that they wouldn't mention. But I don't see any harm in telling you these little stories—which, for all you know, I'm just making up out of thin air as I go."

"Oh, yes," said Word-and-a-Half, with a wink and a nod at the others. "Making them up! Of course you are!"

"Well," said Anita, "there was this time my grandmother wanted a certain piece of furniture—" Anita broke off. "A sort of a chair—we call it an *overstuffed* chair. It's like a grandfather's chair, like a bench with a backrest to it. Only besides that, it's padded so soft, not only on the seat but on the backrest where you lean back against it."

A buzz of interest and astonishment convulsed the group.

"A grandfather chair! And soft?" said Word-and-a-Half in a pleased, but shocked tone of voice. "How did she dare—!"

"Oh, we Shorty females have gotten all sorts of things," said Anita thoughtfully. "And, after all, why shouldn't a female have a grandfather chair? Doesn't she get tired, too?"

"Of course she does!" said No Rest sternly.

"Doesn't a female get old and wise, just like a grandfather?" said Anita.

"Absolutely!" trumpeted No Rest. The circle burst into a mutter of agreement.

"Go on, Dirty Teeth," urged No Rest, quieting the circle with a glance.

"Well, as I say," said Dirty Teeth, carefully watching the knot she was making as she spoke, "my grandmother wanted this chair, but she knew there wasn't much use in asking her man to make it for her. She knew he'd just give some reason for not making it. So what do you suppose she did?"

"Hit him on the head?" suggested Noggle Head hopefully.

"Of course not," said Anita. There was a chorus of

sneers and sniffs from the rest. Noggle Head shrank back into silence. "She realized immediately this was an occasion that called for being sneaky. So one day when her husband was sitting dozing just after lunch, he heard chopping sounds out back. Well, the only ax around the house was his; so he got up and went out to see what was going on. And he saw my grandmother chopping up some lengths of wood.

" 'What're you doing with an ax?' shouted my grandfather. 'Women aren't supposed to use axes! That's *my* ax!'

" 'I know,' answered my grandmother meekly, putting the ax down, 'but I didn't want to bother you. There was this thing I wanted to build. So I just thought I'd try building it myself—'

" '*You* build it!' roared my grandfather. 'You don't know how to use an ax! How would you know how to build anything?'

" 'Well, I went and asked how to do it,' my grandmother answered quietly. 'I didn't want to bother you, so I went down the road here to our next neighbor, and asked her husband—'

"At that my grandfather let out a bellow of rage.

" 'Him? You asked *him*? That lard-head couldn't build anything more complicated than tying one stick to another!' he shouted. 'How did he tell you how to build it? Just tell me—how did he say you ought to do it?'

" 'Well . . .' began my grandmother; and she went on to describe the thing she wanted to build, with its backrest and its padding and all that. But before she was halfway through, my grandfather had grabbed the ax out of her hand and was busy telling her how wrong her neighbor's husband had been in his direction, and he'd started to build the chair himself to prove it."

Anita paused, and sighed and looked up and around at her audience.

"Well, that was it," she said. "Inside of a week my grandmother had the padded chair with the backrest just the way she wanted it."

There was first a titter, then a roar of laughter that gradually built up until some of the females dropped the net, and showed signs of literally rolling about on the floor in an excess of enjoyment.

"I thought you'd like hearing about that," said Anita meekly, working away at the net when they were all silent once more. "—But I ought to tell you that that was only the beginning."

"The beginning?" echoed Noggle Head in awe from across the circle. "You mean afterward he figured out what she'd done to him and—"

"Not likely!" sniffed No Rest. "A man figure out how he'd been made a fool of? He wouldn't want to figure it out. Even if he came close to figuring it out, he'd back away from it for fear he would find out something he wouldn't like!" She turned to Anita. "Wasn't that the way it was, Dirty Teeth?"

"You're right as usual, No Rest," said Anita. "What I meant was, it was just the beginning of what my grandmother had set out to do. You see, this one chair was just the beginning. She wanted a whole house full of furniture like that."

Gasps and grunts of sincere astonishment arose from her audience. Even No Rest seemed a little shaken.

"A whole houseful, Dirty Teeth?" said the outlaw matriarch. "Wasn't that maybe going a little bit too far?"

"My grandmother didn't think so," replied Anita seriously. "After all, a man gets anything he wants, doesn't he? All a woman has is her house and her children, isn't that right? And the children grow up and leave fast enough, don't they?"

"How true," said No Rest, shaking her head sadly. "Yes, every word of it's true. Go on, Dirty Teeth, how did your grandmother get her whole house full of furniture?"

"You'll never guess," said Anita.

"She hit him on the head—" Noggle Head was beginning hopefully, when she was sneered into silence almost automatically by the rest of the audience.

"No," said Anita. "What my grandmother did was to take off one day and go down and visit her neighbor— the same one whose husband she had asked about building the piece of furniture she wanted—because she *had* really asked him, you see."

"Ah," said No Rest meaningfully, nodding her head as if she had known it all the time.

"And," went on Anita, "she quite naturally invited her neighbor up to her house for a bite to eat and to look at her new chair that her husband had built. Well, the neighbor came up and admired the chair very much, and went home again. And what do you think happened before a week was out?"

"That neighbor had her husband make her a chair just like it!" said Word-and-a-Half emphatically. "She told him about the chair, and he went up and saw it and got all fired up, and he came back down and built one just like it!"

"That's exactly right," said Anita quietly but approvingly. "And of course the neighbor invited my grandmother down to see *her* chair. So my grandmother went down and admired it very much."

"So they both had chairs," said Noggle Head. "That was the end, then?"

"No," said Anita. "That was still just the beginning. Because the next day my grandfather came in and saw that the chair he'd built my grandmother wasn't out in the center of the room where it used to be; it was tucked back in a corner where it was dark and pretty well hidden. Well, of course he asked why it was put someplace else. And my grandmother told him about the neighbor's chair. Which made him furious!"

"Why?" asked Noggle Head, blundering in where her older and wiser sisters hesitated to play the role of interlocutor.

"Why," said Anita sweetly, "you see my grandmother was such a modest, kindly, unassuming sort of a Shorty female that she wouldn't for any reason try to hold her head higher than her neighbor. So that when she told my grandfather about the chair her neighbor's husband had built for her neighbor, somehow the way she told it made the chair the neighbor had built seem a lot bigger and grander and softer and higher polished than the one my grandfather had built for my grandmother—almost as if the neighbor's husband had built a better chair than my grandfather had, just to spite my grandfather. So, as I say, my grandfather became furious and what do you suppose he did then?"

"Hit her on the head?" queried Noggle Head, but faintly and with a note of hope that was almost dead, in her voice.

"You think too much of hitting on the head, my girl!" snapped No Rest, in a tone of stern authority. "Only the most helpless sort of a woman tries to handle a husband that way. Little good ever comes of it. Most women don't hit their husbands hard enough, anyway, and it doesn't do anything but make the husbands mad!"

Noggle Head shrank up over her work again, once more properly crushed. No Rest turned back to Anita.

"Well, Dirty Teeth," said Bone Breaker's great-aunt, "go on. Tell us what happened next!"

"Nothing much," said Anita mildly. "Although, by the time it was ended, my grandmother had the best houseful of furniture you have ever seen. But the point is—she continued to put her good sneaky talents to work the rest of her married life with my grandfather. And by the time of his death, he had become one of the richest and best known male Shorties around."

The group considered this conclusion for a long moment in satisfied silence. Then No Rest sighed and placed her seal of approval upon the anecdote.

"There's always a woman behind a man who amounts to anything," she observed sagely.

Outside the window at which he was listening, Bill suddenly jerked his attention away from the aperture in the hide curtains, and strove suddenly with his light-dazzled eyes to pierce the night darkness surrounding him. There was no more time to waste. He had to get Anita outside and away from her net-weaving social circle before the rising moon exposed him to capture. He turned and peered in at the window again. Dilbians, he remembered, because of a difference from humans in jaw structure and lip muscles, could not whistle. Bill took a breath and whistled the first two lines of *"When Johnny Comes Marching Home."*

The results were far greater than anything he had expected. Anita's hands froze suddenly in their movement of making a tie in the net, and her face suddenly went pale in the lamplight. But the effect upon Anita was nothing compared to the effect that the sound of Bill's whistle had on the rest of the Dilbian social circle.

All the Dilbian females in the room checked in midmotion and apparently stopped breathing. They sat like a tableau, listening. For a long moment the silence seemed to ring in Bill's ears. Then Noggle Head began to shiver violently.

"W-what k-kind of a critter's that . . . ?" she whimpered.

"Hush!" ordered No Rest in a harsh whisper, but one so full of terror that Bill himself chilled at the sound of it. "No critter—no bird—no wind in the trees ever made *that* sound!"

Noggle Head's shivers grew until she trembled uncontrollably. Others of the Dilbian females were beginning to cower and shake.

"A Cobbly!" hissed No Rest—and outside the building, Bill stiffened. For a Cobbly was a supernatural creature out of Dilbian legend—a sort of malicious but very powerful elf. "A *Cobbly*," repeated No Rest now. "And it's come for one us women, here!"

The eyes of all the Dilbian females turned slowly and grimly upon Noggle Head.

"You—and your talk about hitting husbands over the head!" whispered No Rest savagely. "You know what

Cobblies do to undutiful females! Now one of them's heard you!"

Noggle Head was shivering so hard she was making the floor creak beneath her.

"What'll we do?" whispered one of the other females.

"There's just one chance!" ordered No Rest, still in a whisper. "Maybe we can still frighten the Cobbly off. I'll give the word, girls, and we'll all scream for help. We'll have men with torches running out of all the buildings before you can wink. I'll count *one, two,* three—and then we'll all yell. All right? Ready now; and take a deep breath!"

Chapter 17

"Wait!" interrupted Anita's voice.

Bill, who had just been about to take to his heels at the prospect of a chorus of powerful female Dilbian lungs shouting for help, checked himself just in time.

"Don't shout," Anita's voice went on, hastily. "You don't want to get the men all roused up and over here, and then find out that the Cobbly's gone before they get here, and there's no way of proving it was here at all. Cobblies don't bother us Shorties. Let me go outside and see if I can get a look at it."

There was no immediate response to Anita's suggestion. Bill turned back to glance in through the tear in the curtain. The assembled Dilbian females were sitting and staring at her. If she had proposed that she try to walk up the wall, across the ceiling, and down the other wall of the room, or casually suggested flying to the top of

285

the cliffs that surrounded the valley they could not have looked more upset. The thought of anyone—let alone a female, whether native or Shorty—facing a Cobbly was evidently so enormous that it had rendered even No Rest speechless. But then that matriarch found her voice.

"Don't bother you?" she echoed, forgetting in her astonishment, to whisper. "But whatever—whatever—" words failed her in an attempt to state the concept of any kind of female world undeviled by Cobblies.

"Oh, we used to have something like Cobblies on our Shorty world," Anita said into the silence. "We had a different name for them, of course. But Cobblies and things like them don't like places where there's been a lot of building and making of things—you know that. You know they like the woods better than the villages and places like here, particularly in the daytime."

There were a few scared, hesitant nods around the circle.

"So our Cobblies sort of faded away," said Anita. "Just the way maybe yours will someday. Anyway, why don't I go outside and look?"

There was another long pause. But then No Rest visibly took a firm hold on herself. She sat up straight and spoke in a decisive voice.

"Very well, Dirty Teeth," she said sternly. "If you're not afraid to go out and look for the Cobbly, we'd all appreciate it very much."

"I'll look all around," said Anita, hastily getting to her feet. "But if I'm not back at the end of fifteen or twenty minutes, then you can always go ahead and shout for the men and torches, the way you were planning to do."

She slipped quickly to the door, opened it, and went out. To Bill, transferring his gaze to the outside, she appeared like a black shadow, slipping through the suddenly lighted opening, which was immediately darkened behind her as the door quickly shut again. The sound of a bar being dropped across it from the inside followed closely upon its closing.

Bill went toward her dark silhouette. She had come down the three steps onto the grass and was standing still—probably trying to adjust her eyes to the darkness outside. Bill came noiselessly up behind her and tapped her on the shoulder.

She gave a sudden gasp—like a choked-off scream—and spun about so abruptly and violently that he backed off a step.

"W-who's there?" she whispered, in English. "Is that you, Pick-and—I mean, Mr. Waltham?"

"*Bill*, blast it! Call me Bill!" whispered Bill fiercely in return. "Come on, let's get away from here to someplace where we can talk."

Without a further word, she turned and began to move off along the building and through several patches of shadow until they came up against the wall of a long, narrow, almost windowless building that was completely dark within.

"This is a storage place—sort of a warehouse," said Anita in a low voice and turning to face him as they stopped. "There won't be anyone around here to hear us. What on earth are you doing in the valley here? Didn't you know any better than to come back here—especially at night?"

"Never mind that!" snapped Bill. He was surprised to find a good deal of honest anger suddenly bubbling up inside him. Here he had risked his neck to find her, and she was adopting the same irritating, authoritative tone she had taken with him on his first visit to the valley. It was the final straw upon the heavy load of frustrations and harrowing experiences which had been loaded upon him ever since he had set foot on Dilbian soil. "I'm here to get some straight answers, and you're going to supply them!"

"Answers?" she replied, almost blankly.

"That's right!" Bill snapped. "Since I saw you last, I've spent an educational fifteen minutes with our Hemnoid friend—with me tied to a tree during the conversation . . ."

and he told her about his kidnapping and rescue of the day before.

"But you don't believe him!" exclaimed Anita, when he was finished. "Mula-*ay*'s a *Hemnoid*! The authorities wouldn't send you here to get killed, just to get themselves out of a tough spot! You *know* that!"

"Do I?" said Bill, between his teeth. "How about the fact that I've been sent here to a job I never trained for? How about the fact the communicator wasn't working when I got here—oh, I found out what was wrong and fixed it . . ." he told her about finding the power lead disconnected. "But who knows how to use a power wrench? No Dilbian, for sure. That leaves you or Lafe Greentree as the only ones who could have disconnected it!"

"How about Mula-*ay*?" she demanded.

"Mula-*ay* doesn't control our relay stations and hospital ship computers. When I got it connected, all I could get was the hospital ship Greentree's supposed to have gone to, and the computer there wouldn't connect me with any live person, or give me anything but a bulletin on his health." Bill told her about his conversation over the communications equipment.

"But—" Anita's voice was unhappy, almost a wail, "it still doesn't prove anything! And the authorities *don't* want to close this project down! Don't you know what the name of the project itself stands for—"

"I know all right!" broke in Bill. "They told me at the reassignment center. 'Spacepaw—*Helping Paw from the Stars*,' in Dilbian translation, because according to the Dilbians they're the only ones who have hands, and we Shorties have 'paws.'" Bill laughed shortly. "Let's try another interpretation, shall we? Project Catspaw—with me as the 'catspaw' that bails our Alien Relations people out of a jam on this world!"

"Bill, you *know* better!" said Anita desperately. "Oh, if you only knew how hard Lafe's worked here, you'd know he'd never have agreed to anything to close this project, let alone helping in making you the catspaw, as you say. It's all coincidence, my being here, and his breaking his leg—"

"Were you there when he broke it?" interrupted Bill.

"Well, I . . . no," admitted Anita grudgingly. "I was away from the Residency. When I got back, he hadn't waited for me. He'd already got a cast on it and called in, asking for transportation to a hospital ship—"

"Then you don't know for sure if he ever did fall and break it," said Bill grimly. "All right, maybe you can tell me what kind of a trick was used when this Half-Pint-Posted I keep hearing about beat up that mountain Dilbian with his bare hands."

"But there wasn't any trick! Honestly—" said Anita fervently. "Or rather, the only trick was that he used his belt. The Half-Pint—I mean, John Tardy—was a former Olympic decathlon champion. He got the Dilbian in the water with him, managed to get behind him and put his belt around the Streamside Terror's neck, and choked him. Outside of using the belt and the fact that he was able to maneuver in the water better than the Streamside Terror, it was a fair fight."

"Well, I'm no Olympic decathlon champion!" said Bill in heartfelt tones. "And if I was, how could I get a duel with swords and shield fought underwater? But I was set up for this duel with Bone Breaker in practically everybody's mind—Human, Dilbian, Hemnoid, and all—before I even got here—"

"But you weren't!" Anita was wringing her verbal hands. "Believe me, Bill—"

"Believe you? Ha!" said Bill bitterly. "You seem to be fitting in right with the rest of the scheme. Here you're supposed to be an agricultural trainee-assistant, but first you get the village females like Sweet Thing and Thing-or-Two all stirred up on opposite sides. Now I find you here stirring up the outlaw females. Why should I believe you any more than I would Greenleaf, or any of the rest who were part of getting me into this mess."

She made an odd, small, choked sound, and he saw the dark shape of her whirl and walk away from him for several paces before she stopped. He stared after her in some astonishment. He was not quite sure what reaction he had expected to his words—but it certainly had not been this. After a moment, when she still did not turn back or say anything, he walked after her and stopped behind her.

"Look—" he began.

"I suppose you think I like it!" she interrupted him without turning about, low-voiced and furious. "I suppose you think I'm doing it all just for my own amusement?"

He stared at the dark back of her head.

"Why, then?" he demanded.

With that, she did swing around to face him. He saw the pale oval of her face, gray in the dimness, without being able to read its expression. But the tone of her voice was readable enough.

"For a lot of reasons you don't even begin to understand!" she said. "But I'll try and make you understand part of it, anyway. Do you know anything about anthropology?"

"No," he said stiffly. "My field's engineering—you know that. Why, what do you know about it? Your field's agriculture, isn't it?"

"I also happen to have an associate's degree in cultural anthropology!" Anita snapped.

"Associate degree—" he peered at her. "But aren't you an agricultural trainee-assistant?" He strove to see her face, through the darkness. He felt bewildered. He would have been ready to swear that she was no older than he was.

"Of course. But—" she checked herself. "I mean, I am. But I've also been under special tutoring and an accelerated study course since I left primary school. For example, I've also got an assistant's certificate in pharmacy, and a provisional research certificate in xeno-biology—"

"*Grk!*" said Bill involuntarily, staring at her through the darkness. She evidently was, he suddenly realized, one of those super-brains customarily referred to as Hothouse Types back in college-preparatory school. Those students with so much on the ball that they were allowed to load up on half a dozen extra lines of study. Well, that was nice. That was all it took in addition to everything else that was making him feel like everybody's prize fool in this Dilbian situation.

"—What?" Anita was asking him puzzledly.

"Nothing. Go on," he growled.

"Well, I'm trying to explain something to you," she went on. "Did you ever hear of the Yaghan—a nearly extinct Indian tribe that used to occupy the south coast of Tierra del Fuego and the islands of Cape Horn at the tip of South America?"

"Why should I?" grumped Bill sourly. "And what's that got to do with the situation, anyway? What I want to know—"

"Just listen!" Anita said fiercely. "The Yaghan were a very primitive tribe, but they were studied by, among other people, a German anthropologist named Gusinde who wrote a monograph on them in 1937. Gusinde found out that the laws or the social rules of existence of the Yaghan were not enforced by any particular specific authority but by what he called the *Allgemeinheit*, meaning the 'group as a whole.' But there had to be some individuals who spoke for this 'group as a whole'; and these speakers were men called *tiamuna* by the Yaghan—and Gusinde describes the *tiamuna* this way—'*men who because of their old age, spotless character, long experience and mental superiority gained such an extent of moral influence that it is equal to a peculiar domination.*'"

Anita stopped speaking. Bill stared through the darkness at her. What relation this lecture had to the subject at hand he had no idea. After a moment he said as much.

"Well, haven't you heard the Dilbians talk about Grandfathers?" demanded Anita. "These Grandfathers are the *tiamuna*-equivalents among the Dilbians. The whole Dilbian culture is a strongly individualistic one—even more individualistic than our human culture. But it keeps itself stable through a very rigid system of unofficial checks and balances. It *looks* as if it'd be easy to introduce new ideas to the Dilbian culture. But the trouble is, introducing any new idea threatens to disrupt the existing cultural system of these checks and balances, and so the new idea gets rejected. There's only one way a new idea can be introduced and that's by getting a *tiamuna*— a Grandfather—to agree that maybe it's a good thing for Dilbians in general. In other words if you want to introduce any element of progress among the Dilbians, you've got to get a Grandfather to back it. And of course, the Grandfathers, because they're old and thoroughly entrenched in the existing system, are highly conservative and not about to give their approval to some change. But that makes no difference—if you want change you've got to find a *tiamuna* to speak up for it!"

"But there aren't any Grandfathers around here," Bill said. "At least there aren't any in the village, or in the outlaw camp, here."

"That's just it!" said Anita urgently. "Nearly all of the Dilbians live up in the mountains, where there *are* Grandfathers, and the Grandfathers *do* control everything. It's only down here in the Lowlands, where old tribal customs have started to relax their hold in the face of the different necessities of an agricultural community that there aren't any Grandfathers to deal with."

"But you said—" fumbled Bill, "that you had to get a Grandfather to accept your new idea before you could get the other Dilbians to accept it. If there aren't any Grandfathers around here—"

"There aren't any *Grandfathers* here," said Anita. "But there *are* *tiamuna*-equivalent individuals. Male Dilbians, who under the proper conditions up in the mountains, or at the proper age, would be Grandfathers."

"You mean," said Bill, his befuddled wits finally

breaking through into a glimmer of the light of under-standing, "someone like More Jam—or Bone Breaker?"

"Not More Jam, of course!" she said. "Bone Breaker is right, enough. But in the village, the closest thing they have to a *tiamuna*-equivalent is Flat Fingers. That's why I told you to get him on your side."

"But More Jam—" began Bill.

"More Jam, nonsense!" Anita said energetically. "I know all the villagers have a soft spot for him, and he carries some weight as the local innkeeper, to say nothing of his former glory as Lowland champion wrestler—Dilbians are very loyal. But him and that enormous stomach of his that he pretends can't stand anything but the daintiest of food—he's a standing joke for miles around. Remember, a leader can never be a figure of fun—"

"Are you sure?" asked Bill doubtfully.

But she was going on without listening to him. Bill's head was whirling. Just as he had seemed to hear a note of something incorrect in what Mula-*ay* had said the day before about Bill's not being likely to feel an empathy with someone like Bone Breaker, now he had just heard the same note again, accompanying Anita's statement about More Jam.

Chapter 18

" . . . I would no more consider you a subject of *sana* on the basis of our casual acquaintance here, *than you would be likely to empathize with—say—Bone Breaker, or any of the Dilbians . . .*"

" . . . More Jam, nonsense! . . . He's a standing joke for miles around. Remember a leader can never be a figure of fun—"

There was something wrong, thought Bill sourly, about both statements. If he could only connect that wrongness with his strange situation here on Dilbia, he had a feeling he might be on the track of handling that situation. Clearly there were some human machinations at work or else he would not be here at all. Clearly Anita knew nothing about them. Also, clearly, the Hemnoids in the person of Mula-*ay* were attempting to exploit the situation. But what none of these individuals and groups seemed to have stopped to consider was that possibly the Dilbians concerned might be grinding some axes of their own in the tangle where all this was going on.

The Dilbians—even the Hill Bluffer, in some obscure way Bill's mind could not at the moment pin down—seemed to have a stake in Bill's situation, of which Hemnoids and humans alike—even Anita, with her anthropological knowledge—seemed to be ignorant.

Without being able to prove all this in any way, Bill still felt it—as he had felt the incorrectness of Dilbian-understanding, first in Mula-*ay* and now in Anita. He felt it in his bones. Anita was still talking. Bill's attention jerked abruptly back to her.

" . . . so forget about More Jam and concentrate on the two important figures of Bone Breaker and Flat Fingers," she was saying. "They're the ones that have to be moved, and I'm trying, just as much as you are, to move them. That's why I've been working with the Dilbian women—in the village as well as here in the valley—the way I have. I suppose you don't understand that, even yet?"

"Ah—no," confessed Bill uncomfortably.

"Then let me tell you," said Anita. "It's because the one person that a *tiamuna* can listen to in the way of advice, without losing face, is his wife! That's because he can talk things over with her privately, and then announce the results in public as if they were his own idea, and she's not going to contradict him. And, of course, because of his physical and social superiority over the other male Dilbians, none of them are going to suggest it isn't his own idea, either."

"Oh," said Bill.

"So you see," Anita wound up, "I know what I'm doing. You don't—and that's why you ought to listen to me when I tell you what to do. And one of the things you shouldn't have done was come into this valley at night, to find me and talk to me. Maybe there *is* something strange about the way you've been left alone to face things. But Lafe didn't have anything to do with it—you can believe me!"

Bill said nothing. Anita, evidently willing to carry the point by default, paused a minute and then went on to other subjects.

"So what you do," she said, "is get back to the village as quickly as you can and *stay there*! Bone Breaker won't come into the village after you—that'd be going too far, even for the Muddy Nosers. And even if Bone Breaker brought all his fighting men with him, there'd still be more villagers than they could handle. So as long as you stay in the village, you're safe. Now do it, and cultivate Flat Fingers as I told you. Now I've got to be getting back to No Rest and the others, before they think the Cobblies have eaten me up! You aren't going to waste any time getting out of the valley now, are you?" A thought seemed to strike her suddenly. "By the way, how did you get in here?"

"Rope," answered Bill absently, still caught up in his new understanding, "down one of the cliffs."

"Well, you get back to that rope and get up it as fast as you can!" said Anita. "Can I trust you to do that?"

"—What?" said Bill, coming abruptly back out of the thoughts that had been occupying him. "Oh, of course. Certainly."

"Well, that's good," said Anita. Her voice softened, unexpectedly. She put her hand on his arm, and he was abruptly conscious of the light touch of it there. "*Please* be careful, now."

She took her hand away with that, turned about, and disappeared into the shadow. For a moment he stood staring into the darkness where she had been, strangely still feeling the touch of her hand even through the thickness of the shirt on his arm. It seemed to him that a little warmth seemed to linger where she had touched him.

Then he shook himself back to awareness. Of course, he was going to head back out of the valley as quickly as he could—but there was still something yet for him to do.

He turned and searched for the large building-shape of the mess hall. He found it and went toward it, keeping in the shadows. Five minutes later he glided up close to the front steps and paused. Here and there a gleam of light still showed between the hide curtains that covered the windows on the inside. But there were no guards standing on either side of the steps leading to the big doors—which were now closed. And the outlaw signal gong hung unguarded.

Bill came up to it and touched it. It was nothing more than a strip of bar iron, hung by a rope from one of the projecting rafter ends that supported the eaves above him. But he suddenly realized that he had made a serious mistake in boasting to the villagers that he would bring this back. For it was at least five feet long and two inches thick. It would be both too awkward and too heavy for him to carry while climbing back up the cliff by means of the rope.

He paused, baffled. If he was right about the Dilbians having their own axes to grind in the present situation, the fact that Bill should be able to produce evidence of having been in the valley this night loomed more importantly than ever. But if he could not carry the gong away with him, as he had promised, what could he do?

An inspiration struck him. He turned to the mess hall wall of peeled and weathered logs just behind the gong. His fingers, searching over its surface, found what he wanted, and unhooked it from the peg that held it by a thong through a hole in one of its ends. He brought it away from the wall, out a little toward the moonlight, so he could examine it. It, like the gong, was simply a length of bar iron. But it was no more than a foot and a half long, with a hole in one end where the thong attached, and below the thong that end was wrapped with cloths to provide a grip for an outsized Dilbian hand. It was, in short, the hammer with which the gong was habitually struck, and something Bill could easily tuck in his belt and take with him back up the cliff to the village.

Tucking his prize through his belt, where the rag-wound end kept it from slipping through, Bill turned and headed back toward the now-visible notch in the moon-lit cliff from which his cord, invisible at this distance, was dangling.

The moon was round and full over the valley by this time, but an intermittent cloudiness hid its face from time to time, so that light became dark. This seemed like a good omen—offering a chance for him to cross the relatively open area between the last of the buildings and the fringe of brush and trees at the base of the cliff, without any chance observer from the outlaw buildings happening to glance out and see him moving. Accordingly, when he reached the edge of the shadow of the final building, he hesitated until a cloud hid the moon, and then made a dash for the nearest place of concealment, a small hollow in the valley floor perhaps fifty yards away.

He made it, and dropped flat, just as the moon came out from behind its cloud. But as he lay hugging the earth, he stiffened suddenly in apprehension.

He was lying face downward, with his head turned to one side and his ear pressed against the still-warm earth beneath the short grass. To that ear there had come the momentary sound of thudding feet—before it abruptly ceased and silence took its place.

The cloud that was just beginning to cover the moon with its fleecy, thin, outer edge was a dark and long one. It looked fully long enough to allow Bill to make it the rest of the hundred yards to the cliff and the cover of the undergrowth at the base of the cliff. He held his breath as the dark part of the cloud began to cover the moon. The light faded abruptly—and all at once it was dark.

At once, Bill was on his feet and running for the cliff. But his ears were alert now, and as he ran he was almost certain that he could hear, in time to his own pounding feet, the thud of heavier ones behind him. Winded and panting, but still under the safe cover of darkness, he saw the deeper shadow of the brush and trees at the foot of the cliff, looming up before him. A second later, he was among them. Ducking off to his right, heedless of the branches that lashed at his face and body, he ran off from the main line of his flight for about thirty feet or so, and stopped, as still as the shadows from the moonlight about him, striving to control the panting of his oxygen-exhausted lungs.

Darkness still held the valley. But now there was no doubt about it. Now that he was stopped, Bill heard plainly the heavy sound of his running pursuer come up to and crash into the undergrowth at the base of the cliff—then stop in his turn.

Suddenly there was silence all around. Bill stood, holding his breath—and, somewhere hidden in the darkness less than twenty or thirty feet away, whoever had been following him was standing, holding *his* breath.

Bill was abruptly conscious of the hard length of the hammer to the valley gong beneath his belt. He backed away along the base of the cliff and looked about, trying to find his rope, or at least the cleft in the top edge of the cliff from which it hung.

However, from this angle of vision—right underneath the cliff, with the bushes and the trees close about him in the now once more brilliant moonlight, the rope seemed nowhere in sight. He hesitated, trying to decide which way he would move to look for it and then, at that moment, he heard a sound that checked him in mid-movement.

It was the sound of a bush rustling less than twenty feet from him.

His pursuer had been closer than he thought. Bill turned desperately to the cliff beside him. It was pitted enough by cracks and holes so that it was just possible he might be able to climb it. He turned to the cliff-face and began to climb.

He went up as noiselessly as he could. For the first eight or ten feet, he made swift and quiet progress. But then, he reached upward with his right leg for a foothold upon a small projection from the cliff-face—and it broke beneath his boot sole.

With a sound that seemed to Bill's tense ears to be like the roar of an avalanche, the broke piece of rock and a few shards of cliff-face it had carried away with it, went cascading down to the bushes below. And with that, everything began to happen very swiftly.

He scrabbled frantically with his unsupported foot for a new resting place. But, as he did so, there was a tearing, rushing sound through the bushes below him, and something that sounded like a snarl of animal triumph. At the same time, the strain of his body weight upon his two hands and remaining foot proved too much for their precarious grasp upon the cliff-face.

The support beneath his other foot gave way suddenly, and he fell, spread-eagled backward, outward into darkness and downward toward the ground, fifteen or twenty feet below.

Chapter 19

As he fell backward through the darkness, Bill instinctively tried to roll himself about in midair as he had learned in Survival School, and land on his feet. But the distance was too short. Even as he tried to relax in expectation of a bone-shattering concussion against the hard ground at the foot of the cliff, his fall was interrupted.

He found himself, unexpectedly, caught in midair—by what appeared to be two very large and capable hands.

"So it's you, Pick-and-Shovel!" the voice of Bone Breaker rumbled above him. "I thought it was you. Didn't I get your promise you wouldn't come back here, except in daylight?"

He set Bill on his feet, as the moonlight broke finally free of all clouds and they saw each other clearly. Bill looked up at the towering, coal-black Dilbian form. His mind was racing. He had never thought faster in his life.

"Well," he said, "I wanted to talk to you privately—"

"Privately? That's a Shorty for you!" said Bone Breaker. "Don't you know that if anybody found out we've been talking together privately, anything might happen? Why, people would be likely to start guessing all sorts of things! But here you show up—"

He broke off abruptly, staring down at Bill.

"By the way," he asked in a tone of puzzlement, "just how did you get here, anyhow? The guards in the gates didn't let you in. And there's no way you could get over the stockade fence in the dark."

Bill took a deep breath and gambled that the truth would serve him better at this point than anything short of subterfuge. He pointed up the wall of the cliff alongside them.

"I climbed down there," he said.

Bone Breaker continued to stare at him for a long moment. Then the Dilbian outlaw chief's eyes moved slowly away from him and lifted, traveling up the sheer face of the cliff.

"You—" the words came out of him slowly with long, incredulous pauses in between, "came down that?"

"Why, certainly!" said Bill determinedly and cheerfully, "we Shorties can climb almost anything. Why, back on my own world once, I—"

"Never mind that," rumbled Bone Breaker. His eyes came back down to focus on Bill's face. "If you came down it, I suppose you can get back up it, again?"

"Well . . . yes," said Bill, a little reluctantly, his fall of a moment before fresh in his mind. "I can climb it, all right."

"Then you better get going," said Bone Breaker—not so much angrily as emphatically. "You don't know how lucky you are it was me who spotted you sneaking around the buildings, back there, instead of it being one of our regular watchmen. It's just a happy chance for you that

I like to take a stroll around myself every evening before I turn in, just to see that everything's all right. Why, you could've spoiled everything!"

"Everything?" echoed Bill frowning.

"Why, certainly," rumbled Bone Breaker reprovingly. "Why would anybody think you'd be here, except to have that duel with me? And what's the point of having a duel at this time of night, with no real light to see by and hardly anybody around? No, no, Pick-and-Shovel. You've got to get this sort of thing straight in your Shorty head. Something like our duel has to be held in broad daylight. With everybody looking on, too. I want everybody up in the valley, and watching. And as many villagers as can get here, as well." His voice took on, strange as it seemed, almost a wistful note. "It's just too bad we can't send runners out with the word so that anyone in the district could drop by. But, I suppose that'd be overdoing it."

"Er—yes," agreed Bill.

"Well, anyway," said Bone Breaker, his voice becoming suddenly brisk, "you'd better get started. Up that cliff with you and out of sight—and remember! Whatever you do, Pick-and-Shovel, make sure it's daylight when you come back again. Full daylight!"

"I will," promised Bill. He turned to the cliff-face without any further hesitation and carefully began to climb. Some ten feet above the ground, he paused to look down. The moon was out from behind its clouds, and by its light he saw the outlaw chief staring up at him. As he watched, Bone Breaker shook his head a little, as if in amazement, and then turned and went off toward the buildings, just as the moon slid once more behind a cloud, and darkness covered the scene.

As soon as the face of the cliff was cloaked in shadow, Bill ceased climbing. Cautiously, feeling his way with hands and feet in the gloom with his heart thudding, Bill climbed back down slowly onto solid ground. When at last he stood firmly upright upon it, he found his face was wet with perspiration. A single misstep on the way down could have set him falling, the way he had done once already. And this time, there would have been no Bone Breaker to catch him.

However, now that he was safely on his feet again, he began to work his way along the base of the cliff until he reached a spot where he was completely hidden by the undergrowth. Here he waited until the moon once more emerged from its cloud, and, looking up, he was able to make out the notch at the top of the cliff from which his rope descended.

It was still a little farther to his right. He continued on and came at last to the rope itself, nearly invisible in the moonlight against the light-colored rock of the cliff-face.

The climb required a number of stops to rest along the way. Whenever he found a spot where he could lean or crouch against the cliff-face to rest those muscles of his arms and legs which had been bearing his weight during the climb, he did so. In spite of this, by the time he could look up and see the bottom of the notch only ten or twelve feet above him, Bill was as exhausted as he could remember being.

He had no idea, as he paused for a final rest upon a ledge of rock outcropping from the vertical face, how long the upward climb had taken. It seemed to have taken hours. However, no alarm had so far been raised that would indicate anyone had caught sight of him. After resting on the rock ledge as long as he dared, without risking the stiffening of his weary muscles, Bill geared up his courage and his remaining energy for the last stretch to the bottom of the notch. Then he began to climb.

It was hard work. With each foot gained upward, he felt the already shallow reserves of his strength ebbing away. Eventually, the bottom of the notch came within view, but still more than an arm's reach away. Bill locked his feet in the rope and started to let go with his right hand in order to reach upward.

—And his exhaustion-weakened left hand almost let go.

Clutching desperately at the rope with both hands, Bill clung to his position. There seemed to be no strength left in him. For a second, a giddy picture of his grip finally loosening on the rope as he hung here, and his plunge to certain death at the foot of the cliff swam through his mind.

—And then he moved.

He moved upward. He and the rope together lifted a good four feet until the notch was almost level with his eyes. Before he could grasp what had happened, the rope lifted again, carrying him with it. Someone above was hauling it upward, pulling him to the safety of the cliff-top.

Wildly and unexpectedly it came to him that possibly the Bluffer had returned, although he was not due until dawn—or had stayed in position above the cliff, and was now bringing him up to safe and level ground. Bill looked upward, expecting to see the dark, furry mass of the Dilbian postman staring down at him. But it was not the Bluffer he saw.

He stared instead into the moonlit, Buddha-like countenance of Mula-*ay*. The hands of the Hemnoid had hold of the rope. The great, heavy-gravity muscles of the alien were bringing it easily in, and there was a smile of pure, gentle joy on Mula-*ay*'s face. Like a hooked fish, Bill was being drawn helplessly upward into the hands of his enemy.

If the shock and dismay that Bill felt were strong, they were overridden just at that moment by the prospect of getting off the cliff-face and onto the level top of the cliff, no matter with whose help. He clung desperately to the rope and let himself be pulled in, until at last he was hauled over the edge of the notch and collapsed weakly upon the soft ground above the vertical rock-face.

For a moment, he simply lay there, almost too weak to move, his arms and legs trembling from the strain they had just endured. Then, painfully, he let go of the rope and struggled to his feet.

Directly in front of him, and less than six feet away, with his arms now folded across his chest within the voluminous sleeves of his yellow robe, Mula-*ay* continued to smile contentedly at him in the moonlight.

"Well, well, my young friend," said Mula-*ay*, with a heavy, liquid chuckle. "And what are you doing here at this time of night?"

Bill had had a chance to collect his wits. As it had in the moment at the foot of the cliff when he first found himself facing Bone Breaker, his mind was racing swiftly, turning up conclusions rapidly as it went.

"Why, I was just out," said Bill, panting slightly in spite of his attempts to appear calm, "for a little sport rock-climbing. Suppose you tell me what you're doing here."

Mula-*ay* laughed again.

"Why, of course I could tell an untruth just like you, my young friend," replied the Hemnoid, "and say I just happened to be out for a moonlight stroll. But people like myself are always truthful—particularly when the truth hurts—and I'll tell you the truth. I was out here looking for you, and, behold, I have found you."

"Looking for me?" queried Bill. "What made you think you might find me here? Particularly, what made you think you might find me here at this time of night?"

"I thought it likely you would want to visit your female confederate down there in the valley before long," chuckled Mula-*ay* thickly. "And I was right."

Bill looked into the round moon-face narrowly. What Mula-*ay* said made sense—but only up to a certain point. His galloping mind seized upon the hole in the Hemnoid's statement.

"You might've been expecting me to try to get in to the valley and see Miss Lyme," said Bill bluntly, "but how would you know that I would try to get in by climbing down the cliffs—and how would you know just where on the cliffs I'd choose to climb down?" His gaze narrowed further. "You've got a robot warning system set up around this valley, haven't you? And that's in violation of the Human-Hemnoid agreement."

He pointed a finger at Mula-*ay*.

"The minute I report this," he snapped, "your superiors will have to pull you from your post here on Dilbia!"

"*If* you tell them, don't you mean, my young friend?" murmured Mula-*ay* comfortably. "I seem to remember something about your not being able to reach your superiors off-planet. And if you did, it would simply be your word against mine."

"I don't think so," retorted Bill grimly. "Any efficient warning system would require power expenditure, and good detection equipment would be able to find traces of power expenditure in this area, once they knew where to look—which they would, as soon as I told them how you had been warned by my entering the valley down the cliff. You must have a sensory ring set up all around the valley."

"And if I have?" Mula-*ay* shrugged. "And if detection equipment actually could find traces? There's still the question of your telling them about it."

These last words were said in the same light and careless tone in which Mula-*ay* had been conversing from the beginning. But something about them sent a sudden chill through Bill. He was abruptly aware of the position in which he stood.

This isolated spot at the cliff's edge, closely and thickly hemmed in by bushes, was now proving to work its former advantages to his present disadvantage. Directly before him, the gross and inconceivably powerful heavy-gravity form of the Hemnoid blocked Bill's only direct route of escape into the nighttime woods. Behind him was the cliff, where one step backward would send him plunging down through emptiness. To right and left the thickly grown bushes formed flanking walls, through which a Dilbian or a Hemnoid might be able to push by brute force, but which would slow down a human like himself, so that he could easily be caught by someone like Mula-*ay*.

These bushes grew almost to the very lip of the cliff. Only perhaps half a foot of crumbling, overhanging turf separated the last of them from the vertical drop. Bill was as neatly enclosed as a steer in a slaughter pen at a meat-packing company. Only his reflexes, which would be faster than the heavy-gravity being facing him—just as they were faster than the Dilbians'—because of his smaller size, remained in his favor. And he did not at the moment see how faster reflexes could help him here.

"You aren't—" he began and hesitated, "you aren't such a fool as to think of actually doing something to me yourself? There'd be bound to be an investigation, and the investigation would be bound to turn up the fact that you were responsible."

Mula-*ay* shook his head.

"I?" he said, and his smile broadened. "Who'd bother to push the investigation in my direction, when it will be plain that your Dilbian postman left you off here for the express purpose of climbing down the cliff? And when your body is found at the very foot of the rope down which you climbed, with every indication that your grip upon it failed so that you fell to your death?"

Mula-*ay* chuckled, and, withdrawing his hands for their sleeves, flexed their thick, wide fingers.

"Oh?" demanded Bill, on what he hoped was a convincing note of scorn, "if that's really what you mean to do, why haven't you just done it, instead of standing around talking to me about it?"

Mula-*ay* chuckled again, continuing to flex his fingers.

"Aren't you forgetting," he replied cheerfully, "that we Hemnoids enjoy the suffering of our victims?" He chuckled. "And mental suffering is so much more delicately satisfying than gross physical discomfort. I wanted to thank you—before pushing you over the cliff, for being so obliging as to put yourself in this exposed and compromising position after you were so lucky as to be rescued from the little execution I arranged for you at the hands of Grandpa Squeaky—"

"All right, Hill Bluffer," interrupted Bill swiftly, looking over Mula-*ay*'s right shoulder. "He's admitted what I wanted him to say. You can grab him now."

Mula-*ay* chuckled again.

"You didn't think you could fool me by saying something like that—" he began. But as he did so, his eyes flickered for a second backward over his right shoulder. And in that second, Bill acted.

Spinning on his heel, he dashed off to his left along the narrow strip between the end of the bushes and the cliff edge. He felt the ground giving under his feet as his weight came upon it—but then he was past, veering into the darkness of the forest beyond and the solid footing farther back. Behind him, he heard Mula-*ay*'s muffled shout, followed by the crashing of the bushes as the tremendously powerful, heavy-gravity body of the other bulldozed through them in pursuit. But without pausing, Bill ran on, taking advantage of every open spot and break in the undergrowth that he could find.

He covered perhaps seventy-five or a hundred yards this way. Then, winded, he stopped. Listening, he heard—quite some distance behind him now—the sound of the Hemnoid blundering and tearing his way through the undergrowth. Panting, and with sweat running off him in rivulets, Bill stood still and kept quiet.

After a few seconds, the sound of the Hemnoid's pursuit also stopped abruptly. Bill could imagine Mula-*ay* standing, listening, waiting for some sound to tell him in which way Bill was trying to escape. But Bill knew better than to give him that clue. Bill continued to stand still, and for the long, drawn-out space of perhaps two and a half minutes nothing but night silence held the clifftop forest.

At the end of that time, Mula-*ay* moved again. He was evidently trying to move quietly, but sound of his passage, of leaves rustling and branches being swept aside by his passage, came clearly and unmistakably to Bill's ears. After perhaps half a minute of this, it must have become obvious to Mula-*ay* as well that he could not move anywhere near as quietly as Bill—nor could he find Bill in the darkened forest this way as long as Bill chose to hide. Amazingly and unexpectedly, the almost ghostly chuckle of the Hemnoid floated through the moonlit undergrowth and trees to Bill's ear. And the voice of Mula-*ay* came quite distinctly, although muted by distance.

"Very good. Very good indeed, my young friend . . ." The ghostly chuckle came again. "But there will be other opportunities and other ways. Good-bye for now—and pleasant dreams."

With the last word, there came the sound of the Hemnoid unmistakably moving off. The rustling and crashing sounds of his departure moved straight away from the edge of the cliff until they were lost in the distance. Bill sat down on a fallen log to catch his breath.

The fact that the Hemnoid had been willing to risk open violence against a representative of the human race here on this neutral world went far to confirm the sudden understanding that had burst upon Bill while he was talking to Anita Lyme in the valley below. There was no doubt now that there was a great deal more at stake between humans and Hemnoids, a great deal more wavering in the balance between them here on Dilbia in this situation than appeared on the surface. Why Bill himself had not been informed of this remained a puzzle.

Bill shook himself abruptly and stood up. A complete silence held the forest. He turned, and moving with a silence that was the result of his long practice and competitions, he found his way back to the cliff edge and followed it around to the valley's entrance. There, working along by moonlight, he measured the angle of the drop from the turn in the trail leading to the stockade gates some fifty yards away and then paced off the distance from the turn to the gates, in order to measure it exactly. Having done this he returned up around the cliff edge to the top of the notch, where Bone Breaker had left him.

Hauling up his rope and once more rewinding it around his waist under his shirt, he scooped out with his hands a small depression in the lea of a large boulder at the cliff top, built a rough bower of branches around it, and then curled up inside the primitive shelter he had so created. It was no worse and a good deal better than many of the same shelters he had created in Survival School, back on Earth. Curled up within it, his own body heat, reflected from the rock behind him and trapped by the enclosing branches, soon made him comfortable . . . and he slept.

Chapter 20

Bill woke to the confused impression that he was flying through the air. The jolt with which he landed brought him fully awake. He found himself being carried. For a moment he hung there, trying to puzzle things out as the mists of sleep evaporated.

Then it came to him. Evidently the Bluffer, coming and finding him asleep, had simply picked him up and plunked him in the saddle without further notice. This was entirely in line with the Dilbian way of doing things. There was even a sort of horrible humor to the situation. Bill opened his mouth and laughed—only the laugh came out more like a croak.

"Alive up there, are you?" queried the Bluffer, without turning his head, or slowing his pace. "You were really sleeping it up, when I found you back there. Have a good night?"

For answer, Bill let go of the Bluffer's straps with his right hand, fumbled under his belt, and brought out the hammer to the outlaw gong, which he held out in front of the Bluffer's eyes.

"Well, well!" said the Bluffer cheerfully. "Thought you were going to bring the gong itself, though?"

"This was easier to carry," said Bill, as indifferently as he could manage. "I suppose it'll do as well as the gong, to prove that I was down in the valley last night?"

"Why, I guess it would," replied the Bluffer judiciously. "You couldn't get either one without going in and out."

The Bluffer's tone of approval it seemed to Bill, however, left something to be desired.

"Why?" asked Bill. "Something wrong with getting into Outlaw Valley by climbing down the cliffs and climbing back up them to get out again?"

"Wrong? No, I wouldn't say so," replied the Bluffer thoughtfully, "but it's just another thing that a Shorty might be able to do that a man couldn't do—not because the Shorty wasn't being better than a man at doing it, but because the Shorty was so small that it was easier for him to do it. Like crawling into a little hole in the ground, one that'd be too small for a real man to crawl into."

"Oh," said Bill, suddenly deflated. He himself knew how hard it had been to get up and down that cliff. It had never occurred to him that the difficulties and dangers involved would mean nothing to a Dilbian—simply because a Dilbian would have no means of duplicating them himself. That took climbing a sheer cliff out of the heroic class and put it into the class of magic to Dilbians. No one expected a human, back on Earth, to swim as well as a fish. After all, he wasn't a fish.

"You see," said the Bluffer, after a moment. "I just thought I'd let you know how things stand, Pick-and-Shovel. It's all very well doing tricks—everybody knows you Shorties have got all kinds of tricks up your sleeves. But what kind of good is it going to do us real men and women and children? *That's* what we want to know! So if you'll go around and climb up on my back again, we'll get going toward the village."

Bill did as the Bluffer suggested, in silence. And that same thoughtful silence he maintained until they entered the main street of the village itself. Nor did the Bluffer seem disposed to interrupt him.

However, when they came in sight of the Residency, and the Bluffer seemed headed past that building on toward the blacksmith shop, Bill roused himself to protest.

"Hey!" he said, leaning forward toward the Bluffer's right ear. "Let me down here. I've got some things to do before I start talking to people—and one of them is getting something in the way of breakfast. I suppose you didn't think of the fact I haven't had anything to eat yet today?"

"You know," said the Bluffer in a tone of wonder, "it did slip my mind at that. Well, I suppose it's natural. If a man's had breakfast himself, he naturally assumes everybody else has too."

"I'll see you in about half an hour, up at the forge," said Bill, heading in toward the Residency.

There were some things he desperately needed to learn before he faced any assemblage of villagers. That was his main reason for stopping—but it was nonetheless true that he did need breakfast. He went first to the kitchen therefore, and it was not until he had surrounded a meal that was almost Dilbian in its proportion that he turned to his search for the information he wanted.

He found it easily enough in the information computer—a complete account of the nursery tale of the Three Little Pigs, and a concise account of methods and tactics in medieval warfare. Having absorbed this information, he put the gong handle through his belt—from which he had removed it for the sake of comfort, while eating breakfast—and went out of the Residency and up the street toward the blacksmithy.

He found not only the blacksmith there with the Hill Bluffer but a fair sprinkling of other citizens of the village, and others began to come out of their various houses and follow him up as he approached the blacksmith shop, until he had quite a crowd surrounding him as he stepped in under the roof of the open shed to greet the Bluffer and Flat Fingers.

"Morning, Pick-and-Shovel," the blacksmith replied, his eyes fastened on the object tucked under Bill's belt. "I've got your blade and buckler ready. Want to try them out?"

"In a minute," replied Bill, with elaborate casualness. "You don't have a nail and a hammer you could lend me, do you?"

"Why, I guess so," replied the blacksmith. He turned to one of the tables nearby, searched among the litter that covered it, and came up with something rather like a short sledgehammer and one of the nails he had made himself from the native iron.

The sledgehammer was difficult to handle with one hand, while holding the nail. The nail itself was some eight inches in length, a triangular sliver of gray native iron, with a bulge at one end for a head and a rather blunt point at the other. Nonetheless, Bill managed to knock it partway into one of the upright posts supporting the shed roof. Then he returned the sledgehammer to the blacksmith, took the gong hammer from his belt, and hung it by the hole in one end of its handle from the nail he had just driven into the pole.

A pleased mutter of deep-voiced and admiring comment went through the crowd that now surrounded the blacksmith shed closely. The blacksmith squinted at the gong hammer.

"Yes," he said, after a minute. "I remember cutting that piece of iron for Bone Breaker, myself. That must have been eight-ten years ago. Before that they were sounding their gong with just a chunk of wood."

He turned to face Bill. Behind and above the singed

fur of the blacksmith's broad right shoulder, Bill saw the face of the Hill Bluffer looking at him expectantly.

"So I guess you really were down in outlaw territory last night, were you, Pick-and-Shovel?" said the blacksmith. "How did you do it?"

"Well, I'll tell you," said Bill. The crowd around the shed had quieted down, and Bill realized that something more than an ordinary relating of the night's activities was expected. This was not a time for modesty. Modesty, in fact, was not considered highly among the Dilbians—except as a cloak for secretive boasting. The Dilbians were like good fishermen, who made it a rule always to exaggerate the size, weight, and number of their catch.

"Well, I'll tell you," he said. "You all know how that valley is. High cliffs all the way around it, the only entrance blocked up by the stockade. And the gates in the middle of the stockade barred shut at sundown. You wouldn't think a fly could get into that valley. But I did. But I'm not boasting about it. You know why?"

He waited for somebody to ask him why. The blacksmith obliged.

"Why, Pick-and-Shovel?" asked Flat Fingers.

"Because it was easy for a Shorty like me," Bill said, keeping in mind the reaction to his climb shown by the Hill Bluffer on the way back to the village. "Even if it would be hard for a real man, the fact that it was easy for me makes it something that I don't need to feel particularly proud about. You asked me how I got into the valley? I'll tell you in just two or three words how I got into that valley. I climbed down one of the cliffs until I was on the valley floor. And when I was ready to leave again, I climbed back up that cliff!"

There was a moment's absolute silence and then a gratifying mutter of incredulity from the audience. Bill interrupted it with an upheld hand.

"No, no—" he said. "As I say, I'm not particularly proud of it. Well, then, you may say—I could be a little

puffed up over having walked into that outlaw camp all
alone, with nobody to help me in case I was discovered.
How many of you would like to do that, especially after
dark?"

Bill paused for an answer. But no volunteers from the
audience spoke up to say that they would have enjoyed
such an excursion.

"But again," went on Bill, after a moment, "I can't take
any credit for that either."

There was a hum of amazement at this new statement that abruptly suggested to Bill the rather ludicrous
picture of the bass droning of a swarm of enormous
bumblebees. He waited for it to die down before he
continued.

"No, I can't feel very proud about that," he said.
"Because I really wasn't worried about going in among
those outlaws all by myself to get this gong handle you
see hanging there. You see, I knew that if I ran into any
of them, I could handle him with no trouble at all."

"What if you ran into a whole bunch of them?"
demanded a voice from the crowd. "How about that, Pick-
and-Shovel?"

"That didn't bother me either," replied Bill. "I could've
handled any number I might've run into." There was a
slight stir in the ranks of the crowd directly before him,
and he saw the incredibly rotund form of More Jam
unobtrusively squeezing into the front rank. "We Shorties know these things. That's why I'm not afraid to face
Bone Breaker in a duel. That's why, in spite of the fact
that we're so much smaller than real men and Fatties,
we Shorties don't have to take a back seat to anybody.
It's because of what we know. And it was because of what
I knew that it didn't bother me to go into that valley and
bring that gong handle out."

Bill stopped. The crowd around the shed, he could now
see from his superior position on top of the barrel, was
as large or larger than it had been the day before when
he had lifted weights with the blacksmith. They were all

staring at him in fascinated interest. He let them stare, waiting for the question that one of them must ask if he was to go on. Finally, it was More Jam in the front rank who put it to him.

"That sounds might interesting, Pick-and-Shovel," said More Jam mildly. "Maybe you wouldn't mind telling us what it is you Shorties know that makes so much difference in handling outlaws? Because," went on More Jam, looking back over his shoulder briefly at his fellow villagers for a moment, and then turning back to Bill, "I don't 'spose most of the real active men around here would like to admit it, but an old fat, decrepit man like myself doesn't mind letting it out. We haven't been able to handle those outlaws, when you get right down to it. They come in a gang all at once upon some single farmer, and there's not much one man can do against a crowd. We never know when they're coming, and by the time we get together to go after them, they're back safe in their valley. So we've just about given up trying to handle them. But you say, Pick-and-Shovel, that there is a way? Maybe you'd like to tell us what that way is?"

"Well," answered Bill, "as you know, we Shorties have an agreement with the Fatties not to go talking out of turn about things back on our home world. If the Fatties don't talk out of turn we don't—and vice versa. So that kind of stops me from telling you plain out what I know."

"You mean, Pick-and-Shovel," More Jam's voice held a strangely silky note that rang a sharp warning bell in the back of Bill's head, "you know something that would help us, here in this village, and you're refusing to tell us what it is?"

"Sorry," said Bill. A low mutter of annoyance began in the crowd, and deepened toward anger. Bill hurried hastily on. "I've given my word not to—just like all the Shorties and Fatties that come here to know you people. But,"—Bill paused, took a deep breath, mentally kicked the Human-Hemnoid Non-Interference Treaty out of the window, and borrowed a page from Anita's book, as he had observed her in Outlaw Valley through the crack in the hide curtain—"let me tell you all a story about my grandfather."

Chapter 21

"It all began because of a story there used to be among us Shorties—" Bill had barely gotten the first words out, when he was interrupted.

"I'll just bet it did!" cried someone in the front of the crowd—and looking down, Bill saw several females standing in a group there, together. He recognized the speaker as Thing-or-Two, flanked by the tall form of Perfectly Delightful. "And it's another story you're going to be telling us all now, we can bet on that too. It's a shame, that's what it is—an absolute shame, the way the men of this village stand around and let the wool be pulled over their eyes by Shorties like you, with no regard for customs and manners and traditions! Why don't some of you speak up and tell this Shorty what he can do with his stories?"

"You shut up!" snapped a new female voice. Looking,

Bill saw that Sweet Thing had appeared beside More Jam and was now looking around his enormous stomach at the older Dilbian female, like a rat terrier growling around the edge of a half-opened door at an intruder. "You just can't wait to get me out of the Inn, so you and Tin Ear can move in on Daddy. Well, I'm not leaving! You let Pick-and-Shovel talk—"

"Did you hear her!" shrieked Thing-or-Two, turning to the crowd. "Did you hear what she said to me—*me*, a woman old enough to be her mother! This is what things have come to! It's a good thing I'm not her mother, I'd—"

"You'd what?" demanded Sweet Thing belligerently, starting around her father toward the older woman. More Jam interposed a heavy arm.

"Now, now, daughter," he rumbled peaceably. "Manners, manners . . ."

Still growling, but complying, Sweet Thing allowed herself to be pushed back to the opposite side of More Jam.

"At the same time," went on More Jam, lifting his voice over that of Thing-or-Two, as she began to speak again, "as I remember it, Pick-and-Shovel was about to tell us something. And I guess I'm probably speaking for most of us when I say that, since he did something pretty interesting in going down into Outlaw Valley to get that gong handle, we ought to at least listen to what he has to say now. Besides, it sounds kind of interesting."

"Well," Bill began, "as I was starting to say, this whole thing came about because of a story we Shorties have. It concerns a sort of Cobbly we Shorties used to have— they've nearly all disappeared nowadays, back where I come from, but we used to have them. The story's about this Cobbly and three brothers."

The crowd had stilled amazingly. Bill was suddenly conscious of all eyes being fixed on him with the particular type of open, fascinated gaze he had occasionally seen in children hearing a story or watching a play.

"This Cobbly—" he stopped to clear his throat, then went on, "had one real powerful habit. He was able to blow rocks—even big boulders—right out of his way. He could even puff hard enough to blow a tree down, the way a storm might do. Well, these three brothers started out to set up their own home. None of them was married yet, so they headed off into the woods, and each one of them picked himself a place to build a house."

Bill paused for a moment to see if he still had the rapt attention of his audience. Gazing down at them, he decided that if anything it was more rapt than ever. He went on.

"You see, they all knew about the Cobbly who lived in this wood, and could blow down trees and things like that, so they were all particularly concerned to build a Cobbly-proof house."

Bill took a breath.

"Well, the first brother was the laziest of the bunch. He thought it would be good enough if he just took a lot of twigs and small branches, wove them together, and made himself a house that way. So he went to work and ran himself up a house in about a day and a half. The only thing he did that didn't call for light branches was to put a stout bar on the inside of the front door—a bar anchored to two doorposts that were set deep in the earth.

" 'Let's see that Cobbly break through that bar!' he said, and rolled himself up for the night.

"Meanwhile, the other two brothers, not having finished their building, had gone back to the nearest village where they'd be safe. Well, the moon came up, and the Cobbly came out and prowled around the woods, and pretty soon he smelled the brother in his house and he chuckled to himself—*because our type of Cobblies used to like to eat people alive, taking their time at it.*"

Bill uttered this last sentence in the most impressive and blood-curdling tone that he could manage. He was gratified to receive in answer a sort of low moan of suspense and terror, particularly from the females in the crowd.

"Yes," went on Bill, in an even firmer and more impressive tone of voice, "this Cobbly was just as hungry as a Cobbly had ever been. So he went up to the door of the house made of woven branches and he tried to open the door—"

Another, somewhat louder, low moan of suspense and anguish from the crowd before him.

"But the door held—" said Bill.

There was a grunt, almost of disappointment, from the crowd this time.

"But the Cobbly," said Bill, fixing his audience with his best glittering eye, "wasn't stopped by that. He knocked at the door—" Bill reached up and sounded his knuckles against a log rafter overhead. The crowd of village Dilbians shivered.

"He knocked again. And again," said Bill. "Finally the sound of his knocking woke the brother who was inside the house.

" 'Who's that, knocking?' asked the brother.

" 'It's just a late traveler, asking if you can't put me up for the night,' answered the Cobbly—"

There was a new moan of excitement from the crowd at the duplicity of this answer. Bill continued.

" 'You can't fool me,' answered the brother. 'I know you're the Cobbly that lives in these woods, and that you'd like to get in so that you could eat me up. But I've put too stout a bar on my door, and you can't get through it. And I'm not going to let you in, either. So go about your business and let me sleep.'

" 'Let me in, I tell you!' shouted the Cobbly at that. 'Let me in—or I'll huff, and puff, and I'll blow your house over!'

"At that, the first brother was very much afraid, and he covered his head with his blanket. But the Cobbly outside began to huff and puff—and before you could wink, he'd blown the house over, snatched up the first brother and eaten him!"

The crowd groaned.

"Well," went on Bill. "The Cobbly, full after the meal he'd just had, went home to sleep until the next night. That next night he went hunting again. The third brother had not yet finished building and he'd gone back into town. But the second brother had finished building his house. And he'd built a pretty good house of logs. So when the Cobbly came up and tested that door, he knew by the feel of it that there was no point even in trying to break in that way. So he called out to the second brother, just as he'd called out to the first, saying he was a traveler who'd like to be put up for the night.

" 'You can't fool me!' shouted the second brother. 'I know you're the Cobbly who lives in this woods and who's already eaten one of my brothers. But you can't get in at my front door.'

" 'In that case,' answered the Cobbly, 'I'll just have to huff and puff until I blow your house down, too.'

" 'You can't blow down a house made of logs!' cried the second brother—but in spite of his brave words, he was afraid, and he covered up his head with his blanket just like the first brother had done.

"Meanwhile the Cobbly took a big lung full of air and began to huff, and puff, and huff, and puff—until at last, bang—a log flew out of the wall in front of him, and then another, and then another—and the next thing you knew he'd blown to pieces the house made of logs, and he got in and gobbled up the second brother!"

The groan that arose from the crowd at this point in the story was the deepest and most sincere tribute that tale had received so far.

"The next night," said Bill, and paused dramatically, "the Cobbly went hunting again. He hunted and he hunted, and though he was sure the third brother was there in the forest, he couldn't seem to find where his house had been built. At last, a little ray of light shining

out through the darkness led him to it. It was no wonder the Cobbly hadn't been able to recognize it as a
house. He had passed it two or three times already.
Because this house was made—" Bill paused again and
his audience held its breath, "of stone!"

For a long moment the villagers continued to hold their
breath in automatic anticipation. But then, slowly, expressions of puzzlement grew on their faces. They began to
breathe again. Many of them were casting sidelong glances
at each other, and a muttering began which spread
through the whole group. Finally, from the rear somebody spoke up.

"Did you say of *stone*, Pick-and-Shovel?"

"That's right," said Bill.

"You mean, of pieces of rock?" asked More Jam from
the front ranks.

"That's exactly right," replied Bill. "The third brother
made his walls by starting with large boulders at the bottom, and working up to smaller and smaller rocks, fitting
them together as he went and packing them tight with wet
clay that dried hard after a little while. He bedded his
rafters in the stone walls at each end and then built a roof
of heavy timbers sloping down from a rooftree mounted
on four posts lined up and sunk in the earth inside."

As far as Bill knew, no Dilbian had ever thought of
making a house with walls of stone. Apparently, he noted
now as he watched and listened from the top of his barrel,
the idea was equally as novel to the villagers. It took some
little time for the buzzings of incredulity and amazement
to die down. But at last, they all quieted like interested
children, and he saw their eyes back on him once again.

"Go on, Pick-and-Shovel," said More Jam. "Here the
third brother was inside his house made of stone, and
there was a Cobbly outside knowing he was in there. What
happened next?"

"Well, I suppose you can guess," said Bill, "that Cobbly
just didn't turn around and go away and leave the third
brother alone."

The villagers hummed their understanding and hearty agreement. It would be no sort of Cobbly at all, they obviously thought, who having gobbled up two of three brothers should leave the third brother in peace.

"The Cobbly knocked at the door—it was a wooden door but three bars held it securely on the inside—" began Bill, but this time he was interrupted from the front rank of the audience.

"*Soheknockedonthedoorandsaidhewasatravelerand-askedifhecouldcome-inandthebrothersaidno—*" exploded Perfectly Delightful, plainly unable to stand the suspense any longer.

"That's right," said Bill quickly, before the rest of the audience could jump on the excited Perfectly Delightful for interrupting. "And, of course, the Cobbly replied the same way he had to the first two brothers, saying he'd huff and he'd puff and he'd blow the house over. And do you know what the third brother said?"

Shaking their heads, his audience replied almost as one Dilbian that they did not—not without some hard glances thrown in Perfectly Delightful's direction, although she was insisting on her ignorance as loudly as the rest of them.

"The third brother said," said Bill, " 'You may huff and puff as long as you want, Cobbly, but you won't be able to blow this house over!' And with that, he turned back to his work, which was putting some final clay around the fireplace he had built into one wall of his house."

"Well," went on Bill, "the Cobbly huffed, and he puffed, and he Huffed and he Puffed! And he HUFFED! But he wasn't able to move that house of stone at all."

Spontaneous cheers rose from the inhabitants of Muddy Nose Village at this information.

"But that Cobbly wasn't giving up—" said Bill when the cheering had died down somewhat. Instantly, a new, complete hush prevailed. He felt the Dilbian eyes hard upon him.

"The Cobbly looked at the door and knew he could never get in there," said Bill. "But then the Cobbly looked up at the roof—and what did he see up there? It was the chimney of a fireplace that the third brother had just built. And in the top of it, was an opening leading right down to the inside of the house. So he jumped up on the roof—"

The audience groaned in new dismay.

"He crept up the logs of the roof until he was at the base of the chimney. He climbed up the chimney. He saw the hole was there. And, without stopping to look, he dived right down it!"

The villagers gasped. Bill stood where he was, in silence, letting the image of the Cobbly's springing down the chimney on a defenseless third brother build itself in their minds. Then he spoke again very slowly.

"But—" he said, and paused again, "the third brother had expected something like this. He had already had some twigs and wood ready in the fireplace underneath his cooking pot, and he had the cooking pot, which was a very large one, full of water. When he heard the Cobbly sneaking around the roof and beginning to investigate the chimney, he had lit the fire under the cooking pot. When the Cobbly dived down the chimney, he dived right into the cooking pot, right into the water and drowned. And the third brother cooked him and had him for dinner, instead!"

It must have been doubtful whether Muddy Nose Village in the Lowlands of Dilbia had ever witnessed such a reaction over the happy ending of a story as took place then. Even Bill himself, half-deafened on top of his barrel, where he deemed it prudent to remain—could hardly believe in his own success as storyteller.

"There's just one thing, Pick-and-Shovel," said More Jam, when order was restored. "Didn't you say something about all this having something to do with your grandfather? How does your grandfather come into it?"

"Actually," said Bill, "he was my grandfather several

times removed. And he actually didn't come into it until quite a few years later. You see, after the story of the three brothers got around, a lot of us Shorties started building houses out of stone. It was back at a time called the 'Middle Ages,' back where I come from. They built some stone houses that were as big as this village, and you just couldn't get into them."

There was a momentary mutter of puzzlement from the crowd at this unfamiliar name, but it quieted quickly. Bill found that their attention was still with him.

"Some Shorties," said Bill, with a heavy emphasis "some," "began to take advantage off these big stone houses of theirs that nobody could get into—sort of the way the outlaws and Bone Breaker take advantage of that valley of theirs. So ways had to be found to get into those stone houses, somehow. So my grandfather came up with an idea. You couldn't walk up too close to one of the walls of the stone houses because they'd throw big rocks and things like that down on you from windows high up in them. There were even some houses that had extra walls around them with platforms inside so that people could throw things down on anyone trying to get over the wall from the outside—"

"That's what those outlaws do," muttered a voice from the crowd.

"But you say your grandfather figured a way around that sort of thing?" put in More Jam mildly. The crowd quieted down, waiting for Bill's answer.

"As a matter of fact, he did," said Bill. "He got to thinking, why not make a sort of big shield you could push ahead of you to keep the rocks off and push it up close to the wall, and then start digging inside the shield and dig down and underneath both the shield and the wall and come up on the inside!"

Bill ended on a bright, emphatic note. Then he waited. But there was no reaction from the villagers. They merely stood, staring at him as the seconds slid away into silence. Bill saw More Jam stir and sneak glances to his right and

left, but the fat Dilbian held his silence. It was Flat
Fingers, who finally broke it.

"Well, I'll be chopped!" exclaimed the blacksmith. "Why
didn't we think of that!"

Flat Fingers' words suddenly released the tongues of
the individuals in the staring audience—it was as if a plug
had suddenly been pulled out of a full barrel—comment
and exclamation gushed forth. Suddenly, all the villagers
were talking at once—more than this, they were breaking up into small groups to argue and discuss the matter among themselves.

A crowd of villagers surrounded Flat Fingers, who was
hoarsely giving directions and expounding upon the practical steps that could be taken to build such a shield.

Bill felt a sudden punch on his elbow that staggered
him. He turned swiftly and found himself facing Sweet
Thing, who was apparently trying to get his attention.

"Pick-and-Shovel, listen!" said Sweet Thing urgently.
"I came up here to tell you but you were talking to
everybody at the time, so I had to wait until you were
through!"

"Tell me what?" asked Bill.

"What I saw, of course!" said Sweet Thing. "What do
you think?"

Bill took a strong grip on his patience.

"What did you see, then," he inquired in as calm a tone
as possible.

"Him, of course!" said Sweet Thing exasperatedly.
"Aren't I telling you? And he was sneaking out of the
Residency. Well, I knew he wasn't supposed to be in there
when you weren't in there, so I came right up here to
tell you about it. But you were so busy talking I had to
wait. So I'm telling you now. That Fatty was up to something, as sure as I'm More Jam's daughter!"

"Fatty?" echoed Bill jolted. "You saw Mula—I mean
Barrel Belly coming out of the Residency just now?"

"Just a little while ago, while you were talking. Probably just after you started talking."

Bill felt a sudden, grim uneasiness clutch at him just under his breastbone.

"I'd better go take a look—" he said, and began to head out through the crowd and down the hill. He discovered that Sweet Thing was coming along with him, and thought briefly of telling her to let him investigate alone. Then it occurred to him that it might be handy to have her along in case there was more information about the sighting of Mula-*ay* at the Residency, which she had not yet managed to get out.

At any rate, she stayed beside him as they reached the Residency, and went in through the front door. Nothing seemed amiss in the reception room, so Bill proceeded to go through the rest of the building. Room after room, he found nothing wrong, no evidence of any reason that would explain a visit by the Hemnoid to the human Residency.

It was not until they got clear back into the warehouse and the workshop corner where the program lathe and other tools were racked and hung on the walls that Bill got his first feeling that something was wrong. He stopped, facing the workshop corner, and slowly ran his eyes over it. What was different about what he was seeing now from what he had seen when he was last here? For a long moment he was unable to identify that difference. Then suddenly an empty space on one of the tool-hung walls seemed to leap at him.

Where the empty space was, the hand-laser welding torch had hung. It hung there no longer.

"What's the matter, Pick-and-Shovel?" demanded Sweet Thing, almost crossly, in his right ear. "What are you just standing there like that for?"

He hardly heard her. Understanding had leaped upon him like a wolf from the underbrush. Mula-*ay* knew that Bill had gone down into the valley the night before. He also knew that now all the village Dilbians knew it, and shortly the whole countryside would know it. The connection between that knowledge and the missing laser

torch flashed suddenly white and clear upon Bill's mind.
That torch could kill, its murderous beam slicing through
the bone and muscle of a Dilbian back to a Dilbian heart,
from as much as fifteen feet away. With that torch, this
coming night, back in the valley, Mula-*ay* could find a
moment when Bone Breaker was out between the houses,
alone in the darkness. He could torch the outlaw chief
from behind, and leave him there with the obviously
Shorty-made weapon beside him. After that no one could
blame the Dilbians for believing that Bill had once more
reentered the valley and avoided a duel by killing his
opponent in the most cowardly and treaty-breaking way
possible.

Bill jerked suddenly out of his thoughts and spun on
one heel. He had to catch Mula-*ay* before Mula-*ay* could
get back into the outlaw valley.

Then his shoulders sagged, and his spirits with them.
He remembered now how long he had gone on talking
after first spotting Sweet Thing in the crowd, standing
beside More Jam. Mula-*ay* would have too much of a
head start. There was no hope of Bill catching him before
he was safe back behind the gates and the stockade of
Outlaw Valley. And the villagers would never be able to
finish making their shield, get it up against the outlaw
wall, and dig in to the valley under the stockade wall
before night would put a halt to that operation.

Mula-*ay* would be left safely behind that stockade wall
in Outlaw Valley as night came down. And a word from
him to Bone Breaker would be enough to set sentinels
on watch, so that Bill could not safely climb down the
cliffs a second time to warn the outlaw chief.

Chapter 22

Sweet Thing was still demanding to know what was wrong with him. Bill collected his wits. He pointed at the empty space on the wall.

"There's a thing gone," he said to her. "A sort of a Shorty thing, but if Mula-*ay* uses it, he could hurt somebody. And he's already got a head start toward the valley so that we couldn't catch up with him and get it back from him."

"But what'll we do now?" said Sweet Thing.

"Why don't you tell your father to wander out and into the outlaw camp," suggested Bill. "He can keep an eye on Mula-*ay* without letting anyone know what's up, and if Mula-*ay* tries to do anything with the thing, he can set up an alarm."

"Set up an alarm, huh!" said Sweet Thing scornfully. "If Barrel Belly tries anything with that thing, whatever it is, my dad would just jump him—from behind, of course, so as not to get hurt by the thing—and squash him!"

"Ah—yes," agreed Bill warily. Personally, he had little faith that any Dilbian, even Bone Breaker himself, would come close to being a match with the massive, heavy-gravity muscles of the Hemnoid. More Jam may have been something of a terror in his youth, but he was old now, and he was fat—there was no gainsaying those two points. Bill did not share Sweet Thing's daughterly confidence in More Jam's physical abilities. But on the other hand, More Jam was as wily as anyone among the Dilbians, and not likely to let himself be trapped into a match with somebody who could easily overpower him.

"I'll go right away," said Sweet Thing, and not wasting any time about it, she turned and barreled out of the room. Well, he thought, that was that. But it was not much. The situation called for more active measures than simply sending More Jam to keep an eye on Mula-*ay*.

It was still only midmorning, but there was no hope of getting the villagers up to and under the stockade barring the entrance to the valley before night fell. And once night had fallen, it was an odds-on chance that Mula-*ay* would be able to evade More Jam long enough to kill Bone Breaker.

Something must be done—and it must be done before sundown. Bill thought about the plan of attack on which he had sold the villagers, running over it in his mind to see if there was not some way by which it might be speeded up so that they could take the valley this same day, while daylight lasted. But it was just not possible.

Suddenly he jumped to his feet with an almost Dilbian-like snort of triumph. It was true the mantelet and sapping operation . . . which was the technical, military term for the tactic he had explained to the villagers—would not breach the Outlaw Valley's defenses before nightfall. But he had forgotten entirely that the Middle Ages had had other, even simpler ways of taking castles by storm.

He had forgotten, in fact, the most obvious one of them all.

He turned and hurried out of the Residency, and back up the road to the blacksmith shop, which was now a-swarm with male Dilbians from the village and the farms around, most of them with weapons of some sort— ranging from actual swords down to axes, and heavy-handled native scythes. The Bluffer was looking on interestedly as Flat Fingers supervised the construction of the mantelet, or shield, which Bill had described. Bill slowed his headlong pace and sauntered up to the group. As usual, it was a few seconds before the Dilbians looked down and noticed him standing there.

"Oh, there you are, Pick-and-Shovel," said the blacksmith. What do you think—shouldn't the skids be longer, there, under the back of the shield?"

Bill examined the structure. It looked to his human eye to be nearly as tall, wide, and heavy as the actual stockade fence of the outlaws themselves. Only the brute muscles of the Dilbians could entertain the thought of using such a thing, let alone transporting it through the several miles of woods that separated the village from the valley entrance. It was evidently designed to be moved on three pointed logs which served as its base and would operate as skids or runners on which the weight of the shield would bear, as it would push toward the wall. The shield was set just behind the points of these logs, slop-ing backward, and was heavily braced, towering to per-haps fifteen feet above the logs at its upper edge. Bill smiled agreeably at the sight of it, and nodded his head vigorously.

"That's just fine, Flat Fingers," he said. "The men pushing it certainly ought to be safe behind that, as they go up to the wall. Yes, it'll be good protection, that shield. There's nothing like being *safe*, when you attack a bunch like those outlaws."

"Well, it'll get us in close all right," said the blacksmith, though he frowned a little at Bill's second repetition on the word "safe." "Then once we're close, we'll dig under and tear into them."

That's the spirit!" said Bill enthusiastically. "Guard yourself as much as possible until you get inside, and then tear into them. Don't be disappointed if it takes a little while to dig under the wall. Better to be safe than sorry, I always say."

"Oh, we won't be disappointed, Pick-and-Shovel," rumbled Flat Fingers grimly. "We've been waiting to tangle with those outlaws too long to cool down, just because we have to do a little digging to get at them."

"Good, good!" said Bill strongly. "I know you are. But it doesn't do any harm to play safe, does it?"

"What do you mean *'play safe'*?" exploded the village blacksmith. "What's all this about, 'playing safe' you keep talking about. We're going in there to tangle with those outlaws, the sooner the better!"

"Of course you are!" replied Bill hastily. He saw the Bluffer's face approach and peer interestedly down at him over the left shoulder of the blacksmith. Bill went on. "There's just no point in getting any more men hurt than have to be. That's why I suggested this way of getting into the valley. After all, it's the safest way, even if it does take a longer time than some other ways."

"What other ways?" roared Flat Fingers. "You mean to say there's other ways—quicker ways? Ways you didn't tell us about because you thought we were worried about keeping *safe*?"

"There's lots of other ways, of course," said Bill. "But after all, as I understand it, man for man those outlaws are a lot tougher than you are—"

"Who says so?" roared one of the Dilbians who had been working on the shield. He was holding an ax which he flourished in Bill's direction in a way that made Bill's throat go dry. Suddenly there was bedlam, all of the village males shouting at Bill. Flat Fingers bellowed them all back into silence, then turned ominously back to face Bill.

"Now, you listen to me, Pick-and-Shovel!" said Flat

Fingers. "We're all Muddy Nosers, here—the sort of men here who'd tear that wall down with our bare hands, if we thought it could be done that way! Are you trying to start trouble—or something?"

"Why, no—of course not!" said Bill hastily. "Why, I'll be glad to tell you of the quicker ways to get in through the gates in that stockade. As I say, there's lot of them—"

"What's the quickest?" demanded Flat Fingers.

"The quickest?" echoed Bill. "Well, the quickest would be to use a tree trunk."

The assemblage of Dilbians stared at him blankly. It was hard for Bill to believe that their minds did not spring immediately from his suggestion of using a tree trunk to the idea of using it as a battering ram against the gates. The concept was so obvious to him that it was hard to see how it could not be obvious to these Dilbians.

"You take a log," explained Bill. "You trim off all the branches, except for a few that you leave along its length for handholds. Then you get as many men to pick up the log all at the same time as you can. Then, holding the log, they run at the gates in the stockade end-on."

To his surprise, the Dilbians continued to stare at Bill, after he had stopped speaking, with blank or puzzled looks.

"And what'll that do, Pick-and-Shovel?" asked Flat Fingers finally.

"Stop and think," answered Bill, "and you can imagine it for yourself. Suppose we had a bunch of men pick up one of those logs over there"—he pointed to the pile of loose logs on which he climbed the day before to hang the block and pulley from the rafter—"and ran that log at you, end-on, as hard as they could. What do you think the end of that log would do to you—or to anything else that it hit?"

For a long moment, it seemed that Flat Fingers still did not understand. Then, very slowly, his expression began to change. His eyes opened wide, his jaw dropped, his nostrils spread—and without warning he let out a war whoop that seemed to split Bill's eardrums—and leave him slightly deaf for several seconds.

At that, it was probably just as well that he did not have the full sense of his hearing in the moments that followed. Because, in a second Flat Fingers was explaining to the rest of the villagers, and inside of two minutes the area was bedlam again. Villagers whooped, hollered, roared with laughter, and pounded each other on the back as they described the principle behind the use of a tree trunk as a battering ram.

"Let's go!" trumpeted Flat Fingers, making himself heard over the rest of the din. "We don't need to take a log to them. We can chop one down when we get there!"

Take off, they did. Bill, staring after them in a sort of deafened wonder, was in danger of being left behind as they streamed off from the village into the woods at a pace that his shorter human legs could not match. But, abruptly, he felt himself snatched up and sailed through the air to land with a thud in the saddle on the Hill Bluffer's back.

"Hang on, Pick-and-Shovel!" the postman shouted, infected himself by the general excitement. "We'll be up with the ones in the lead in two minutes."

Chapter 23

Having said this, the Bluffer proceeded to increase Bill's steadily growing respect for him by proving himself almost as good as his word. In his ride on the Bluffer before, Bill had somehow come to assume that the pace at which they traveled was pretty close to the practical limit for the Dilbian beneath him, considering the burden he was bearing on his back. In short, Bill had not experienced the Hill Bluffer's running before. But now the postman set out to stretch his legs—and the result from Bill's point of view was awesome. The landscape whizzed by at something between twenty-five and thirty-five miles an hour. And the jolting threatened to shake Bill out of the saddle within the first fifty yards.

Luckily for him, however, once the Bluffer had caught up with the leaders of the group, he dropped back to a rapid walking pace, which was a good deal easier on his rider.

Bill unlocked his legs and arms from the straps and sat

up. He looked back over his shoulder. The whole village seemed to be streaming after them. The citizens of Muddy Nose were on the march at last against the outlaws.

In the front strode the biggest and best males of the community, literally tramping out a path through the brush, and chopping down small trees that impeded their way. They detoured only around the larger trunks. Behind them came the younger members of the community and the village women, flanked on both sides and followed by a rear guard of lesser and older Dilbian males. Then Flat Fingers began to sing, and the others took it up until the whole party was joining in.

The subject matter of the song—or chant—was nothing remarkable. It seemed to deal with an individual who had a perfect mania for throwing other individuals and things down his well. But it seemed to please its singers vastly.

> *Souse-Nose's wife's old uncle*
> *He liked his grub real well.*
> *One day he came to visit,*
> *And said, "I'll stay a spell."*
> *"Oh, no you won't!" said Souse-Nose*
> *And he threw him down the well!*

> *—Threw him down the well!*
> *Now wasn't that a sight?*
> *He threw him down the well so far*
> *That he was out of sight!*

> *Souse-Nose's wife saw him do this*
> *And she let out a yell.*
> *"What do you mean by doing that?*
> *I love my uncle well!"*
> *"Then go with him!" said Souse-Nose*
> *And he threw her down the well!*

> *—Threw her down the well . . . etc.*

After disposing of his wife's uncle and his wife, Souse-Nose rapidly threw down the well, according to the song, a number of other relatives, some neighbors he didn't like, a hammer that had dropped on his toe the week before, the family cooking pot (because it was empty)—and then proceeded to start throwing down the well various individuals among the marching villagers themselves, as the singers began to pick on each other.

It was all apparently hilariously funny to the Dilbians—but at the same time, Bill felt a slight shiver run down his back. The song was a humorous song, but it was also a grimly humorous one, and the tone in which it was sung was very nearly more grim than it was humorous. In fact, for all the comedy in the words, Bill realized that what he was listening to was the Dilbian equivalent of a war song. The villagers were working themselves up emotionally for combat with the outlaws. For the first time, Bill began to feel some misgivings about the forces he had set in motion. Leaning forward, he spoke into the Hill Bluffer's right ear.

"Bluffer—" he said. "Bluffer, listen to me for a moment, will you. I'd like to ask you something—"

But he might as well have been speaking to some ten-foot-high boulder rumbling at the head of an avalanche. The Bluffer was roaring out the song about Souse-Nose with the rest, completely carried away by it.

Bill sat back in the saddle, abruptly prey to a new fear. If the Bluffer was beyond his control—how about Flat Fingers and the rest of the villagers? The rolling chant of the voices around him was hypnotic—even Bill himself felt his breath coming quicker and the blood pounding in his ears.

He was still fighting for self-control, when the Bluffer beneath him, with the other leaders of the village party, rounded the turn into the narrow ravine that led down to the entrance to the valley, and stopped.

Before them, the gates in the stockade were already shut and barred, and the heads of outlaws, as well as the

upper rims of shields were showing over the points at the
upper end of the upright logs which made up the stockade. There was nothing surprising in finding the valley
prepared in this way. Singing and marching as they had
been, the villagers undoubtedly had been heard a good
half-mile or more off. Now, a few furry arms swung in
the air above the stockade, and a few good-sized stones
sailed toward the front rank of the villagers—but fell short.
In reply, the villagers crowded into the narrow entrance
of the valley and began to sing about outlaws being thrown
down the well. The outlaws shouted back insults and
challenges, but the solid chorus of the villagers overwhelmed them.

> ... *Throw you down the well so far,*
> *That you are out of sight* ...

—chanted the villagers.

Meanwhile, Flat Fingers had ceased singing and was
rapidly issuing orders. A team of axmen had already
headed off into the woods nearby, and the sound of
chopping could occasionally be heard in the moments of
relative silence between the singing of the villagers and
the insults hurled by the outlaws. Shortly, there was the
crash of falling timber—followed by a male-voiced cheer
that drowned out even the singing.

Then the sound of chopping began again. Shortly, the
team returned, carrying at least thirty feet of tree trunk
two feet in diameter. Here and there along the trunk, they
had left the stubs of branches for handholds. But most
of those carrying the logs simply had one large hairy arm
wrapped around it, and they grinned savagely at each
other and at the outlaws.

The Bluffer squatted down and let Bill slip off his back.
Bill started to approach Flat Fingers—but at this moment
there was a sudden crashing sound from the forest behind
them, as if a second tree was falling and everybody turned
around. A moment later, a second party came trotting up,

carrying a second trunk stripped down to little stubs of branches for handholds.

"No you don't!" roared Flat Fingers, waving them back. "One at a time! Here, lay that other pole up against the side of the cut, and give us some room."

The blacksmith's huge finger indicated the vertical rock wall that formed one side of the narrow entrance to the valley. Reluctantly, the second batch of Dilbians leaned their log up against this and fell back.

"All right, the rest of you!" shouted the Bluffer to the rest of them standing around. "Here we go! Ready with those rocks!"

Bill had noticed these others arming themselves with rocks—and in some cases, the very ones that had been thrown at them from behind the stockade. Now, looking again, he saw that almost everyone who was not on the battering-ram crew had at least two or three of these missiles in his or her hands.

"Shields, here!" bellowed Flat Fingers. Those of the battering-ram crew who already had shields swung them up into position overhead. The rest hastily borrowed shields from friends or relatives standing around and did likewise.

"All right, then!" cried the blacksmith, taking his place at the head of the battering-ram crew. "Here we go-o-o . . ."

The last word ended in a long, drawn-out howl, as the battering-ram crew started off at full speed toward the gate of the stockade. In a black furred wave behind them, surged the rest of the Dilbians—but they surged only to within throwing distance of the stockade wall, and began to loose a literal barrage of rocks.

The heads of the outlaws to be seen above the points of the stockade ducked hastily down out of sight as the first flight of stones reached them. They stayed down. Meanwhile, the battering-ram crew was carrying on full tilt for the gate in the very center of the stockade. For a moment, they seemed to be galloping away and making no progress. But a moment later, they loomed over the gate, and a second later, they struck it. The results were all but unbelievable.

The gate split from top to bottom with a sound like a crack of thunder. But this was the least spectacular of the results of the impact. The battering-ram crew, shaken loose by the impact, piled up against the gate and the walls of the stockade themselves, like so many Dilbian-furred missiles. As a result, not merely the gate but the whole stockade wall quivered and shook like a fence of saplings.

There were glimpses of hairy arms thrown in the air briefly above the stockade's points, as the outlaws on the catwalk inside were shaken loose and dumped backward. Evidently, not one of them up there had been able to retain his grip, for although the stones had stopped flying from the crowd of Muddy Nosers, not one head made its reappearance above the stockade wall.

"*All right—up and at it!*" Flat Fingers was shouting, down by the gate, as he scrambled himself to his feet. "*On your feet and let's hit it again!*"

The battering-ram crew recollected itself, picked up its log, and began to swing its front end rhythmically against the cracked gate. With each blow, the entrance to the valley resounded, and gate and wall shivered together. Slowly the crack widened, and another crack split the door into three pieces. Around Bill, back at a stone's throw distance from the gate, the rest of the villagers were going wild with triumph, and the din was deafening.

A cold feeling clutched suddenly at Bill's chest. He had not fully imagined the violence and excitement that surrounded him now. He had not planned to get outlaws and villagers killed or maimed—

The sudden, hard poke by something rigid behind him, sent him stumbling forward half a step. He spun about, swiftly and angrily, to find himself confronting Sweet Thing. She was carrying a rectangular shield and a sword slung in its supporting strap, both of which were too small for any Dilbian's use.

"Well, put them on!" hissed Sweet Thing, almost in his ear. "Flat Fingers left them behind, but I went back and got them. They're yours, Pick-and-Shovel! Put them on, will you? You can't fight Bone Breaker without them, and you're the only one who can stop the war by fighting him!"

She thrust shield and sword at Bill. Bill found himself numbly taking them and strapping the sword around him. The shield, fitted with an elbow loop and a hand grip and made of inch-thick wood covered with half-inch hide, dragged his left arm groundward when he tried to hold it up in proper fashion.

He—? Stop the war—? His head whirling, he stared about him at the shouting, leaping villagers as they cheered on the battering ram crew down at the gates.

Of course! Suddenly the whole Dilbian picture fell into place. Suddenly he understood everything, including why he had been assigned here and then apparently abandoned by Greenleaf and his other superiors! He turned and looked about him. The second battering ram still leaned against the rock wall of the valley entrance, a little ways off.

"Here, hold this," Bill grunted, shoving the sword and shield back into Sweet Thing's hands. He turned and ran for the tree trunk leaning against the cliff, and went quickly up it, using the handholds almost as the rungs on a ladder. Twenty feet above the heads of the Dilbians below he stared down and over the top of the stockade into the valley beyond.

He saw that there were no outlaws inside the gate now. The tall, coal-black figure of Bone Breaker was in the center of a line that was drawn up perhaps halfway between the gate and the outlaw buildings. They were all armed and ready. The noon sun glinted on six-foot swords, and the shiny metal of an occasional piece of body armor or protective cap. Behind the line, back

by the buildings themselves, was a small knot of outlaw women, and close to them was a round figure in
a yellow robe whom Bill had no difficulty in recogniz-
ing as Mula-*ay*. As he watched, Mula-*ay* lifted something
to his face that winked in the sunlight in Bill's direction. A second later, the Hemnoid's hands lifted and
flicked outward in a human, military-type of salute. It
was the kind of gesture only a human being would be
able to recognize for what it was. Mula-*ay* was thumbing
his nose at Bill from the distance, and, having done so,
Mula-*ay* turned about and disappeared around the corner
of the eating hall.

In spite of his new understanding, the coldness in Bill's
chest tightened into a hard, unmeltable lump. Bluff and
bluster made up a large part of the Dilbian nature, but
only up to a point. Now, neither the villagers nor the
outlaws were bluffing—or at least, only half-bluffing.

Mula-*ay* had caught Bill neatly in a trap. He had known
that taking the laser-welding gun might stampede Bill into
inciting the villagers to just such an attack as this. An
attack in which both outlaws and villagers would be killed
or hurt. It was not necessary for the Hemnoid to risk
killing Bone Breaker himself in order to get rid of Bill
and discredit humans on Dilbia. All he had to do was wait
for the attacking villagers to come to grips with the outlaws—and this Mula-*ay* must have planned from the very
moment in which he decided to take the laser-welding
gun.

There was only one solution to the situation now. The
hard way out that had been available to Bill from the
beginning. Only at the beginning he had not understood
the way Dilbian minds worked. Now he was sure he did,
and it was that extra knowledge that gave him his advantage over the Hemnoid, who not only did not understand,
but was racially incapable of understanding.

Bill skidded hastily down the tree trunk. He ran back
to Sweet Thing and snatched the shield from her. It was
quite true, what she had said. Only he could stop the war.

"Where's the Hill Bluffer?" he demanded urgently. "Help me find him!"

"There he is!" she shouted, and started for him. Bill ran after her.

The lanky postman was standing a little apart from the group, his eyes fixed and all his attention riveted on the battering-ram crew, which had now widened the original split in the gate to the point where only the bars beyond it were holding its planks together. Sweet Thing punched the Bluffer unceremoniously in the ribs, and he twisted about, angrily.

"Pick-and-Shovel!" said Sweet Thing economically, jerking her thumb back at Bill as he came pounding up.

"Bluffer," panted Bill, "I've got to get down into the valley before anybody else does, so I can reach Bone Breaker first. Can you get me to him?"

For a moment the Hill Bluffer stared as if he did not understand. Then, with a sudden whoop of joy and excitement, he reached out, picked up Bill and all but tossed him over a furry shoulder into the saddle. Bill grabbed for the straps, as the Bluffer pivoted on one heel and ran down toward the gate, which was beginning to disintegrate under the impact of the battering-ram crew.

It did, in fact disintegrate, falling apart in a shower of broken wood, just as the Bluffer reached the crew. Without pausing, the Bluffer hurdled the nearest member of the crew, who had collapsed, out of breath, wheezing on the grass, and ran directly toward the center of the armed and ready outlaw line, where the massive, black-furred figure of Bone Breaker towered, waiting with shield and sword.

Bill glanced over his shoulder, waited until they were midway between the gate and the outlaw line, and then shouted to the Bluffer to halt. As the postman did so, Bill jumped from the saddle and landed clanking with shield on the turf. Turning so that he could face first left toward the outlaws and then right toward the villagers who were now beginning to pour through the broken doorway, Bill shouted to them all—and a second later the powerful Dilbian lungs of the Hill Bluffer took up his shout and repeated it, so that it was plainly to be heard in the silence that had fallen over both attackers and defenders.

"Stop the war!" he shouted. "None of you are going to tangle on either side until I've first had my own personal crack at Bone Breaker!"

Chapter 24

It was only then that Bill realized he did not have his sword.

He had left it back in the hands of Sweet Thing. However, it seemed that the apparent ridiculousness of one unarmed small Shorty standing between opposing lines of armed giants and calling on them to give over the idea of fighting, apparently did not strike home to the Dilbians. Even as Bill looked, the outlaws on either side of Bone Breaker were relaxing, sheathing their swords and ambling forward. Looking in the other direction, he saw the villagers pouring through the broken gate, but also without signs of hostility. Two groups met and mingled around Bill as with the Hill Bluffer he went forward toward Bone Breaker, who stood still, waiting.

When Bill and the Bluffer reached him, the outlaw chief turned abruptly on his heel.

"Come on!" he said to Bill, and strode off toward the buildings. Bill, the Bluffer, and everybody else followed.

Bone Breaker stopped at last beside a long, narrow building, with only one or two windows, and a door at each end. Bill recognized it as the storehouse into the shadow of which Anita had led him that night when he had climbed down the cliff to see her. It was here that they had talked. Now Bone Breaker had brought him back here for their duel. Close up, now, he loomed over Bill like a mountain.

"Here's your sword—" muttered Sweet Thing's voice abruptly in his ear, and he half-turned to receive the hilt of his sword thrust into his palm. The leather-wrapped hilt was cold to his grasp and the weight of the sword seemed to drag down at his arm, even though it was less than half the length of Bone Breaker's great blade. In spite of his certainty that he had now figured matters out, it was a calculated gamble he was taking here; and the fact that it was calculated did not lessen the fact that it was a gamble.

"All right, Bone Breaker," he said, speaking as loudly and scornfully as he could, "how do you want it?"

"I'll tell you how I want it," retorted Bone Breaker. He pointed at the warehouse beside them. "I had the windows in there blocked off yesterday. The place is full of stuff, but there's room to get from one end to the other. I'll go in at this end—you go in at that. And the first one out the other end on his two feet wins. Right?"

"Right!" said Bill, glancing at the storehouse with a queasy feeling. He heard the crowd behind him making guesses as to the outcome of the duel. Although there was a small minority that seemed to feel that you should never sell a Shorty short, most of them seemed firmly convinced that Bone Breaker would have no trouble at all encountering Bill in the gloom of the darkened building, and chopping him into small pieces.

Meanwhile, there was no hanging back. Bone Breaker had already headed off toward one end of the building.

Bill turned, with the Bluffer beside him, and headed for the other. The crowd made way for him as he went. They came to the end of the building and rounded it to find three wooden steps leading up to a heavy door. With a tight throat, which his inner confidence did not seem to help, Bill mounted the steps.

"Good luck—" he heard the Bluffer say. Then he had opened the door and was through it, stepping into a darkness heavy with a mixed odor of leather, wood, root vegetables, and other dusty smells.

The door banged shut behind him.

He stood. The sword was in his hand now, and now its handle felt slippery in his grasp. He waited for his eyes to adjust somewhat to the darkness, but for a couple of long minutes it seemed that even with their pupils at full dilation he would not be able to make out any of his surroundings. Then, slowly, vague shapes of darker black began to emerge out of the general gloom. He made out finally that he stood in a little cleared space, facing what seemed to be a corridor between ten- to fifteen-foot piles of assorted, unidentifiable objects.

The rattle of something displaced and rolling across a wooden floor sounded distantly, without warning, from the far end of the building. Bill froze. For a moment he was conscious only of the heavy pounding of his heart, and the heavy weight of the sword and shield on his arms. Then he began to breathe again.

That sound, unintentional or not, was adequate announcement that Bone Breaker was coming in his direction. Bill could not simply stay here and wait for him. It was necessary to go and meet the outlaw chief.

Cautiously, Bill began to inch his way forward down the corridor between the high piled contents of the storehouse.

The corridor was nothing but a lane connecting a series of spaces between stored goods. Occasionally the lane widened out into areas that were certainly big enough to give room for a sword fight between a Dilbian and a human. Again, it narrowed down so that a Dilbian, at least, would have had to go sideways to make his way through. But there was never any more than the one path among the things piled up. There was to be no chance, apparently, for Bill to sneak past his larger opponent without meeting him face to face.

Bill heard no more sounds from the far end of the building to inform him of Bone Breaker's progress toward him. But under Bill's own feet, the boards of the building's flooring occasionally creaked, and once or twice he stumbled over something lying in the path, with some little noise.

Each time he did so, he stopped still, sweating and listening. But there was nothing to be heard from the far end of the building to let him know whether Bone Breaker had heard him, or not.

By this time, Bill had covered some little distance. He found himself wishing that he had measured the building with his eye before going in, and then counted his steps once he was in, so that he would have an approximate idea of how far along its length he had traveled. It seemed to him that he must have reached the middle of the building by this time. But he had not yet encountered Bone Breaker, and certainly the outlaw chief would meet him at least halfway?

Bill went on, making his way, sword extended point first, before him along the narrow aisle of darkness. Still— there was no sign of the outlaw chief. By now, Bill was sure that he had covered at least half the length of the building. The only possible conclusion was that somewhere up ahead of him the huge Dilbian was waiting at some convenient place of his own choosing. And still, in the face of that conclusion, there remained nothing for Bill to do but to keep moving forward.

Surprisingly, however, this new conclusion of Bill's did not increase his tension or his emotion. In fact, a good deal of the downright fear and uncertainty he had felt on stepping into the dark building was beginning to slip away from him now. The handle of the sword no longer felt slippery with perspiration in his grip. His heart had slowed and calmed in its beating. There was even beginning to kindle in him now a sort of warm grimness of purpose—a readiness, foolish as it seemed—to be ready to fight back, if Bone Breaker should, after all, suddenly spring upon him out of the further shadows.

The Dilbian was huge—but that very hugeness, thought Bill, out of this new grim warmth inside him, made the outlaw chief clumsy in comparison with a human. If Bill could manage to dodge the first devastating blow of that man-long sword in Bone Breaker's grasp, it might be that he could get in under the other's guard and do something with his own small sword before his opponent could recover. If it came to that, it would probably be wise to throw away his shield the minute they came together, thought Bill. A shield was of some use to a Dilbian who could use it to deflect a blow from another's sword blade, but for a human to even be brushed by such a Dilbian weapon would be disaster. Bill would do a better job of running and dodging without the shield on his arm. Inspiration struck him suddenly—as long as he had to throw it, he would throw it at Bone Breaker. There might be a way of gaining some small advantage out of the surprise element of such a maneuver. What were the terms of the duel, as Bone Breaker had said before they went in the building?

"The *first* one out of the building on his feet . . ."

If it were possible for Bill to dodge the first assault of Bone Breaker, trip the big Dilbian up somehow, and get past him; a quick rush could carry Bill to the door at the end of the building and out—

Less than fifteen feet in front of Bill, there was a sudden rattle of something set rolling by the movement of an incautious foot.

Bill checked, suddenly taut in nerves and muscles. Directly in front of him, the corridor was narrow, but a little beyond—Bill screened his eyes against the dimness—

it seemed as if the corridor might open up again into one of its wide spaces. If that were true, it was from that wide space that the sound Bill had heard had just now come. It was there that Bone Breaker was waiting for him.

Bill reached out with the back of his sword hand to explore by touch both sides of the aisle, without letting go of his weapon. To his left were sacks full of some hard, lumpy objects, too heavy to lift, and stacked clear to the ceiling—he had had some thought of climbing up on them and approaching the open space across their top. To his right, was a stack of logs, their farther ends reaching off ahead of him into darkness. These were not stacked more than halfway to the ceiling, barely above Bill's head—their top would be shoulder-high on Bone Breaker. Bill took hold of one of them, testing it by putting his weight on it—and it shifted slightly.

Hastily, he let go. A log rolling from under him, as he attempted to creep along it, would not only destroy the surprise approach he planned, but possibly leave him helpless at Bone Breaker's feet. There was nothing forward but to continue creeping along the aisle as quietly as possible and hope to steal upon the waiting Dilbian, before Bone Breaker knew he was close.

Accordingly, Bill inched forward, setting his feet down lightly and only gradually shifting his weight upon them. He was lucky—no boards creaked as that weight came on them. Slowly, in this manner, he stole forward until he reached the point where the aisle widened.

Unexpectedly, the foot he reached forward stubbed its toe against something hard above floor level. Bill stopped, trying to hover in mid-air and bent forward to inspect by touch what he had encountered. It was the end of a log, evidently fallen off the pile and angling up ahead into the darkness. Cautiously, Bill began to circle around it, holding his breath.

Where was Bone Breaker? The wide space in which Bill stood now, was more open than any he had encountered so far. To his left the sacks of hard lumpy objects had completely disappeared. It was evidently clear to the far wall of the narrow building. To his right the logs appeared to have changed their orderly piling for a dim tangle, from which several of them had rolled out onto the floor. Bill began carefully to pick his way among them.

Suddenly, he stopped. His foot had come down on something yielding. He snatched it up again and stood on one leg, like a crane.

But nothing happened. After a moment he reached down with the back of his sword hand toward the object on which he had stepped.

For a moment he felt nothing, then the skin on the back of his hand came in contact with the coarse curly fur of a Dilbian. It was motionless to his touch. Shock raced through him. Hastily he shifted his sword to his shield hand, and reached down to feel what he had touched.

It was a large, motionless, Dilbian foot pointing up at the ceiling and attached to a leg stretched out upon the floor.

"What—" began Bill, incautiously speaking out loud. Then, abruptly, everything happened at once.

With an ear-splitting roar and a rumble, the murky tangle of logs at his right suddenly seemed to disintegrate, falling and rolling about with great noise. Bill leaped away from the pile, but, curiously, none of the logs rolled in his direction. After what seemed like several minutes, but was only probably a second or two, the sound and motion ceased. But now the darkness was reinforced by a thick cloud of dust raised by the falling logs. Bill sneezed loudly.

It was a moment before he got his wits back. When he did, he stepped back and searched about for the Dilbian foot and leg with which he had been in contact just before the logs fell. After some groping he found it, lying just as motionless as before. He groped his way up along it, and eventually made out that what he was touching was Bone Breaker, lying silent and apparently unconscious underneath a log.

Bill stood up quickly. He had no intention of looking a gift horse in the mouth. Taking his sword in his right hand, he turned and raced toward the farther entrance of the building, that one through which the outlaw chief had entered. That door, with the line of light around it, dimly illuminating that end of the building to Bill's now darkness-adjusted eyes, loomed in a little open space of its own, not more than twenty feet away. Bill made that opening in three running strides—and burst out from the mouth of the narrow aisle just in time to catch sight, out of the corner of his right eye, of the glint of whirling steel descending upon him.

He jumped away, throwing up his own sword instinctively. In the same instant it was hammered from his grasp, as if that grasp had been the grip of a child, and sent flying against the wall behind him. Something terrifically hard crashed against the side of his head, and he staggered back until the wall itself stopped him from falling.

Blood was streaming down onto his face, half blinding him.

He grabbed his sword from the floor instinctively, and raised his head to face his attacker. The end of the building was swimming around him, but the sight that greeted his eyes from the leakage of daylight around the door, brought him to a halt.

Facing him, half-held in mid-air and with Bone Breaker's great sword just now dropping from his paralyzed grasp, was the yellow robed figure of Mula-*ay*. But he was neither attacking nor making a sound—and for very good reason.

Around his waist, pinning one arm to his side and enclosing the wrist of the other, sword-carrying arm in a crushing grip, was a black-furred forearm the size of a young watermain. Another black-furred arm encircled the Hemnoid's thick throat in a choke hold, and above that choke hold Mula-*ay*'s eyes were popping and his mouth was gasping for breath. Over the Hemnoid's shoulder grinned the ferociously cheerful, round features of More Jam.

For just a moment, Bill goggled at the sight. He would not have believed that any Dilbian on the planet could not only have overpowered Mula-*ay*, but lifted him right off his feet in the process. If More Jam was capable of something like this now, what indeed had he been like as a wrestler in the days of his youth?

But it was not a sight that Bill could stay to enjoy. The building was swaying around him now like a ship upon heavy seas, and his strength was beginning to desert him. At all costs he must make it out of the door of the building.

He turned and staggered toward the door. He had to drop his shield to get it open, but he hung onto his grip on his sword as he staggered down the steps, into the blinding, sudden sunlight. Into the center of a circle of black, furry faces that danced and wavered around him.

Barely, he heard the mounting cheer that went up from those faces. Suddenly, the whole earth and crowd and sunlit sky whirled about him; and he tumbled, sprawling forward into darkness.

At some indefinable time later, he swam up briefly from the darkness to find himself lying on a human-style bed, within the white walls of a room. The walls shimmered, advancing and retreating to his unsteady eyes. A face moved into his field of vision. It was the face of Anita and it seemed to Bill to be the most beautiful face he had ever seen. It too wavered in unreliable fashion.

There was a touch of something cold and wet against his forehead and the side of his head. Anita seemed to be sponging him off with something.

"Is this a hospital ship?" he croaked.

"Certainly not!" replied Anita, and her voice was strangely choked. "You're back at the Residency. You don't need a hospital ship. There's nothing wrong with you I can't fix. I've got a medical assistance certificate."

He looked at her wonderingly.

"Is there anything you haven't got?" he asked her.

To his surprise, she burst into tears.

"Oh shut up!" she said, threw the cloth, or whatever it was she had in her hand, into the basin where she had been dampening it, and ran out of the room.

Startled, baffled, dismayed, Bill tried to push himself up on his elbows to call after her. But as he lifted his head, a heavy weight seemed to swing from the inside front of his skull and smashed dizzyingly against the inside of the same skull at its back. Unconsciousness rose and sucked him down into it once more.

Chapter 25

"—Then you'll be going back to Earth with me for debriefing?" asked Bill, delighted.

"I will be traveling on the same ship, if that is what you mean," replied Anita, very coldly and distinctly.

She turned and marched off toward the courier ship lying lengthwise on the grass in the center of the meadow. It was a sleek, heavily built ninety-footer, capable of interstellar travel on its own; and its size, which was several times that of the usual shuttle boat, had attracted the attention of several Dilbians, who were now examining it curiously.

Bill gazed after the retreating shape of Anita wistfully. How could he talk to her if she would not talk to him? Recovering from the blow on the head he had gotten from Mula-*ay*, he had admitted to himself that he liked her. Liked her a good deal in fact. In short, the idea of parting company with her was suddenly very painful.

But even as he had come to realize this, his relationship with her had seemed to be getting worse and worse. It had started with that unfortunate question of his, about there being anything she didn't have, when he had just come to and she was sponging his head. He had tried to explain later that he had actually meant it as a compliment. He realized that she was a hothouse type and he was a pretty ordinary sort of individual. In fact, he had just sort of muddled through to a fortunate conclusion of the situation, while she was attacking it properly with all the unusual resources of her unusual mind and training. He wasn't trying to pretend he was anything like her equal, or anything like that.

But the more he had tried to explain, the more displeased Anita had become. It was as if every time he opened his mouth, he dug himself in that much deeper.

"Well, Pick-and-Shovel—" the voice of the Hill Bluffer interrupted his thoughts and Bill started guiltily. He had completely forgotten he had been talking to the postman when Anita had passed by, just now on her way to the ship. She was, he saw, being met in a very familiar way by a tall man who had just stepped out of the hatchway. The tall man was himself vaguely familiar. Bill peered at him somewhat grimly.

"—So I guess I'll be off, back to the mountains," the Bluffer's voice boomed on Bill's ear. "They'll all be wanting to hear up there if you turned out the way I said you would."

"They will?" Bill was startled. Then he remembered how he had speculated on the Hill Bluffer's having some stake of his own in the outcome of the situation in which Bill had been trapped. Bill looked sharply up at the lanky Dilbian.

"Why, sure," said the Hill Bluffer comfortably. "They all remember the Half-Pint-Posted, but there was considerable discussion about whether you Shorties could do it twice in a row."

"Twice in a row?" echoed Bill. "Do what?"

"Come out one up on a Fatty, of course," replied the Bluffer. "You know, like him!"

He nodded over at the far side of the meadow, behind Bill. Bill turned and saw the yellow-robed figure of Mula-*ay* standing solitary in the shadow of the trees in his yellow robes. The heavy-gravity figure was not likely to slump in this Dilbian gravity, but there was something defeated about its isolation.

"Word is, a flying box like yours is coming in anytime now," said the Bluffer, "—only one run by Fatties—to take him out. That's probably the last we'll see of old Wasn't Drunk around these parts."

"Who?" Bill blinked at the distant figure. He had been sure that it was Mula-*ay*. In fact, he still was. "But that's Barrel Belly over there, isn't it?"

The Bluffer snorted with contemptuous good humor.

"Not any more. Got his name changed," he said. "You didn't hear—?"

"No," said Bill.

"Why, after your hassle with Bone Breaker was over, it turned out that More Jam had found old Wasn't Drunk passed out cold behind the eating hall, with half a barrel of beer spilled down his front. It was pretty plain for everyone to see that he'd figured the villagers swarming down on the valley would keep the outlaws so busy he could sneak a bellyful. So he'd poured most of a barrel of beer down himself on the sly and passed out." The Bluffer stopped to laugh uproariously. "Result was, he missed all the fun, just by getting drunk at the wrong time!"

"Fun?"

"Why, your duel with Bone Breaker. He missed all that!" said the Hill Bluffer. "So, after More Jam found him and brought everybody to see, they poured some water over him to bring him to, and he sat up to find everyone laughing at him. After all his talk about how tough the Fatties were! Turned out he'd rather drink than fight!"

The Bluffer chortled again, at the memory.

"But," said Bill, "how did his name—"

"Oh, that!" interrupted the Bluffer. "That's the funniest part of all. When he sat up with all that water streaming off him and everybody started kidding him about getting drunk and missing the duel, he lost his head and tried to say it wasn't so. Why, if he'd only kept his mouth shut, or admitted it and laughed at himself—but he had to go and claim he wasn't drunk. *'But I'm not drunk!'* That's the very first words he used. Only when they asked him how come he was out cold, he didn't have any good answer. Tried to come up with some weak story about maybe tripping and hitting his head on the side of the building. Well, you know that's a lie, Pick-and-Shovel. No one's going to trip and hit his head on a log wall hard enough to knock himself out. So, naturally, he got his name changed."

"Naturally," echoed Bill automatically. He was aware enough of Dilbian attitudes now to realize that Wasn't Drunk was as much a liability of a name as Barrel Belly had been an advantage to Mula-*ay*. What it boiled down to was that the Hemnoid had become a figure of fun to the Dilbians and his usefulness to the Hemnoid purpose on Dilbia was at an end. No wonder he was being withdrawn. Bill could even find it in himself to feel a little sorry for Mula-*ay*, now that he had come to understand how the Dilbian mind worked.

Remembering the vagaries of Dilbian thought, he woke abruptly now to the fact that the Hill Bluffer, in the oblique Dilbian way, was trying to tell him something.

"But you were saying," said Bill hastily, "that the people up in the mountains were interested in how I worked things out down here? Why would they be interested?"

"Oh, lots of reasons, Pick-and-Shovel," said the Bluffer carelessly. "Some of them might've been wondering, of course, just how things might work out, with you helping these Muddy Nosers to grow all kinds of stuff. Of course, Lowland folk like this don't count for much in the minds of mountain people, but they're still real people down here, just the same, and a lot of Upland folk were kind of interested to see who the Muddy Nosers'd end up going along with—you or the Fatty. Just in case they ran into the same sort of situation themselves, some day."

"I see," said Bill. It was pretty much as he expected, he thought, interpreting what the postman was saying in the light of his newfound Dilbian knowledge. The Hill Bluffer had been more than a hired companion for Bill. He had been an unofficial—almost everything practical was unofficial among the Dilbians—observer for the Uplanders, with the duty of reporting back on the feasibility of accepting Shorty, rather than Hemnoid, help in agricultural and other matters. And the Bluffer was now delicately informing Bill of that fact.

"How do you suppose they'll feel at the way things turned out?" Bill asked the postman.

"Well," said the Bluffer judiciously, "I think there might be some people, maybe quite some people, who'll be kind of pleased things worked out the way they did. Guess I'm one of them myself." Abruptly, the tall Dilbian changed the subject. "By the way, I passed the word to Bone Breaker the way you told me. I said to him you'd like to see him before you leave."

"You did?" Bill looked hastily off in the direction of the village. He had seen no sign of the former outlaw chief, and had assumed that Bone Breaker had not got the message, or had refused to come—though that was unlikely. "He said he wouldn't come?"

"Oh no. He's coming," said the Bluffer. "He started out with me when I left Muddy Nose."

"Started out?" Bill, staring about, could still not see any sign of Bone Breaker. "What happened—"

"Oh, well, I sort of outwalked him, you know," said the Hill Bluffer comfortably. "He's slowed down a mite.

Not that he ever could have kept up with me before either, if I'd been minded to leave him behind. There's no man living who could do that."

"I believe you," said Bill honestly. And he did.

"There he is now," said the Bluffer, nodding over Bill's head at the courier ship. "Must have circled around to look at that flying box of yours."

Bill turned. Sure enough, there was Bone Breaker, towering amidst the other Dilbians examining the ship. As Bill watched, the former outlaw chief turned and ambled in Bill's direction.

"Well," said the Bluffer's voice, "guess I'll be throwing my feet. See you again, maybe, sometime, Pick-and-Shovel."

Bill turned back to the postman.

"I hope so," said Bill.

"Right. So long," replied the Hill Bluffer. He turned and went—his abrupt farewell being quite in accordance with Dilbian lack of ceremony over both meetings and partings. Bill stared after the tall, striding figure for a moment. Being human, himself, he would have liked to have made a little more out of the process of saying good-bye, particularly since he had come to have a strong feeling of friendship for the Bluffer. But the other was already dwindling in the distance and a moment later he disappeared among the trees not far from where the solitary figure of Mula-*ay* was standing.

"Well, Pick-and-Shovel!" said a different, deep, bass voice, and looking around, Bill saw that Bone Breaker was indeed upon him. "I heard you were asking around about me since you got back on your feet. So I told the wife I'd step over and see what you had on your mind before you took off."

"The wife?" echoed Bill. "Sweet Thing?"

"Who else?" replied Bone Breaker, patting his stomach gently in a manner vaguely resembling More Jam's favorite gesture. "Yes, I'm an innkeeper now, Pick-and-Shovel, and I guess the old gang in the valley's just about broken up. Most of them came to the village with me, and the rest lit out for parts unknown. But what were you asking for me, about?"

"Just a little idle curiosity about something," said Bill, approaching the subject obliquely in the best Dilbian manner. "So you gave up outlawing after all and settled down, did you?"

"What else could I do?" sighed Bone Breaker sadly, "after the way you licked me in a fair fight the way you did, Pick-and-Shovel? Not that I miss the old days too much, though. There's been some compensations."

"There have?" asked Bill.

"Why, sure there have," said Bone Breaker. "There's that little wife of mine, for one—what a prize she is, Pick-and-Shovel." Bone Breaker lowered the volume of his kettledrum bass voice confidentially, "Not only is she the best cook around, but she can lick any other two females, hands-down. She may not be the best-looking female in the region—"

"She isn't?" said Bill, considerably surprised. It was true Perfectly Delightful had called Sweet Thing stubby and little, but Bill had put this down more to jealousy than fact. His human eyes of course were no judge of Dilbian beauty, but he had taken it for granted that Bone Breaker, being the locality's most eligible bachelor, would naturally take an interest only in the better-looking of the available females.

"I wouldn't admit this to any other man," said Bone Breaker, still confidentially, "but you're a Shorty, so of course you don't count—my little wife isn't *exactly* the world's best-looking. No. But what's the good of getting someone with a figure like Perfectly Delightful's, for instance, if you've got to take the rest of her along with it? No, Sweet Thing's the wife for me, on all counts— to say nothing of getting a daddy-in-law like More Jam, thrown in. That old boy's *smart*, Pick-and-Shovel—"

Bone Breaker's nose twitched in the Dilbian equivalent of a wink.

"—As I guess you know," he went on. "Between him and me, I suppose we can get most of the people in Muddy Nose to agree to just about anything we want. So, you can see I'm pretty well off, in spite of the fact my outlawing days are over. I guess that was what you wanted to know, come to think of it, wasn't it, Pick-and-Shovel?"

"Why, I guess that was part of it, anyway," said Bill slowly.

He and Bone Breaker were eyeing each other like fencers. What Bone Breaker had said was, indeed, only part of what Bill wanted to get the ex-outlaw chief to say. In total, the admission Bill wanted was necessary ammunition for a certain private and entirely non-Dilbian hassle toward which he was eagerly pointing.

He was going to make someone pay for what had been done to him. To do that, he needed Bone Breaker to admit certain things. Bone Breaker knew that Bill knew that these things were true. But the big Dilbian was not necessarily going to admit them, just for that reason.

That was not the Dilbian way, Bill had learned. Even though, in a sense, Bone Breaker owed Bill the admission and that was why he was here. The necessary words would be forthcoming only if Bill was clever enough to trap Bone Breaker into a position between them and an outright lie.

"Yes, I guess that was part of it," Bill went on, cautiously. "I did wonder how you were making out. After all, it's a pretty free and easy life, being an outlaw—going out and taking whatever you wanted when you wanted it. It must be pretty dull after that, just being an innkeeper."

"Well now, it is, at times," said Bone Breaker easily. "I won't try to deny it."

"Of course," said Bill thoughtfully. "More Jam managed to settle down to it, all right, in his time."

"That's true," said Bone Breaker, nodding. "I imagine he had a pretty high old life for a while there, when he was younger."

"I'd guess so," said Bill. "And that's what got me wondering—about More Jam, now that I stop to think of it. There must have come some sort of time when he made a decision. Somewhere along the way, he must have said to himself something like—'*Well, it's been fun and all that, but sooner or later I'll be getting along in years; and it'd be nice to quit while I was ahead.*'—Do you suppose he might have thought something like that?"

"Well, of course I don't know," said Bone Breaker, "but I'd guess he might well have, Pick-and-Shovel."

"I mean," said Bill, "he might have thought what it would be like if he just kept on going until he started to slow down and some young buck came along and took him some day in a regular, fair, man-to-man tussle out in the daylight where everybody could see. Then, all of a sudden, the fun and reputation would be gone and he wouldn't have anything to show for it."

"I guess he might," said Bone Breaker.

"He might even have thought," said Bill, "how smart it would be to settle down and get married to Sweet Thing's mother and become an innkeeper ahead of time. Only, of course it must have been a problem for him, because he couldn't quit just like that, without an excuse. People would have figured he'd lost his nerve. Luckily, about that time, his stomach must have started going delicate on him, and that solved the problem for him. He didn't have any choice but to marry Sweet Thing's mother to make sure he had her to cook for him—and of course that meant he had to take up innkeeping and give up wrestling, and all. Of course, I don't *know* it happened that way. It just seems to me it might have."

"Well, that's pretty surprising, Pick-and-Shovel," rumbled Bone Breaker, "as a matter of fact, that's just what did happen with More Jam."

"You don't say?" said Bill. "Now, that's interesting— my hitting the nail on the head just like that. But, of course, much of it isn't hard to figure out, because almost any man with a terrific reputation as a fighter would have trouble quitting. Wouldn't you say that?"

"Yes," said Bone Breaker, staring off across Bill's head at the distant courier ship, "I guess I'd have to say that. A man can't just give up being Lowland champion wrestler without some kind of good reason."

"Or," said Bill, "being outlaw chief."

"Well, that too," admitted Bone Breaker.

"Yes," said Bill thoughtfully, "I guess you might have had your problems too along that line if luck hadn't turned out the way it did. You had Sweet Thing on your side, and she knows a thing or two—"

"She," said Bone Breaker, "surely does."

"To say nothing of her old daddy, who's as tricky as they come; and who probably wouldn't have objected at all getting a real tough cat for a son-in-law to help him with the innkeeping business."

"Well, now that it's all over," said Bone Breaker, "I have to admit More Jam's pretty much been on my side all along."

"But there wasn't much they could do directly to help you," said Bill. "So it was sort of handy—my coming along. You couldn't very well quit outlawing without being licked in a fair fight. And you couldn't very well let yourself get licked by any other real man, especially from around these parts, and still keep your reputation after you retired. But of course, if a Shorty like me won a fight with you, and I flew out of here a few days later, that'd still leave you top dog—locally, at least. Of course, you didn't *have* to quit outlawing just because a Shorty beat you. It wasn't as if I was a real man."

"No, but it was a sign to me—you winning like that," said Bone Breaker sadly. "I was getting slow and weak, Pick-and-Shovel, and it was only a matter of time until somebody else took me. I could tell that."

"Oh, you don't look all that old and weak yet," said Bill.

"Nice of you to say so, Pick-and-Shovel," said the Bone

Breaker. "Oh, I might stand up to any other real man around here for a few years yet. But I sure can't stand up to a fire-eating Shorty like you."

"Well, it's particularly nice to hear you say that," pounced Bill. Bone Breaker's gaze centered on him remained calm and innocent. "Because this mixed-up memory of mine's been giving me all sorts of trouble about that fight."

"Memory?" queried Bone Breaker, with rumbling softness.

"That's right." Bill shook his head. "You remember you must have hit me quite a clip in that storehouse, even if I did get out of it on my feet, first. I was laid up for a few days afterward. And that knock on the head seems to have got my memory all mixed up. Would you believe it, I find myself thinking that I touched your leg, lying on the floor, *before* all those logs came tumbling down, and covered you up."

"My!" Bone Breaker shook his head slowly. "I really did clip you one, then, didn't I, Pick-and-Shovel? Now, what would I be doing lying down on the floor, waiting for some logs to roll down on me?"

"Well, I guess you'll laugh," said Bill. "But it just seems to stick in my head that you were not only lying there, but that you pulled those logs down on yourself, and it was that that made folks think I'd won. But anyone knows you wouldn't do that. After all, you were fighting for your old free way of life. The last thing you wanted was to get married and settle down to innkeeping. So I tell myself I shouldn't think that way. *Should I?*"

Bill shot the last two words hard at the big Dilbian. Bone Breaker breathed quietly for a second, his eyes half-closed, his expression thoughtful.

"Well, I'll tell you, Pick-and-Shovel," he said at last. "As long as it's just you, and you being a Shorty, I don't guess I mind your thinking that, if you want to. After all, your thinking it happened like that doesn't do *me* any harm as long as you're getting in that flying box there and going away. So, you go ahead and think that, if you like and I won't mind."

Bill let out a deep breath in defeat. Bone Breaker had managed to weasel out of it.

"But I'll tell you something," went on Bone Breaker, unexpectedly. "I'll tell you how I like to think of our fight."

"How's that?" asked Bill, suspiciously.

"Why, I like to think of how I was tiptoeing along in the darkness there—and suddenly you came at me like a wild tree-cat," said Bone Breaker. "Before I was half-ready, you were on me. Next thing I knew you'd knocked my sword spinning out of my fist and split my shield. Then you picked up a log and hit me. And then you hit me with another log and the whole pile came tumbling down as you threw me through the wall of the storehouse, jumped outside and threw me back in through another part of the wall, just as the rest of the logs came tumbling down and covered me."

He stopped speaking. Bill stared at him for a long moment before he could find his voice.

"Threw you through the wall, *twice*?" echoed Bill, his voice cracking. "How could I? There weren't any holes made in the storehouse walls!"

"There weren't!" said Bone Breaker, on a note of surprise, rearing back. "Why, now, that's true, Pick-and-Shovel! I must be wrong about that part. I'll have to remember to leave that part out when I tell about our fight. I certainly am obliged to you, Pick-and-Shovel, for pointing that out to me. I guess my memory must have gotten a little mixed-up—just like yours did."

"Er—yes," said Bill.

Suddenly, a great light burst upon Bill. Anything a Dilbian said had to be interpreted—and he had been looking for Bone Breaker to admit the truth about the duel in a different way. *This*, then, was the admission—in the shape of a story about Bill's prowess too wonderful to believe. So he had picked up this nine-hundred-pound hulk before him and thrown it through a wall of logs, not once, but twice, had he?

"But, after all," Bone Breaker was going on, easily, "there's no reason for us to go picking on each other's memories. Why don't I just remember the fight the way I remember it, and you remember it your way, and we'll let it go at that?"

Bill grinned. He could not help it. It was a violation of the rules of Dilbian verbal fencing, which called for a straight face at all times, but he hoped that his human face would be alien enough to Bone Breaker so that the Dilbian would not interpret the expression.

Whether this was the case or not, Bone Breaker did not seem to notice the grin.

"All right," said Bill. Bone Breaker nodded in satisfaction.

"Well, I guess I'll be rolling home for dinner, then," he said. "You know, Pick-and-Shovel, you're not bad for a Shorty. Something real manly about you. Pleased to have met you. So long!"

He turned and left—as abruptly as had the Hill Bluffer. Watching him go, Bill saw him stop to speak to another male Dilbian who had been examining the courier ship, but who now hurried to intercept the ex-outlaw chief.

There was something undeniably respectful about the way the other Dilbian approached the big, black-furred figure. Whatever other changes had occurred in Bone Breaker's life as a result of his losing the fight to Bill and taking up innkeeping, it was plain to see that he had not lost anything of his local stature and authority in the process.

But just at that moment, out of the corner of his eye, Bill caught sight of the tall, lean man who had been talking to Anita by the open hatch of the ship, picking up what was evidently a suitcase and turning as if to head off through the woods.

"Hey!" shouted Bill, starting to run toward him. "No, you don't! Hold up, there! I've got some talking to do to you!"

Chapter 26

The man stopped and turned as Bill ran up to the ship. Anita, who had been just about to go in through the hatch, also stopped, turned and waited—thereby presenting Bill with a small problem. He had wanted a clear ring for his encounter with the tall man.

"If . . . you don't mind," said Bill, stammering a little with breathlessness from his run, "this is a private . . ."

"Oh, all right!" she exploded furiously. "Go on, make a perfect fool of yourself! See if I care!"

She turned and stamped up the steps, through the hatch and into the ship. Bill looked after her, unhappily. There was the sound of a chuckle behind him.

"I wouldn't worry about it," said the voice of the tall man. "She'll come around shortly."

Bill turned sharply. Facing him was the same lean, long-nosed figure he had first met as the reassignment officer who had changed his course from Deneb-Seventeen to Dilbia. The man was smiling with an altogether unjustified cheerfulness. Bill did not smile back.

"What makes you so sure?" Bill snapped.

"For one thing," answered the tall man, "the fact I know her better than you do. For another, I know some other facts you don't know. For one thing, it's a pretty fair guess she's in love with you."

"She—*what*?" said Bill, jerking himself up in midsentence. He goggled at the tall man.

"She can't help it," said the tall man, the smile spreading across his face under the long nose. "You see, at heart she's a Dilbian. And so are you."

"Dilbian?" Bill was completely adrift on a sea of bafflement.

"Oh, your body and mind are human enough," said the tall man. "But you're strongly Dilbian—especially you, Bill—in your personality characteristics. Both of you were carefully chosen for that. You've got roughly the personality of a Dilbian hero-type, as closely as a human can have it. And Anita has a complementary Dilbian heroine-personality. You can hardly help being attracted to each other—"

"Oh?" interrupted Bill, grimly cutting the other short and hauling the conversation back to the main topic he had in mind. "Let's forget that for the moment, shall we? You're Lafe Greentree, aren't you?"

"I'm afraid so," said the tall man, still smiling.

"You never were a reassignment officer? And you never really did break your leg, did you?"

"No, I'm afraid those were both bits of necessary misinformation we had to give you." Greentree laughed. "And it was worth it—what you've done here is breathtaking. You see, you were being used without your knowing it—"

"I figured that out, thanks," said Bill harshly. "In fact I figured out a little more than you figured I would. I know what the real story was here, and I can guess from that what kind of a scheme you sold your superiors on, to get me assigned here. Mula-*ay* told me I was thrown in here, all untrained and unbriefed, deliberately to mess up the situation and give you a chance to close down a stalemated project without losing face. *That's* the idea you sold your superiors on. But what you had in mind was a little bit more than that, wasn't it?"

The smile faded into a puzzled look on Greentree's long face.

"More than that—" he began.

"That's right!" snapped Bill. "You didn't just want me to mess things up here; you wanted me *killed*!"

"*I* wanted you killed?" repeated Greentree, in a tone of astonishment. "But Mula-*ay* wouldn't try anything like that, unless—"

"I'm not talking about Mula-*ay* and you know it," snarled Bill. "I'm talking about Bone Breaker and the duel!"

"But we never thought you'd actually fight the duel!" protested Greentree. "All you had to do was hole up in the Residency. Bone Breaker and his outlaws wouldn't have come into the village after you. You'd have been quite safe—"

"Sure," said Bill, "that's what you told your superiors, wasn't it? Only you knew better. You knew that I'd have been gotten to that duel if Sweet Thing had to kidnap me herself and carry me to it!"

"Sweet Thing?" said Greentree. "What's Sweet Thing got to do with it?"

"Don't try to pretend you didn't know. Anita didn't know—I thought at first she did, but it was plain she didn't understand the male Dilbians at all. She thought More Jam was just a figure of fun, instead of being the leading male in the Village. And Mula-*ay* didn't know. But *you* must have figured it out some time before and realized that you'd been doing things exactly the wrong way around with the Dilbians. Officially, the Alien Cultures Service couldn't fault you for not finding out sooner how the Dilbians worked—but unofficially, the way you'd been made a fool of would have been a joke from one end of the Service rankings to the other. And that joke could just about kill any hopes of promotion for you, later. So you set me up to be killed—so the project wouldn't merely be closed 'temporarily' but hushed up, and its records buried in the files; and that way no one would find out how you'd been fooled!"

"Wait a minute—" said Greentree bewilderedly. "As I said, you've been used here without your permission or knowledge. I admit that. But the rest of all this—I give you my word I'm no more a villain than Anita is, except that I knew why you were sent here and she didn't. Now, what's all this about Sweet Thing carrying you to that duel with Bone Breaker?"

"As if you didn't know!" snapped Bill, getting hold of himself just in time as his voice threatened to scale upward to a shout that would be heard inside the courier ship. "Do you think you can talk me out of what I know? You set me up too beautifully for it to be an accident; and if you set me up, you had to have the Dilbians figured out; and if you'd figured them out, you couldn't help knowing just what Bone Breaker was after!"

"I don't—"

"Oh, cut it out!" said Bill. "You know it as well as I do. Bone Breaker wanted to quit outlawing and settle down before he began to lose his speed and strength. He wanted to quit and become a villager while he was still on top, but he couldn't just abdicate as outlaw leader without a good reason—unless he wanted to lose face, tremendously—and face is what the Dilbian community runs on. So he settled on marrying Sweet Thing; and More Jam, by way of dowry, cooked up a scheme to get him out of being outlaw chief without loss of face."

"What scheme?" Interest had begun to dawn on Greentree's face beneath the frown of puzzlement.

"You know!" growled Bill. "All Dilbia knew that a Dilbian—the Streamside Terror—had once fought a human and lost, so, More Jam planned to get Bone Breaker in a duel with a human, so Bone Breaker could pretend to lose, too. Since it would be a human he'd be losing to, he'd still be top dog among his fellow Dilbians; but he could use the loss as an excuse to give up outlawing, and go to live in Muddy Nose. It was you More Jam planned on Bone Breaker fighting, but you saw the duel coming, so you ducked out and got me stuck with it instead. That was supposed to kill two birds with one stone—get the project closed up, and also get you off Dilbia before the duel took place. Because if you went through with the duel and survived, you'd have to explain to your superiors how you did it—and the whole business of your understanding the Dilbians and keeping the fact a secret would come out!"

Bill stopped. Greentree was staring at him strangely.

"Admit it!" demanded Bill. "I've got you cold and you know it!" But, though his words were angry as ever, a slight uneasiness was beginning to stir in Bill. It was incredible that Greentree could go on pretending to be innocent this way, in the face of what Bill had told him. Unless he really was innocent—but with what Bill knew, that was impossible.

"Maybe you'll tell me," said Greentree in an odd voice, "just what it was—this understanding of the Dilbians you say I have?"

"You know!" snarled Bill.

"Tell me anyway," urged Greentree.

"All right, if you want it spelled out, so you can be sure I've seen through the whole thing!" said Bill furiously. "What you found out was what I finally figured out—just in time to tip off Bone Breaker that I understood, by pushing the duel through after all. If he hadn't understood that I understood, he might have had to make a real fight out of it. Just to make sure I didn't tell the other Dilbians afterward that he'd deliberately lost to me. And that a real duel would have left me very dead indeed!"

"But," said Greentree, "you still haven't told me what this knowledge about the Dilbians was."

"Why, it's their different way of doing everything, of course!" burst out Bill, exasperated. "A Dilbian never lies, except in desperate circumstances—"

"We know that—" began Greentree. "It's a capital offence under the tribal laws in the mountains—"

"—But he never tells the exact, whole truth, either, if he can possibly twist it or distort it to give a different impression!" said Bill. "He admits nothing, and acknowledges nothing. He exaggerates in order to minimize, and minimizes in order to exaggerate. He blusters and brags when he wants to be modest, and he practically quivers with modesty and meekness when he's issuing his strongest warning to another Dilbian to back off or prepare for trouble. In short—the Dilbians do everything backward, inside out, and wrong-way-to, on principle!"

Greentree's face lit up.

"So that's how—" he broke off, sobering. "No, that can't be the answer. We concluded a long time back that the Dilbians had some kind of overall political system, or understanding, that they wouldn't admit to—they worked too well together as individuals and communities for them not to have something like that. But what you're talking about can't be the answer. No political system could exist—"

"What're you talking about?" said Bill harshly. "They've got a perfect political system. What they've got here on Dilbia is a one hundred percent, simon-pure, *classic* democracy. Nobody tells anybody else what to do among the Dilbians. Under cover of a set of apparently iron-clad visible rules like that one about not lying, there's a set of invisible, changeable rules that really govern their actions. Also, no matter what the circumstances, every Dilbian has an equal right to persuade any other Dilbian to agree with him. If he gets a majority to agree, the new invisible, unacknowledged rule that results is applied to all Dilbians. That's what makes More Jam and Bone

Breaker top dogs in their community—they're champion persuaders—in short, makers of invisible laws."

Greentree stared.

"That's hard to believe," he said, at last, slowly. "After all, as chief outlaw, Bone Breaker headed a strong-arm band—"

"Which only took from the villagers what the villagers could spare!" snapped Bill. "And if they took more, the villager complained to Bone Breaker who made the outlaws who took it give it back."

"But obviously—"

"*Obviously!*" Bill snorted. "The whole point of the way the Dilbians do things is that whatever is obvious is a smoke screen for the real thing—" he broke off suddenly. "What're you doing here? Trying to make me sound as if I'm telling you all this? You know as well as I do the Dilbians were running a test case on you and Mula-*ay*, to see which of you would win out in the end—instead of you and he competing to sway the primitive natives to your side, as you thought at first—and that was the joke you wanted so badly to bury. Even if you had to get me killed to do it."

"A test case?" Greentree had stared at Bill before during this conversation, but not the way he stared now. "A *test case?*"

"You know that," said Bill, but with suddenly lessening conviction. Either, he began to think, Greentree was telling the truth—or he was the best actor ever born.

"Tell me," said Greentree in a hushed voice.

"Why . . . the whole idea of the agricultural project in updating Dilbian farming methods was a debatable question. The Dilbians wondered if the advantages you claimed for it were all true, or if there weren't hidden disadvantages. So they took sides—the way they always do. The villagers took your side, and those who took the other joined the outlaws and cosied up to Mula-*ay*. Then they all sat back to see which one—human or Hemnoid—would break the stalemate wide open in his own favor.

Look," said Bill, almost pleading now. "You know this. You know all this!"

Greentree slowly shook his head.

"I swear to you," he said, slowly, "I give you my word— I didn't know it. No one in the Alien Cultures Service knew it!"

It was Bill's turn to stare now.

"But—" he said after a long moment, "if you didn't know, how could *I* find out—"

He checked, baffled. Looking again at Greentree, he saw the beginnings of a smile starting to dawn again beneath the long nose.

"I'll tell you—if you'll listen now," said Greentree.

"Go ahead," said Bill, cautiously.

"You found out—" began Greentree, and the smile was breaking out now like gleeful sunshine across the tall man's face, "because you're the most unique subject of the most important experiment in the duplication of alien psychologies that's ever been tried!"

Bill scowled suspiciously.

"It's the truth!" said Greentree energetically. "I was going to tell you all about it—but you started talking and now it turns out that you're even more of a success than we dreamed you'd be. You see, you *were* sent here to Dilbia to break up a stalemate between the project and Hemnoid opposition. And you've done that— but you've also given us a whole new understanding of Dilbian nature, and proved that we've got a tool in dealing with other alien races that the Hemnoids can't match!"

Bill scowled harder. It was all he could think of to do, in view of the tall man's words.

"*You* weren't just pitched into the Dilbian situation without consideration," Greentree said. "But somebody else once was. It was John Tardy, the one the Dilbians called the Half-Pint-Posted. It was sheer accident, and our lack of understanding of the Dilbians, that caused him to be caught in an impossible situation—faced with a fight against the Streamside Terror, and the Terror really wanted to win *his* fight."

"I don't get it, then," said Bill feebly.

"Well you see," said Greentree, "John Tardy managed—almost miraculously—to come out on top. He managed to win his battle with the Terror and solve the situation. It was something that by all the rules simply could not have happened. And figuring out how it could have happened became a Number One priority project that took several years. Finally, they came up with an answer—a sort of an answer."

"What?"

"The one thing that came out of all the investigation," said the tall man, with deep seriousness, "was the fact that John Tardy by accident happened to fit the Dilbian personality very closely with his own. The point was raised that he had perhaps been able to solve his situation on Dilbia because he was able to think more like Dilbians than the rest of us. In short, that perhaps he had been just exactly the right man in the right place at the right moment. And a new concept was born; a concept called the Unconscious Agent."

"Unconscious—" even the words sounded silly in Bill's mouth.

"That's right," said Greentree. "Unconscious Agent. A man who's had absolutely no briefing—and therefore has no visible ties to his superiors, but who so exactly fits the situation he meets and the personalities in that situation, that he's ideally fitted to improvise a solution to it. The difference between an Unconscious, and an ordinary, Agent is something like that between the old-fashioned sea-diver with his helmet and air hose tethering him to a pump on the surface, and a free-swimming scuba diver of the mid-twentieth century."

Bill shook his head again.

"The Unconscious Agent isn't only free to improvise," went on Greentree. "He's *forced* to improvise. And, being ideally suited to the situation and the characters in it, he can't fail—we hope—to come up with the ideal solution."

The last two words of this penetrated deeply into Bill.

"You hope—" he echoed bitterly. "So I was an Unconscious Agent, was I?"

"That's right," said Greentree. "The first one—of what will probably be many, now. Of course, we insured our bet on you by supplying you with a hypnoed storehouse of general Dilbian information and another complementary Dilbian-like human who was Anita. But the solution was all your own. And now I'm finding out you've also come up with an insight into the Dilbian character and culture we've never had before. But best of all is that you've proved the workability of something we have that the Hemnoid can't match."

Bill frowned.

"Why?" he asked. "You mean—they can't find and send in personality-matched Unconscious Agents of their own? Why?"

"Because of a lack in their own emotional structure!" Greentree's smile hardened a little. "Don't you know? The Hemnoid character has a cruel streak (as we would call it) that prohibits their having anything but the most rudimentary capacity for empathy. Empathy—the ability to put yourself in somebody else's shoes, emotionally. That's what we humans have, that they haven't. And that's why your likeness to the Dilbians paid off the way it did. Your being like them wouldn't have helped, if you hadn't instinctively tried to think the way they did, in order to figure out what they were doing!"

Of course, thought Bill, suddenly. All at once he remembered his first clue to the fact that perhaps there was more to Dilbian nature than even a trained Hemnoid agent like Mula-*ay* seemed to know. He remembered how Mula-*ay* had taken it for granted that Bill did *not* empathize with someone like Bone Breaker, and had even used that as an example in explaining his own, Hemnoid nature. But Greentree was still talking.

"—if you only knew," he was saying to Bill, "how many millions of individuals on Earth and even on the newly settled worlds were screened to find you, as the closest Dilbian-like human. And how much of our future dealings with alien races has been riding on your success or failure here. Did you know you can just about write your own ticket as far as future work or study goes, after this? Did you know at the moment you're currently the most valuable man off-Earth in the whole Alien Cultures area . . ."

He went on talking, and slowly Bill's spirits began to rise, in spite of himself, like a cork released in deep water and headed for the surface. Within himself—though he was far from admitting it to Greentree, yet—he had to face the fact that he was not the revengeful type, and if there had been a shadow of an excuse for what he had believed Greentree had done, he would probably never have pushed matters to the point of filing charges against the tall man, anyway. Particularly since, after all, Bill had come out of the situation on Dilbia without harm, and even with some benefits in the way of new knowledge and experience.

Certainly, therefore, now that it was turning out that there were strong extenuating circumstances, there was no reason why he shouldn't sit back and ride with the situation. Was that his Dilbian-like nature counseling him how to act? As he stopped to question himself, suddenly a new aspect of the situation burst upon him like sunlight through an unexpected break in a heavy cover of clouds.

If he was Dilbian-like and Anita was Dilbian female-like, he saw at once why she had been so intractable and upset these last few days. Of course! Here, when he was in charge of the situation, he had been going around pretending he had done nothing, and was nothing—at just the time when Anita had expected him to show his authority and strength.

Sweet Thing, now that he stopped to think of it, had

provided him with considerable insight into the way Anita's mind might be working. He woke from his thoughts to find that Greentree was shaking his hand and saying good-bye.

" . . . You'll understand in the long run, Bill, I know," the tall man was saying. "I've got to go now. Somebody's got to hold down the situation at the project here, for the moment. But I'll be following you and Anita to Earth shortly. We'll talk some more then. So long . . ."

"Good-bye," said Bill. He watched the tall man move off towards the woods where Barrel Belly—Wasn't Drunk, that is, Bill corrected himself—was still standing discon-solately. Poor old Mula-*ay*, thought Bill; he was the real loser—and the only real villain there had been in the whole situation. But then Bill shivered, suddenly, remem-bering the episode with Grandpa Squeaky; and, later on, the cliff-edge above Outlaw Valley, where only a light shove from the Hemnoid had been needed to send Bill plunging to his death. Mula-*ay* had been a real enough villain and enemy, at that. Bill shifted his gaze to another part of the meadow. The sun was moving into later afternoon position between the trees, and Bone Breaker, having finished his talk with the smaller Dilbian male, was finally headed off toward Muddy Nose and his dinner table. Bill stared after the big Dilbian, his attention suddenly caught.

"Bill!" It was Anita's voice calling exasperatedly from the open hatch of the courier ship behind him. "Come *on*! We're ready to go!"

"Just a minute!" he shouted back.

He squinted impatiently against the sunlight, striving to catch the tall figure of Bone Breaker in silhouette again. Yes, there it was. There was no doubt about it.

Marriage was apparently being good to the Bone Breaker. It was visible only when you caught him blackly outlined against the sun this way, but it was undeniably a fact, all the same.

Bone Breaker had begun to put on weight.

The Law-Twister
Shorty

The Law-Twister Shorty

"He's a pretty tough character, that Iron Bender—" said the Hill Bluffer, conversationally. Malcolm O'Keefe clung to the straps of the saddle he rode on the Hill Bluffer's back, as the nearly ten-foot-tall Dilbian strode surefootedly along the narrow mountain trail, looking somewhat like a slim Kodiak bear on its hind legs. "But a Shorty like you, Law-Twister, ought to be able to handle him, all right."

"Law-Twister . . ." echoed Mal, dizzily. The Right Honorable Joshua Guy, Ambassador Plenipotentiary to Dilbia, had said something about the Dilbians wasting no time in pinning a name of their own invention on every Shorty (as humans were called by them) they met. But Mal had not expected to be named so soon. And what was that other name the Dilbian postman carrying him had just mentioned?

"Who won't I have any trouble with, did you say?" Mal added.

"Iron Bender," said the Hill Bluffer, with a touch of impatience. "Clan Water Gap's harnessmaker. Didn't Little Bite back there at Humrog Town tell you anything about Iron Bender?"

"I . . . I think so," said Mal. Little Bite, as Ambassador Guy was known to the Dilbians, had in fact told Mal a great many things. But thinking back on their conversation now, it did not seem to Mal that the Ambassador had been very helpful in spite of all his words. "Iron Bender's the—er—protector of this Gentle . . . Gentle . . ."

"Gentle Maiden. Hor!" The Bluffer broke into an unexpected snort of laughter. "Well, anyway, that's who Iron Bender's protector of."

"And she's the one holding the three Shorties captive—"

"Captive? What're you talking about, Law-Twister?" demanded the Bluffer. "She's *adopted* them! Little Bite must have told you that."

"Well, he . . ." Mal let the words trail off. His head was still buzzing from the hypnotraining he had been given on his way to Dilbia, to teach him the language and the human-known facts about the outsize natives of this Earth-like world; and the briefing he had gotten from Ambassador Guy had only confused him further.

" . . . Three tourists, evidently," Guy had said, puffing on a heavy-bowled pipe. He was a brisk little man in his sixties, with sharp blue eyes. "Thought they could slip down from the cruise by spaceliner they were taking and duck into a Dilbian village for a firsthand look at the locals. Probably had no idea what they were getting into."

"What—uh," asked Mal, "were they getting into, if I can ask?"

"Restricted territory! Treaty territory!" snapped Guy, knocking the dottle out of his pipe and beginning to refill it. Mal coughed discreetly as the fumes reached his nose.

"In this sector of space we're in open competition with a race of aliens called Hemnoids, for every available, habitable world. Dilbia's a plum. But it's got this intelligent—if primitive—native race on it. Result, we've got a treaty with the Hemnoids restricting all but emergency contact with the Dilbians—by them or us—until the Dilbians themselves become civilized enough to choose either us or the Hemnoids for interstellar partners. Highly illegal, those three tourists just dropping in like that."

"How about me?" asked Mal.

"You? You're being sent in under special emergency orders to get them out before the Hemnoids find out they've been there," said Guy. "As long as they're gone when the Hemnoids hear about this, we can duck any treaty violation charge. But you've got to get them into their shuttle boat and back into space by midnight tonight—"

The dapper little ambassador pointed outside the window of the log building that served as the human embassy on Dilbia at the dawn sunlight on the cobblestoned Humrog Street.

"Luckily, we've got the local postman in town at the moment," Guy went on. "We can mail you to Clan Water Gap with him—"

"But," Mal broke in on the flow of words, "you still haven't explained—why me? I'm just a high school senior on a work-study visit to the Pleiades. Or at least, that's where I was headed when they told me my travel orders had been picked up, and I was drafted to come here instead, on emergency duty. There must be lots of people older than I am, who're experienced—"

"Not the point in this situation," said Guy, puffing clouds of smoke from his pipe toward the log rafters overhead. "Dilbia's a special case. Age and experience don't help here as much as a certain sort of—well—personality. The Dilbian psychological profile and culture is tricky. It needs to be matched by a human with just the proper profile and character, himself. Without those natural advantages the best of age, education, and experience doesn't help in dealing with the Dilbians."

"But," said Mal, desperately, "there must be some advice you can give me—some instructions. Tell me what I ought to do, for example—"

"No, no. Just the opposite," said Guy. "We want you to follow your instincts. Do what seems best as the situation arises. You'll make out all right. We've already had a couple of examples of people who did, when they had the same kind of personality pattern you have. The book anthropologists and psychologists are completely baffled by these Dilbians as I say, but you just keep your head and follow your instincts . . ."

He had continued to talk, to Mal's mind, making less and less sense as he went, until the arrival of the Hill Bluffer had cut the conversation short. Now, here Mal was—with no source of information left, but the Bluffer, himself.

"This, er, Iron Bender," he said to the Dilbian postman. "You were saying I ought to be able to handle him all right?"

"Well, if you're any kind of a Shorty at all," said the Bluffer, cheerfully. "There's still lots of people in these mountains, and even down in the lowlands, who don't figure a Shorty can take on a real man and win. But not me. After all, I've been tied up with you Shorties almost from the start. It was me delivered the Half-Pint Posted to the Streamside Terror. Hor! Everybody thought the Terror'd tear the Half-Pint apart. And you can guess who won, being a Shorty yourself."

"The Half-Pint Posted won?"

"Hardly worked up a sweat doing it, either," said the Hill Bluffer. "Just like the Pick-and-Shovel Shorty, a couple of years later. Pick-and-Shovel, he took on Bone Breaker, the lowland outlaw chief—of course, Bone Breaker being a lowlander, they two tangled with swords and shields and that sort of modern junk."

Mal clung to the straps supporting the saddle on which

he rode below the Hill Bluffer's massive, swaying shoulders.

"Hey!" said the Hill Bluffer, after a long moment of silence. "You go to sleep up there, or something?"

"Asleep?" Mal laughed, a little hollowly. "No. Just thinking. Just wondering where a couple of fighters like this Half-Pint and Pick-and-Shovel could have come from back on our Shorty worlds."

"Never knew them, did you?" asked the Bluffer. "I've noticed that. Most of you Shorties don't seem to know much about each other."

"What did they look like?" Mal asked.

"Well . . . you know," said the Bluffer. "Like Shorties. All you Shorties look alike, anyway. Little squeaky-voiced characters. Like you—only, maybe not so skinny."

"Skinny?" Mal had spent the last year of high school valiantly lifting weights and had finally built up his five-foot-eleven frame from a hundred and forty-eight to a hundred and seventy pounds. Not that this made him any mass of muscle—particularly compared to nearly a half-ton of Dilbian. Only, he had been rather proud of the fact that he had left skinniness behind him. Now, what he was hearing was incredible! What kind of supermen had the computer found on these two previous occasions—humans who could outwrestle a Dilbian or best one of the huge native aliens with sword and shield?

On second thought, it just wasn't possible there could be two such men, even if they had been supermen, by human standards. There had to have been some kind of a gimmick in each case that had let the humans win. Maybe, a concealed weapon of some kind—a tiny tranquilizer gun, or some such . . .

But Ambassador Guy had been adamant about refusing to send Mal out with any such equipment.

"Absolutely against the Treaty. Absolutely!" the little ambassador had said.

Mal snorted to himself. If anyone, Dilbian or human, was under the impression that *he* was going to get into any kind of physical fight with any Dilbian—even the oldest, weakest, most midget Dilbian on the planet—they had better think again. How he had come to be selected for this job, anyway . . .

"Well, here we are—Clan Water Gap Territory!" announced the Hill Bluffer, cheerfully, slowing his pace.

Mal straightened up in the saddle and looked around him. They had finally left the narrow mountain trail that had kept his heart in his mouth most of the trip. Now they had emerged into a green, bowl-shaped valley, with a cluster of log huts at its lowest point and the silver thread of a narrow river spilling into it from the valley's far end, to wind down into a lake by the huts.

But he had little time to examine the further scene in detail. Just before them, and obviously waiting in a little grassy hollow by an egg-shaped granite boulder, were four large Dilbians and one small one.

Correction—Mal squinted against the afternoon sun. Waiting by the stone were two large and one small male Dilbians, all with the graying fur of age, and one unusually tall and black-furred Dilbian female. The Hill Bluffer snorted appreciatively at the female as he carried Mal up to confront the four.

"Grown even a bit more yet, since I last saw you, Gentle Maiden," said the native postman, agreeably. "Done a pretty good job of it, too. Here, meet the Law-Twister Shorty."

"I don't want to meet him!" snapped Gentle Maiden. "And you can turn around and take him right back where you got him. He's not welcome in Clan Water Gap Territory; and I've got the Clan Grandfather here to tell him so!"

Mal's hopes suddenly took an upturn.

"Oh?" he said. "Not welcome? That's too bad. I guess there's nothing left but to go back. Bluffer—"

"Hold on, Law-Twister," growled the Bluffer. "Don't let Gentle here fool you." He glared at the three male Dilbians. "What Grandfather? I see three grandpas—

Grandpa Tricky, Grandpa Forty Winks and—" he fastened his gaze on the smallest of the elderly males, "old One Punch, here. But none of them are Grandfathers, last I heard."

"What of it?" demanded Gentle Maiden. "Next Clan meeting, the Clan's going to choose a Grandfather. One of these grandpas is going to be the one chosen. So with all three of them here, I've got the next official Grandfather of Clan Water Gap here, too—even if he doesn't know it himself, yet!"

"Hor!" The Bluffer exploded into snorts of laughter. "Pretty sneaky, Gentle, but it won't work! A Grandfather's no good until he's *named* a Grandfather. Why, if you could do things that way, we'd have little kids being put up to give Grandfather rulings. And if it came to that, where'd the point be in having a man live long enough to get wise and trusted enough to be named a Grandfather?"

He shook his head.

"No, no," he said. "You've got no real Grandfather here, and so there's nobody can tell an honest Shorty like the Law-Twister to turn about and light out from Clan Territory."

"Told y'so, Gentle," said the shortest grandpa in a rusty voice. "Said it wouldn't work."

"You!" cried Gentle Maiden, wheeling on him. "A fine grandpa you are, One Punch—let alone the fact you're my own real, personal grandpa! You don't have to be a Grandfather! You could just tell this Shorty and this long-legged postman on your own—tell them to get out while they were still in one piece! You would have, once!"

"Well, once, maybe," said the short Dilbian, rustily and sadly. Now that Mal had a closer look at him, he saw that this particular oldster—the one the Hill Bluffer had called One Punch—bore more than a few signs of having led an active life. A number of old scars seamed his fur; one ear was only half there and the other badly tattered. Also, his left leg was crooked as if it had been broken and badly set at one time.

"I don't see why you can't *still* do it—for your granddaughter's sake!" said Gentle Maiden sharply. Mal winced. Gentle Maiden might be good looking by Dilbian standards—the Hill Bluffer's comments a moment ago seemed to indicate that—but whatever else she was, she was plainly not very gentle, at least, in any ordinary sense of the word.

"Why, Granddaughter," creaked One Punch mildly, "like I've told you and everyone else, now that I'm older I've seen the foolishness of all those little touches of temper I used to have when I was young. They never really proved anything—except how much wiser those big men were who used to kind of avoid tangling with me. That's what comes with age, Granddaughter. Wisdom. You never hear nowdays of One Man getting into hassles, now that he's put a few years on him—or of More Jam, down there in the lowlands, talking about defending his wrestling championship anymore."

"Hold on! Wait a minute, One Punch," rumbled the Hill Bluffer. "You know and I know that even if One Man and More Jam do go around *saying* they're old and feeble nowdays, no one in his right mind is going to take either one of them at their word and risk finding out if it is true."

"Think so if you like, Postman," said One Punch, shaking his head mournfully. "Believe that if you want to. But when you're my age, you'll know it's just wisdom, plain, pure wisdom, makes men like them and me so peaceful. Besides, Gentle," he went on, turning again to his granddaughter, "you've got a fine young champion in Iron Bender—"

"Iron Bender!" exploded Gentle Maiden. "That lump! That obstinate, leatherheaded strap-cutter! That—"

"Come to think of it, Gentle," interrupted the Hill Bluffer, "how come Iron Bender isn't here? I'd have thought you'd have brought him along instead of these imitation Grandfathers—"

"There, now," sighed One Punch, staring off at the

mountains beyond the other side of the valley. "That bit
about imitations— That's the sort of remark I might've
taken a bit of offense at, back in the days before I developed wisdom. But does it trouble me nowdays?"

"No offense meant, One Punch," said the Bluffer. "You
know I didn't mean that."

"None taken. You see, Granddaughter?" said One
Punch. "The postman here never meant a bit of offense;
and in the old days I wouldn't have seen it until it was
too late."

"Oh, you make me sick!" blazed Gentle Maiden. "You
all make me sick. Iron Bender makes me sick, saying he
won't have anything against this Law-Twister Shorty until
the Law-Twister tries twisting the Clan law that says those
three poor little orphans belong to me now!" She glared
at the Bluffer and Mal. "Iron Bender said the Shorty can
come find him, any time he really wanted to, down at
the harness shop!"

"He'll be right down," promised the Bluffer.

"Hey—" began Mal. But nobody was paying any attention to him.

"Now, Granddaughter," One Punch was saying, repro-
ingly. "The Bender didn't exactly ask you to name him
your protector, you know."

"What difference does that make?" snapped Gentle
Maiden. "I had to pick the toughest man in the Clan to
protect me—that's just common sense; even if he *is* stubborn as an I-don't-know-what and thick-headed as a log
wall! I know my rights. He's got to defend me; and
there—" she wheeled and pointed to the large boulder
lying on the grass, "—there's the stone of Mighty Grappler, and here's all three of you, one of who's got to be
a Grandfather by next Clan meeting—and you mean to
tell me none of you'll even say a word to help me turn
this postman and this Shorty around and get them out
of here?"

The three elderly Dilbian males looked back at her
without speaking.

"All right!" roared Gentle Maiden, stamping about to turn her back on all of them. "You'll be sorry! All of you!"

With that, she marched off down the slope of the valley toward the village of log houses.

"Well," said the individual whom the Hill Bluffer had called Grandpa Tricky, "guess that's that, until she thinks up something more. I might as well be ambling back down to the house, myself. How about you, Forty Winks?"

"Guess I might as well, too," said Forty Winks.

They went off after Gentle Maiden, leaving Mal—still on the Hill Bluffer's back—staring down at One Punch, from just behind the Bluffer's reddish-furred right ear.

"What," asked Mal, "has the stone of what's-his-name got to do with it?"

"The stone of Mighty Grappler?" asked One Punch. "You mean you don't know about that stone, over there?"

"Law-Twister here's just a Shorty," said the Bluffer, apologetically. "You know how Shorties are—tough, but pretty ignorant."

"Some *say* they're tough," said One Punch, squinting up at Mal, speculatively.

"Now, wait a minute, One Punch!" the Hill Bluffer's bass voice dropped ominously an additional half-octave. "Maybe there's something we ought to get straight right now! This isn't just any plain private citizen you're talking to, it's the official postman speaking. And *I* say the Shorties're tough. *I* say I was there when the Half-Pint Posted took the Streamside Terror; and also when Pick-and-Shovel wiped up Bone Breaker in a sword-and-shield duel. Now, no disrespect, but if you're questioning the official word of a government mail carrier—"

"Now, Bluffer," said One Punch, "I never doubted you personally for a minute. It's just everybody knows the Terror and Bone Breaker weren't either of them push-overs. But you know I'm not the biggest man around, by a long shot; and now and then during my time I can remember laying out some pretty good-sized scrappers, myself—when my temper got away from me, that is. So

I know from personal experience not every man's as tough as the next—and why shouldn't that work for Shorties as well as real men? Maybe those two you carried before were tough; but how can anybody tell about this Shorty? No offense, up there, Law-Twister, by the way. Just using a bit of my wisdom and asking."

Mal opened his mouth and shut it again.

"Well?" growled the Bluffer underneath him. "Speak up, Law-Twister." Suddenly, there was a dangerous feeling of tension in the air. Mal swallowed. How, he thought, would a Dilbian answer a question like that?"

Any way but with a straight answer, came back the reply from the hypnotrained section of his mind.

"Well—er," said Mal, "how can I tell you how tough I am? I mean, what's tough by the standards of you real men? As far as we Shorties go, it might be one thing. For you real men, it might be something else completely. It's too bad I didn't ever know this Half-Pint Posted, or Pick-and-Shovel, or else I could kind of measure myself by them for you. But I never heard of them until now."

"But you think they just *might* be tougher than you, though—the Half-pint and Pick-and-Shovel?" demanded One Punch.

"Oh, sure," said Mal. "They could both be ten times as tough as I am. And then, again— Well, not for me to say."

There was a moment's silence from both the Dilbians, then the Bluffer broke it with a snort of admiration.

"Hor!" he chortled admiringly to One Punch. "I guess you can see now how the Law-Twister here got his name. Slippery? Slippery's not the word for this Shorty."

But One Punch shook his head.

"Slippery's one thing," he said. "But law-twisting's another. Here he says he doesn't even know about the stone of the Mighty Grappler. How's he going to go about twisting laws if he doesn't know about the laws in the first place?"

"You could tell me about the stone," suggested Malcolm.

"Mighty Grappler put it there, Law-Twister," said the Bluffer. "Set it up to keep peace in Clan Water Gap."

"Better let me tell him, Postman," interrupted One Punch. "After all, he ought to get it straight from a born Water Gapper. Look at the stone there, Law-Twister. You see those two ends of iron sticking out of it?"

Mal looked. Sure enough, there were two lengths of rusty metal protruding from opposite sides of the boulder, which was about three feet in width in the middle.

"I see them," he answered.

"Mighty Grappler was just maybe the biggest and strongest real man who ever lived—"

The Hill Bluffer coughed.

"One Man, now . . ." he murmured.

"I'm not denying One Man's something like a couple of big men in one skin, Postman," said One Punch. "But the stories about the Mighty Grappler are hard to beat. He was a stonemason, Law-Twister; and he founded Clan Water Gap, with himself, his relatives, and his descendants. Now, as long as he was alive, there was no trouble. He was Clan Water Gap's first Grandfather, and even when he was a hundred and ten nobody wanted to argue with him. But he worried about keeping things orderly after he was gone—"

"Fell off a cliff at a hundred and fourteen," put in the Bluffer. "Broke his neck. Otherwise, no telling how long he'd have lived."

"Excuse me, Postman," said One Punch. "But I'm telling this, not you. The point is, Law-Twister, he was worried like I say about keeping the clan orderly. So he took a stone he was working on one day—the stone there, that no one but him could come near lifting— and hammered an iron rod through it to make a handhold on each side, like you see. Then he picked the stone up, carried it here, and set it down; and he made a law. The rules he'd made earlier for Clan Water

Gappers were to stand as laws, themselves—as long as that stone stayed where it was. But if anyone ever came along who could pick it up all by himself and carry it as much as ten steps, then that was a sign it was time the laws should change."

Mal stared at the boulder. His hypnotraining had informed him that while Dilbians would go to any lengths to twist the truth to their own advantage, the one thing they would not stand for, in themselves or others, was an out-and-out lie. Accordingly, One Punch would probably be telling the truth about this Mighty Grappler ancestor of his. On the other hand, a chunk of granite that size must weigh at least a ton—maybe a ton and a half. Not even an outsize Dilbian could be imagined carrying something like that for ten paces. There were natural flesh-and-blood limits, even for these giant natives—or were there?

"Did anybody ever try lifting it, after that?" Mal asked.

"Hor!" snorted the Bluffer.

"Now, Law-Twister," said One Punch, almost reproachfully, "any Clan Water Gapper's got too much sense to make a fool of himself trying to do something only the Mighty Grappler had a chance of doing. That stone's never been touched from that day to this—and that's the way it should be."

"I suppose so," said Mal.

The Bluffer snorted again, in surprise. One Punch stared.

"You giving up—just like that, Law-Twister?" demanded the Bluffer.

"What? I don't understand," said Mal, confused. "We were just talking about the stone—"

"But you said you supposed that's the way it should be," said the Bluffer, outraged. "The stone there, and the laws just the way Mighty Grappler laid them down. What kind of a law-twister are you, anyway?"

"But . . ." Mal was still confused. "What's the Mighty Grappler and his stone got to do with my getting back these three Shorties that Gentle Maiden says she adopted?"

"Why, that's one of Mighty Grappler's laws—one of the ones he made and backed up with that stone!" said One Punch. "It was Mighty Grappler said that any orphans running around loose could be adopted by any single woman of the Clan, who could then name herself a protector to take care of them and her! Now, that's Clan law."

"But—" began Mal again. He had not expected to have to start arguing his case this soon. But it seemed there was no choice. "It's Clan law if you say so; and I don't have any quarrel with it. But these people Gentle Maiden's adopted aren't orphans. They're Shorties. That's why she's going to have to let them go."

"So that's the way you twist it," said One Punch, almost in a tone of satisfaction. "Figured you'd come up with something like that. So, you say they're not orphans?"

"Of course, that's what I say!" said Mal.

"Figured as much. Naturally, Gentle says they are."

"Well, I'll just have to make her understand—"

"Not her," interrupted the Bluffer.

"Naturally not her," said One Punch. "If *she* says they're orphans, then it's her protector you've got to straighten things out with. Gentle says 'orphans,' so Iron Bender's going to be saying 'orphans,' too. You and Iron Bender got to get together."

"And none of that sissy lowland stuff with swords and shields," put in the Hill Bluffer. "Just honest, man-to-man, teeth, claws, and muscle. You don't have to worry about Iron Bender going in for any of that modern stuff, Law-Twister."

"Oh?" said Mal, staring.

"Thought I'd tell you right now," said the Bluffer. "Ease your mind, in case you were wondering."

"I wasn't, actually," said Mal, numbly, still trying to make his mind believe what his ears seemed to be hearing.

"Well," said One Punch, "how about it, Postman? Law-Twister? Shall we get on down to the harness shop and you and Iron Bender can set up the details? Quite a few folks been dropping in the last few hours to see the two of you tangle. Don't think any of them ever saw a Shorty in action before. Know I never did myself. Should be real interesting."

He and the Hill Bluffer had already turned and begun to stroll down the village.

"Interesting's not the word for it," the Bluffer responded. "Seen it twice, myself, and I can tell you it's a sight to behold . . ."

He continued along, chatting cheerfully while Mal rode along helplessly on Dilbian-back, his head spinning. The log buildings got closer and closer.

"Wait—" Mal said desperately, as they entered the street running down the center of the cluster of log structures. The Bluffer and One Punch both stopped. One Punch turned to gaze up at him.

"Wait?" One Punch said. "What for?"

"I—I can't," stammered Mal, frantically searching for an excuse, and going on talking meanwhile with the first words that came to his lips. "That is, I've got my own laws to think of. Shorty laws. Responsibilities. I can't just go representing these other Shorty orphans just like that. I have to be . . . uh, briefed."

"Briefed?" The Bluffer's tongue struggled with pronunciation of the human word Mal had used.

"Yes—uh, that means I have to be given authority—like Gentle Maiden had to choose Iron Bender as her protector," said Mal. "These Shorty orphans have to agree to choose me as their law-twister. It's one of the Shorty freedoms—freedom to not be defended by a law-twister without your consent. With so much at stake here—I mean, not just what might happen to me, or Iron Bender, but what might happen to Clan Water Gap laws or Shorty laws—I need to consult with my clients, I mean those other Shorties I'm working for, before I enter into any—er—discussion with Gentle Maiden's protector."

Mal stopped speaking and waited, his heart hammering away. There was a moment of deep silence from both the Bluffer and One Punch. Then One Punch spoke to the taller Dilbian.

"Have to admit you're right, Postman," One Punch said, admiringly. "He sure can twist. You understand all that he was talking about, there?"

"Why, of course," said the Bluffer. "After all, I've had a lot to do with these Shorties. He was saying that this isn't just any little old hole-and-corner tangle between him and Iron Bender—this is a high-class hassle to decide the law; and it's got to be done right. No offense, One Punch, but you, having been in the habit of getting right down to business on the spur of the moment all those years, might not have stopped to think just how important it is not to rush matters in an important case like this."

"No offense taken, Postman," said One Punch, easily. "Though I must say maybe it's lucky you didn't know me in my younger, less full-of-wisdom days. Because it seems to me we were *both* maybe about to rush the Law-Twister a mite."

"Well, now," said the Bluffer. "Leaving aside that business of my luck and all that about not knowing you when you were younger, I guess I had to admit perhaps I *was* a little on the rushing side, myself. Anyway, Law-Twister's straightened us both out. So, what's the next thing you want to do, Law-Twister?"

"Well . . ." said Mal. He was still thinking desperately. "This being a matter that concerns the laws governing the whole Water Gap Clan, as well as Shorty laws and the stone of Mighty Grappler, we probably ought to get everyone together. I mean we ought to talk it over. It might well turn out to be this is something that ought to be settled not by a fight but in—"

Mal had not expected the Dilbians to have a word for

it; but he was wrong. His hypnotraining threw the proper Dilbian sounds up for his tongue to utter.

"—court," he wound up.

"Court? Can't have a court, Law-Twister," put in the Bluffer, reprovingly. "Can't have a Clan court without a Grandfather to decide things."

"Too bad, in a way," said One Punch with a sigh. "We'd all like to see a real Law-Twister Shorty at work in a real court situation, twisting and slickering around from one argument to the next. But, just as the Bluffer says, Twister, we've got no Grandfather yet. Won't have until the next Clan meeting."

"When's that?" asked Mal, hastily.

"Couple of weeks," said One Punch. "Be glad to wait around a couple of weeks far as all of us here're concerned; but those Shorty orphans of Gentle Maiden's are getting pretty hungry and even a mite thirsty. Seems they won't eat anything she gives them; and they even don't seem to like to drink the well water, much. Gentle figures they won't settle down until they get it straight that they're adopted and not going home again. So she wants you and Iron Bender to settle it right now—and, of course, since she's a member of the Clan, the Clan backs her up on that."

"Won't eat or drink? Where are they?" asked Mal.

"At Gentle's house," said One Punch. "She's got them locked up there so they can't run back to that box they came down in and fly away back into the sky. Real motherly instincts in that girl, if I do say so myself who's her real grandpa. That, and looks, too. Can't understand why no young buck's snapped her up before this—"

"You understand, all right, One Punch," interrupted an incredibly deep bass voice; and there shouldered through the crowd a darkly brown-haired Dilbian, taller than any of the crowd around him. The speaker was shorter by half a head than the Hill Bluffer—the postman seemed to have the advantage in height on every other native Mal had seen—but this newcomer towered over everyone else and he was a walking mass of muscle, easily outweighing the Bluffer.

"You understand, all right," he repeated, stopping before the Bluffer and Mal. "Folks'd laugh their heads off at any man who'd offer to take a girl as tough-minded as Gentle, to wife—that is, unless he had to. Then, maybe he'd find it was worth it. But do it on his own? Pride's pride . . . Hello there, Postman. This is the Law-Twister Shorty?"

"It's him," said the Bluffer.

"Why he's no bigger'n those other little Shorties," said the deep-voiced Dilbian, peering over the Bluffer's shoulder at Mal.

"You go thinking size is all there is to a Shorty, you're going to be surprised," said the Bluffer. "Along with the Streamside Terror and Bone Breaker, as I recollect. Twister, this here's Gentle's protector and the Clan Water Gap harnessmaker, Iron Bender."

"Uh—pleased to meet you," said Mal.

"Pleased to meet you, Law-Twister," rumbled Iron Bender. "That is, I'm pleased now; and I hope I go on being pleased. I'm a plain, simple man, Law-Twister. A good day's work, a good night's sleep, four good meals a day, and I'm satisfied. You wouldn't find me mixed up in fancy doings like this by choice. I'd have nothing to do with this if Gentle hadn't named me her protector. But right's right. She did; and I am, like it or not."

"I know how you feel," said Mal, hastily. "I was actually going someplace else when the Shorties here had me come see about this situation. I hadn't planned on it at all."

"Well, well," said Iron Bender, deeply, "you, too, eh?" He sighed heavily.

"That's the way things go, nowdays, though," he said. "A plain simple man can't hardly do a day's work in peace without some maiden or someone coming to him for protection. So they got you, too, eh? Well, well— life's life, and a man can't do much about it. You're not a bad little Shorty at all. I'm going to be real sorry to tear your head off—which of course I'm going to do, since I figure I probably could have done the same to Bone Breaker or the Streamside Terror, if it'd ever happened to come to that. Not that I'm a boastful man; but true's true."

He sighed again.

"So," he said, flexing his huge arms, "if you'll light down from your perch on the postman, there, I'll get to it. I've got a long day's work back at the harness shop, anyway; and daylight's daylight—"

"But fair's fair," broke in Mal, hastily. The Iron Bender lowered his massive, brown-furred hands, looking puzzled.

"Fair's fair?" he echoed.

"You heard him, harnessmaker!" snapped the Bluffer, bristling. "No offense, but there's more to something like this than punching holes in leather. Nothing I'd like to see more than for you to try—just try—to tear the head off a Shorty like Law-Twister here, since I've seen what a Shorty can do when he really gets his dander up. But like the Twister himself pointed out, this is not just a happy hassle—this is serious business involving Clan laws and Shorty laws and lots of other things. We were just discussing it when you came up. Law-Twister was saying maybe something like this should be held up until the next Clan meeting when you elect a Grandfather, so's it could be decided by a legal Clan Water Gap court in full session."

"Court—" Iron Bender was beginning when he was interrupted.

"We will *not* wait for any court to settle who gets my orphans!" cried a new voice and the black-furred form of Gentle Maiden shoved through the crowd to join them. "When there's no Clan Grandfather to rule, the Clan goes by law and custom. Law and custom says my protector's got to take care of me, and I've got to take care of the little ones I adopted. And I'm not letting them suffer for two weeks before they realize they're settling down with me. The law says I don't have to and no man's going to make me try—"

"Now, hold on there just a minute, Gentle," rumbled Iron Bender. "Guess maybe I'm the one man in this Clan, or between here and Humrog Peak for that matter, who could make you try and do something whether you wanted it or not, if he wanted to. Not that I'm saying I'm going to, now. But you just remember that while I'm your named protector, it doesn't mean I'm going to let you order me around like you do other folk—any more than I ever did."

He turned back to the Bluffer, Mal and One Punch.

"Right's right," he said. "Now, what's all this about a court?"

Neither the Bluffer nor One Punch answered immediately—and, abruptly, Mal realized it was up to him to do the explaining.

"Well, as I was pointing out to the postman and One Punch," he began, rapidly, "there's a lot at stake, here. I mean, we Shorties have laws, too; and one of them is that you don't have to be represented by a law-twister not your choice. I haven't talked to these Shorties you and Gentle claim are orphans, so I don't have their word on going ahead with anything on their behalf. I can't do anything important until I have that word of theirs. What if we—er—tangled, and it turned out they didn't mean to name me to do anything for them, after all? Here you, a regular named protector of a maiden according to your Clan laws, as laid down by Mighty Grappler, would have been hassling with someone who didn't have a shred of right to fight you. And here, too, I'd have been tangling without a shred of lawful reason for it, to back me up. What we need to do is study the situation. I need to talk to the Shorties you say are orphans—"

"No!" cried Gentle Maiden. "He's not to come *near* my little orphans and get them all upset, even more than they are now—"

"Hold on, now, Granddaughter," interposed One Punch.

"We all can see how the Twister here's twisting and slipping around like the clever little Shorty he is, trying to
get things his way. But he's got a point there when he
talks about Clan Water Gap putting up a named protector,
and then that protector turns out to have gotten into a
hassle with someone with no authority at all. Why they'd
be laughing at our Clan all up and down the mountains.
Worse yet, what if that protector should lose—"

"*Lose?*" snorted Iron Bender, with all the geniality of
a grizzly abruptly wakened from his long winter's nap.

"That's right, harnessmaker. *Lose!*" snarled the Hill
Bluffer. "Guess there just might be a real man not too
far away from you at this moment who's pretty sure you
would lose—and handily!"

Suddenly, the two of them were standing nose to nose.
Mal became abruptly aware that he was still seated in the
saddle arrangement on the Bluffer's back and that, in case
of trouble between the two big Dilbians, it would not be
easy for him to get down in a hurry.

"I'll tell you what, Postman," Iron Bender was growling.
"Why don't you and I just step out beyond the houses,
here, where there's a little more open space—"

"Stop it!" snapped Gentle Maiden. "Stop it right now,
Iron Bender! You've got no right to go fighting anybody
for your own private pleasure when you're still my protector. What if something happened, and you weren't able
to protect me and mine the way you should after that?"

"Maiden's right," said One Punch, sharply. "It's Clan
honor and decency at stake here, not just your feelings,
Bender. Now, as I was saying, Law-Twister here's been
doing some fine talking and twisting, and he's come up
with a real point. It's as much a matter to us if he's a
real Shorty-type protector to those orphans Maiden
adopted, as it is to him and the other Shorties—"

His voice became mild. He turned to the crowd and
spread his hands, modestly.

"Of course, I'm no real Grandfather," he said. "Some
might think I wouldn't stand a chance to be the one you'll

pick at the next Clan meeting. Of course, some might think I would, too—but it's hardly for me to say. Only, speaking as a man who *might* be named a Grandfather someday, I'd say Gentle Maiden really ought to let Law-Twister check with those three orphans to see if they want him to talk or hassle, for them."

A bass-voiced murmur of agreement rose from the surrounding crowd, which by this time had grown to a respectable size. For the first time since he had said farewell to Ambassador Joshua Guy, Mal felt his spirits begin to rise. For the first time, he seemed to be getting some control over the events which had been hurrying him along like a chip swirling downstream in the current of a fast river. Maybe, if he had a little luck, now—

"Duty's duty, I guess," rumbled Iron Bender at just this moment. "All right, then, Law-Twister—now, stop your arguing, Gentle, it's no use—you can see your fellow Shorties. They're at Gentle's place, last but one on the left-hand side of the street, here."

"Show you the way, myself, Postman," said One Punch.

The Clan elder led off, limping, and the crowd broke up as the Hill Bluffer followed him. Iron Bender went off in the opposite direction, but Gentle Maiden tagged along with the postman, Mal, and her grandfather, muttering to herself.

"Take things kind of hard, don't you, Gentle?" said the Hill Bluffer to her, affably. "Don't blame old Iron Bender. Man can't expect to win every time."

"Why not?" demanded Gentle. "I do! He's just so cautious, and slow, he makes me sick! Why can't he be like One Punch, here, when *he* was young? Hit first and think afterward—particularly when I ask him to? Then Bender could go around being slow and careful about his own business if he wanted; in fact, I'd be all for him being like that, on his own time. A girl needs a man she can respect; particularly when there's no other man around that's much more than half-size to him!"

"Tell him so," suggested the Bluffer, strolling along, his long legs making a single stride to each two of Gentle and One Punch.

"Certainly not! It'd look like I was giving in to him!" said Gentle. "It may be all right for any old ordinary girl to go chasing a man, but not me. Folks know me better than that. They'd laugh their heads off if I suddenly started going all soft on Bender. And besides—"

"Here we are, Postman—Law-Twister," interrupted One Punch, stopping by the heavy wooden door of a good-sized log building. "This is Gentle's place. The orphans are inside."

"Don't you go letting them out, now!" snapped Gentle, as Mal, relieved to be out of the saddle after this much time in it, began sliding down the Bluffer's broad back toward the ground.

"Don't worry, Granddaughter," said One Punch, as Mal's boots touched the earth. "Postman and I'll wait right outside the door here with you. If one of them tries to duck out, we'll catch him or her for you."

"They keep wanting to go back to their flying box," said Gentle. "And I know the minute one of them gets inside it, he'll be into the air and off like a flash. I haven't gone to all this trouble to lose any of them, now. So, don't you try anything while you're inside there, Law-Twister!"

Mal went up the three wooden steps to the rough plank door and lifted a latch that was, from the standpoint of a human-sized individual, like a heavy bar locking the door shut. The door yawned open before him, and he stepped through into the dimness. The door swung shut behind him, and he heard the latch being relocked.

"Holler when you want out, Law-Twister!" One Punch's voice boomed through the closed door. Mal looked around him.

He crossed the room and tried the right-hand door at random. It gave him a view of an empty, kitchenlike room with what looked like a side of beef hanging from a hook in a far corner. A chopping block and a wash trough of hollowed-out stone furnished the rest of the room.

Mal backed out, closed the door, and tried the one on his left. It opened easily, but the entrance to the room beyond was barred by a rough fence of planks some eight feet high, with sharp chips of stone hammered into the tops. Through the gap in the planks, Mal looked into what seemed a large Dilbian bed chamber, which had been converted into human living quarters by the simple expedient of ripping out three cabin sections from a shuttle boat and setting them up like so many large tin boxes on the floor under the lofty, log-beamed roof.

At the sound of the opening of the door, other doors opened in the transplanted cabin sections. As Mal watched, three middle-aged people—one woman and two men—emerged each from his own cabin and stopped short to stare through the gaps in the plank fence at him.

"Oh, no!" said one of the men, a skinny, balding character with a torn shirt collar. "A kid!"

"Kid?" echoed Mal, grimly. He had been prepared to feel sorry for the three captives of Gentle Maiden, but this kind of reception did not make it easy. "How adult do you have to be to wrestle a Dilbian?"

"Wrestle . . . !" It was the woman. She stared at him. "Oh, it surely won't come to that. Will it? You ought to be able to find a way around it. Didn't they pick you because you'd be able to understand these natives?"

Mal looked at her narrowly.

"How would you have any idea of how I was picked?" he asked.

"We just assumed they'd send someone to help us who understood these natives," she said.

Mal's conscience pricked him.

"I'm sorry—er—Mrs. . . ." he began.

"Ora Page," she answered. "This—" she indicated the thin man, "is Harvey Anok, and—" she nodded at the other, "Zora Rice." She had a soft, rather gentle face, in contrast to the sharp, almost suspicious face of Harvey

Anok and the rather hard features of Zora Rice; but like both of the others, she had a tanned outdoors sort of look.

"Mrs. Page," Mal said. "I'm sorry, but the only thing I seem to be able to do for you is get myself killed by the local harnessmaker. But I do have an idea. Where's this shuttle boat you came down in?"

"Right behind this building we're in," said Harvey, "in a meadow about a hundred yards back. What about it?"

"Good," said Mal. "I'm going to try to make a break for it. Now, if you can just tell me how to take off in it, and land, I think I can fly it. I'll make some excuse to get inside it and get into the air. Then I'll fly back to the ambassador who sent me out here, and tell him I can't do anything. He'll have to send in force, if necessary, to get you out of this."

The three stared back at him without speaking.

"Well?" demanded Mal. "What about it? If I get killed by that harnessmaker it's not going to do you any good. Gentle Maiden may decide to take you away and hide you someplace in the mountains, and no rescue team will ever find you. What're you waiting for? Tell me how to fly that shuttle boat!"

The three of them looked at each other uncomfortably and then back at Mal. Harvey shook his head.

"No," he said. "I don't think we ought to do that. There's a treaty—"

"The Human-Hemnoid Treaty on this planet?" Mal asked. "But, I just told you, that Dilbian harnessmaker may kill me. You might get killed, too. Isn't it more important to save lives than worry about a treaty at a time like this?"

"You don't understand," said Harvey. "One of the things that Treaty particularly rules out is anthropologists. If we're found here—"

"But I thought you were tourists?" Mal said.

"We are. All of us were on vacation on a spaceliner tour. It just happens we three are anthropologists, too—"

"That's why we were tempted to drop in here in the first place," put in Zora Rice.

"But that Treaty's a lot more important than you think," Harvey said. "We can't risk damaging it."

"Why didn't you think of that before you came here?" Mal growled.

"You can find a way out for all of us without calling for armed force and getting us all in trouble. I know you can," said Ora Page. "We trust you. Won't you try?"

Mal stared back at them all, scowling. There was something funny about all this. Prisoners who hadn't worried about a Human-Hemnoid Treaty on their way to Dilbia, but who were willing to risk themselves to protect it now that they were here. A Dilbian female who wanted to adopt three full-grown humans. Why, in the name of all that was sensible? A village harnessmaker ready to tear him apart, and a human ambassador who had sent him blithely out to face that same harnessmaker with neither advice nor protection.

"All right," said Mal, grimly. "I'll talk to you again later—with luck."

He stepped back and swung closed the heavy door to the room in which they were fenced. Going to the entrance of the building, he shouted to One Punch, and the door before him was opened from the outside. Gentle Maiden shouldered suspiciously past him into the house as he emerged.

"Well, how about it, Law-Twister?" asked One Punch, as the door closed behind Gentle Maiden. "Those other Shorties say it was all right for you to talk and hassle for them?"

"Well, yes . . ." said Mal. He gazed narrowly up into the large furry faces of One Punch and the Bluffer, trying to read their expressions. But outside of the fact that they both looked genial, he could discover nothing. The alien visages held their secrets well from human eyes.

"They agreed, all right," said Mal, slowly. "But what they had to say to me sort of got me thinking. Maybe you can tell me—just why is it Clan Water Gap can't hold its meeting right away instead of two weeks from now? Hold a meeting right now and the Clan could have an elected Grandfather before the afternoon's half over. Then there'd be time to hold a regular Clan court, for example, between the election and sunset; and this whole matter of the orphan Shorties could be handled more in regular fashion."

"Wondered that, did you, Law-Twister?" said One Punch. "It crossed my mind earlier you might wonder about it. No real reason why the Clan meeting couldn't be held right away, I guess. Only, who's going to suggest it?"

"Suggest it?" Mal said.

"Why, sure," said One Punch. "Ordinarily, when a Clan has a Grandfather, it'd be up to the Grandfather to suggest it. But Clan Water Gap doesn't have a Grandfather right now, as you know."

"Isn't there anyone else to suggest things like that if a Grandfather isn't available?" asked Mal.

"Well, yes." One Punch gazed thoughtfully away from Mal, down the village street. "If there's no Grandfather around, it'd be pretty much up to one of the grandpas to suggest it. Only—of course I can't speak for old Forty Winks or anyone else—but I wouldn't want to be the one to do it, myself. Might sound like I thought I had a better chance of being elected Grandfather now, than I would two weeks from now."

"So," said Mal. "You won't suggest it, and if you won't I can see how the others wouldn't, for the same reason. Who else does that leave who might suggest it?"

"Why, I don't know, Law-Twister," said One Punch, gazing back at him. "Guess any strong-minded member of the Clan could speak up and propose it. Someone like Gentle Maiden, herself, for example. But you know Gentle Maiden isn't about to suggest anything like that when what she wants is for Iron Bender to try and take you apart as soon as possible."

"How about Iron Bender?" asked Mal.

"Now, he just might want to suggest something like that," said One Punch, "being how as he likes to do everything just right. But it might look like he was trying to get out of tangling with you—after all this talk by the Bluffer, here, about how tough Shorties are. So I don't expect Bender'd be likely to say anything about changing the meeting time."

Mal looked at the tall Dilbian who had brought him here.

"Bluffer," he said, "I wonder if you—"

"Look here, Law-Twister," said the Hill Bluffer severely. "I'm the government postman—to all the Clans and towns and folks from Humrog Valley to Wildwood Peak. A government man like myself can't go sticking his nose into local affairs."

"But you were ready to tangle with Iron Bender yourself, a little while ago—"

"That was personal and private. This is public. I don't blame you for not seeing the difference right off, Law-Twister, you being a Shorty and all," said the Bluffer, "but a government man has to know, and keep the two things separate."

He fell silent, looking at Mal. For a moment neither the Bluffer nor One Punch said anything; but Mal was left with the curious feeling that the conversation had not so much been ended, as left hanging in the air for him to pick up. He was beginning to get an understanding of how Dilbian minds worked. Because of their taboo against any outright lying, they were experts at pretending to say one thing while actually saying another. There was a strong notion in Mal's mind now that somehow the other two were simply waiting for him to ask the right question— as if he had a handful of keys and only the right one would unlock an answer with the information he wanted.

"Certainly is different from the old days, Postman," said One Punch, idly, turning to the Bluffer. "Wonder what Mighty Grappler would have said, seeing Shorties like the

Law-Twister among us. He'd have said something, all right. Had an answer for everything, Mighty Grappler did."

An idea exploded into life in Mal's mind. Of course! That was it!

"Isn't there something in Mighty Grappler's laws," he asked, "that could arrange for a Clan meeting without someone suggesting it?"

One Punch looked back at him.

"Why, what do you know?" the oldster said. "Bluffer, Law-Twister here is something to make up stories about, all right. Imagine a Shorty guessing that Mighty Grappler had thought of something like that, when I'd almost forgotten it myself."

"Shorties are sneaky little characters, as I've said before," replied the Bluffer, gazing down at Mal with obvious pride. "Quick on the uptake, too."

"Then there is a way?" Mal asked.

"It just now comes back to me," said One Punch. "Mighty Grappler set up all his laws to protect the Clan members against themselves and each other and against strangers. But he did make one law to protect strangers on Clan territory. As I remember, any stranger having a need to appeal to the whole Clan for justice was supposed to stand beside Grappler's stone—the one we showed you on the way in—and put his hand on it, and make that appeal."

"Then what?" asked Mal. "The Clan would grant his appeal?"

"Well, not exactly," said One Punch. "But they'd be obliged to talk the matter over and decide things."

"Oh," said Mal. This was less than he had hoped for, but still he had a strong feeling now that he was on the right track. "Well, let's go."

"Right," said the Bluffer. He and One Punch turned and strolled off up the street.

"Hey!" yelled Mal, trotting after them. The Bluffer turned around, picked him up, and stuffed him into the saddle on the postman's back.

"Sorry, Law-Twister. Forgot about those short legs of yours," the Bluffer said. Turning to stroll forward with One Punch again, he added to the oldster, "Makes you kind of wonder how they made out to start off with, before they had flying boxes and things like that."

"Probably didn't do much," offered One Punch in explanation, "just lay in the sun and dug little burrows and things like that."

Mal opened his mouth and then closed it again on the first retort that had come to his lips.

"Where you off to with the Law-Twister now, One Punch?" asked a graying-haired Dilbian they passed, whom Mal was pretty sure was either Forty Winks or Grandpa Tricky.

"Law-Twister's going up to the stone of Mighty Grappler to make an appeal to the Clan," said One Punch.

"Well, now," said the other, "guess I'll mosey up there myself and have a look at that. Can't remember it ever happening before."

He fell in behind them, but halfway down the street fell out again to answer the questions of several other bystanders who wanted to know what was going on. So it was that when Mal alighted from the Bluffer's back at the stone of Mighty Grappler, there was just he and the Bluffer and One Punch there, although a few figures could be seen beginning to stream out of the village toward the stone.

"Go ahead, Law-Twister," said One Punch, nodding at the stone. "Make that appeal of yours."

"Hadn't I better wait until the rest of the Clan gets here?"

"I suppose you could do that," said One Punch. "I was thinking you might just want to say your appeal and have it over with and sort of let me tell people about it. But you're right. Wait until folks get here. Give you a chance to kind of look over Mighty Grappler's stone, too, and put yourself in the kind of spirit to make a good appeal . . . Guess you'll want to be remembering this word for word, to pass on down the line to the other clans, won't you, Postman?"

"You could say I've almost a duty to do that, One Punch," responded the Bluffer. "Lots more to being a government postman than some people think . . ."

The two went on chatting, turning a little away from Mal and the stone to gaze down the slope at the Clan members on their way up from the village. Mal turned to gaze at the stone, itself. It was still inconceivable to him that even a Dilbian could lift and carry such a weight ten paces.

Certainly, it did not look as if anyone had ever moved the stone since it had been placed here. The two ends of the iron rod sticking out from opposite sides of it were red with rust, and the grass had grown up thickly around its base. That is, it had grown up thickly everywhere but just behind it, where it looked like a handful of grass might have been pulled up, recently. Bending down to look closer at the grass-free part of the stone, Mal caught sight of something dark. The edge of some indentation, almost something like the edge of a large hole in the stone itself—

"Law-Twister!" The voice of One Punch brought Mal abruptly upright. He saw that the vanguard of the Dilbians coming out of the village was almost upon them.

"How'd you like me to sort of pass the word what this is all about?" asked One Punch. "Then you could just make your appeal without trying to explain it?"

"Oh—fine," said Mal. He glanced back at the stone. For a moment he felt a great temptation to take hold of the two rust-red iron handles and see if he actually could lift it. But there were too many eyes on him now.

The members of the Clan came up and sat down, with their backs straight and furry legs stuck out before them on the grass. The Bluffer, however, remained standing near Mal, as did One Punch. Among the last to arrive was Gentle Maiden, who hurried up to the very front of the crowd and snorted angrily at Mal before sitting down.

"Got them all upset!" she said, triumphantly. "Knew you would!"

Iron Bender had not put in an appearance.

"Members of Clan Water Gap," said One Punch, when they were all settled on the grass and quiet, "you all know what this Shorty, Law-Twister here, dropped in on us to do. He wants to take back with him the orphans Gentle Maiden adopted according to Clan law, as laid down by Mighty Grappler. Naturally, Maiden doesn't want him to, and she's got her protector, Iron Bender—"

He broke off, peering out over the crowd.

"Where is Iron Bender?" the oldster demanded.

"He says work's work," a voice answered from the crows. "Says to send somebody for him when you're all ready to have someone's head torn off. Otherwise, he'll be busy down in the harness shop."

Gentle Maiden snorted.

"Well, well. I guess we'll just have to go on without him," said One Punch. "As I was saying, here's Iron Bender all ready to do his duty; but as Law-Twister sees it, it's not all that simple."

There was a buzz of low-toned, admiring comments from the crowd. One Punch waited until the noise died before going on.

"One thing Law-Twister wants to do is make an appeal to the Clan, according to Mighty Grappler's law, before he gets down to tangling with Iron Bender," the oldster said. "So, without my bending your ears any further, here's the Law-Twister himself, with tongue all oiled up and ready to talk you upside down, and roundabout— Go ahead, Law-Twister!"

Mal put his hand on the stone of Mighty Grappler. In fact, he leaned on the stone and it seemed to him it rocked a little bit, under his weight. It did not seem to him that One Punch's introductory speech had struck quite the serious note Mal himself might have liked. But now, in any case, it was up to him.

"Uh—members of Clan Water Gap," he said. "I've been

disturbed by a lot of what I've learned here. For example, here you have something very important at stake—the right of a Clan Water Gap maiden to adopt Shorties as orphans. But the whole matter has to be settled by what's really an emergency measure—that is, my tangling with Iron Bender—just because Clan Water Gap hasn't elected a new Grandfather lately, and the meeting to elect one is a couple of weeks away—"

"And while it's not for me to say," interrupted the basso voice of the Hill Bluffer, "not being a Clan Water Gapper myself, and besides being a government postman who's strictly not concerned in any local affairs—I'd guess that's what a lot of folks are going to be asking me as I ply my route between here and Wildwood Peak in the next few weeks. 'How come they didn't hold a regular trial to settle the matter, down there in Clan Water Gap?' they'll be asking. 'Because they didn't have a Grandfather,' I'll have to say. 'How come those Water Gappers are running around without a Grandfather?' they'll ask—"

"All right, Postman!" interrupted One Punch, in his turn. "I guess we can all figure what people are going to say. The point is, Law-Twister is still making his appeal. Go ahead, Law-Twister."

"Well . . . I asked about the Clan holding their meeting to elect a Grandfather right away," put in Mal. A small breeze came wandering by, and he felt it surprisingly cool on his forehead. Evidently there was a little perspiration up there. "One Punch here said it could be done all right, but it was a question who'd want to *suggest* it to the Clan. Naturally, he and the other grandpas who are in the running for Grandfather wouldn't like to do it. Iron Bender would have his own reasons for refusing; and Gentle Maiden here wouldn't particularly want to hold a meeting right away—"

"And we certainly shouldn't" said Gentle Maiden. "Why go to all that trouble when here we've got Iron Bender perfectly willing and ready to tear—"

"Why indeed?" interrupted Mal in his turn. He was

beginning to get a little weary of hearing of Iron Bender's
readiness to remove heads. "Except that perhaps the
whole Clan deserves to be in on this—not just Iron
Bender and Maiden and myself. What the Clan really
ought to do is sit down and decide whether it's a good
idea for the Clan to have someone like Gentle Maiden
keeping three Shorties around. Does the Clan really want
those Shorties to stay here? And if not, what's the best
way of getting rid of these Shorties? Not that I'm trying to suggest anything to the Clan, but if the Clan should
just decide to elect a Grandfather now, and the Grandfather should decide that Shorties don't qualify as
orphans—"

A roar of protest from Gentle Maiden drowned him
out; and a thunder of Dilbian voices arose among the
seated Clan members as conversation—argument, rather,
Mal told himself—became general. He waited for it to
die down; but it did not. After a while, he walked over
to One Punch, who was standing beside the Hill Bluffer,
observing—as were two other elderly figures, obviously
Grandpa Tricky and Forty Winks—but not taking part in
the confusion of voices.

"One Punch," said Mal, and the oldster looked down
at him cheerfully, "don't you think maybe you should quiet
them down so they could hear the rest of my appeal?"

"Why, Law-Twister," said One Punch, "there's no point
you going on appealing any longer, when everybody's
already decided to grant what you want. They're already
discussing it. Hear them?"

Since no one within a mile could have helped hearing them, there was little Mal could do but nod his head
and wait. About ten minutes later, the volume of sound
began to diminish as voice after voice fell silent. Finally,
there was a dead silence. Members of the Clan began
to reseat themselves on the grass, and from a gathering in the very center of the crowd, Gentle Maiden
emerged and snorted at Mal before turning toward the
village.

"I'm going to go get Bender!" she announced. "I'll get those little Shorties up here, too, so they can see Bender take care of this one and know they might just as well settle down."

She went off at a fast walk down the slope—the equivalent of about eight miles an hour in human terms.

Mal stared at One Punch, stunned.

"You mean," he asked him, "they decided not to do anything?"

A roar of explaining voices from the Clan members drowned him out and left him too deafened to understand them. When it was quiet once more, he was aware of One Punch looking severely down at him.

"Now, you shouldn't go around thinking Clan Water Gap'd talk something over and not come to some decision, Twister," he said. "Of course, they decided how it's all to go. We're going to elect a Grandfather, today."

"Fine," said Mal, beginning to revive. Then a thought struck him. "Why did Gentle Maiden go after Iron Bender just now, then? I thought—"

"Wait until you hear," said One Punch. "Clan Water Gap's come up with a decision to warm that slippery little Shorty heart of yours. You see, everyone decided, since we were going to elect a Grandfather ahead of time, that it all ought to be done in reverse."

"In reverse?"

"Why, certainly," said One Punch. "Instead of having a trial, then having the Grandfather give a decision to let you and Iron Bender hassle it out to see whether the Shorties go with you or stay with Gentle Maiden, the Clan decided to work it exactly backward."

Mal shook his head dizzily.

"I still don't understand," he said.

"I'm surprised—a Shorty like you," said One Punch, reprovingly. "I'd think backward and upside down'd be second nature to a Law-Twister. Why, what's going to happen is you and Bender'll have it out *first*, then the best decision by a grandpa'll be picked, then the grandpa whose decision's been picked will be up for election, and the Clan will elect him Grandfather."

Mal blinked.

"Decision . . ." he began feebly.

"Now, my decision," said a voice behind him, and he turned around to see that the Clan's other two elderly members had come up, "is that Iron Bender ought to win. But if he doesn't, it'll be because of some Shorty trick."

"Playing it safe, eh, Forty Winks?" said the other grandpa who had just joined them. "Well, *my* decision is that with all his tricks, and tough as we've been hearing Shorties are, that the Law-Twister can't lose. He'll chew Iron Bender up."

The two of them turned and looked expectantly at One Punch.

"Hmm," said One Punch, closing one eye and squinting thoughtfully with the other at Mal. "My decision is that the Law-Twister's even more clever and sneaky than we think. My decision says Twister'll come up with something that'll fix things his way so that they never will tangle. In short, Twister's going to win the fight before it starts."

One Punch had turned toward the seated crowd as he said this, and there was another low mutter of appreciation from the seated Clan members.

"That One Punch," said Grandpa Tricky to Forty Winks, "never did lay back and play it safe. He just swings right in there twice as hard as anyone else, without winking."

"Well," said One Punch himself, turning to Mal, "there's Gentle Maiden and her orphans coming up from the village now with Iron Bender. You all set, Law-Twister?"

Mal was anything but set. It was good to hear that all three grandpas of Clan Water Gap expected him to come out on top; but he would have felt a lot better if it had been Iron Bender who had been expressing that opinion. He looked over the heads of the seated crowd to see Iron Bender coming, just as One Punch had said, with Gentle Maiden and three, small, human figures in tow.

His thoughts spun furiously. This whole business was crazy. It simply could not be that in a few minutes he would be expected to engage in a hand-to-hand battle with an individual more than one and a half times his height and five times his weight, any more than it could be that the wise men of the local Clan could be betting on him to win. One Punch's prediction, in particular, was so farfetched . . .

Understanding suddenly exploded in him. At once, it all fitted together: the Dilbian habit of circumventing any outright lie by pretending to be after just the opposite of what an individual was really after; the odd reaction of the three captured humans who had not been concerned about the Human-Hemnoid Treaty of noninterference on Dilbia when they came *into* Clan Water Gap territory, but were willing to pass up a chance of escape by letting Mal summon armed human help to rescue them, now that they were here. Just suppose—Mal thought to himself feverishly—just suppose everything is just the opposite of what it seems . . .

There was only one missing part to this whole jigsaw puzzle, one bit to which he did not have the answer. He turned to One Punch.

"Tell me something," he said, in a low voice. "Suppose Gentle Maiden and Iron Bender *had* to marry each other. Do you think they'd be very upset?"

"Upset? Well, no," said One Punch, thoughtfully. "Come to think of it, now you mention it, Law-Twister— those two are just about made for each other. Particularly seeing there's no one else made big enough or tough enough for either one of them, if you look around. In fact, if it wasn't for how they go around saying they can't stand each other, you might think they really liked each other quite a bit. Why do you ask?"

"I was just wondering," said Mal, grimly. "Let me ask you another question. Do you think a Shorty like me could carry the stone of Mighty Grappler ten paces?"

One Punch gazed at him.

"Well, you know," he said, "when it comes right down to it, I wouldn't put anything past a Shorty like you."

"Thanks," said Mal. "I'll return the compliment. Believe me, from now on, I'll never put anything past a real person like you, or Gentle Maiden, or Iron Bender, or anyone else. And I'll tell the other Shorties that when I get back among them!"

"Why thank you, Law-Twister," said One Punch. "That's mighty kind of you—but, come to think of it, maybe you better turn around now. Because Iron Bender's here."

Mal turned—just in time to see the towering figure of the village harnessmaker striding toward him, accompanied by a rising murmur of excitement from the crowd.

"All right, let's get this over with!" boomed Iron Bender, opening and closing his massive hands hungrily. "Just take me a few minutes, and then—"

"*Stop!*" shouted Mal, holding up his hand.

Iron Bender stopped, still some twenty feet from Mal. The crowd fell silent, abruptly.

"I'm sorry!" said Mal, addressing them all. "I tried every way I could to keep it from coming to this. But I see now there's no other way to do it. Now, I'm nowhere near as sure as your three grandpas that I could handle Iron Bender, here, with one hand tied behind my back. Iron Bender might well handle *me*, with no trouble. I mean, he just might be the one real man who can tangle with a Shorty like me, and win. But, what if I'm wrong?"

Mal paused, both to see how they were reacting and to get his nerve up for his next statement. If I was trying something like this any place else, he thought, they'd cart me off to a psychiatrist. But the Dilbians in front of him were all quiet and attentive, listening. Even Iron Bender and Gentle Maiden were showing no indications of wanting to interrupt.

"As I say," went on Mal, a little hoarsely as a result of working to make his voice carry to the whole assemblage, "what if I'm wrong? What if this terrific hassling ability that all we Shorties have gets the best of me when

I tangle with Iron Bender? Not that Iron Bender would want me to hold back any, I know that—"

Iron Bender snorted affirmatively and worked his massive hands in the air.

"—But," said Mal, "think what the results would be. Think of Clan Water Gap without a harnessmaker. Think of Gentle Maiden here without the one real man she can't push around. I've thought about those things, and it seems to me there's just one way out. The Clan laws have to be changed so that a Shorty like me doesn't have to tangle with a Clan Gapper over this problem."

He turned to the stone of Mighty Grappler.

"So—" he wound up, his voice cracking a little on the word in spite of himself, "I'm just going to have to carry this stone ten steps so the laws can be changed."

He stepped up to the stone. There was a dead silence all around him. He could feel the sweat popping out on his face. What if the conclusions he had come to were all wrong? But he could not afford to think that now. He had to go through with the business, now that he'd spoken.

He curled his hands around the two ends of the iron rod from underneath and squatted down with his knees on either side of the rock. This was going to be different from ordinary weight lifting, where the weight was distributed on the outer two ends of the lifting bar. Here, the weight was between his fists.

He took a deep breath and lifted. For a moment, it seemed that the dead weight of the stone refused to move. Then it gave. It came up and into him until the near face of the rock thudded against his chest; the whole stone now held well off the ground.

So far, so good, for the first step. Now, for the second . . .

He willed strength into his leg muscles.

Up . . . he thought to himself . . . up . . . He could hear his teeth gritting against each other in his head. Up . . .

Slowly, grimly, his legs straightened. His body lifted,

bringing the stone with it, until he stood, swaying, the weight of it against his chest, and his arms just beginning to tremble with the strain.

Now, quickly—before arms and legs gave out—he had to take the ten steps.

He swayed forward, stuck out a leg quickly, and caught himself. For a second he hung poised, then he brought the other leg forward. The effort almost overbalanced him, but he stayed upright. Now the right foot again . . . then the left . . . the right . . . the left . . .

In the fierceness of his effort, everything else was blotted out. He was alone with the stone he had to carry, with the straining pull of his muscles, the brightness of the sun in his eyes, and the savage tearing of the rod ends on his fingers, that threatened to rip themselves out of his grip.

Eight steps . . . nine steps . . . and . . . ten!

He tried to let the stone down easily, but it thudded out of his grasp. As he stood half-bent over it, it stuck upright in its new resting place in the grass, then half-rolled away from him, for a moment exposing its bottom surface completely, so that he could see clearly into the hole there. Then it rocked back upright and stood still.

Painfully, stiffly, Mal straightened his back.

"Well," he panted, to the silent, staring Dilbians of Clan Water Gap, "I guess that takes care of that . . ."

Less than forty minutes later he was herding the three anthropologists back into their shuttle boat.

"But I don't understand," protested Harvey, hesitating in the entry port of the shuttle boat. "I want to know how you got us free without having to fight that big Dilbian— the one with the name that means Iron Bender?"

"I moved their law stone," said Mal, grimly. "That meant I could change the rules of the Clan."

"But they went on and elected One Punch as Clan Grandfather, anyway," said Harvey.

"Naturally," said Mal. "He'd given the most accurate

judgment in advance—he'd foretold I'd win without laying a hand on Iron Bender. And I had. Once I moved the stone, I simply added a law to the ones Mighty Grappler had set up. I said no Clan Water Gapper was allowed to adopt orphan Shorties. So, if that was against the law, Gentle Maiden couldn't keep you. She had to let you go and then there was no reason for Iron Bender to want to tangle with me."

"But why did Iron Bender and Gentle decide to get married?"

"Why, she couldn't go back to being just a single maiden again, after naming someone her protector," Mal said. "Dilbians are very strict about things like that. Public opinion *forced* them to get married—which they wanted to do anyhow, but neither of them had wanted to be the one to ask the other to marry."

Harvey blinked.

"You mean," he said disbelievingly, "it was all part of a plot by Gentle Maiden, Iron Bender, and One Punch to use us for their own advantage? To get One Punch elected Grandfather, and the other two forced to marry?"

"Now, you're beginning to understand," said Mal, grimly. He started to turn away.

"Wait," said Harvey. "Look, there's information here that you ought to be sharing with us for the sake of science—"

"Science?" Mal gave him a hard look. "That's right, it was science, wasn't it? Just pure science, that made you and your friends decide on the spur of the moment to come down here. *Wasn't it?*"

Harvey's brows drew together.

"What's that question supposed to mean?" he said.

"Just inquiring," said Mal. "Didn't it ever occur to you that the Dilbians are just as bright as you are? And that they'd have a pretty clear idea why three Shorties would show up out of thin air and start asking questions?"

"Why should that seem suspicious to them?" Ora Page stuck her face out of the entry port over Harvey's shoulder.

"Because the Dilbians take everything with a grain of salt anyway—on principle," said Mal. "Because they're experts at figuring out what someone else is really up to, since that's just the way they operate, themselves. When a Dilbian wants to go after something, his first move is to pretend to head in the opposite direction."

"They told you that in your hypnotraining?" Ora asked.

Mal shook his head.

"No," he said. "I wasn't told anything." He looked harshly at the two of them and at the face of Rice, which now appeared behind Harvey's other shoulder. "Nobody told me a thing about the Dilbians except that there are a few rare humans who understand them instinctively and can work with them, only the book-psychiatrists and the book-anthropologists can't figure out why. Nobody suggested to me that our human authorities might deliberately be trying to arrange a situation where three book-anthropologists would be on hand to observe me— as one of these rare humans—learning how to think and work like a Dilbian, on my own. No, nobody told me anything like that. It's just a Dilbian sort of suspicion I've worked out on my own."

"Look here—" began Harvey.

"You look here!" said Mal, furiously. "I don't know of anything in the Outspace Regulations that lets someone be drafted into being some sort of experimental animal without his knowing what's going on—"

"Easy now. Easy . . ." said Harvey. "All right. This whole thing was set up so we could observe you. But we had absolute faith that someone with your personality profile would do fine with the Dilbians. And, of course, you realize you'll be compensated for all this. For one thing, I think you'll find there's a full six-year scholarship waiting for you now, once you qualify for college entrance. And a few other things, too. You'll be hearing more about them when you get back to the human ambassador at Humrog Town, who sent you here."

"Thanks," said Mal, still boiling inside. "But next time

tell them to ask first whether I want to play games with the rest of you! Now, you better get moving if you want to catch that spaceliner!"

He turned away. But before he had covered half a dozen steps, he heard Harvey's voice calling after him.

"Wait! There's something vitally important you didn't tell us. How did you manage to pick up that rock and carry it the way you did?"

Mal looked sourly back over his shoulder.

"I do a lot of weight lifting," he said, and kept on going.

He did not look back again; and, a few minutes later, he heard the shuttle boat take off. He headed at an angle up the valley slope behind the houses in the village toward the stone of Mighty Grappler, where the Bluffer would be waiting to take him back to Humrog Town. The sun was close to setting, and with its level rays in his eyes, he could barely make out that there were four big Dilbian figures rather than one, waiting for him by the stone. A wariness awoke in him.

When he came up, however, he discovered that the four figures were the Bluffer with One Punch, Gentle Maiden, and Iron Bender—and all four looked genial.

"There you are," said the Bluffer, as Mal stopped before him. "Better climb into the saddle. It's not more than two hours to full dark, and even the way I travel we're going to have to move some to make it back to Humrog Town in that time."

Mal obeyed. From the altitude of the saddle, he looked over the Bluffer's right shoulder down at One Punch and Gentle Maiden and level into the face of Iron Bender.

"Well, good-bye," he said, not sure of how Dilbians reacted on parting. "It's been something knowing you all."

"Been something for Clan Water Gap, too," replied One Punch. "I can say that now, officially, as the Clan Grandfather. Guess most of us will be telling the tale for years to come, how we got dropped in on here by the Mighty Law-Twister."

Mal goggled. He had thought he was past the point of surprise where Dilbians were concerned, but this was more than even he had imagined.

"*Mighty* Law-Twister?" he echoed.

"Why, of course," rumbled the Hill Bluffer, underneath him. "Somebody's name had to be changed, after you moved that stone."

"The postman's right," said One Punch. "Naturally, we wouldn't want to change the name of Mighty Grappler, seeing what all he means to the Clan. Besides, since he's dead, we can't very well go around changing his name and getting folks mixed up, so we just changed yours instead. Stands to reason if you could carry Mighty Grappler's stone ten paces, you had to be pretty mighty, yourself."

"But—well, now, wait a minute . . ." Mal protested. He was remembering what he had seen in the moment he had put the stone down and it had rocked enough to let him see clearly into the hole inside it, and his conscience was bothering him. "Uh—One Punch, I wonder if I could speak to you . . . privately . . . for just a second? If we could just step over here—"

"No need for that, Mighty," boomed Iron Bender. "I and the wife are just headed back down to the village, anyway. Aren't we, Gentle?"

"Well, *I'm* going. If you want to come too—"

"That's what I say," interrupted Iron Bender. "We're both just leaving. So long, Mighty. Sorry we never had a chance to tangle. If you ever get some spare time and a good reason, come back and I'll be glad to oblige you."

"Thanks . . ." said Mal. With mixed feelings, he watched the harnessmaker and his new wife turn and stride off down the slope toward the buildings below. Then he remembered his conscience and looked again down at One Punch.

"Guess you better climb down again," the Bluffer was saying, "and I'll mosey off a few steps myself so's not to intrude."

"Now, Postman," said One Punch. "No need for that. We're all friends here. I can guess that Mighty, here, could have a few little questions to ask or things to tell—but likely it's nothing you oughtn't to hear; and besides, being a government man, we can count on you keeping any secrets."

"That's true," said the Bluffer. "Come to think of it, Mighty, it'd be kind of an insult to the government if you didn't trust me—"

"Oh, I trust you," said Mal, hastily. "It's just that . . . well . . ." He looked at One Punch. "What would you say if I told you that the stone there is hollow—that it'd been hollowed out inside?"

"Now, Mighty," said One Punch, "you mustn't make fun of an old man, now that he's become a respectable Grandfather. Anybody knows stones aren't hollow."

"But what would you say if I told you that one is?" persisted Mal.

"Why, I don't supposes it'd make much difference you just *telling* me it was hollow," said One Punch. "I don't suppose I'd say anything. I wouldn't want folks to think you could twist me that easily, for one thing; and for another thing, maybe it might come in handy some time later, my having heard someone say that stone was hollow. Just like the Mighty Grappler said in some of his own words of wisdom—'It's always good to have things set up one way. But it's extra good to have them set up another way, too. Two ways are always better than one.'"

"And very good wisdom that is," put in the Bluffer, admiringly. "Up near Wildwood Peak there's a small bridge people been walking around for years. There *is* a kind of rumor floating around that it's washed out in the middle, but I've never heard anybody really say so. Never know when it might come in useful to have a bridge like that around for someone who'd never heard the rumor— that is, if there's any truth to the rumor, which I doubt."

"I see," said Mal.

"Of course you do, Mighty," said One Punch. "You

understand things real well for a Shorty. Now, luckily we don't have to worry about this joke of yours that the stone of Mighty Grappler is hollow, because we've got proof otherwise."

"Proof?" Mal blinked.

"Why, certainly," said One Punch. "Now, it stand to reason, if that stone were hollow, it wouldn't be anywhere near as heavy as it looks. In fact, it'd be real light."

"That's right," said Mal, sharply. "And you saw me— a Shorty—pick it up and carry it."

"Exactly!" said One Punch. "The whole Clan was watching to see you pick that stone up and carry it. And we did."

"And that proves it isn't hollow?" Mal stared.

"Why, sure," said One Punch. "We all saw you sweating and struggling and straining to move that stone just ten paces. Well, what more 1proof does a man need? If it'd been hollow like you say, a Shorty—let alone a mighty Shorty like you—would've been able to pick it up with one paw and just stroll off with it. But we were watching you closely, Mighty, and you didn't leave a shred of doubt in the mind of any one of us that it was just about all you could carry. So, that stone just *had* to be solid."

He stopped. The Bluffer snorted.

"You see there, Mighty?" the Bluffer said. "You may be a real good law-twister—nobody doubts it for a minute—but when you go up against the wisdom of a real elected Grandfather, you find you can't twist him like you can any ordinary real man."

"I . . . guess so," said Mal. "I suppose there's no point, then, in my suggesting you just take a look at the stone?"

"It'd be kind of beneath me to do that, Mighty," said One Punch, severely, "now that I'm a Grandfather and already pointed out how it couldn't be hollow, anyway. Well, so long."

Abruptly, as abruptly as Iron Bender and Gentle Maiden had gone, One Punch turned and strode off down the slope.

The Hill Bluffer turned on his heel, himself, and strode away in the opposite direction, into the mountains and the sunset.

"But the thing I don't understand," said Mal to the Bluffer, a few minutes later when they were back on the narrow trail, out of sight of Water Gap Territory, "is how . . . What would have happened if those three Shorties hadn't dropped in the way they did? And what if I hadn't been sent for? One Punch might have been elected Grandfather anyway, but how would Iron Bender and Gentle Maiden ever have gotten married?"

"Lot of luck to it all, I suppose you could say, Mighty," answered the Bluffer, sagely. "Just shows how things turn out. Pure chance—like my mentioning to Little Bite a couple of months ago it was a shame there hadn't been other Shorties around to watch just how the Half-Pint Posted and Pick-and-Shovel did things, back when they were here."

"You . . ." Mal stared, "mentioned . . ."

"Just offhand, one day," said the Bluffer. "Of course, as I told Little Bite, there weren't hardly any real champions around right now to interest a tough little Shorty— except over at Clan Water Gap, where my unmarried cousin Gentle Maiden lived."

"Your *cousin* . . . ? I see," said Mal. There was a long, long pause. "Very interesting."

"Funny. That's how Little Bite put it, when I told him," answered the Bluffer, cat-footing confidently along the very edge of a precipice. "You Shorties sure have a habit of talking alike and saying the same things all the time. Comes of having such little heads with not much space inside for words, I suppose."

The Honor Harrington series:

On Basilisk Station

" . . . an outstanding blend of military/technical writing balanced by superb character development and an excellent degree of human drama . . . very highly recommended. . . ." —*Wilson Library Bulletin*

The Honor of the Queen

"Honor fights her way with fists, brains, and tactical genius through a tangle of politics, battles and cultural differences. Although battered she ends this book with her honor, and the Queen's honor, intact."
—*Kliatt*

The Short Victorious War

The people who rule the People's Republic of Haven are in trouble and they think a short victorious war will solve all their problems—only this time they're up against Captain Honor Harrington and a Royal Manticoran Navy that's prepared to give them a war that's far from short . . . and anything but victorious.

Field of Dishonor

Honor goes home to Manticore—and fights for her life on a battlefield she never trained for, in a private war that offers just two choices: death—or a "victory" that can end only in dishonor and the loss of all she loves. . . .

continued

DAVID WEBER

<u>The Honor Harrington series:</u> *(cont.)*

Flag in Exile
Hounded into retirement and disgrace by political enemies, Honor Harrington has retreated to planet Grayson, where powerful men plot to reverse the changes she has brought to their world. And for their plans to succeed, Honor Harrington must die!

Honor Among Enemies
Offered a chance to end her exile and again command a ship, Honor Harrington must use a crew drawn from the dregs of the service to stop pirates who are plundering commerce. Her enemies have chosen the mission carefully, thinking that either she will stop the raiders or they will kill her . . . and either way, her enemies will win. . . .

In Enemy Hands
After being ambushed, Honor finds herself aboard an enemy cruiser, bound for her scheduled execution. But one lesson Honor has never learned is how to give up!

Echoes of Honor
"Brilliant! Brilliant! Brilliant!"—*Anne McCaffrey*

Ashes of Victory
Honor has escaped from the prison planet called Hell and returned to the Manticoran Alliance, to the heart of a furnace of new weapons, new strategies, new tactics, spies, diplomacy, and assassination.

continued

When it comes to the best
in science fiction and fantasy,
Baen Books has something for *everyone!*

IF YOU LIKE . . .
YOU SHOULD ALSO TRY . . .

IF YOU LIKE ...
YOU SHOULD ALSO TRY ...

Lackey's "SERRAted Edge" series .... Rick Cook, *Mall Purchase Night*

Dungeons & Dragons™ .... "Bard's Tale"™ Novels

Star Trek .... James Doohan & S.M. Stirling, "Flight Engineer" series

Star Wars .... Larry Niven, David Weber

Jurassic Park .... Brett Davis, *Bone Wars* and *Two Tiny Claws*

Casablanca .... Larry Niven, *Man-Kzin Wars II*

Elves .... Ball, Lackey, Sherman, Moon, Cook, Guon

Puns .... Rick Cook, Spider Robinson Harry Turtledove, *The Case of the Toxic Spell Dump*

Alternate History .... Gingrich and Forstchen, *1945* James P. Hogan, *The Proteus Operation* Harry Turtledove (ed.), *Alternate Generals* S.M. Stirling, "Draka" series Eric Flint & David Drake, "Belisarius" series Eric Flint, *1632*

SF Conventions .... Niven, Pournelle & Flynn, *Fallen Angels* Margaret Ball, *Mathemagics* Jerry & Sharon Ahern, *The Golden Shield of IBF*

Quests .... Mary Brown, Elizabeth Moon, Piers Anthony

Greek Mythology .... Roberta Gellis, *Bull God* Roberta Gellis, *Thrice Bound* Eric Flint & Dave Freer, *Pyramid Scheme*